We

MW00948840

Forges of the Federation:
Part VI
Hunter

A Forges of the Federation Novel

By
Julie Weil Thomas
Inspired by
Raymond L. Weil
USA Today Best Selling Author

Forges of the Federation: Hunter

Books in the Forges of the Federation Series

Forges of the Federation: Part I Explorer
Forges of the Federation: Part II Oasis
Forges of the Federation: Part III Rebel One
Forges of the Federation: Part IV Spirit of Rebellion
Forges of the Federation: Part V Defender
Forges of the Federation: Part VI Hunter
Forges of the Federation: Part VII Guardian (December 2024)

Website: http://raymondlweil.com/

Dedication

This book is dedicated to my parents. The older I get, the more appreciative I am of the way I was raised. I hope someday my kids will think the same thing. Thanks for being such a great example. I'm thankful both of my kids had the pleasure of knowing their grandparents. We love you, and we miss you.

Forges of the Federation Part VI: Hunter

Chapter One

Alarms rang out, waking me from my fitful sleep. It took me a moment to realize where I was. Why would sensor alarms be sounding? We weren't near Federation space yet.

I quickly got up and headed for the Command Center. Was Admiral Adali even on duty? We should still be in hyperspace. Had our hyperdrive malfunctioned? That thought brought back a flood of memories. Ones that I pushed from my mind. I needed to know why those alarms were sounding. Was it the Jatarians? Had they already made their move? No, it was too soon. It couldn't possibly be them.

If it was a hyperdrive malfunction, were rebels on board? Was this a rescue operation? My heartbeat sped up at the possible implications. I couldn't let my mind run wild. Once I arrived at the Command Center, I would know more about what we were dealing with.

I arrived at the same time as Admiral Adali. "What's going on?" I asked him, as we stood at the door to the Command Center.

Adali shrugged. "I haven't a clue. I was sound asleep when the alarms rang out."

"Me too," I replied.

Adali punched in the code to allow us access to the Command Center. I stood back and allowed him to enter first. He was the admiral, after all.

"What do we have?" Adali asked, as we walked into the Command Center. Adali took his seat and surveyed the viewscreens that filled the front of the room.

"It's the Druin fleet, Admiral, or what's left of it," the tactical officer answered.

"What are they doing here?"

"They're hiding," I answered.

"From what?" Adali asked.

"The Human Empire fleets. I'm sure when the Empire eliminated all of the Morag ships, the Empire moved on to the Druin ones. No doubt the Empire will attack all the major Druin systems on their way out of the Confederation. This Druin fleet doesn't want to be there to face the Empire," I explained.

"Why don't they defend their systems?" asked the tactical officer.

"They don't have the ships to challenge the Empire fleets. They know it, so they hide here and wait for their enemy to leave."

"Has there been any change in their formation since our arrival?" Adali asked.

"No. It seems they haven't sensed us. We never had any indication that the Druins sensed us back in the Golan Four system either. Nothing has changed," reported the sensor officer.

"Yet," Adali pointed out, "it's not a stretch to think that our stealthed capabilities have been compromised, considering that something went wrong with our systems to cause us to exit hyperspace here. This was not a scheduled stop."

"You're right, Admiral. We had a malfunction in our hyperdrive. When our ship exited hyperspace, the rest of the fleet followed. Our stealthed systems are still fully operational."

"I need a report on our hyperdrive stat," Adali commanded.

"I'll go check," I volunteered, "if you don't mind. Back in my day, I helped fix a hyperdrive a time or two."

"I'm sure they've changed a bit since then, but feel free to have a look."

I nodded and headed out of the Command Center. On my walk to the engineering section, I couldn't help but feel a little disappointed. A part of me hoped this was an extraction mission, with the rebels here to rescue me. Did I need rescued? Were there still rebels? What about the rebel bases? Had they ever been found?

Did I still have family out there? Would anyone remember me or know my name if I someday made my way to one of our rebel villages?

I sighed. I hoped one day I would have my answers to those questions. Right now the only answer I needed was what was wrong with the hyperdrive.

As I reached the door to the engineering section, I closed my eyes, and a flood of memories poured through my mind. I shook my head and took a deep breath. I had to stay in the present. At least for now.

I opened the door. I was surprised at how little the engineering room had changed over the last one thousand years. I noted more screens with more readouts on them, but mostly it looked the same. I felt a little twinge of peace, while looking around the room.

No one looked familiar though. Everyone who I had known was dead and had been for a very long time. It wasn't something I wanted to dwell on. I would rather think they were out there somewhere, safe, living a happy and full life at one of the refugee villages. I think that's why I had such a strong desire to see if the villages still remained.

"Can I help you?" one of the crew asked me, pulling me from my thoughts of the past.

I cleared my throat and replied, "Captain Adali sent me to see what was amiss and how long it would take to fix it."

"And you are?" he asked.

"Slade Erickson."

The man looked me over really well, once I had given him my name. "Are you really the Slade Erickson who's over one thousand years old?"

"Yes, sir. I don't feel that old though," I said, with a grin.

"Why did Adali send you?"

I shrugged. "I volunteered. Back in my day, I knew my way around the engineering section of a ship pretty well. Don't worry. I realize that's been a while ago. I'm not planning to try to help." I gave the man a big smile. He seemed to be trying to determine something. I wasn't sure what it was.

"You can tell the admiral that we have already identified the issue and will have it fixed within the hour."

I nodded and replied, "Thank you."

As I turned to go, the man said, "My name is Marcus Erickson."

I slowly turned around. Was this a descendant of Bryce or one of his brothers? Or even perhaps one of my descendants? I was at a loss for words, while I considered the possibilities. I looked up at this man, Marcus. "Any relation to me or anyone I used to know?"

Everyone in the room had stopped what they were doing and were now intently watching the exchange between Marcus and me. Silence filled the room. The anticipation grew.

Marcus answered, "I have a very distant relative named Wyatt. Wyatt Erickson. I believe you may have known him."

My face lit up. It took every ounce of composure I had for me *not* to close the distance between me and Marcus and envelop him in a hug. "Wow. I did know Wyatt. I served with him for many years. He also worked in engineering, like you."

Marcus nodded and smiled. "Yes, that's what I've heard."

"I would love to sit down and hear what you know of Wyatt, but I realize that, right now, you are rather busy. Maybe we can catch up some other time," I said. I didn't like everyone watching. I was dying to know what had happened to Wyatt and the rest of the Erickson family. This man might have those answers.

It was tough for me to turn toward the door again to leave. I wanted nothing more than to ask Marcus about my friends. Now was not the time. I would search out Marcus later. Just knowing the answers to many of my questions were so close gave me a sense of hope.

"It was nice to meet you, Slade," Marcus said, as I opened the door.

Once outside in the corridor, I stopped and took a deep breath. I knew where the answers to many of my questions were. Right here on this ship. What were the chances of that?

As I returned to the Command Center, I was surprised when I saw Empire Admiral Cleemorl walking toward me.

"Slade, what's going on? Are we in danger? Is it the Morag?" Cleemorl asked me, fear evident in his tone.

I shook my head. "No need to worry. Our hyperdrive malfunctioned, and we ended up in the same system as the leftover Druin fleet. That's why the alarms sounded. I just checked with engineering, and they should have the repairs finished soon."

"What about the Druins?" Cleemorl asked.

"Our stealthed capabilities are still functional, so they can't sense us," I answered. I stopped short of reminding Cleemorl that I could easily control the Druins. Maybe he didn't need to be reminded of that at this moment.

"That's a relief."

"After I report to Admiral Adali about what I found in engineering, I'll update everyone on the situation."

Cleemorl nodded. "Thanks, I appreciate that."

I put my hand on Cleemorl's shoulder and said, "Admiral Cleemorl, I am not your enemy. You have nothing to fear from me."

"I believe you. It's everyone else I don't trust. And you've been out of touch with the leaders of the Federation for over one thousand years. So please forgive me for questioning the motives behind bringing Layla to the Federation and for destroying the surface of Golan Four."

"I've lived most of my adult life being paranoid, so I can relate to your feelings. I realize that likely doesn't alleviate your fears, but believe me when I say that I've considered all the angles and possibilities. I know you will too. I'll come to Layla's quarters after I finish in the Command Center. I know you all have more questions for me."

Cleemorl nodded. "We will be expecting you."

I turned and walked the rest of the way to the Command Center. When I entered, Adali looked at me expectantly. I wondered if he realized that I had a past connection to one of the engineers.

"What did you find out?" Adali asked.

"The engineers have identified the problem and expect to have it working within the hour."

"Good." Adali's attention returned to the viewscreen.

I glanced over at the viewscreen myself. Not many ships remained of this once-powerful Druin fleet. Was this all they had left? The Human Empire had managed to fracture the Confederation and, in doing so, had weakened all the fleets that would have stood between them and the Jatarians.

What would we do now? Had the Federation managed to accumulate a massive fleet that could contend with the Jatarians? The only way to find out was to venture back to Jatarian space and see what they had managed to build in secret over the past one thousand years. I had no doubt they were preparing for war.

I shook my head. Adali must have noticed.

"Is something wrong?" he asked me.

"I was just thinking about the Jatarians and what they may have accomplished in secret while I was away," I replied.

"The Morag have been watching them. I doubt you have anything to worry about," Adali replied.

"The Morag were also watching the Human Empire. Look what they managed to build up in secret. Now the Human Empire has essentially wiped out the entire Morag warfleet in the galaxy."

"Except for the one stationed in the Jatarian systems. The Jatarians have no idea anything has changed. They have no reason to question the status quo. All they see is that the Morag fleet still patrolled their systems. The Jatarians pose no threat to us."

A chill ran down my spine. Adali was wrong, and I knew it. I hoped the Federation would be ready for what was to come. "I'll check on our guests. I'm sure they're curious about what's going on," I said, as I left.

Adali said nothing as I walked out. I took a deep breath once outside in the corridor. If only Adali were right. He was underestimating the Jatarians. I hoped his sentiment wasn't widespread among the other Federation admirals.

I walked slowly to Layla's quarters. I didn't want to think of the Jatarians. I knew though that my story needed to continue.

In all honesty, I had been avoiding Layla's quarters. The next part of the story would do nothing but give them more cause for concern. To bring to light just how powerful the Jatarians really were was also the part of the story I would rather not relive. Plus the part where Amelia left this life for the next.

I knocked on the door, and Cleemorl quickly answered. Layla walked over and hugged me. "What was that for?" I asked, surprised by the move.

"You are my brother, after all. You have no other family or friends left. They all have been gone for a long time. I thought maybe you needed a hug," Layla explained.

"I just met a man in engineering who is a descendant of Wyatt, one of Bryce's brothers. I'm looking forward to hearing what he knows about what happened to my friends."

"Wow, that's amazing," Layla replied.

I nodded. It really was.

"We've been anxious to hear more of your story, Soren. We are all curious to know what happened next with the Jatarians and Aunt Amelia."

I nodded. "I know. I've been putting off this part, telling you about what happened to Amelia. I would much rather not relive it. I understand though that you need to know. The story of my life here in the Federation needs to be concluded before we arrive at Falton Two."

Everyone found a seat and looked to me to continue my story. I took a deep breath and closed my eyes.

-

Everything was quiet in the Federation for the next two years. We spent some good quality time with our families. Why the Jatarians didn't attack during this time, we didn't know. We could only imagine they were building up their fleets. Had they used a majority of their fleet numbers in the attacks on the Federation? We also speculated that perhaps they were fighting a war on another front. Was someone else out there attacking the Jatarians?

That was a scary road to let my mind wander down. What if another race was out there that was even more aggressive and more dangerous than the Jatarians? Were they holding them at bay? What if we destroyed the Jatarians just to find an even more formidable enemy?

In the interim, Alex was busy building us a larger stealthed ship to hunt down the Jatarians. One that would be more comfortable to live in for a longer period of time. It would also require a slightly larger crew.

As for Amelia, she was still holding on. Her health had improved slightly while at Elmania. She had managed to spend the majority of her time with Jeffery and his family. She reluctantly requested that I return to Elmania to take her back to Falton Two. She had decided it was time.

I had spent the past two years doing various missions for the rebels. I managed to visit Amelia and Jeffery at least once a month. I dreaded returning Amelia to Falton Two. Even the thought gave me numerous nightmares.

The day had come, and Bryce and I prepared to leave our families again. It would be a relatively short mission, but it grew increasingly hard to leave behind our wives and children. We both knew space travel could be very dangerous. We also both agreed that the sleeping giant could strike at any moment. How long would the Jatarians wait before they strike again? With every passing day, I knew that day was imminent.

The Federation had placed even more early warning buoys out there, hoping to get a heads-up of when the next attack would occur. We knew where all of them were, thanks to our spies and to Amelia.

Amelia also informed us of where the scout ships had searched. So far they had turned up nothing.

As for the Jatarian colony in the Dove Two system, it still thrived. The scout ships had followed multiple ships from the system but had no luck in finding any other Jatarian colonies. Let alone their homeworld.

The Federation finally had developed a way to sense stealthed ships. This technology had been passed to us, with the help of a couple rebel spies. Each of our ships had been retrofitted with this detection system. Other stealthed ships showed up in blue now on the tactical display.

We had debated on which ship to use to take Amelia back to the Federation. Now that the Federation Protection Unit could sense our stealthed ships, they weren't quite the advantage they once were. At least not where the FPU was concerned.

In the end, we elected to take my transport vessel, the *Spirit of Rebellion*. We hoped to blend in with the other transport vessels traveling to and from Falton Two. The plan was to drop off Amelia and Theodore at one of the main ports and be on our way, before Amelia and Theodore reached the palace. If we could leave the Falton Two system before the FPU realized we were there, perhaps we could get away without being followed.

Amelia had agreed that, in the worst case, she would order the FPU to stand down if they caught wind of my presence in the system. It was slightly reassuring. The nagging knowledge that most of the FPU would take orders from the Emperor over Amelia kept me from having peace about the situation.

Knowing I would be so close to Phoebe and yet again unable to visit her saddened me deeply. It had been so long since I'd seen Phoebe face-to-face. I missed her. One day she would likely come to live with me at one of the refugee villages—once Amelia was no longer with us, when Jeffery and Eloise took over. I tried not to dwell too long on that thought.

My crew loaded on the *Spirit of Rebellion* and set off toward Elmania. The trip went smoothly. We were like a well-oiled machine. We had done enough missions together over the years to work together pretty seamlessly.

As we neared the Elmania system, I reached out to Kami to double-check that no ships were in the system. *Kami, this is Slade. We are nearing the system. Are we clear to make our way out of hyperspace?*

Yes, Slade. All is clear. Proceed to the landing bay quickly.

Are you aware of any particular threats in the area?

No, we remain vigilant. We all feel a Jatarian strike is imminent.

I agree. We will see you soon.

"Connor, confirm scans are clear," I ordered.

"Scans are clear, Captain."

I nodded. "Once we enter the system, we will make a short hyperspace jump to get us closer to Elmania. We want to land on the surface quickly. No use lagging around and putting the settlement in any danger."

I felt the familiar twinge in the pit of my stomach as the *Spirit of Rebellion* exited hyperspace in the Elmania system. Shortly after our arrival, we made our microjump to get us closer to Elmania.

Due to the increase in refugee populations in our available colonies, a new colony had now been started on another moon in the Elmania system. This settlement was called Kamian, named in honor of the leader of Elmania, Kami. The population grew slowly but steadily.

Once our ship entered the atmosphere of Elmania, I felt myself relax a little. I expertly landed the ship in the cave, and we all exited the ship. Kami waited for us at the end of the ramp.

"Welcome back," Kami said, with a smile.

"It's good to be back. Any updates from Alex?" I asked.

"Yes. He's done. He is running the ship through some tests before he will be ready to take it up."

"Wow. It sounds like he's ahead of schedule. That's great news."

"Alex hopes to have it ready for you to take on some test flights, by the time you return from this next mission," Kami explained.

"That sounds good to me," I said. Kami's mention of this next mission filled me with apprehension again. I was always nervous about going anywhere near Falton Two and the Emperor.

"I'm sure you're anxious to see your aunt. I'll let you get to it. Any idea when you plan to head out?" Kami asked.

"I'll speak with Amelia and then will let you know."

Kami nodded. The rest of the crew had gone on ahead to find friends and entertainment. I would visit Amelia and Jeffery on my own.

I took my time walking to the village. I was in no hurry to get underway and to head to Falton Two. I knew Amelia had mixed feelings about it. She had said as much multiple times.

When I finally arrived in front of Amelia's little cottage, Theodore sat on the porch. "It's a beautiful day," I called out, knowing he hadn't noticed me yet.

Theodore smiled and replied, "Yes, it is. I'm just trying to soak it all in. It won't be like this when we return to Falton Two."

I walked onto the porch and sat down. "I'm guessing you aren't looking forward to returning to Falton Two?"

Theodore laughed. "I missed it at first, but this change of pace has grown on me. I've enjoyed my time here. I'm sad that it has to come to an end. I'm afraid many dangers await us back on Falton Two."

The hairs on my arms stood up, and goose bumps rose across my body. "Anything in particular you are worried about?"

"The Emperor, for one. He's had a majority of the power while Amelia's been away. He won't appreciate her taking it back."

"No, but he will still have more than if she were no longer with us," I added.

"But less than what he's had. I fear for Amelia's health, for two. She hasn't gotten any worse while we've been here. I'm afraid things will change when we return."

"Do you think poison made her sick?" I asked.

"Yes, I do. I also believe the Emperor is behind it."

"And you believe the Emperor will continue to poison her again once she returns?"

"Yes, unfortunately I do."

"Is there any way that you and she can be hypervigilant about her food and clothes being free of poison?" I asked.

"We tried that before, but it didn't work."

"It has to be someone close to her, someone she trusts."

"I agree. We trust only a handful of people."

"Maybe someone is being threatened into carrying out the crime. I don't see any other way that someone would betray her, at least not someone she trusted. Unless something was in it for them. Maybe look into the motivations of those you trust. Look into their families and ensure none of them are being held captive—or stand to profit from Amelia's demise and Jeffery or Eloise's rise." Even as I said that last part, Theodore and I looked at each other, realizing what was happening.

"Eloise," we both said in unison.

"It's her parents or someone close to them. I'm guessing they have a staff of people who used to work for them and are still employed inside the palace," I commented.

Theodore stood up and paced across the porch. "We are on to something here. The Averys must be paying someone or promising someone something big to help them pull this off. They stand to gain the most," Theodore said.

"So the Emperor has never been the one behind it," I said, as the realization sunk in. "But how is Lord Avery in contact with someone on Falton Two? His gift is not that strong. I couldn't even communicate with Fritz when he traveled to the Bacchus region of space. We both know I'm more powerful with the gift than Avery."

"What ship took him out there? Maybe he has a contact on that ship. Each time it takes prisoners to Earth, Avery could make contact with that person on the ship," Theodore suggested.

"Right now the *how* is not as important as *who* is acting on his behalf. You and Amelia need to make a list of her most trusted aides and servants. Then we have to search for any connection to the Averys. Now that we know who is ultimately behind this plot, we can more easily make the connection," I said excitedly. Maybe now we could stop Lord and Lady Avery, once and for all.

"I hope we can figure it out. We should keep this revelation from Eloise. I'm not sure how she would react to the news," Theodore added.

"You're right. We will speak with Amelia about this later. Perhaps on the ship on our way to Falton Two," I replied.

"We have a plan. That's a step in the right direction, Slade."

"I never want to see Lord Avery again. Eloise will want her parents returned when she and Jeffery take over one day. If I can prevent that from happening, I will."

"Good. I agree. It would be a travesty for them to return. We don't need Lord Avery trying to influence Jeffery. I am really impressed with the relationship you've been able to build with him. I hope he will remember it down the line. He will need you one day."

I nodded. "I've gotten to know Jeffery on a level that would never have been possible if he had stayed in the Federation. I think being here has changed him. A change for the better. Maybe even Eloise too. Although I'm afraid that, when they return to the Federation and are surrounded by their old friends and advisors, they will return to their old ways," I expressed.

"I'm afraid of that too. All we can do is keep building those relationships. Do the best we can. Some things are beyond our control, I'm afraid," Theodore stated.

"I know you're right." I sighed. "I wish you and Amelia didn't have to leave here. It's been great getting to see you."

Theodore smiled. "It's been a much-needed respite for the both of us. Now it's time to get back to work."

"On that note, I'll head over to Jeffery's. I would like to know Amelia's timetable for when she intends to leave."

"Do we need to keep it from Jeffery? He may inform his father and have the FPU watching for you and your ship," Theodore mentioned.

"Jeffery will know she's leaving. Perhaps if we say we will visit the colonies between here and there first, the timetable would be more questionable."

19

"Maybe Jeffery would keep his mouth shut to protect you," Theodore suggested.

"Perhaps, but are we willing to chance that? I don't think I am. Not where my crew is concerned. They are my family too. I would do anything to assure their safety, as far as it's in my control."

"I agree. Let's say we plan to visit a few of the colonies then," Theodore agreed.

I looked over toward Jeffery's cottage. It was just beginning to get dark. I took in a deep breath and savored the aroma of dinner cooking over at the cafeteria. My stomach growled.

I exchanged a glance with Theodore and then headed toward the cottage. I was aware that my time with Amelia was dwindling quickly. Once she returned to Falton Two, I would likely never see her face-to-face again. I needed to soak in what time I had remaining with her. You never know what the future may hold.

Chapter Two

I took a deep breath and raised my hand to knock on the door. It opened before I could. Jeffery stood there, a big smile on his face. "Slade, it's so good to see you. Come on in."

I couldn't help but wonder if Jeffery knew I was here to take Amelia back to Falton Two. He would likely never see her again. Based on his demeanor, I assumed he had no idea. "How are the kids?" I asked, as we made our way to the backyard.

"Growing fast as ever."

"And the baby?"

"She's amazing. Slade, I really hope you have kids one day. It's changed my life."

I smiled. Having kids changed my life too. Jeffery still had no idea I had kids though, and I intended to keep it that way. My children would be threats to his children, especially since my gift was stronger than Jeffery's.

Bryce and I had debated telling Jeffery. We entertained the idea that, if Jeffery grew close to me and my wife, and my kids and his kids became close, Jeffery would have a hard time with the idea of eliminating them. In the end we decided it was best not to take the chance. After all, Jeffery had, in some fashion, agreed with the devastating hit on his own brother.

I heard the kids and Amelia's laughter before we reached the backyard. I took a moment to soak it in.

When the kids noticed us walking outside, they stopped what they'd been doing and ran my way. I scooped each of them up in a big bear hug. I loved these kids. They were family after all. One of them might be a future ruler of the Federation. Thankfully no one had told them.

"Slade, it's nice to see you. You're looking as handsome as ever," Amelia said, as she walked over and enveloped me in a hug.

"It's good to see you, Amelia," I replied. It felt good to be here in this moment.

"So how long are you here?" Jeffery asked.

I glanced at Amelia. She shook her head slightly. "I'm not sure but definitely long enough to stay for supper."

We all sat and idly chatted, while the kids played. When the aroma of dinner overwhelmed us, we made our way to the cafeteria. It was refreshing to see Jeffery and Eloise's kids play with the kids of the village.

I sat with Jeffery during dinner. It was always nice to chat with him.

Once the kids had finished their meal and then ran off to play with their friends, Jeffery asked, "Have you been to any new worlds lately?"

"No, I've mostly been doing supply runs between the colonies," I replied. "Nothing exciting."

"No sign of the Jatarians, I assume."

"No, not that I'm aware of. Have the scout ships found any Jatarian colonies?" I asked.

"No, I'm beginning to wonder if we ever will. How are we not finding them?"

"It's a massive galaxy. Yet I am surprised we haven't found them. I think that's one of my next missions. To go on the hunt for the Jatarians."

"You'll be gone a long time when you go on that mission, right?" Jeffery asked.

"I imagine so. Long enough to find what we are looking for."

"I'm sure it will be a great adventure," Jeffery said.

"It will. It always is."

"Is that why you are here? To prepare for your trip?"

"No, not quite yet. I would imagine within a couple weeks, we will set off. A few more things need to be done first," I explained.

"I don't suppose I could go with you?" Jeffery asked.

I thought about it for a moment. "I'm not sure, Jeffery. We would be gone a long time. I have no idea how long. What if something happens, and we get stranded out there somewhere?"

Jeffery sighed. "I know it's dangerous. However, I think that I would learn a lot from the experience. It would make me a better leader. I just want to see more of what's out there. Gain an even larger perspective than I currently have."

"I'll give it some thought, Jeffery. I know you've always wanted to get up there to the stars and explore some. I'm not sure this is the right mission for that, but I don't know that one ever will be. There's always danger with space travel. It's unpredictable. What if we were gone for a year? What about Eloise and the kids?"

"I will admit it would work better if it were a shorter mission. What if you do find the Jatarians though? Then we will take the battle to them. What an amazing learning experience it would be for me to see a battle firsthand. If I'm to take over this Federation one day, it would be beneficial for me to have at least witnessed a battle."

"I'll think about it, Jeffery. I see the point of what you're saying. I agree with you. If it were a shorter mission, I would be all for it. It's the unknown length and destination I'm most concerned with."

"Almost everyone on your crew has a family who they're leaving behind. What makes me leaving mine any different?"

Jeffery did have a point. I knew he did. "Let me do some more calculations on how far we plan to search and how long we intend to be gone. Then we can discuss it further."

"That sounds good to me."

"What would your father think?" I asked.

"I have no intention of telling him."

"Won't he realize something is wrong when he can't communicate with you? I assure you that we will be out of range of both of our gifts."

"You do have a point there. I would probably need to tell him. I don't want him to worry about me."

"I'm sure he always worries about you. He is your father, after all—even if he's the Emperor of the Federation."

Jeffery smiled. "You do make a good point."

The kids returned then, and our conversation turned to more mundane things. Jeffery's kids were growing up fast. I couldn't help but wonder which one of them would one day take over for their father. I prayed there would be no fighting or plotting among them. What if none of them had the gift? Then what?

I turned to Jeffery and asked quietly, "Do you and Eloise plan to have more children?"

Jeffery smiled. "Yes. Eloise wants to have many. The more we have, the more likely at least one of them will have the gift."

I nodded. Leave it to Eloise to stack the odds in her favor.

"What about you, Slade? When will you settle down and have kids?" Jeffery asked.

I took a deep breath and shrugged. "Your guess is as good as mine."

"I could set you up on some dates, if you like," Jeffery teased.

I laughed. "No thanks, Jeffery. I can handle that myself." Jeffery went quiet. I looked over at him. He seemed deep in thought. "Are you okay?" I asked.

"Yes. I was just thinking about how great it's been living here and raising my kids here." Jeffery glanced over to where Amelia was playing with the kids. "I hope we're able to stay here for many more years. She seems to be doing better since she came here, don't you think?"

"I think so," I agreed.

"She'll want to return to Falton Two soon. I can feel it. It's almost like a cloud is hanging over her head. She doesn't want to go back, but she knows it's her duty."

I remained quiet and watched Amelia too. She looked so happy, playing with her grandkids. This was how I wanted to remember her—happy and healthy and doing what she loved. I took a deep breath and replied, "She does look happy."

"I'm afraid of what will happen when she returns to Falton Two, Slade."

"What do you mean?" I asked.

"Whoever was poisoning her will start again. Then her health will deteriorate. It already took a heavy toll on her from the last time."

"I'm sure Amelia will remain vigilant where her health is concerned."

"I am not sure that's enough," Jeffery replied sadly. "These last two years with her have been amazing. I'm not ready for her to leave and return to Falton Two."

"Would you ever be ready?"

"Probably not," Jeffery answered.

Eloise gathered up her children. She had been chatting with a few of the other mothers. It appeared they were friends. Imagine that. Eloise had friends. Friends who she wasn't using for anything. At least I could fathom no reason she could use any of those women to her advantage here at Elmania.

We headed back toward their cottage. I enjoyed the evening air and the peaceful moments. I knew these would be harder to find, especially for these members of my family.

Once back at the cottage, I sat and relaxed, as Jeffery and Eloise got the kids ready for bed. Amelia sat with me.

"It's quite remarkable, isn't it?" Amelia asked.

"What?"

"How those two make such great parents. I would have never imagined Eloise to thrive in her role as a mother like she has."

I laughed. "Me neither. She seems to have made friends here too."

"They fit in nicely here. I'm happy they have this time to grow close as a family. These times are precious. There will come a time when this place is only a distant memory to them and to the children."

"Hopefully they have a few more years left to enjoy this time together," I added, while closely watching Amelia.

Amelia smiled. "I hope so too."

Once Jeffery and Eloise returned from putting the kids to bed, we chatted about the village for a few minutes. I could tell that both Jeffery and Eloise were tired. I knew from experience that taking care of kids takes a lot of energy.

"So how many more kids do you plan to have?" I asked Eloise.

"Who knows? Two or three, I suppose," Eloise answered.

Amelia smiled. We all knew why she wanted to have so many. Amelia said, "I hope your children don't turn on each other when they become adults."

I was slightly shocked Amelia had said that. An awkward silence followed. I was racking my brain for how to break the silence.

Amelia added, "I'm not sure what you can do as parents to help prevent that. Whatever it is, you might want to figure it out. I obviously can't tell you since I was unsuccessful in that endeavor."

"I didn't try to kill Gabriel, Mom," Jeffery said, obviously shaken by his mother's words.

"Maybe not, but you possibly could have prevented it. That's something I'll never know. He will never trust you."

"What happens when Eloise and I move back to the palace?" Jeffery asked. "Gabriel won't want to be there with me."

"That's a very true statement. I've made some arrangements myself for Gabriel. No need to worry."

"I worry," Eloise chimed in. "I worry Gabriel will take revenge on us or our children for something we didn't do."

I couldn't stop myself from laughing a little. Eloise gave me a death stare. "I don't think Gabriel would harm the children. Now *you* might not be so safe."

"They cannot remain when we return. We must feel safe in our own home," Eloise stated.

"You made them feel unsafe in their home first," I pointed out. I didn't really like where this conversation was headed. I had spent years trying to put this behind me. Now it was rearing its ugly head again.

I did my best to calm my growing anger. I closed my eyes and counted backward from twenty. It's something my mother had taught me years ago. It surprisingly worked. When I opened my eyes again, everyone was staring at me. I took a deep breath and slowly let it out.

"It's a sad thing that brothers can't get along and can't live together peacefully. There might come a day, Eloise, when you will wish for Gabriel and Phoebe's support," I said.

Jeffery sighed. "I don't think Gabriel will ever even consider forgiving us for what he thinks we did. Yet we had no involvement at all," Jeffery said.

"You're right. I think you've lost the relationship with your brother forever. As for Emma, who knows? I guess in the back of her mind she wonders if she's next," I said.

I knew my words were hurting Jeffery. I didn't care as much about Eloise's feelings as I did for Jeffery's. "I'm sorry if that hurts your feelings, Jeffery. That's not my intention. I'm being honest and not sugarcoating the truth."

"I do appreciate that, Slade," Jeffery replied slowly.

"I have plans for Gabriel. So hopefully everything will work out," Amelia said.

"What are these plans?" Eloise asked.

"It doesn't matter. Perhaps with more time, the wounds and the mistrust will heal, and you guys could get along better. That's what I hope for," Amelia said.

I shrugged. "I don't think Gabriel will ever move past it. Every time he tries to walk and struggles to get across the room, he's reminded of what happened," I explained. "Reminded of what caused him his pain and struggles."

Jeffery stared at the floor. Eloise focused on the window behind me.

Amelia added, "I think the best way to move forward is separately. Gabriel and Phoebe will have their home, and the two of you will have a separate home. Currently that means you are here, and they are at the palace. When you return, that will change."

"They will come here?" Eloise asked.

"That has not yet been determined. Slade will see to it that they live someplace where they can be happy and away from what the two of you are doing at Falton Two."

"Will the rebels rally behind Gabriel and try to put him above Jeffery?" Eloise asked worriedly.

"What rebels are you referring to?" I asked. "These people who you have lived among for the past six years? Eloise, you know that these people are *refugees*. No one here wants any harm to come of the Federation. They only seek to live their lives in peace, away from the Federation. You know this."

Eloise looked at me. "I know that is true of this village. I cannot speak to the others."

"Well, I can. The others are the same. Plus you and Jeffery have lived here with these refugees for years. They know very little of Gabriel and Phoebe. I think it would be wise to stop seeing enemies where there aren't any. You're starting to sound like the Emperor," I said.

"I like that sound of that," Eloise replied, with a smirk.

"You shouldn't. It's not a compliment."

Amelia laughed. "The Emperor does have his positive qualities. I will agree with Slade on this one though. I don't see any rebels here. I see a group of people who fled or were forced to flee a place that they were not happy with. I've seen no evidence of any plotting against the Federation here.

"Plus they have let us stay here, with no obvious complaints. I'm the Empress of the Federation, and you are the future leader of the Federation. No threat is here. The rebel threat that the Emperor believes in is irrelevant. It doesn't exist. The threat is a few individuals who have extreme ideas. That's not the norm. Those few people are the outliers. There will always be people unhappy with how things are going.

"As a leader, the blame gets put on your shoulders. You begin to see enemies where there shouldn't be, which makes the situation even worse. No one is plotting to attack the Federation, other than the Jatarians. That's the enemy we should protect ourselves from, not our fellow Humans. *Not* our brothers."

I added, "Jeffery, you asked me why I haven't had a family. Do you want to know the honest truth as to why that is? My children would be seen as threats to yours someday. Part of me worries about what that would look like and how that would play out. Would my children be in hiding, like I am essentially from the Emperor? All because he perceives me as a threat to his children? Would you one day perceive my children as threats? What about Gabriel's children or Emma's children?"

Jeffery put his head in his hands. "I'm so sorry, Slade. I would never wish you or your children harm."

"I believe you, but things change. When you feel your children are threatened, parents will do some pretty crazy things. My case in point is the Emperor. He pinned the blame for his assassination attempt on me to discredit me. He knew I had no involvement. Yet he blamed me anyway. He perceived me as a threat and acted on it.

"Regardless, Jeffery, I count you as my friend. I'm glad we've had this time together, and I hope it continues for years to come. My view of you has changed dramatically since I rescued you from Tyrus. However, I do worry about the future and your eventual return to Falton Two," I replied.

Jeffery nodded. Eloise remained silent. We had hurt both of them with our words tonight, and that was not my intention. I knew it wasn't what Amelia had wanted either.

"I'll value our friendship while I have it and hope it lasts the rest of our lives. I'm glad I've gotten to know you better and to watch you become a father. You are a remarkable father. It's amazing to see," I said.

"Thanks," Jeffery replied.

Amelia stood. "Well, I'm getting tired. I'll head home and rest. Slade, could you walk with me?" Amelia asked.

I nodded and stood. "Of course."

Jeffery and Eloise stood too. Amelia gave each of them a hug. "I love you both. We meant no harm from our discussion tonight. We only mean to help you see a different perspective, to open your eyes to things you may have been blind to. We are in your corner. We are rooting for you to succeed."

Jeffery and Eloise nodded. I hugged Jeffery and nodded to Eloise.

Once Amelia and I were outside, and the door closed behind us, I said, "That's not exactly how I imagined the night to go."

Amelia didn't reply, not until we neared her cottage. "Slade, I have a question."

"What's that?"

"You already have children, don't you? You're just keeping them secret to keep them safe, aren't you?"

I smiled at Amelia and winked. "I'll never tell."

Amelia patted me on the back and said, "I'll never tell a soul. I feel much better believing you do have a family of your own. Keep them safe. You are wise to keep it a secret."

"I am happy you've had the chance to see Jeffery as a father."

"Me too. I know you told me that he'd changed, but it's easier to believe it when you see it for yourself. Thanks for not mentioning why you're really here."

"You're welcome. When will you tell them?" I asked.

"Tomorrow, while the kids are at school."

"I hope they don't think it has anything to do with our conversation tonight," I added.

"I will explain that's why you had to come to Elmania. To take me back home. At my request."

"It might be best to mention we plan to check in on the colonies on our way back to Falton Two. That way, if Jeffery does mention to the Emperor that you are returning, he won't know our timetable."

"I intend to ask Jeffery not to mention anything about my departure to his father. No use endangering you or your crew. I do appreciate the added thought of mentioning going to the colonies, although that might put the colonies on a closer watch."

"The last few times I've been spotted was in our stealthed ship. That's what they'll be looking for. This trip, we're taking my transport vessel. We intend to blend in."

"Wise choice," Amelia replied.

"Also much more spacious."

"I'm thankful I've had this time with Jeffery, Eloise, and the children. I needed it. I feel much more at peace now, when I think about Jeffery taking over for me one day."

"I'm glad this worked out for you to visit. I know you never intended the visit to last quite this long," I joked.

"No, I did not."

"How has the Emperor handled things with you gone?"

"I think he's realized how much I actually handled. He is looking forward to my return."

"Do you think your absence will bring the two of you closer when you return?"

Amelia shrugged. "I'm not sure. We've grown apart over the years. Plus knowing in the back of my mind that he may be responsible for making me sick doesn't help matters."

"Oh, Theodore and I talked earlier, and we believe we've figured out who is truly behind it."

Amelia stopped in her tracks. "Who?"

"Lord and Lady Avery. They stand to gain from your demise."

"Yes, but they are far removed from the palace and Falton Two," Amelia replied, yet also considering the possibility.

"They have many connections. I'm guessing some of their staff still work inside the palace?" I asked.

"I would assume so," Amelia replied, now deep in thought.

We walked the rest of the short distance to her cottage in silence, as the news I had shared sunk in.

Theodore saw us approach and stood to greet us. "Is everything okay?"

"I let Amelia in on our new suspicions about the Averys."

Theodore nodded in understanding. "I've been working on a list of all the people who come in contact with you or work closely with you on a regular basis, those who would have the access to carry out their task," Theodore commented.

"I just don't see how the Averys could organize such a mission from such a remote location," Amelia responded.

"My guess is they have a contact on the transport vessel that brings prisoners to Earth. They relay their orders to that contact, who then relays them to the next person when they return," I replied.

"I guess it would only take a handful of people, given the right motivations," Amelia expressed.

"The Averys could promise them a status change when they return, once their daughter is crowned Empress. Or they could be using blackmail or threats," I said.

Amelia sat on the porch swing and considered what we had told her. "The more I think about it, the more it makes sense.

The Averys are the ones most likely to be behind the plot to poison me. They do stand to gain the most. A return to the Federation and their daughter in the position they always expected her to have? I wish there were a way they wouldn't win their hearts' desire."

"I do know the captain of that transport vessel," I said. "When the time comes to bring the Averys home, the ship could get lost and might have to drop off his passengers at another remote location."

Amelia turned to me and smiled. "Is he a rebel then?"

"No, not exactly. Just a father of someone we rescued from being killed by the Lamothians. A father who feels he owes us a favor for saving his daughter," I explained.

"This is wonderful news, Slade. I do not want the Averys to return to Falton Two. I do not want them to triumph."

"Don't worry. I'll ensure they don't."

Amelia smiled and sat back and relaxed a little. "Now to figure out who is a part of this plot to kill me. That's treason. Maybe if we could somehow prove the Averys' involvement, we could have them tried for treason. Then they would be executed and could not bother anyone in the future. I definitely don't want their influence on Jeffery after I'm gone."

"I imagine it will be almost impossible to prove that the Averys are, indeed, the masterminds behind the plot," I said.

"You're right. Perhaps if we can get the Emperor on our side, it would be helpful," Theodore added.

"First, we have to narrow down our list of suspects and their connection with the Averys," Amelia commented.

"Here's my list. See if you can add anyone else to it," Theodore said, as he handed Amelia a piece of paper.

I was curious who was on the list, but I would know very few of them. One familiar name would be on that list, *Phoebe*. She was related to the Averys but would have no reason to help them. She loved Amelia and thought of her as a mother figure. She would never do anything to harm her.

Amelia surveyed the list and added a few more names.

I wouldn't be any help, so I said, "I'll head to my quarters and get some rest. I won't be much help in narrowing down that list. I'll check in tomorrow sometime and see what you two have accomplished."

"Thanks, Slade, for everything you've done to help me and my family," Amelia said, as she stood to hug me.

"What's your time line for returning to Falton Two?" I asked.

"I need two more days, if you don't mind," Amelia replied.

"I can handle that. I have a few things I can do to keep me occupied," I commented.

"Like spending time with your family?" Amelia suggested.

"Yes, I promise I will do that too. I also have a new ship to try out. It's the one I will use to hunt for the Jatarians," I explained.

"What makes you think you will be successful in finding the Jatarians? We've had numerous ships searching for years, all with no luck," Amelia responded.

"I have a particular knack for finding them. I don't know what it is. It's as if a magnet pulls me to them."

"You do have a point there. You've always been the one who finds them. Well, I hope you're successful and safe. Is your new ship stealthed?" Amelia asked.

"It's supposed to be," I answered.

"Let's hope the Jatarians haven't figured out a way to detect stealthed ships in the last two years," Amelia noted.

It was something I hadn't really thought much about. Now I would definitely be paranoid about it. "The Jatarian colony has not been visited by any stealthed ships, have they?" I asked.

"Not that I'm aware. I will check when I return to Falton Two."

I nodded. "It could explain why the Federation scout ships have been unable to follow any of the Jatarian ships back to their other systems. Perhaps they are meeting with stealthed ships. Or stealthed ships freely come to and from the colony system from their home systems all the time, right under our noses."

"I don't like the sound of that," Amelia said, looking up at the sky.

I didn't either. It opened another door of possibilities and reasons for me to worry. Were they watching us now? Did they know of our refugee villages? I let out a deep breath.

Amelia added, "I wish I had the chance to see Colin."

"Me too. It's been many years since I've seen him."

"He's stuck somewhere, isn't he?" Amelia asked.

I shrugged. "I can't tell you where he is."

"But you do know where he is, right?" Amelia asked.

"Yes, I do."

"Is there any way you could take me to him?"

I could possibly use the stealthed striker to sneak her into the Dove Two settlement, but we had avoided that system since the Jatarians arrived. We didn't want to chance the Jatarians sensing the ship and realizing that Humans lived right there, so close to their colony. That's the last thing we needed to have happen. "No, not safely."

"He's in the system where the Jatarian colony is, isn't he?" Amelia asked.

I didn't say anything to confirm or deny her suspicions. I just said, "He's safe. You don't have to worry about him."

"Jeffery is suspicious of why Colin hasn't come to visit him all these years he's been here. He suspects the same thing I do—that Colin is at a settlement in the same system as the Jatarian colony."

I swallowed the nervousness building inside me. Had he mentioned these suspicions to his father? "Colin is a busy man."

"I'm sure he is. I just wish I could see him one last time."

I nodded. "Hopefully you will have that chance before too much longer."

"I hope so. Well, I will let you get back to your quarters. We will see you tomorrow," Amelia said.

As I walked away, I had a great deal to think about. From who was poisoning Amelia to the Jatarians having stealthed ships. Also the Dove Two settlement. Was it safe from the Federation? Did the Emperor suspect we had a settlement there? Should we evacuate it when we have the chance? I was glad I wasn't the one to make these decisions. I would inform Colin of what Amelia had said. He could speak with Akari, and they could discuss it with the Leadership Summit.

Chapter Three

My walk helped me sort out things a little. Once I reached the mountain, I headed to find Alex. If I would be here for a few days, while Amelia said her goodbyes, I wanted to see this new ship. The ship Bryce and I would use to find the Jatarian home system.

I knew I would find Alex in the research and development area of the mountain. I quickly took a detour to the hangar where the stealthed strikers were housed. Eight were now in our fleet. Progress was definitely being made. It wasn't enough to fend off an attack from the Jatarians, but we were headed in the right direction.

I ended up running into Alex in the hallway. "Just the man I've been looking for," I said, when I saw him.

Alex smiled. "I'm guessing you want to see your new ship?"

"Of course."

"Follow me," Alex said.

I fell into step beside him. "How much longer until I can take it up?"

"Soon. We are testing all the systems now."

"I'm glad you made a larger ship. The *Defender* would've been pretty cramped for an extended trip, as I imagine our next one to be."

"Any idea where you will start your search?" Alex asked.

"Bryce and I have been working with Maro on where we should look. His planet is a two-week hyperspace jump away. Maro knows that area of space. He can rule out a few systems, although I do realize that the Jatarians may have set up new colonies since Maro's planet was destroyed. I am interested to know where these colonies are, but my main goal is to find the Jatarian homeworld."

"It seems Maro will be a good asset. Is he planning to tag along on the mission?"

"Yes, he is. That's one of the things I need to determine, how large of a crew I need."

We had come to a closed door. Alex punched in a string of numbers on the key pad, and the door slowly opened. Alex stepped through the door, and I followed closely behind. Then I stopped in my tracks.

"Here it is," Alex indicated the reasonably large ship in the hangar.

"It's larger than I thought. I assumed it would be only slightly larger than the *Defender*. This is only a bit smaller than some of the transport vessels I've been on."

"You know the Federation is making stealthed warships. The technology is there. We must utilize it."

"Well, I'm thoroughly impressed. Have you taken it out at all?"

"We intend to tomorrow. That's why we're running all our systems checks now."

"Any way I can be on it?"

"I can give you a tour now, but I don't want you on the first few test flights. Just in case anything goes wrong," Alex answered.

"Okay. I would like that tour though." I understood Alex's hesitation to let me on the initial test flights. It could be risky. I hoped things went well. If not, it could put our mission off even farther. I'd already been waiting so long for this mission. I didn't think I would handle a setback very well.

"Right this way," Alex said, as he headed toward the ship.

We made our way all around the outside. I was astonished by its size. I might need my entire crew for this mission. I had not been expecting that.

After we toured the outside of the ship, we made our way on board. Everything was new and state-of-the-art. "Wow, Alex. You really outdid yourself this time."

"I can't take all the credit. We've had a large team of people working on it for a few years now. From the beginning we wanted to make larger stealthed ships. They just take longer and use up more of our resources. This is the only one of its kind."

"It's quite remarkable. Does it have weapons?" I asked. I wasn't sure which answer I was hoping for. On one hand, the ability to defend ourselves if need be was a positive, especially way out in unexplored space. On the other hand, we would be perceived as a threat. Not only to any alien race we came in contact with but also to any Federation ships we came across.

"Yes, it does. We've taken the time to hide the weapons turrets, so, to an outside ship, it appears as if it's unarmed. Not that any outside ship will actually see your ship, not unless you want them to."

I nodded. We had weapons if we needed them. Alex showed me everything. He was so proud of the ship he had created. "Will you be going up on its maiden voyage?" I asked.

"No. I'll keep my feet firmly on the surface. Space is no place for me."

I had to laugh. "I can't wait to show my crew this ship. It will definitely keep us comfortable for a long-term mission."

"You will appreciate this next room," Alex said, as he opened a door.

We walked in, and a smile crossed my face. "You put in a recreation room?"

Alex smiled. "We understood what you intended to do with this ship. We knew that finding the Jatarians might take years. We wanted you and your crew to be comfortable."

"Thank you," I said, as I surveyed the different activities in the room.

"We also have a workout facility and a theater."

"This ship reminds me in many ways of the *Explorer*, with all these amenities. Don't get me wrong. This ship is much smaller than the *Explorer*, but I know it will be every bit as comfortable. Thank you, Alex, for thinking of these things. It will make our time in hyperspace much more pleasant."

Alex beamed with pride. "Let me show you to your office and quarters."

I liked the sound of that. It turned out my office was adjacent the Command Center. My quarters were attached to my office. I had to smile. "You really thought of everything, Alex."

"So you approve?"

"Yes, very much. I'm also afraid that, after this, my crew will not be willing to return to our transport vessel." I laughed.

Alex chuckled. "I'm glad you approve. We will start our test flights first thing in the morning. We hope to have this ship ready for you in a few weeks."

"It's time we find the Jatarians' homeworld," I said.

"Do you find it odd that we haven't seen or heard from them in the last couple years? Other than their one known colony?" Alex asked.

"Yes. And it makes me even more afraid that another attack from the Jatarians could happen at any time."

"What if you're out hunting for their homeworld, and they attack the Federation? From what I hear, you were instrumental in controlling the Morag and keeping Falton Two safe."

I shrugged. "It didn't work out for the other colonies."

"You didn't have the ships. I'm sure the Morag have rebuilt their fleet by now."

"They have. I've been keeping tabs on them. I have large fleets placed near the Federation that we can call on, if need be."

"What if you are out of range of your gift?" Alex asked, the worry evident in his expression.

The questions Alex asked were not new to me. I'd spent many hours worrying about these things already, and countless hours of worry and planning had resulted. Amelia knew where the Morag fleets were, as did Jeffery and the Emperor. I had to believe they could handle the situation, if it arose.

"I've thought that over and have placed Morag fleets nearby. The Emperor can handle it. Jeffery and Amelia will help too. Everything will work out." I portrayed confidence, even though, deep down, I wasn't sure.

"I assumed you had a plan. I guess the fate of the Federation should be in the Empress and the Emperor's hands, not yours."

I smiled. "So does this ship have a name?"

"*Hunter*," Alex said, as he beamed with pride.

"I like the sound of that. I'm confident we will find them, Alex."

"Me too."

"Can I be in the Flight Command Center with you tomorrow, as the ship goes through these flight tests?"

"Yes, but it is pretty boring stuff. I would imagine you'll find more important things to do. But do feel free to check in at any time. I'll ensure the staff knows they are to admit you, if you come by."

"Okay. I will find Bryce and figure out what crew we need."

Alex nodded. "Have a good night."

As I left the hangar where my new ship was, I couldn't help but feel eager for our mission. I would find the Jatarian homeworld, no matter how long it took.

My thoughts changed to my family. I would miss Hadassah and the kids deeply, but, if I wanted to keep them safe long-term, this was a necessary step in the right direction—even though it meant I would miss out on many things with my family while I was gone.

I headed to find Bryce. It didn't take me long to find him. He was in our quarters.

"How are things with Amelia and Jeffery?" Bryce asked, when I walked in.

"Good. Amelia wants to leave in a couple days. I just got back from seeing our new ship."

"Were you impressed?"

"Yes, it's much larger than I had imagined."

Bryce smiled. "I know. I saw it earlier."

"You did?"

"Yes, I ran into Alex shortly after we arrived. I managed to talk him into showing me the ship. I hope you don't mind, but I've been working on a list of who we might want to take as our crew."

"Sometimes it's a little scary how well you know me, Bryce. That's exactly why I was coming to find you. We need to figure out who's coming with us."

"Here's my list," Bryce said.

I took the piece of paper and looked it over. I had to smile. "It's pretty much our entire crew from the *Spirit of Rebellion*."

"Yes. I thought it would be prudent for us to have Wyatt and Samson in engineering. We will be far away from any help, should something malfunction."

"Good point. It would be good to get both of them here to work with Alex and his team. The more familiar they can get with the ship before we head out, the better."

"I'll send Wyatt over there tomorrow, and I'll find out where Samson is and get him here," Bryce said.

"Good. If Samson and Wyatt can get familiar with the ship, while we take a few days to return Amelia, we might as well do it. The rest of the crew will catch up after we have dropped off Amelia."

"I agree."

"Jeffery wants to come," I said, as I sat down.

"Will you let him?"

"I don't know. If it wouldn't be such a long trip, I would consider it more seriously. I just don't think Jeffery can be away that long. What if something happens to Amelia? What if the Jatarians attack? We might need his strong gift to help here," I explained, as I ran my fingers through my hair.

"He would learn a lot by going into space. And you two would get even closer. What does Eloise think?"

"I have no idea. I'm not sure how Amelia feels about it either."

"What will you do?"

"I'm not sure. Maybe I'll mention it to Amelia and get her take on it."

"If we find the Jatarians, Jeffery would get to witness a battle and how all that comes together firsthand. That could be pretty valuable in the future."

"I know, but what if we are gone for one year or more?"

"We are starting farther out than the scout ships are. My guess is the Jatarians are even farther out than we think."

"What if we went to the edge of the galaxy and then made our way back in? Then the scout ships are exploring from one end, and we are from the other," I suggested.

"That's something to consider," Bryce replied.

"How long of a jump is it to the edge of the galaxy?" I asked.

"I have no idea. No one has ever explored that far," Bryce said.

"Exploring the unknown," I began. "What could possibly go wrong?"

"Maybe we shouldn't go all the way to the outskirts of the galaxy. We will be on a new ship. Maybe at first we shouldn't venture so far," Bryce answered.

"You're right. We should be a little more cautious on our first voyage. Let's go out farther than Maro's planet though."

"I can't believe we're finally looking for the Jatarian homeworld. It seems like we've waited forever for this mission."

"First, we have to get Amelia home," I said.

"I'll talk to the crew tomorrow and get Samson here. You worry about Amelia and Jeffery."

"Okay, I can do that."

"What did you think of the ship's name?" Bryce asked.

"It's fitting. That's exactly what I intend to do, hunt down the Jatarians."

Bryce stood and said, "I'll go find some of the crew and see who I can get on those test flights tomorrow."

I nodded. I needed to talk to Colin. I wasn't really looking forward to it. Both Amelia and Jeffery suspected Colin was in the refugee system where the Jatarian colony was. What did this mean for the future? Was the refugee settlement in danger? Would it one day be when Jeffery becomes the Emperor?

Once Bryce walked out the door, I closed my eyes and focused on my gift.

How are things going with you, Slade? Colin asked.

I've seen my new ship and am excited to get underway on my mission of hunting down the Jatarians.

I have no doubt you are. How's Amelia?

I'm here to take her home.

She mentioned that. I really wish I would've had the opportunity to see her in person. I'm afraid I never will.

Amelia mentioned that she suspects you are in a settlement in the same system as the Jatarians' colony. She also said Jeffery expects the same thing.

I was afraid of that. It's the only logical reason why I wouldn't have visited either one of them by now. Something has kept me away. They can both still communicate with me, so it's not that I'm too far away.

So what does this mean for the long-term safety of Dove Two? I asked.

I'm honestly not sure. You know Jeffery at this point better than I do. What do you think?

I don't know. I guess a lot can happen between now and when it will matter. Not much we can do about it at the moment.

Colin replied, *You're right. We will keep it in our minds, but, first, the Jatarians must be destroyed.*

About that, I replied. *Jeffery wants to tag along on the mission. I think he would learn many valuable lessons that could be useful. Yet I'm not sure how long we will be gone.*

Does he realize how long of a mission it might be?

He does. He's hesitant because of it. I'm not sure how much longer I'll have to take him on a mission like this, one where he could hopefully realize that many other races are out there—races that aren't our enemies. I think it would really open his eyes to the vastness of our galaxy and to the smallness of the Federation. Perhaps he will realize not all things revolve around the Federation—or Humans, for that matter.

What makes you hesitant to take him on such an extended mission? Colin asked.

What if something happens to Amelia?

46

Do you know something I don't?

Theodore and I believe the Averys are behind her deteriorating health. We are concerned it will continue when she returns.

How could the Averys be behind it?

You know better than do I how connected they were. Is someone willing to help them get back to the Federation by hastening the scenario where their daughter is the Empress? The first thing Eloise would do would be to bring her parents back.

Slade, I'm afraid you may be on to something there. I don't like it, not one bit. I hadn't even considered the Averys as suspects. They do have the most to gain from Amelia's demise.

Theodore and Amelia were working on a list of people who are close to her and then will cross-reference the list with those who once worked for Lord and Lady Avery, I explained.

It could be someone who has no viable ties to Avery. This task may be challenging.

I agree. Especially if they have the gift, and there may not be any traceable evidence.

They need to get the Emperor involved in this. That will ensure, if something happens, the blame gets placed in the right direction and not in ours. If the Emperor blames the Averys for Amelia's death, he will work to ensure they do not return. Plus he could possibly narrow the suspect list better than Amelia or Theodore.

You're right about that. The Emperor may end up on our side on this one. That will be a change.

Who will tell him?

I'll leave that to Amelia, I replied.

What about Jeffery? Do you plan to tell him that we suspect his in-laws are responsible for poisoning his mother?

I don't know. He and Eloise are removed from the situation. They would have no involvement, right? I knew Jeffery could connect with other gifted people as far away as Falton Two. Surely he had no involvement.

I would assume they weren't involved. The Averys have been gone from Falton Two for a long time, but they would still have more of those loyalties and connections that could make this happen. Eloise and Jeffery are pawns in their game.

Do you think they had anything to do with Gabriel's attack, or do you think it was solely Lord and Lady Avery? I asked.

You know Eloise and Jeffery better than I do. Perhaps they're only pieces in the game the Averys are playing. Maybe Eloise and Jeffery are just victims.

It's hard to picture either one of them as a victim.

If Jeffery realizes who is behind the attempt to poison Amelia, then maybe he would prevent the Averys from returning to the Federation when the time comes, Colin said.

When do you propose I tell him?

I'm not sure. He will tell his father, once he hears. If we want to let Amelia pass along that information, we better wait to tell Jeffery.

Okay.

I really wish I could've seen Amelia while she was there at Elmania. As for Jeffery's suspicions of us having a refugee settlement here, we will deal with that later. Thanks for keeping me informed, Slade.

You're welcome, Colin.

Be careful when you return Amelia to Falton Two. Never trust the Emperor where you're concerned. Remain vigilant always.

I will. Thanks for the reminder though.

Good luck, Slade.

After my conversation with Colin, I sat and thought long and hard about Jeffery. God forbid, what if something happened to Amelia, once she's back home at the palace? Worst case we would return Jeffery to Falton Two before we found the Jatarian homeworld. That would slow down our mission but wouldn't derail it.

Would this mission be the last time Jeffery had the opportunity to come along? If he did, what could possibly go wrong? That train of thought led down a rabbit hole of possibilities that I would rather not consider.

Could Eloise manage the kids here at Elmania, without Jeffery's help? She did have a village to assist her. She appeared to have friends. Was that enough? Would she feel more isolated? That was a conversation Jeffery must have with her.

As the captain of the ship, did I have any reason why bringing Jeffery might be a bad idea? We had the room and the resources. It would be a great experience for him. It would help bring the two of us closer. That was good for my future and for those around me.

I got up and left my quarters. A quick walk and some fresh air might help me think clearer. I didn't want to end up back down in the village, so I stayed near the mountain.

In the end, I decided that the decision was ultimately Jeffery's. I had no real reason to say no. I could point out the hesitations I had, but the final decision would fall to him. Him and Eloise.

I resolved to talk to Jeffery about it more in the morning. That would give him and Eloise plenty of time to discuss it, while I returned Amelia to Falton Two.

By the time I reached my quarters again, I felt a sense of peace. It felt good. It was only temporary, however. Before long my mind would find something else to worry about. As for whether or not Jeffery would tag along on our mission to find the Jatarian homeworld, I would leave that up to him.

Chapter Four

The next few days flew by. The test flights of
the *Hunter* went well. A few things needed fine-tuning but
nothing drastic. My crew was heavily involved with the test
flights and spent most of the day familiarizing themselves with
our new ship.

I found myself getting more excited by the day, anticipating
our mission to search for the Jatarians. We would find countless
other races and planets while we searched for the Jatarians. This
was basically an exploration mission. We wouldn't be exploring
planets for colonization, but my guess was that we would find
more out there.

We planned to start farther out than we've ever been. To my
knowledge, it was farther out than any Human had ever gone
before. It was exhilarating to think about.

Jeffery and I had talked extensively about the mission and
the positives and negatives of him tagging along. He had already
started discussing it with Eloise. I personally don't think she
liked the idea, not when it meant she would be stuck here at
Elmania, alone with the children. If this scenario had come up
while Amelia was here, Eloise might have been more receptive to
the idea. Now that Amelia was leaving, Eloise had no family to
help.

I suggested that perhaps we could pick up Emma while we
were at Falton Two, dropping off Amelia. That would be
someone who could help Eloise. Amelia wasn't keen on the idea.
She hadn't had the opportunity to spend time with her daughter
since she'd been here at Elmania. So that idea was out.

I tried not to let it distract me much. This was Jeffery's
problem to solve, not mine. I left my children behind all the time

to do my job as captain of a transport vessel, yet never for as long as we expected this mission to be. I tried not to dwell much on it. We had a village of people to help Hadassah though. Did Eloise and Jeffery have that?

The day finally came for us to leave, returning Amelia and Theodore to Falton Two. Jeffery had agreed not to mention anything about Amelia's return to his father. The Emperor would find out when she walked into the palace. This helped ease some of my fears but not all.

The goodbyes were hard for Amelia and the kids. Jeffery kept a positive attitude in front of the children, while sending off his mother. He knew what I knew. This would likely be the last time he saw his mother. He stayed strong.

Once we were all loaded on the transport vessel, I closed the back ramp, while Jeffery, Eloise, and the kids waved from a safe distance.

Amelia had tears in her eyes. I gave her a hug to comfort her. Then I showed her to her quarters. The ship took off and entered hyperspace while I was doing this. Connor was in charge when I wasn't in the Command Center. The ship was in good hands.

After assuring myself that Amelia was comfortable, I headed to the Command Center. It felt good to sit in my command chair and to see my command crew. I trusted these people. This was my extended family in a sense.

I took a deep breath and slowly let it out. We were headed to Falton Two. As much as I tried to calm my mind from the fears that threatened to overtake me, I couldn't quite shake the unease. Every time I went to Falton Two, I was in danger—which meant my crew was also in danger.

After sitting at my post for a few hours, I checked on Amelia. We would be in hyperspace for a few days, and I wanted to ensure she was comfortable.

I found her in the cafeteria, chatting with Captain Parker. I couldn't help but smile, as I sat down at the table with them. "Captain Parker is quite the storyteller, isn't he?" I asked.

"Yes, I'm fascinated by his stories of his life on Leanessa. His story of survival and perseverance is remarkable," Amelia commented.

"It is. He should write a book, and that book should be required reading in flight school. Anything can happen while traveling in space. We all need to be at least somewhat prepared for how to handle things, should we crash-land on a remote planet."

"I'm glad I have a few more days to hear more of your stories, Captain Parker," Amelia said. "And to enjoy your granddaughter's cooking."

Parker beamed with pride. "It's such an honor to have the opportunity to meet you and to speak with you."

"I believe I will learn many things from you, Parker," Amelia added.

"I know I have," I commented. "Are you settled, Amelia? Is there anything you need?"

"I'm doing great. Thank you, Slade. Your crew has been very helpful. I'll enjoy this trip back home. Plus I enjoy getting to know these people who have basically become your family. I am filled with pride to hear them talk about you. You've done well, Slade. You've managed to surround yourself with an amazing group of individuals, and that's not an easy thing to accomplish," Amelia shared.

"It's not been easy, but it's definitely been worth it. This crew, with a few extras, will accompany me on our hunt to find the Jatarians."

"Yes, Captain Parker mentioned your friend Maro will be traveling with you. I wish I had the opportunity to meet him. He sounds like an amazing individual, one I'm sure has many stories I could learn from as well."

I was tempted to make a stop at Dove One and pick up Maro and introduce Amelia to my family, but I couldn't risk it. The safety of my children had to be my top priority. "Maro means a great deal to us, as does his family. He knows the area of space closer to where his people's homeworld was. That's where we will start our hunt for the Jatarians' homeworld. We will be farther out than any of the scout ships."

"Their routine searching patterns don't seem to be the fastest way to find what we're searching for. I am confident you and your crew will be the ones to find the Jatarians, Slade. Where would we be without you? I shudder to even think about it," Amelia said.

"You would be fine, I'm sure," I replied.

Amelia shook her head. "I hope that, when the time comes, you will serve Jeffery as you have served me, Slade. Give him wise counsel when asked. I know you will always do what's best for the greater good of Humans in general. Your mother would be so proud of the man you've become. The Empire would greatly benefit from your leadership. Have you considered returning?"

"No. This is my home. These are my people. Hunting down and destroying the Jatarians helps the Empire too. I'm saving them from an enemy they aren't even aware exists."

"Well, your mother knows but not your father. I wish your father could see you now. He has no idea where you are. Your mother has kept the truth from him, since he has no knowledge of the Human Federation's existence."

"What do you think he would do if he found out?" I asked.

Amelia laughed. "He would want an alliance. Maybe even bring us together under his rule. Most rulers want to expand their dominion, some out of necessity but most to increase the power it gives them."

"The Empire and the Federation are too far apart to be ruled by one leader. That would never work."

"I agree. This is one of the numerous reasons we've agreed to keep the Federation's existence a secret from your father. It would only complicate things."

"The wisest choice, I'm sure. So does the Emperor want to expand his influence and territory?" I asked.

"Yes, of course. This is why he wanted to start new colonies. He's learned that, when we start a new colony, we must also have the means to protect its citizens. I've explained how your people use the caves and mountains to stay hidden from the Jatarians. When we start new colonies again, we should use this method. We must keep our people safe. If we can't, no one will volunteer to go to these new colonies—not when it means they have a good chance of being killed by hostile aliens," Amelia explained.

I didn't like that the Emperor now knew that we hid in caves and mountains to stay hidden from the Jatarians. Would this help him find us eventually? I took a deep breath. Keeping any and all Humans safe was my priority. If the Federation could use this strategy to keep their new colonies safe, it would be a good thing.

Inwardly I sighed. Outwardly I smiled. "We did this with Maro's people too. When we rescued the survivors from his world and took them to a new planet to live, we suggested they use the caves and mountains to remain hidden from their enemies."

Weil Thomas

"What other enemies would they have, besides the Jatarians?" Amelia asked.

"The Federation. If the Federation found them and realized they had the technology to travel through hyperspace, even in unarmed ships, they would be marked as a threat."

Amelia looked down at her hands. "You are right, Slade. I'm not sure where the line is in determining whether a race is peaceful or dangerous. Is the presence of military ships not a criteria that must be met before they are destroyed?"

"I believe the presence of military technology or the ability to travel in hyperspace are both triggers to call in the Morag. Then the Morag just takes over and destroys their ships and makes the survivors slaves to their needs and wants."

"It sounds like these are policies you do not agree with."

"I don't agree. I've seen numerous alien civilizations, yet only two of them has been hostile—the Jatarians and the Lamothians. I guess, without my gift, I would count the Morag as hostile too. Still, I can't help but wonder how many aliens have been destroyed throughout the centuries because they might one day become a threat," I replied.

"It's hard to determine who will or won't be a threat down the line. We do our best. Perhaps after we've found and dealt with the Jatarians, we can examine our alien policies more closely and see how they can be improved. Jeffery could gain a lot of experience going with you on your mission and witnessing these situations for himself. It might help make the future of this Federation a better one. I don't think it would hurt," Amelia said.

"I agree. I'm not sure Eloise agrees, however."

"I think she sees your influence on Jeffery as a threat to hers. She's had her parents telling her, since the day you arrived, that you are a threat to the Federation. I'm sure, in the back of her mind, she still believes this."

"Eloise is definitely not a fan of mine. She just tolerates my presence."

"I'm certain she's also worried about what would happen if Jeffery didn't return to Falton Two. She would lose her chance to be the Empress of the Federation. That's the role she's been raised to fulfill all her life. She doesn't think she can risk it."

"That does make sense. I'm leaving that problem to Jeffery. I've agreed that he can come along with us. Making Eloise comfortable with it is up to him," I replied.

"I agree. I think it would be good for Jeffery, an experience he will never have the opportunity to witness again. He can't pass it up, in my opinion. I took the liberty to express that very opinion to him and Eloise. Whether it will work or not on Eloise remains to be seen."

"It's out of our hands. We've done all we could," I commented.

Amelia nodded.

"Are you excited to be headed home?" I asked.

"Yes and no. I'm excited to see the rest of my family and to resume the rest of my duties. I'm nervous for the future and what that looks like."

"Did you and Theodore narrow down the list of people who could be trying to poison you?"

"Yes. We have narrowed it down to three. Hopefully we can figure out the culprit, and I won't have to worry about it further," Amelia replied.

"I hope so. Will you tell the Emperor?" I asked.

"Yes. It's one of the things I will discuss with him when I return."

"Good. He needs to know who we think is behind it."

"I agree."

"Did you tell Jeffery?"

"No. Not much he can do about it. The Emperor maybe can. He will know even better than I do which connections the Averys have."

"Seems we are at least taking steps in the right direction," I said.

"Yes. I will keep in contact with you as long as possible. I know you will eventually go farther into the galaxy than we can communicate with our gifts."

"Yes, I'm afraid so."

"Please be careful out there, Slade. Whether or not Jeffery goes with you, I hope you won't take too many risks."

"I won't. This crew is my responsibility. It's my job to keep them safe. They are my family. I won't take any unnecessary risks." I looked over at Parker and smiled.

He smiled back. Parker was like a grandfather to me. He was great to have around. Always full of wise advice.

"I better get back to the Command Center. I'll let Parker entertain you with more of his life stories."

"Thanks for checking on me, Slade."

I made my way to the Command Center. Everything appeared to be operating as usual. I hoped that would continue, since we had Amelia on board. This was not the time for something to go wrong. I said a quick prayer that everything would go smoothly.

"How's Amelia?" Bryce asked, interrupting my thoughts.

"She's sitting with Parker in the cafeteria."

Bryce laughed. "So she's being entertained."

"Yes."

"Do we have a plan for where we will land, once we arrive at Falton Two?" Bryce asked.

"Yes. Colin has made arrangements for us to land at Star Station twenty. It's staffed mostly by rebel sympathizers. So we should be safe there."

"What about Theodore and Amelia? Will they be safe?"

"Yes. Colin has a driver who's supposed to meet us. It's someone he trusts. He didn't say who."

"I'm glad Colin still has all these connections, even though he hasn't stepped foot off Dove Two in years," Bryce said.

"Me too. I don't have many connections on Falton Two."

"Good thing we have Colin then," Bryce said. "Still, you are very well connected, aren't you?"

I had to laugh. "I do know many people at the top," I joked.

Hearing that, Graham laughed. "We know a lot of people on Falton Two. That's the dock we usually use to smuggle people out. Are we picking up any passengers?" Graham asked.

"Not that I'm aware of," I replied. "Maybe when we get closer, I'll check in with Colin and get more specifics on his plans."

"We know who we can trust there," Graham added. "No need to worry."

I nodded. "I'm glad you are familiar with the area and the people. That'll make it all easier."

"Glad we can help," Graham replied.

I felt better after Graham reminded me of that. They knew their way around. They were connected to the rebels. Maybe this mission would go better than I feared. I usually let my imagination run wild with all the ways things could go wrong. Expect the best, but prepare for the worst. That's usually what I did.

After manning my post for a few hours, I headed to my quarters to rest. This trip would last a few days. There was plenty of time to rest.

I spent the remaining days of our journey to Falton Two trying to soak up as much time as possible with Amelia. This would likely be the last time I would see her. I had no intentions of returning to Falton Two. I did wish I could see Phoebe, but it was too risky. I held out hope that, one day, I would see her again.

Amelia and I had shared some deep conversations about the past and the future. I looked forward to the moments I had to visit with her.

As we grew closer to Falton Two, my sense of dread increased. If something bad happened, it would be disastrous for me and my crew and possibly even the future of the Federation.

Amelia reminded me so much of my own mother. It felt so good to be around her. I dreaded watching her walk down the ramp.

I was comforted that Phoebe was getting Amelia back. I knew Phoebe missed her deeply. As did Phoebe's children. I knew Amelia would enjoy still being surrounded by her other grandkids.

When the time neared, I headed to the Command Center. Amelia joined me. She thought it would be interesting to see Falton Two from space.

"Bryce, how far are we from the Falton Two system?" I asked.

"Fifteen minutes," Bryce replied.

My heart beat faster. I took a deep breath to calm my nerves. It didn't really work. "Connor, run the scans," I ordered, once five minutes had passed.

We had no idea what to expect regarding the number of ships we would find in the system. Would the Emperor want a show of strength to any ships that may pass the system? Would we find hundreds of ships? Or would he hide his strength and only leave a minimum number of ships in the system? I would lean to a minimum number of ships, if it were me. As I wasn't the Emperor, we really had no idea which way he would lean.

"Scans are coming," Connor announced.

The Command Center grew silent, as we awaited Connor's report. We all looked to Connor for the results of his scan.

"Scans show a minimal number of ships in the system. Only twenty-one ships show on the scans," Connor reported.

"That's a relief," I said, as I slowly let out a deep breath of air.

"Do we know how many are military ships?" Amelia asked.

"No, unfortunately we cannot discern that from outside the system," I answered.

"What about the stealthed military ships?" Amelia asked slowly.

I took in a sharp breath. I had forgotten about them. "They also won't show on the scans from outside the system. Once we exit, we should hopefully see them on our scans. They'll show up as blue icons on the tactical display right here." I pointed to the tactical display, now represented on one of the large screens at the front of the Command Center.

"Do you expect to find many of these stealthed ships?" Connor asked her.

"I do," Amelia answered.

I didn't like the sound of that. "No need to worry," I reminded the crew. "We are a transport vessel, one that is expected at our designated port. We have an identification that is sound. We will be the transport vessel *Liberty*. The *Liberty* is an almost identical ship to ours. We have covered all the scenarios. We've made our plans. We're ready for this."

My words seemed to comfort the command crew. I did my best to look calm and confident.

The twinge in the pit of my stomach signaled our exit from hyperspace. My gaze moved immediately to the tactical display, as did everyone else's in the room.

I felt the bile rising in my throat and stood up. There on the tactical display was an overwhelming number of blue icons. Stealthed warships. The Federation had been busy, very busy building warships.

A hush fell over the crew in the Command Center. The system was filled with warships that couldn't be seen. It made me wonder if the Jatarians could sense stealthed ships. I prayed they couldn't. Two years was a lot of time to develop the technology though. That was a worry for another day, so I pushed it out of my mind, at least for now.

Soon after we exited hyperspace, Graham said, "We are receiving a communication from Falton Two, asking us to identify ourselves."

"Tell them that we are the transport vessel *Liberty* and are expected at Star Station twenty," I ordered.

Graham nodded and sent over the information.

We all tensely waited for a response. After a few moments, Graham replied, "We are to proceed to Star Station twenty."

Everyone breathed a sigh of relief. One hurdle down. Everything needed to go exactly according to plan. There was no room for error.

"I love seeing Falton Two from this perspective," Amelia said. "It helps remind me that this planet and our Federation is so small compared to what this galaxy holds. We are only a minuscule part of it. I think sometimes we forget that and think that everything revolves around us. That we, as Humans, are superior to other races. That's just not the case. I wish everyone had the opportunity to see it from here."

"You do make an excellent point, Amelia. We are not the only ones who live in this galaxy. We must remember our place in it and be intentional in our dealings with other alien races to ensure that Humans are painted in a positive light and not a negative one," I added.

"Spoken like a true leader, Slade. Are you sure you don't want to reconsider ruling the Federation?" Amelia asked, as she laughed.

"I'm sure," I quickly replied. "Don't even consider it. I would turn it down."

"I know. I do hope you will help Jeffery when the time comes, Slade. An advisor like you would be invaluable."

"As long as it can be done remotely, I'm fine with that."

"Good. Jeffery will need it," Amelia replied.

I moved my attention from Amelia back to the viewscreens at the front of the room. I couldn't stop myself from looking at the tactical display. So many blue icons were represented there. I shivered. These stealthed warships were a huge asset for our fight against the Jatarians. Yet the idea that, one day, they could be used against the refugees, the so-called rebels, made me very uneasy.

After exiting hyperspace, it took us a few hours to get to Falton Two. It was very unnerving, knowing so many warships were in the system, but we couldn't see them with our own eyes.

The tactical display showed all the blue icons holding their positions. So far, no one had raised any alarm, we hadn't been discovered as an imposter of the true transport vessel *Liberty*. At least not yet.

"The planet is so beautiful from here," Amelia commented, as we made our final approach to the planet.

I nodded and replied, "It is." Yet I knew it was full of danger. It also held one of my best friends, Phoebe. I wished I could reach out and could tell her that I was here and could see her face-to-face. It was out of the question though.

As we entered the atmosphere, Korah came into view. Every time I saw the city, it seemed to have grown. We quickly made our way to Star Station twenty.

Once we touched down, I turned to Amelia. "Are you ready?"

Amelia nodded. "I'm ready."

I nodded and stood up. "Everyone stay at your post. We want to be ready in the event we need to leave quickly."

I knew that scenario would never turn out well for us. Numerous stealthed ships in orbit would follow us.

I pushed the thought from my mind and led Amelia out of the Command Center. Theodore was waiting for us near the rear ramp. I gave Amelia a big hug. "Take care of her, Theodore," I said, as I shook his hand.

"I will. You stay safe, Slade. I hope to see you again one day."

"Me too." I reached for the button that would open the ramp. I imagined what might be on the other side of it—an entire company of Federation Protection Unit soldiers. I pushed the button anyway.

I held my breath as the ramp lowered. What I saw stopped me in my tracks. I took in a sharp breath, and tears came to my eyes. Phoebe. Phoebe was standing on the dock.

I ran down the ramp and enveloped Phoebe in a giant hug. I couldn't help the tears that slipped down my cheeks. It had been so long since I'd seen her. "What are you doing here?" I asked.

"I'm here to take Amelia back home. Colin contacted me and told me when and where to be. He said it was a secret. I was to let no one know where or why I was leaving."

"So what was your excuse to leave the palace?" I asked.

"I don't need an excuse. I'm not under house arrest. I go shopping. I go walking."

Phoebe turned to Amelia and smiled.

Amelia said, "It's so good to see you, Phoebe. Thank you for coming to get us. I'm sure we need to make this short, before someone recognizes what's going on."

I looked around. Everyone was watching. "Too late for that," I said. I hoped all these people were rebels and wouldn't turn me into the FPU.

Phoebe looked around and nodded. "We better be on our way."

I gave Phoebe another big hug and then turned to Amelia. "Until next time," I said.

Amelia smiled. "Until next time. Thank you, Slade."

"Good luck," I replied. Then I shook hands with Theodore one more time. I watched as the three of them walked away. It wasn't easy to stand here and watch them leave, knowing I might not ever see any of them again.

I glanced around again. Everyone was still watching. I asked, "Do we have any cargo to load up?"

People of all ages began to appear from behind crates and various other objects. I nodded and turned around and walked back on the ship.

Graham and Hayes stood at the top of the ramp. They began greeting all our new passengers. I headed back to the Command Center.

When I walked in, Bryce said, "It appears Colin had more plans at work than we realized."

"You didn't get to see her," I said sadly.

"It's okay. I saw Phoebe on the video feed. She looked good. Healthy and happy."

"Yes, she did." I sat in silence, watching the security footage from the rear of the ship. When at last our cargo was all on board, Graham and Hayes returned to the Command Center.

"Cargo is loaded. We are ready to head out," Graham reported, as he sat down at his console.

"Let's get out of here," I ordered.

As our ship began its ascent into space, my nerves increased. Would we be followed? Did the FPU know what had happened here? Had they implanted a spy? Would they track us? I shook my head. I had to stop seeing danger at every turn. It was not a healthy way to live.

I remained on the edge of my seat as we moved through the atmosphere of Falton Two. If we made it out this time, I hoped it would be years before I had to return here.

The tactical display was still full of blue icons, the stealthed warships. Would one be assigned to follow us?

"We are ready to enter hyperspace," Cole said.

"Let's return to Elmania. We have a lot of cargo to unload."

As I felt our ship make the transition into hyperspace, my gaze stayed glued to the tactical display. Would we be followed?

I waited what seemed like an eternity before asking, "Connor, are we being followed?"

"No, Captain. We are in the clear."

I knew however that if a stealthed ship were following us, we wouldn't know. I quickly confirmed with Colin, through his contacts that none of the stealthed ships in the Falton Two system had left. We were truly in the clear.

I sat back and breathed a sigh of relief. We had done it. Amelia was safely back on Falton Two. We had a ship full of new refugees who needed a safe place to live. Life was good, at least for now.

Forges of the Federation: Hunter

Chapter Five

The trip back to Elmania went smoothly. Kami expected the influx of refugees and was ready for them. I was anxious to speak to Alex and iron out our timetable for taking the *Hunter* on our first mission. I also needed to talk to Jeffery.

It just so happened that I ran into Alex shortly after we unloaded all our cargo. "How is the new ship?" I asked him.

Alex smiled. "It's ready. I would like to get this part of your crew in there, so they can start familiarizing themselves with the ship."

"I'm sure they're ready. We are all anxious to get underway."

"I heard your return to Falton Two went well," Alex commented.

"It did, as well as I could have hoped."

"Good. We can get all of your crew now on the ship first thing in the morning. I estimate one week will be sufficient enough to prepare for your mission."

"That sounds promising. I'll talk to my full crew, and we will report first thing in the morning," I said excitedly.

"Samson has already been here, working on the ship, so he has a bit of a head start."

"I don't have a problem with that. The more Samson knows, the better, as far as I'm concerned."

"I'll see you first thing in the morning then, Slade."

"See you then."

I quickly found Bryce and updated him on our timetable. He agreed to inform the rest of the crew. I planned to head down to the village and speak with Jeffery.

On my walk, I decided to reach out to Amelia. It had been a few days since her return to Falton Two. I had yet to check in with her.

I assume you made it back to Elmania safely.

Yes, with a ship full of refugees.

After what I've witnessed here over the past few days since my return, I'm not surprised. The people without the gift are still being persecuted. It is no wonder they're still leaving. It makes me sad, but I'm glad they have somewhere to go. At this rate, the refugee villages are growing in population faster than Falton Two.

Why does the Emperor do this?

I have tried to talk to him about this. An ever-growing gap continues between those with the gift and those without the gift. I would like to find ways to bridge that gap. It's something I am working on. Having seen the other side, I feel even more compelled to bring all of us together and to not further separate us.

Was the Emperor happy to see you?

Yes, surprisingly he was. It was such a delight to see Gabriel, Phoebe, their children, and Emma again.

I was thrilled to see Phoebe too. It was unexpected.

I guess Colin had a few surprises awaiting you. You got to see Phoebe and got a group of refugees to take to safety.

Leave it to Colin to organize something like that, I said. *Have you discussed with the Emperor our suspicions about the Averys?*

No, I have not had the opportunity yet. I am being cautious though. We are on the lookout for our three suspects. The sooner we can get to the bottom of this, the better.

Good. Stay vigilant, Amelia. We need you alive and well.

Are you preparing for your hunt for the Jatarians?

Yes. We are making our final preparations now.

Will Jeffery be joining you? Amelia asked.

I'm on my way to speak with him now.

Good luck. Stay in touch, Slade.
I will. Stay safe.
You too.

I enjoyed the rest of my walk to the village. Fall was just beginning to show its beauty in the forest around the village. It was a breathtaking sight. Fall was a beautiful time of year. It did lead to winter, which was a much harder season to get through here at Elmania. Yet how could I not notice the beauty surrounding me?

Once I reached Jeffery's cottage, I paused for a moment. I wasn't sure what I was hoping for. Would he stay, or would he go? I guessed it was time to get the answer.

I knocked, and it didn't take long for Eloise to open the door. She seemed obviously disappointed that it was me. "Were you expecting someone else?" I asked, as she moved to the side to let me in.

"Yes, I have a friend coming over," Eloise replied.

I couldn't help but raise an eyebrow at that. It didn't go unnoticed.

"What? Are you surprised I have friends?"

"No, I'm not, Eloise. Last time I was here, I noticed you seemed to have numerous friends. I'm glad for you."

Eloise didn't appear convinced. Another knock sounded at the door. Eloise gave me a look that made me head off to find Jeffery. I was curious who this friend was but wasn't willing to stick around and find out.

It was easy to find Jeffery. I just followed the sound of the children's laughter. I found him playing with his children in the backyard. A feeling of pride swept over me. This man—who I had thought was just as evil as his father—had turned out to be an amazing dad. Times had changed and had changed for the better.

I watched quietly from the doorway, until the children noticed me. It also reminded me of what I was missing back on Dove One.

"How long have you been standing there?" Jeffery asked.

"Not long. I didn't want to interrupt. You guys were having such a great time."

The kids all ran over and wanted my attention for a few minutes. Eventually they lost interest in me and returned to the game they'd been playing.

"I take it Amelia is back, safe and sound?" Jeffery asked quietly.

"Yes, she is."

"Good. Everything went according to plan then?"

"Yes. What about you and Eloise? Have you made your decision?"

"We have. I will go with you. We agreed that I could not pass up this opportunity. Kami has helped us find a few people who can help Eloise with the children. Eloise is comfortable with it."

"I have to admit that I am a little surprised. I never thought she would agree to it," I said.

"Me neither, but I think she realized how important it is for me. So when do we leave?"

"My best guess at this point is about one week. We have a new ship. My crew will begin familiarizing themselves with it first thing in the morning," I explained.

"Is it stealthed?"

"Yes, it is. The biggest one we've built. The only one of its kind. It has been specifically designed for this particular mission."

"Is there room for me?"

"Yes, there is."

"Will you give me some job to do, so I can be useful on the ship?" Jeffery asked.

"Do you want a job?"

"Yes, I do. I want to be a part of the crew, doing my part."

"I will give it some thought and will let you know."

"I would appreciate that, Slade. Have you had dinner?"

"No, not yet."

"You are more than welcome to tag along with us."

"I would like that. Thank you."

The evening passed quickly, as I sat back and enjoyed my time with Jeffery and his family. I had grown used to hearing my own children's laughter. It would be quite some time before I would hear them again. But I hoped that, when I did, we would have already eliminated the greatest threat to their future, the Jatarians. The sound of Jeffery's children playing warmed my heart. If I closed my eyes and cleared my mind, it sounded very similar to my own children.

I savored the walk back to the mountain. I wasn't sure when we would make it back here again. The opportunity to enjoy the fresh air would be limited, once we left for our hunt for the Jatarians.

The next morning I woke bright and early, ready to get started on familiarizing myself with our new ship. It seemed I wasn't the only one ready to get started. The entire crew nearly beat me there.

We spent the next few days going over everything on the ship. The more we could learn, the better. I spent a considerable amount of time with Wyatt and Samson in engineering. I knew that's where the heart of the ship was. If anything could go wrong, that's where it would be. I wanted to soak up as much information as I could, given the time we had.

After a few days of learning about the ship and its nuisances, it was finally time to take it up for a test flight.

I stood in front of the command chair, and we did all our systems checks. Everything was operating as it should be. Once we were cleared for takeoff by Alex and his crew, we slowly guided the ship out of the landing bay.

Leaving the protection of the mountain, we activated our stealthed systems. No need to take any chances that our refugee settlement would be discovered by any passing ship.

We spent the next few days testing all the systems we could. Each time we took the ship out, we became more and more comfortable with it. By the end of the week, I felt as if we were ready to begin the final preparations for our mission.

I spent my days on the ship and my evenings with Jeffery and his family.

As we made our final preparations for our mission, I became even more excited. I knew we would find the Jatarians. I had no doubt about it.

Maro arrived on the morning of our departure. Hadassah brought him. It was nice to spend an evening with my wife before we left. She updated me on the kids and everything happening at Dove One.

I woke up early, ready to get underway. The crew all arrived and got into their positions. We had agreed to fly the ship down to the village to pick up Jeffery. We had managed to keep the secrets of the mountain from him all these years. No need to change that now.

Eloise and the kids were waiting there with Jeffery. They looked apprehensive. Jeffery could barely contain his excitement.

I landed the ship and walked to the rear of the ship to let Jeffery come on board. I lowered the ramp and walked out toward them. "Don't worry, Eloise. I'll keep him safe."

"You better, or you will have to answer to me," Eloise replied.

I was tempted to point out that, if something happened to Jeffery, I would likely be in the same predicament, but I kept that thought to myself.

Jeffery added, "Everything will be fine, Eloise. This is a stealthed ship. No one can see it. The Jatarians won't even know we are there."

"Is that true?" Eloise asked me.

I nodded. "If you stay and watch, we will activate the stealthed systems, once we take off. You will see it disappear from view yourself." I turned and walked back on the ship. I wanted to give Eloise and Jeffery privacy for their goodbyes.

"I'm ready," Jeffery said, once he had climbed up the ramp.

I turned and hit the button to close the ramp and then headed for the Command Center. "I'll show you to your room, after we've entered hyperspace."

"Can I watch?" Jeffery asked.

I hesitated. Would Jeffery discern enough information about the system to recognize it later? Probably not. "Follow me." I quickly punched in the codes to gain access to the Command Center. I doubted Jeffery could figure out the code very easily.

Once inside, I showed Jeffery where he could sit, and then I took my position in my command chair. "All systems check," I called out.

After everyone reported all systems were a go for takeoff, I slowly guided the ship off the ground. When we were slightly above the surface, I said, "Engage the stealthed systems."

Cole confirmed my order, and soon our ship disappeared from view. I had zoomed in on Eloise and the kids to see their expressions when the ship disappeared. The shock was evident on all of their faces. I couldn't help but smile at that.

"I guess Eloise was surprised when you engaged the stealthed capabilities," Jeffery said, from behind me.

"I knew she would be. It's an amazing thing to witness a ship disappearing before your eyes," I answered.

The ship continued on through the atmosphere and into the space above Elmania. We wasted no time entering hyperspace. We had a mission to accomplish. The sooner we found the Jatarians, the sooner we could return home, return home to our families.

"How long will we be in hyperspace?" Jeffery asked.

"Two weeks. We will stop in and check on Maro's planet. Have you met Maro yet, Jeffery?" I asked.

"I have not."

"You'll enjoy listening to his stories and Captain Parker's."

"Maro's planet was destroyed by the Jatarians?"

"Yes. We rescued over one thousand survivors and took them to a new planet to start over. It's been a few years since then. I'm interested to see what the planet looks like now. The Jatarians only bombed the larger cities," I explained.

"Do you think the Jatarians have plans for these planets? Or do they only destroy the main cities to preserve more of their weapons?" Jeffery asked.

"That's a good question. Unfortunately it's one we don't have the answer to. If the Jatarians are in the system where Maro's planet is, that might help us put together more pieces of the puzzle. Perhaps the Jatarians intend to enslave the survivors or harvest particular resources from the planet, after the dust settles. We might not like what we find in Maro's system."

"Are any Federation scout ships out that far?" Jeffery asked.

"No, not yet. I'm unsure of where the *Explorer* is. It is too far away for me to contact with my gift."

"Could the *Explorer* have found something?"

"The *Explorer* is not a stealthed ship. If they did find numerous ships in a system, they wouldn't exit hyperspace. They would make a note of it and then send in a scout ship or the Morag to investigate."

Jeffery replied, "That makes sense. What happens if the ships aren't Jatarian?"

"Federation policy states that, if the ships can travel in hyperspace or have weapons, they are to be destroyed, whether they pose a threat or not. Either one of those things the Federation considers as enough of a threat to eliminate them."

"Have you ever encountered a race where it would be wrong for us to assume they are our enemies?" Jeffery asked.

"Two come to mind. The Zator people and Maro's people, the Gormanians. Maro's people can travel in hyperspace. They were a peaceful people and had never developed any type of weapons for their ships. When the Jatarians showed up, negotiation was the Gormanians only weapon. They could do nothing to save their planet because the Jatarians weren't willing to negotiate. So the Gormanian planet was bombed. As for the Zator, they defended the Zenyan system from the Jatarians multiple times, saving countless Human lives."

"So you believe the Federation policy is wrong then?"

I sighed. How could I explain it? "Not necessarily wrong. The policy exists for the right reasons. It's there to help protect the Federation from future threats. It's not a stretch to think that a race that developed weapons for their ships could also develop the means to travel in hyperspace or vice versa. What today might not pose a threat could one hundred years from now. I don't know what the right answer is. I just don't necessarily believe it's something that should be applied across the board all the time. There can be exceptions. How we determine that, I have no idea."

"These are the type of things I'll have to figure out when I become the Emperor, right?"

I nodded. "I don't know what the right answer is, Jeffery."

"I'm guessing many things out here have rules created by individuals who've never left the surface of Falton Two and have no idea what really happens out here," Jeffery commented.

"Very insightful, Jeffery."

"I have a feeling that I'll learn many things on this trip."

"I think we all will."

"Will we stop before we get to Maro's system?" Jeffery asked.

"None are planned. We will keep our long-range scans on, as we travel by other systems. If anything suspicious shows up, we will investigate," I explained.

"So what do we do in the meantime?" Jeffery asked.

"This is the boring part of space travel. However, the guy who designed this ship knew we would spend an extended amount of time in hyperspace, so he included some ways of entertaining ourselves."

"Oh, like what?" Jeffery asked, intrigued.

"Connor, you're in charge. I'll go show Jeffery around the ship."

Connor smiled and stood. He made his way to sit in the command chair.

I led Jeffery out of the Command Center. "I guess I should show you where you'll be staying."

Jeffery nodded. "This ship is pretty nice, Slade."

"This is the mission it was designed for—a long-term search, where we need the stealthed capabilities to keep our presence a secret."

"What about weapons?" Jeffery asked.

My heart skipped a beat. I couldn't tell him that we had weapons. He would see it as a threat to the Federation. "We don't need weapons since we have the stealthed capability. The Jatarians won't even know we are there."

"I guess that's true. I'm glad we at least have that."

After showing Jeffery to his quarters, I gave him a tour of the ship. We ended up in the recreation room.

"Wow. This is great. It will give us something to do when we get bored. What about a job for me? I feel a need to contribute," Jeffery said.

"I have thought about that. I decided it would be beneficial for you to learn many different jobs. Spend some time in each department, learning the ropes, so to speak. What do you think about that?"

"That sounds like a great idea, Slade. That will help me learn more about the crew and their jobs. I'm excited. Where will I start?"

"You will start in engineering, with Wyatt and Samson. There's a lot to learn there about how the ship works and the various systems that keep us alive and traveling through space safely. I've always enjoyed spending time in there, learning more myself. Some people don't enjoy it as much as I do, but I thought that would be a good place to start."

"Sounds like a great idea."

"I'll take you there now and introduce you to Wyatt and Samson."

"Do either of them have the gift?" Jeffery asked.

"Samson does. Wyatt is a brother to my good friend, Bryce. Bryce and his family are the ones who I came with from the Empire. They are like brothers to me. You'll get along well, I have no doubt."

I knew that Jeffery would figure out many of our connections. There was no need to hide them from him. I had a long talk with the crew once we realized Jeffery was, indeed, tagging along with us. I had presented them with my idea to let Jeffery learn the ropes. Samson and Wyatt had volunteered to have him with them first.

Once we arrived in the engineering section, we quickly found Samson and Wyatt. After the introductions, I left Jeffery there, so he could get a tour of where he would be spending his time. We agreed to meet for lunch in a couple hours.

I was encouraged that Jeffery's time on our ship would help teach him many things, not only about the policies affecting space travel and exploration but also about how crew members on ships live and work. I suspected the Emperor had no experience in the lives of any of his average citizens. My father didn't either, for that matter. I intended for that to be different for Jeffery.

Chapter Six

Jeffery met me in the cafeteria a couple hours later. When he walked in, he seemed excited. I watched as he scanned the room until he found me.

He came right over. "I hope you haven't been waiting on me long. I lost track of time."

"That's okay. How was it?" I asked, a little surprised by Jeffery's enthusiasm.

"It's amazing. I'm going to love it in engineering." Jeffery pulled out a chair and sat down.

I had to smile. "I'm glad. I was surprised at how much I enjoyed it too. It was a nice change from the command crew. I'm really glad you like it."

Jeffery turned serious for a moment and leaned in. "Slade, what if I find my passion here on the ship? What if I find what I love to do?"

I raised an eyebrow. "Then hopefully you can continue to do it as long as possible." It's not what I had expected to hear. Of course this was the first day. Maybe the more mundane day-to-day operations of space travel would change his mind after a few weeks. What if Jeffery did find his passion and then refused to take over for Amelia? Then what? I shook the thought from my head. That was a worry for another day.

"I'm hungry. Anything good to eat?" Jeffery asked.

"Yes. I'll take you through the line. It's usually a buffet-type meal, with a few options to choose from. I'm sure you'll find something you like." I stood and took Jeffery over to the line. While we waited, I introduced him to a couple of the crew members who were beside us in line.

So far everyone seemed to be treating Jeffery like one of the crew. I was glad. That's what he needed.

After filling our trays, we made our way over to Maro's table. I had yet to introduce Jeffery to Maro. Maro was, of course, sitting with Captain Parker.

"Mind if we join you two?" I asked, as we walked up to the table.

Captain Parker smiled. "Not at all. Pull up a seat."

I made the introductions and then sat back and watched as Maro and Parker took turns telling Jeffery stories of their lives. I never grew tired of hearing their tales of survival. From the look on Jeffery's face, I could tell he felt the same way.

After lunch, Jeffery still eating and enjoying Maro's and Parker's company, I made my way back to the Command Center. Connor had everything under control. "How much longer until we pass by our first system?" I asked Bryce.

"We still have another six hours. I don't expect to find anything there. We've traveled this path before, when we went to rescue Maro and the survivors from his planet. I don't expect to find anything different," Bryce replied.

"I don't either, but I would like to have that peace of mind that the Jatarians haven't established a new colony in this area of the galaxy," I replied.

"Good point. I wonder why the Jatarians are trying to expand their territory?" Bryce asked.

"Power, resources, influence, who knows. We have to stop them. Or rather we have to use the Morag to stop them, before they can mount another attack on the Federation."

"Why do you think they've stayed away for two years?" Graham asked.

"Your guess is as good as mine. I would imagine they're rebuilding their fleet and perhaps improving their technology. Maybe even developing stealthed technology," I said.

A hush fell over the Command Center. The crew's gazes were on me.

"You think they may have developed stealth technology?" Cole asked slowly.

I shrugged. "It's always a possibility. We will be cautious. Don't tell me the thought hadn't crossed your minds."

Most of the crew shook their heads no.

Connor said, "You must always be prepared for the worst-case scenario. I'm not surprised that it's crossed your mind, Slade. That's what makes you a good leader. You think things through and plan for the possibilities, whether they be good or bad. I'm glad you're our captain."

"Thanks, Connor," I replied.

Everyone else nodded and returned their attention to their consoles.

Graham added, "Thanks for being honest, Slade."

I nodded to Graham. I hoped my honesty didn't cause the crew any unnecessary worry. I usually did a good job of keeping my paranoia to myself, or at least between Bryce and Connor. I don't know why I let my guard down there. I shrugged it off. Not much I could do about it now.

"I'll be in my office if anyone needs me," I said, as I walked over to my office door, which was connected to the Command Center.

Once inside I sat down and pulled up the holographic display. Our path would take us right by the system where we had found Phoebe's parents. We didn't plan to stop in that system, but I would feel better if the system was void of any ships. It would still be a few days before we reached that location.

I studied the display for a few minutes. What would we discover on this trip? What adventures would we have? Would we find what we were searching for?

My thoughts moved to Fritz. I wondered where the *Explorer* was and what they'd found. Fritz was still out of the range of my gift. Maybe before this trip was over, I could reach him.

I tapped my fingers on my desk. It was still hours before we passed by a system. Maybe I should take the time to check in with the different parts of the ship. Talk to all of the crew who I don't usually interact with on a daily basis. It definitely wouldn't hurt.

I got up and left my office. First, I peeked into the cafeteria to see if Jeffery was still listening to Maro's and Parker's stories. He was, and I wasn't surprised.

I headed on to the maintenance area of the ship. This was the crew that kept the ship looking good. After chatting with them briefly, I headed back to the cafeteria. This time Jeffery saw me and waved for me to come over.

"How's it going in here?" I asked.

"I can tell I'll spend a lot of time with Maro and Parker," Jeffery replied, "but I probably should get back to engineering."

"I'll walk with you," I said.

"Wow, the stories those two have are mind-blowing. They've seen things I could never even dream of seeing," Jeffery said, as we walked.

"That's true. I hope I never experience getting stranded on a moon, far from the Federation."

"That moon we went to after you rescued us from Tyrus was where you found Maro, right?" Jeffery asked.

I felt a pang of guilt, as I remembered that I had intended to leave Jeffery and Eloise there. "That's right. That's where we found him. His ship had crash-landed on the surface. He was the only survivor."

"I must admit that today is the first day I've ever met a nonhuman."

"Really?" I asked, surprised.

"I've rarely had the opportunity to leave the palace growing up," Jeffery said.

"I will admit I do know what that feels like. I was the same way. Then I started figuring out ways to escape and to explore the city."

Jeffery smiled slyly. "Gabriel and I did too. We never found any aliens though."

"Maybe remember that, when your kids want to leave the palace. Don't make that palace a prison for them. We both know they'll find a way out."

"Thinking of it from a father's perspective, I can understand the desire to keep your children safe. I'm scared to take them back to Falton Two. They're safe on Elmania. At Falton Two, many people with numerous motivations might decide to kidnap them or to harm them. I see why my father wanted to keep us under lock and key."

I nodded. I understood too, although I couldn't say as much. Not without giving away the fact that I had children as well. I was keeping them a secret from Jeffery to protect them. "You're probably right. Speaking of your father, did you tell him you were coming with me?"

"I did."

"What did he say?" I asked, anxiously anticipating the answer.

"He said, if I were to explore space, you would be the best person to do it with. He has no doubt we will succeed in finding the Jatarians. It's only a matter of how long it will take."

"No warnings against me?" I asked, surprised.

"Not really. My father knows you are an important asset to the Federation, whether he likes it or not. You have the most experience with the Jatarians. You have an uncanny knack for finding them. He said I would learn a lot and would have an adventure all at the same time. I would experience things he'd never even dreamed of."

"I'm still waiting for the negative comments," I commented.

"He just warned me to be careful and to check in when I could. I told him that we would move out of the range of our gifts eventually but not to worry. He just said, *Find the Jatarians.*"

"Have the scout ships had any luck yet?" I asked.

"No. Do you want to know where they've searched? That could help us."

"I'm pretty sure we are going farther out than the scout ships have gone. You are welcome to check with them to see the farthest-out point they've gone to so far. It should be wherever their current locations are. We don't have that information. And, if it makes you and the Emperor feel more comfortable, you don't have to tell us where they are, just if where we're going is farther or not."

"I will work on that later today, after I finish in engineering. Thanks again, Slade, for letting me come, plus giving me something to learn and to do."

"I'm glad you're here, Jeffery." We had reached engineering, so I watched as Jeffery went inside.

Amelia had given me the information she could on the scout ships. Jeffery might have the ability to access more up-to-date information. In fact the Emperor might be willing to give us even more information, given that our goal was the same as the Federation's—to find the Jatarians.

I returned to my office to look at our maps and the information we had on the scout ships. We had a huge galaxy to search. We might as well work together with the Federation. We would find the Jatarians faster if we did.

That was the first step in this mission—to find the Jatarians. Then we would organize an attack. Hopefully the Jatarians would be taken by surprise. What if they'd had the opportunity to develop stealth technology? What would we do then? We would be in serious trouble.

I took a deep breath and took my maps to review with Maro. He could narrow down where we should search. The Jatarian homeworld would not be in any system Maro's people had been to. It had to be farther out but how far?

Maro and Parker were still right where I'd left them earlier. "Maro, let's look at the maps," I said, as I sat down.

Between Maro, Parker, and me, we spent hours poring over the star maps. We had a good idea where we would head next, after we checked on Maro's homeworld. It made me feel much better that we had a plan.

Jeffery eventually joined us. He had gathered some information on where the scout ships had searched. He was still waiting on a few more contacts to get more information for him. "You know, I've never seen a star map like this. Where is Falton Two?" Jeffery asked.

"It's right here," I said, as I pointed.

"Where are we now?" Jeffery asked.

"I can't tell you that, but I can show you the vicinity we are headed," I said.

"So I guess you won't tell me where Elmania is on this map either, then will you?" Jeffery asked.

I turned to Maro and asked, "Maro, do you know where Elmania is on this map?"

Maro replied, "No, I don't."

I then turned to Parker. "Parker, do you know where Elmania is on this map?"

"No, I don't."

"See, Jeffery? It's not anything against you personally. We don't share the location of our refugee villages with anyone. I don't even know where all of them are. Neither does anyone else here. It's a tightly held secret. It's what keeps the villages safe."

Jeffery seemed a little surprised that neither Parker nor Maro knew where Elmania was. "How many people on this ship know where Elmania is?"

I thought it over for a minute. "My best guess is four, including me."

"Okay. I just wanted to ensure it wasn't only you. What if something happened to you? We couldn't find our way back home."

"Good point. No need to worry. It's not just me."

"I don't expect anything to happen to you, but just in case."

"I understand. This is the area where we will start our search." I pointed to an area of the galaxy a good three weeks away.

"That's a long way from the Federation," Jeffery said, amazed. "We are going to find them. I can feel it."

"Don't get too excited. It's a large area to cover," I warned.

"Who knows what else we will find? Perhaps more allies," Jeffery said excitedly.

"Or more enemies," I added.

"How far away will the Morag be?" Jeffery asked.

"We have most of their fleets stationed near the Federation—in case the Jatarians attack. A small task group is closer to us, but it would take them weeks to get to where we will be."

"So let's say we do find the Jatarians, way out here somewhere," Jeffery said, as he pointed to the area we intended to search. "If it will take us three weeks to get there and, let's say, two weeks to find the Jatarians, and then we have to wait another three weeks before the Morag could respond to our position, I can see why you said this mission could last a while."

I nodded. "It will be an adventure, no doubt about it."

"One that will hopefully end with us witnessing the destruction of the Jatarian homeworld," Jeffery said.

"What if the Jatarians have multiple core planets, similar to the Empire?" Parker asked.

I had talked with Parker extensively about the Empire over the years, as we had traveled together. He had been fascinated that so many other Human planets were out there. "We must destroy them all," I answered.

"What about negotiations? Is that completely off the table?" Parker asked.

I looked over at Jeffery. Who would handle negotiations, if there were any? Me or him? "I don't think it will come down to negotiations. The Jatarians have been unwilling to contemplate that scenario this far. Why would that change?"

"Perhaps when their own planets and citizens are threatened, they will change their tune," Parker said.

It was something to consider. While I didn't believe it was a probable scenario, there was at least a remote possibility it could happen. "I don't see the Federation being happy with a negotiation that ended in any way other than the Jatarians having no more warships. Otherwise we always have to worry if they'll return one day, after building a large warfleet, strong enough to destroy us."

"I agree. Perhaps we will discover what the Jatarians' motivations are for their actions," Jeffery commented.

"My guess is they need more resources, those that their planets no longer have," Maro suggested.

"It could be, or it may just be their quest for expansion and total galaxy domination," I added.

None of us liked the sound of that.

"They have a long, hard road ahead of them, if that's their goal," Parker said.

"I agree," I replied.

"I'm a little concerned to see what the Jatarians have managed to develop in their military technology, since the last battle in the Federation," Parker said.

"Me too. There has to be a good reason we haven't seen them attack the Federation again. They had us at a disadvantage—if they had more ships to spare to press our diminished ship numbers, that is. That makes me think they had pretty-much exhausted the resources of their military. It's the only thing that makes sense," I reasoned.

"I'm glad our ship is stealthed. Who knows what we might find when we do locate the Jatarians' home system," Jeffery commented.

"There are a lot of unknowns, which makes this adventure that much more exhilarating, not to mention mentally exhausting. Considering all the possibilities and how we could react to them, it's a lot to process," I replied.

"You are not alone, Slade. We are here anytime you need us to reason out your thoughts," Maro said.

"Thanks, Maro," I replied.

"Is it about time for us to pass our first system yet?" Jeffery asked.

I looked down at my watch. "Actually it is."

"Do you mind if we tag along?" Parker asked. "I know we aren't likely to find anything, but I am curious."

"That's fine. Follow me," I replied.

Parker, Maro, and Jeffery followed me to the Command Center. As we approached the door, it opened. Bryce was coming out. "I was just coming to find you. We are nearing the first system."

"That's why we were coming. We are all curious to see if anything is in the system," Parker said.

We all filed into the Command Center. I took my seat, and the others stood behind me. "How far are we from the first system?" I asked.

"Fifteen minutes," Bryce answered.

"We will commence long-range scans of the system in five minutes," Connor reported.

We all waited, as the five minutes ticked slowly by. Finally Connor said, "Commencing scans."

The silence continued, while we waited for the results.

Would we find anything? I sincerely hoped not. I didn't want to think of the implications if we did. I shook my head, trying to keep my mind from spiraling down that road. I swallowed to soothe my parched throat. I looked over at Connor, waiting for his report.

"Scans show no ships in the system," Connor reported, his relief evident in his tone.

"That's a relief," Bryce said.

I sat back in relief too. If there had been ships, we would stop and investigate. I had hoped we would find no ships anywhere near this area of space. If a sizeable Jatarian fleet was out here somewhere, I didn't want to find it for a couple weeks. The Federation would need as much time as possible to prepare and for the Morag to get to their positions to defend the Federation. "How much farther is the next system?" I asked.

"Eighteen hours, Captain," Bryce replied.

"Okay. We have plenty of time to start our six-hour rotations, so everyone can get some sleep and some downtime. Augusta, you have the first shift as captain," I ordered.

Augusta nodded and moved to my seat. I walked Parker, Maro, and Jeffery out of the Command Center.

"What will you do now?" Jeffery asked.

"I'll get some sleep. I suggest you do the same. Do you remember how to get to your quarters?" I asked.

Jeffery nodded. "I do. I guess I'll see you in a few hours then."

"Good night," I said, as I headed to my own quarters. Once inside, I sat down and breathed a sigh of relief. I hoped I didn't have this level of anxiety with each system we passed. Surely once we got farther away from our home, I would have less anxiety about finding the Jatarians and more anticipation about it.

I showered, then lay down to rest. Many things were on my mind. Almost all of them were beyond my control.

So far, Jeffery tagging along had been a wise decision. He was expanding his knowledge and understanding of many things. I hoped that he wouldn't figure out where Elmania was. It was not labeled on any map or tactical display in the ship. Neither were any of the other systems which held refugee villages. I didn't think he had an extensive knowledge of the star maps, so we were more than likely safe in that respect.

As far as the Jatarians were concerned, I had no way to predict what we would find or how soon we would find them. I would deal with that when the time came. No use worrying about it now.

We had plenty of supplies to last us through one whole year. If we hadn't found anything by then, we would need a resupply, whether from foraging or meeting a supply ship. I hoped it wouldn't come to that, but it was a possibility. That was one problem we did have at least an idea of how to solve.

I wasn't sure how far out my gift would work. I would have communication with Colin longer than I would with Amelia and Phoebe. It would still be a while before I had to worry about that.

I decided to reach out to Colin. If nothing different were happening at the Jatarian colony, then I would feel more at ease.

Have you found anything yet, Slade? Colin asked.

No, thankfully not. I hope we don't find anything until we get a couple weeks out. If we do, then an attack is imminent.

That's true. How's Jeffery?

He's doing really well. I have him learning the ropes in engineering. So far, he is enjoying it.

Wow. That's a good sign. It's smart that you have him doing something to help. Otherwise I'm afraid he would get bored and then get into trouble.

I plan to have him rotate through many positions. He can learn many things while he's here. How are things at Dove Two?

Things are fine here. The Jatarian colony continues to grow.

Any changes that seem unusual in their activity? I asked.

No. We keep a watch out for that. Any change in their behavior might mean an attack is coming.

I'm glad nothing points to an attack yet. Please keep me posted. I will worry while I'm gone that the Jatarians will attack, and I won't be there to help.

Try not to worry, Slade. Plenty of people now have at least some experience with the Jatarians, including the Emperor. Let him worry about the defense of the Federation. That's not your responsibility. All of the refugee villages are well hidden. We are safe.

Thanks for the reassurance, Colin. I appreciate it.
I know you are a worrier. I'll let you know if anything changes here at Dove Two. Good luck finding the Jatarian's home system.
Thanks, we will need it.

After talking to Colin, I felt a little better. Shortly after that, I calmed my mind enough to finally get some rest.

Chapter Seven

The next few days passed by relatively quickly. Each time we neared a system, we anxiously waited to see if any ships were present. So far we had found none, but to truly locate any stealthed ships, we must drop in each system, which we weren't doing. The farther out we got, the more I couldn't shake the feeling we were getting closer to finding what we were searching for.

We neared the system with the hidden Human settlement, where Phoebe's parents were. I had already reminded the crew not to say anything that would make Jeffery aware of this settlement. It was vital we kept this place secret from the Federation.

I couldn't help but wonder if the Federation scout ships had found this planet. Also what would happen if they did? The Federation finding them was a better alternative to the Jatarians finding them. It was only a matter of time before Phoebe's parents and the others with them were found.

Jeffery joined us in the Command Center as we neared the next system, as did Parker and Maro. We all waited for Connor's scans to come back.

I found myself thrumming my fingers on the armrest of my chair. I made a conscious effort to stop. I didn't want to seem nervous. I didn't want Jeffery to know that this system was any different than the others.

"Scans are coming in. Eight ships show on the scans, Captain," Connor reported.

Now what? Were these Human ships? Jatarian ships? We had no way to know. We had to investigate though. "I guess we need to see whose ships they are," I said. "It's obviously not a warfleet. It could be a scout group though."

Was this a Jatarian scout group? Had they found the Human settlement? Had they destroyed it? We had to find out. "Prepare to exit hyperspace. Cole, are our stealthed systems online?" I asked.

"Yes, Captain, stealthed systems are online," Cole answered.

"Preparing to exit hyperspace," Bryce reported.

I held my breath. These ships could belong to the Human settlement. At least Jeffery didn't know where we were, if this did turn out to be Human ships from the settlement.

I felt the twinge in my stomach as we exited hyperspace. I moved to the edge of my seat. What would we find? Whose ships were these? Was the settlement destroyed?

"Scans show eight Jatarian ships in the system, Captain," Connor said worriedly.

"Can we determine what they are doing?" I asked.

Out of the corner of my eye, I saw Jeffery step forward. He hadn't had the opportunity to see a Jatarian ship yet.

"Let's move in closer and see if we can figure out what they're doing here," I said. I wasn't sure I wanted to know. Either they had already destroyed the settlement or were looking for it. Could we stop them? How close were the Morag? Could I send a message to the surface without the Jatarians intercepting it?

I stood up and walked closer to the viewscreens at the front of the room. We weren't close enough yet to see the ships. "Which planet are they closest to?" I asked.

"The one we've been to before," Connor reported slowly.

"Damn. Can you scan the surface yet to see if they've already destroyed it?" I asked.

I knew Jeffery had questions, but I guess he realized now wasn't the time to ask.

"Not yet, Captain," Connor replied.

"Let's do a microjump to get closer," I ordered. If I called in the Morag, the Jatarians would realize this system was important. If they'd already found the Human settlement here, it wouldn't matter though.

After the microjump, the eight Jatarian ships came into view. They were warships. This was not looking good. What could I do? "Is there any damage to the surface of the planet?" I asked.

"No, there's not," Connor reported.

"Well, that's a relief. Graham, is there any communication between the Jatarians and the surface?" I asked.

"No," Graham replied.

I studied the screens and the information represented there. What should we do? Was there a chance the Human settlement hadn't been discovered yet?

I closed my eyes and reached out to the Humans below. Would any of them have the gift? I searched and searched but didn't find anyone I could communicate with.

"Are the Jatarian ships running scans of the surface?" I asked.

"No. But, once the surface grows dark, any city lights will give them away, if they haven't already been discovered," Connor said.

He did have a point, a very good one. What should we do? I ran various scenarios through my mind. If the Jatarian ships already knew of the settlement, they would have already destroyed it. With the warships they had, they could easily eliminate the settlement. So what were they waiting on?

"Captain, our communications are being jammed," Graham said worriedly.

94

"Cole, are our stealthed capabilities still online?" I asked hurriedly.

"Yes, Captain," Cole replied.

"Graham, are they only jamming our communications or the Jatarians too?" I asked.

"What makes you think it's not the Jatarians who are jamming our communications?" Connor asked.

"Because last time we were here, they alluded to the ability to protect themselves. I assumed that's what this is," I answered. "Let's move back a little. If something is about to happen, I don't want to be caught in the crossfire."

I felt the ship move, as Bryce navigated the ship away from the area. Everyone silently watched the screen, waiting for whatever was about to unfold. I crossed my arms over my chest.

"Look at the screen. Weapons fire is coming from that rock orbiting the planet," Cole said.

"That's no rock," I said, with a smile. "That's a defensive satellite."

All ten of these *rocks* launched weapons fire at the eight Jatarian warships. Two quickly succumbed to the onslaught of the attack. As it was unexpected, the Jatarians had not activated their energy shields. They did now.

Multiple other ships had sustained significant damage. These ships were now targeting the defensive satellites and eliminating them. In the process, the Jatarians lost two more ships. Now only four remained.

Everyone in the Command Center watched the screens, stunned to witness this small battle unfold. All rooted for the death of the Jatarians.

I ran my fingers through my hair. What would happen next? How would the Humans destroy the four remaining ships?

"I'm sensing more ships on the tactical display," Connor called out.

"Are they Jatarian?" I asked.

"No, they are launching from the surface," Connor confirmed.

I couldn't help but smile. The Humans had warships. It still remained to be seen how strong they would be when going up against the might and strength of the Jatarians. "How many ships?" I asked.

"Twenty. They appear to be smaller ships," Connor reported.

"The Jatarians are already taking aim at the new threat," I commented.

Weapons fire erupted from the four remaining Jatarian ships. Could these smaller ships eliminate the much larger Jatarian ones?

I practically held my breath, awaiting the weapons launch by these smaller ships. What type of weapons would they have?

The Human ships dodged the incoming enemy fire as they closed the distance between them. So far, the Human ships had yet to launch their weapons.

"What are they waiting for?" Jeffery asked.

"Their optimal firing range. If they launch their weapons fire too early, the Jatarians will just shoot down their missiles. If they wait, the Jatarians have less time to react and to target the incoming firepower," I explained.

It was important to teach Jeffery what I could at every opportunity. This was his first battle to witness in person. Even if the enemy only had eight ships, they were still a threat to this planet.

"They're firing," Connor reported.

My gaze refocused on the viewscreen in front of me. The twenty Human ships had engaged the four Jatarian ships, only they waited until they were at close range.

I told Jeffery, "If they can get close enough, the Jatarians will have a hard time targeting them. It's the same case with the Federation's devastators. That's where they are the most effective, up close and personal with the enemy warships."

"Are these ships the same size as the devastators?" Jeffery asked.

"I would guess they're a little bigger. See where the energy screen of the Jatarian ships glows brighter and brighter," I pointed out. "Eventually the screens will fail, and the ships will be vulnerable to the weapons fire."

We watched as one of the Jatarian energy screens failed, and the Human ships capitalized on the opportunity to hit the hull of the enemy ship with their weapons fire. Small explosions began to erupt across the Jatarian ship. More and more weapons fire hit the exposed ship, until the small explosions erupted into a giant one that consumed the ship.

The Human ships then focused on the remaining three Jatarian ships. Another energy screen failed, and the Humans pushed the advantage. Soon another Jatarian ship fell. Two down and two to go.

The last two didn't take long for the remaining Human ships to finish off. When the final Jatarian ship exploded in a shower of fiery projectiles, I breathed a sigh of relief. "How many ships did they lose?" I asked.

"Only two," Connor replied.

"Did they have energy screens?" I asked.

"Yes, very powerful ones apparently," Connor said.

"I wonder if that's all the ships they have," I thought out loud.

"I hope not. The Jatarians will return sooner or later," Bryce commented. "They'll wonder what happened to their missing warships."

"Maybe they'll assume they ran into Morag ships or Human ships," Jeffery said.

I took a deep breath. "Actually, Jeffery, these were Human ships."

"What?" Jeffery asked, confused.

"We found this planet accidentally on our way to rescue Maro. Our hyperdrive malfunctioned and put us in this system. We scanned the planets, while making our repairs. We found a large settlement of Humans on it. They are not part of our refugee settlements. I'm not sure how they ended up here."

"Wow. How far is this from the Federation?" Jeffery asked.

"Over a week," I answered.

"Are we going to make contact?" Graham asked.

I shook my head. "When we first found them, they made it very clear that they wanted to be left alone. We have already warned them of the threat of the Jatarians. We have nothing more to add. Are they still jamming communications?"

"The jamming has stopped," Graham confirmed.

"So they must not sense us," I commented.

"Shall we move in closer and see what other types of defenses they have?" Connor asked.

"No. We don't want to risk them sensing us. They aren't in danger at the moment. We do know the Jatarians are in the area though. We might be making a lot more stops. How much longer do we have before our hyperdrive is charged?" I asked.

"Half an hour," Cole replied.

I took a deep breath. "Let's move in a little closer. I would like to see if anything has changed since our last visit. We must be careful not to set off any of their defenses." I moved back to my command chair and sat down.

"Are there more Human planets out there?" Jeffery asked.

"I don't know. This is the only one we are aware of," I replied.

I watched as the planet again grew larger on the viewscreen. When we got close enough, the main city came into view. Night had fallen, and the area was glowing from the lights of the city. It looked slightly larger than before, but it was hard to tell.

"They don't live much differently than we do, do they?" Jeffery asked.

"Nope."

"Do any of them have the gift?" Jeffery asked.

"I tried to find someone with the gift when we were here last but came up empty. So I guess not. At least not any who don't know how to guard their minds," I answered.

"Did they give you any indication of where they came from?" Jeffery asked.

"No, they did not."

"This defensive satellite idea is something we hadn't considered. We need these in the Federation. Especially around all the planets and moons where the Jatarians already know we have settlements," Jeffery said. "I will speak to my father about it."

"These Humans don't want to be involved with the Federation. So maybe, when you mention the idea to your father, don't mention it was a Human planet where you witnessed the defensive satellites," I suggested.

"I wonder why they don't want to be involved with the Federation," Jeffery asked.

"Maybe they like their independence and aren't interested in being ruled by someone far removed from their area of space," I suggested. "They didn't tell us that, but that's what I deduced from what they did say."

"I guess that makes sense," Jeffery said slowly. "I guess the Federation would have to offer them something they needed in order to bring them under our rule. Like protection or something."

"Which they may not need," I replied. "They did well against the Jatarians. This was only an enemy task group of eight ships though, not hundreds."

"We can't risk using our resources elsewhere at this point either. We need all our ships to protect the Federation," Jeffery added.

"We will try to stop back by here after we've eliminated the Jatarians," I said. "I would like to confirm that the planet is safe."

"Me too," Jeffery agreed.

I hoped his motivations stemmed from the right place, not the desire to expand the Federation. I had no way to tell, however.

"Captain, our hyperdrive is charged," Cole reported.

"Let's get on our way then. We need to find these Jatarians and their homeworld, before they destroy any more worlds," I said.

Shortly after that, we were back in the safety of hyperspace.

Connor said, "My guess will be that we will see small task groups of Jatarians in many of the systems from now on."

"I agree. Should we call in the Morag to take care of the task groups? Or do we wait until we find the home system and take them by surprise?" I asked, already knowing the answer.

"We take them by surprise in their home system," Jeffery suggested. "We don't want to give them a warning that we are coming. If we do, they'll be harder to defeat, and we will lose more assets. After we take the Jatarians' home system, the Morag can hunt down all the small task groups," Jeffery said.

I smiled with pride at Jeffery. "You're right, Jeffery. We must take the Jatarians by surprise."

Jeffery smiled in return.

"How long until we pass the next system?" I asked Bryce.

"Eight hours, Captain."

"Okay. Let's go back to our rotations. I'll be in my office," I said, as I stood. Jeffery followed me there. I wasn't surprised.

"Nice office," Jeffery said, as he sat down.

"Thanks. It's convenient since it's so close to the Command Center."

"Do you think those Humans are a threat to us?" Jeffery asked.

"Honestly, no. I think they want to be left alone and have developed ways to protect themselves from intruders."

"Did you go to the surface when you were here before?"

"No. I only talked to their leader via video communication. He didn't sound very welcoming. We agreed we wouldn't reveal their location. And I won't. So don't ask."

"I have no intention of asking. I know you're a man of your word, Slade. You protect Humans, all Humans, no matter where they are from. I respect you for that. I'll have my hands full with the problems of the Federation when I, one day, take over. I don't have the desire to force anyone to join us if they don't want to. It would only lead to more problems. We have enough problems of our own."

"I agree completely. My father has worked on expanding the Human Empire his entire adult life. All I saw was the problems that it brought. A larger area to protect and more people to ensure they are behaving as they should. Resources spread thin, and more people are unhappy with you. Not a job I want," I replied.

"We need to fix our existing problems and protect our existing colonies, before trying to expand any further. I know my father is currently consumed with this Jatarian situation. I do worry about what happens after that is over. Once we've neutralized this threat, what will he turn his attention to next? The rebels? He's always thought they're a threat to him. Right now the Jatarians pose the greater threat, but don't think for a moment he's forgotten about the rebels."

"I know. Jeffery, I hope you believe me when I say I've never met anyone who wanted to do harm to the Federation. Only people who want to live their lives on their terms and without the preferential treatment of those people who have the gift. No Human is planning to attack the Federation. No one that I've ever met. I'm not naive enough to think those people don't exist, but I do believe they are the exception, not the standard. I would never stand behind anyone who wanted to harm the Federation or any other Human settlement. There's just no reason for it," I explained.

"I believe you, Slade. It's what I've come across too. Everyone at Elmania was very welcoming to us and accepted us, even though they know who I am and who I will one day be."

"I'm glad. I was honestly a little worried some might be rude or ignore you. I'm glad that wasn't the case."

"Me too," Jeffery replied. "Thanks again for letting me come along on this mission, Slade. It has already been an adventure."

I smiled. "We're just getting started."

"I know. Do you think we will find more Jatarian scout groups in this sector of the galaxy, since the one was here?"

"I imagine so. Hopefully those Humans back there can eliminate them when they happen by their area. Even eight at a time could make a difference over the long haul," I replied.

"Won't the Jatarians wonder what's happening to their task groups?"

"Yes, but my guess is they'll blame the Morag or us."

"I wonder how many ships the Jatarians have," Jeffery commented.

"My guess is more than we can even imagine."

"That's not a good way to think."

"I prefer to think it's thousands but find only hundreds than the opposite."

"Would the Morag have enough ships to defeat thousands of Jatarian ships?" Jeffery asked.

"I don't know, but a coordinated attack from the Morag, the Zator, and the Federation might be what we need. We might have to work together on this one. We won't know until we find the Jatarains, see their homeworld, count their ships. That might still be months from now."

"What if we found a Jatarian task group and just followed them?" Jeffery suggested.

"They might not return home. They may be scout groups that stay out for years at a time. Perhaps one of the Federation scout ships can take that strategy, when they come across a Jatarian scout group. I don't think that strategy will work fast enough though. That's why we aren't doing it. Scout ships have followed Jatarian ships from their known colony system numerous times. They've never led them back to their home system."

"That's true. Also very puzzling. What if their home system has already been destroyed by another aggressive alien race, and all that is left of the Jatarians are smaller colonies, with a limited number of warships. This may be why they've refrained from another massive attack on the Federation," Jeffery suggested.

"I hadn't considered that possibility. It is something to think about. I appreciate you sharing your theory with me. I usually have a bunch of them swarming around in my mind. It's nice to share them and to discuss them sometimes."

"There are so many possibilities. It's a little overwhelming to think about," Jeffery stated.

"It is. It's something I've thought about for years. The possibility that I may, in the near future, have some of the answers is very gratifying and a little hard to believe."

"Then what?" Jeffery asked.

"I don't know. The Jatarians have consumed my thoughts and plans for so long. I'm not sure how I will feel when we've defeated them. I guess we will cross that bridge when it comes. Maybe I can be an explorer again. That would be nice."

"Sounds fun. I hope I can join you," Jeffery said sincerely.

"Me too, Jeffery."

"I guess I better go get some rest before we reach our next system. Who knows what we might find."

"You'll find our schedules aren't always so cut and clear. We've got to sleep while we are in hyperspace and be prepared for anything. You never know when something might malfunction. Get some rest, and I'll see you in a few hours."

Jeffery nodded and left my office.

Shortly after that, I headed to my quarters too. I might as well listen to my own advice. I needed sleep while I could get it.

Chapter Eight

The next few systems we passed turned up empty of any ships. We would near Maro's system by the end of the day. Before then we would pass by one more system. I was hoping it would be empty. I knew the Jatarians' home system was not near here. I didn't want to waste any time investigating ships that weren't in the Jatarian home system or a colony system.

The past two weeks had gone by pretty slowly, with not much adventure or excitement—other than the one system where the Humans live.

I was relieved that we hadn't found multiple scout groups in the area. Perhaps the one we had found was the farthest group from their home system. If the Jatarians were now searching planets for inhabitants, we might have a bigger problem.

I had spent many hours wondering what had caused the Jatarians to find that Human settlement. Did the Humans have ships in orbit? Or had the Jatarians scanned every inhabitable planet? I wouldn't have an answer to my question unless we stopped and asked the Humans on our way back to Elmania. Hopefully we wouldn't need to. Hopefully by then the Jatarians would be destroyed.

When the time came to pass by the last remaining system before Maro's, we all made our way to the Command Center. With the many disappointments we had had over the last two weeks, we weren't expecting to find anything.

We all watched and waited for Connor to confirm that *no* ships were in the system. Instead he said, "Captain, ships detected in the system. Over one hundred of them."

A cold shiver ran down my spine. One hundred ships? Was this a warfleet headed to the Federation? It wasn't enough to get the job done, but perhaps this was where they were rendezvousing. "Let's exit hyperspace and see what's going on. Cole, are our stealthed systems activated?"

"Yes, Captain, they are," Cole reported.

"Good. Keep a watch on it. We would be in a world of hurt if that malfunctioned, especially if these are Jatarians warships."

Cole nodded.

I felt the familiar pang in my stomach as our ship exited hyperspace. I held my breath, waiting for the report from Connor. Were these Jatarian ships?

"Captain, these are Jatarian ships. The fleet appears to be a mixture of transport vessels and warships. They seem to be congregated around the fourth planet," Connor reported.

"A new colony perhaps? Let's move in slowly and see what we can figure out."

Why were the Jatarians starting new colonies? Had their planet been destroyed, and the survivors were spread out to try to survive? Or were these forward bases on the way to their ultimate destination? If so, what was their target destination? Was it the Federation? Or was their ultimate goal larger than just defeating the Federation?

We moved slowly toward the fourth planet, all the while watching the Jatarian ships' movements.

"Should we do a microjump, Captain?" Bryce asked.

"Let's move in slowly, until our hyperdrive is fully charged. I want to be prepared to make a quick getaway, if need be."

I stood and moved closer to the viewscreens at the front of the room. What exactly were these ships doing? "How long at sublight speed will it take us to reach the fourth planet?"

"Six hours," Bryce replied.

"Let me know once our hyperdrive is charged. We will do a microjump then."

"It might be safer to continue at sublight speed, Captain," Connor suggested. "It's harder to shield our energy emissions when we exit hyperspace. As we would be doing that near all those ships, it might be too risky."

I nodded. "Good point, Connor. We will continue at sublight speed."

It was a little eerie watching the Jatarians. My heart thudded in my chest.

"There has been no reaction to our presence in this system. Is that correct?" I asked. I hadn't noticed any change in the Jatarian ships' movements since we had arrived. It didn't appear to me that anyone had noticed our arrival. I wanted to confirm that though.

"That is correct," Connor agreed.

"That's a relief," I replied.

We continued to close in on the fourth planet. As time slowly passed, I moved back to my chair. Six hours was a long time to stand.

No one left the Command Center. We were all a little on edge. What would we find? A mining operation perhaps? We speculated what might be on the fourth planet. Most of us agreed that it would be another colony.

It had been a few years since we'd come this way to rescue Maro and his people from their home planet, after it had been attacked by the Jatarians. At that time, no ships had been in this system.

Why had the Jatarians picked this particular system? Were their colonies spaced pretty evenly apart? I didn't think we had enough data to make that assumption. We knew of only one other colony. This might not even be a colony. We had yet to confirm that.

The fourth planet grew more prominent on our viewscreen as we neared it. Could we run scans of the surface without raising an alarm? I wasn't sure.

"Did we ever test to see if running scans of the surface would raise any alarms?" I asked.

Connor replied, "We didn't test that."

"I guess we will find out soon enough. Our hyperdrive is charged, so we could make a quick getaway, if need be. Cole, when the time comes, you need to help Connor keep watch on the ships, while we run the scans. If you see any change in their behavior, we need to know immediately," I said.

"I've found a different structure in the space above the planet. It doesn't appear to be a ship. Look, right here," Connor said, as he zoomed in closer to one object on the tactical display.

"If it's a ship, it has an odd shape," Bryce added.

I was puzzled and a little worried about this new discovery. What could it be? Was it a new warship that would be even more dangerous than the others?

Our ship continued to move toward the unidentified object and the planet. It wouldn't be much longer now until Connor could run more detailed scans.

When the time came, I moved closer to the viewscreens. Jeffery followed.

"What do we look for?" Jeffery asked.

"When we run the scans, we watch all the ships in this area. We will watch for them to change positions or to stop what they were doing. Also keep a watch on that unidentified object. If it moves or changes course, we need to know. Cole, is our energy screen activated?"

"Yes, Captain," Cole replied.

I racked my brain for anything else we needed to have ready in the event the Jatarians realized they weren't alone in the system. I had covered all my bases though. We were ready, as ready as we would ever be. "Start the scans of that unidentified object. Let's see what it is we're dealing with," I ordered.

My gaze stayed glued to the tactical display and the viewscreen that showed the ships near us. Would any of them react to our scans? The adrenaline coursed through my veins.

The Command Center went silent, as we all collectively held our breaths, hoping to remain undetected.

"Scans show it's a large shipyard. They're building warships here," Connor said, awestruck.

"A shipyard," I repeated. "It's huge."

"Here are the detailed scans," Connor said, as he put them on the viewscreen for us all to see.

"Is this a military base then?" I asked.

"We'll know once we scan the planet's surface," Connor said slowly.

The images of the shipyard were impressive.

"Can we send these back to the Federation?" Jeffery asked.

"We could, but, if we built one of these, it would be the first thing the Jatarians would destroy. It's an easily identifiable target," I replied.

"I think it's armed," Connor said. "Look at this area here and here," he said, as he pointed out both places. "I believe these are weapons turrets."

"They're all along the side here," Bryce added.

"I would say it's heavily armed. Does it have an energy screen?" I asked.

"Hard to confirm at present but I think this right here might be a shield generator," Connor answered.

"I don't like the looks of this," I said.

"Me neither," Jeffery agreed.

"Is this the only one that they have orbiting the planet?" I asked.

"It appeared they are in the process of constructing another one over here," Connor said, as he showed us what he was talking about.

"I think you're right," I replied. I took a deep breath and slowly let it out. "We need to see what's on the surface. Is this a colony that builds warships, or is this a military base?"

"Running the scans of the planet now," Connor said.

"Slade, the ships have all stopped moving," Jeffery said.

"What?" I asked, as I moved my gaze to the viewscreen

"Do you think they've sensed our scans?" Jeffery asked.

"Graham, do you hear anything unusual on the comms?" I asked quietly.

Graham shook his head.

We watched, waiting to see what would happen.

"Captain," Connor said suddenly. "The shipyard is opening its weapons turrets."

"That's not good. Let's move back a little. Away from where we initiated the scans," I ordered. Could they sense us? Or was this just a reaction to something else? Were we about to be fired on?

My gaze moved to Cole's console. I could see clearly our energy shield and our stealthed capabilities were online. My breathing quickened, as I waited for the Jatarians to make their next move.

"Should we do something?" Jeffery asked worriedly.

I shook my head. "Let's just watch and see what they do."

"The shipyard is running a scan of the area," Connor reported.

Had the Jatarian technology advanced enough to sense stealthed ships? I hoped not. If so, we were in a heap of trouble.

The Command Center was so quiet that I could hear my heart thudding in my chest.

"What's that?" I asked, as I saw something leave the shipyard.

"I can't tell without running a scan," Connor replied. "I don't think we should do that right now."

"I agree. Can we zoom in on one to get a better look at it?" I asked. I moved closer to the viewscreen. Dozens of small round orbs were surrounding the shipyard.

"Are those a defensive mechanism or some sensing device?" Jeffery asked.

I shrugged. "I have no idea." One thing was certain. The Jatarians had advanced their technology since the last time we had battled them. What we would face in battle, we weren't sure of yet.

"What if we moved closer to one of these transport vessels and then scanned those things?" Bryce asked. "The Jatarian vessel might mask our scan. If not, they surely wouldn't shoot at one of their own ships."

"We do need to find out what we are dealing with here. If we plan to attack the Jatarians, the more information we can gather on them, the better chance we have of coming out on top of this war," I replied. "Let's do it. Move the ship in closer to this transport vessel. Then we will run our scans."

The *Hunter* slowly moved in closer to the nearest transport vessel. Once in position, Connor initiated the scans of the orbs.

I was anxious as the scans began. My gaze was glued to the viewscreen, which showed a close-up of one of the orbs. Was it some tracking device? Or perhaps a small weaponized device?

The orb that the screen was focused on suddenly moved. The viewscreen camera backed up and tried to locate the device. It was headed toward our location.

111

"How much longer until the scan is complete?" I asked Connor.

"One more minute."

"I'm not sure we have that. Six of the devices are closing in on our location," Cole reported, looking at Connor's consoles.

I glanced at the tactical display. Sure enough, numerous of the small devices were closing in on our location. "Once the scans are complete, let's move away from our current location," I said.

"Twenty more seconds," Connor called out.

I held my breath as the orbs closed in on our location. What would they do when they got here? Explode?

"The transport vessel is moving away from this location," Cole reported.

"Scan complete," Connor yelled.

"Follow that transport vessel. Stay close to it," I ordered. "It might save us from being discovered." I didn't know what those orbs did, but I definitely didn't want to be surrounded by them.

When they arrived at our previous location, each one began to scan the area. What were they looking for? Could they sense anything?

"Are we recording this?" Jeffery asked.

"Yes," I answered.

"We need to send this back to the Federation to be analyzed," Jeffery said.

"I agree. Once we leave this system, we will send the information. It will take a while to get there."

"We can send it to the nearest scout ship, and they can relay the information," Jeffery suggested.

"Good idea," I replied. "Connor, what did our scans of the devices show?"

"They have many different sensors on them. They must somehow pinpoint the location of a stealthed ship, based on whatever type of information that thing is made to detect," Connor said.

"Do you think we are in danger?" I asked.

"I would advise that we don't do any more scans and continue moving slowly out of this area."

"I think we've got what we came here for. We've scanned the shipyard, the surface, and these new devices. We can analyze the data more, once we're in the safety of hyperspace," I said.

"They know we are here. They just don't know where," Connor said. "We will need to be more careful in the future."

"We will learn as we go. How much farther do we need to go before we can make our jump into hyperspace?" I asked.

"Ten more minutes to clear the area where these ships are congregated," Bryce answered.

It would be a long ten minutes. I continued to watch the orbs. They moved around and scanned another area. They did seem to be following us, although we were moving faster than they were. I wondered what would happen if they thought they had located our ship.

We had moved away from the nearest Jatarian ships. The orbs were still actively scanning the areas where we had been. How were they still able to detect where we'd been? What were they using to do it?

"How much longer until we can make our jump into hyperspace?" I asked, beginning to get more worried about what these orbs might do if they thought they had found something.

"Four more minutes and we should be good to make our jump," Bryce replied.

We all watched the screen which focused on the orbs.

"Could we release something that the orbs would sense, so we can see what happens?" Jeffery asked.

"Maybe some waste?" Connor suggested.

"They would get a more accurate read on our actual location," I replied.

"We need to know what these things can do," Jeffery said.

"True. Can we release some waste and remain stealthed?" I asked.

"I'm not sure. We've never tried that," Bryce said. "Maybe wait until we are clear to enter hyperspace first."

"I agree. We will wait a few more minutes, release some waste, and see what happens. Let's be prepared to enter hyperspace if our stealthed systems deactivate," I said. We needed to know what these orbs were capable of. I just didn't want to risk my crew and my ship to find out.

"What if we release our waste and then do a microjump to get out of the area?" Bryce suggested. "Then we can see from a safer distance what happens next."

"I like that idea. How much time do we have left?" I asked.

"We're ready," Bryce replied.

"Okay, let's do it. Cole, prepare to dump the waste. Bryce, plot our microjump."

"Ready," reported Cole.

"Ready," Bryce agreed.

"On my count. In three, two, one."

I watched as Cole hit the button to release the waste. Almost immediately Bryce initiated our microjump.

Once everything settled, we refocused in on the area where we'd been. The orbs arrived to the location. Then they spread out, and one by one detonated themselves.

My eyes grew wide, and my mouth fell open. A cold chill washed over me. If we hadn't done that microjump, we wouldn't have been far enough away. Those explosions would have impacted us. How I wasn't sure.

"Wow," Bryce said, as he was the first one to regain his composure.

"I guess we know what they can do," Jeffery said slowly.

"How much longer until our hyperdrive is charged again for us to leave the system?" I asked.

"After that microjump, about fifteen minutes," Cole replied.

"Let's keep a watch for any more of those little orbs. They hopefully think we left the system," I said.

"We've got to warn the Federation," Jeffery said.

"We will but not until we're out of the system. Unless you want to use your gift to tell your father now," I said.

"I'll wait until we're out of the system. I don't want to miss anything," Jeffery replied.

I nodded. I couldn't blame him for that. "Do we know how many of those devices are left?" I asked Connor.

"Not without doing a scan," Connor replied.

"Let's not do that. We will just watch and see what happens now from here," I replied.

The fifteen minutes went slowly, as we watched for any sign of the orb devices. From our far-out vantage point, the orbs were not visible.

"Can we review our scans and see how many orbs were deployed to begin with?" I asked.

"Yes. Do you want me to do that now?" Connor asked.

"No, wait for our jump into hyperspace," I answered.

Connor nodded.

I needed his attention on what was happening now, in case one of those orbs made an appearance near us again.

Cole finally announced, "Hyperdrive is charged."

"Good. Let's get out of here," I ordered. Shortly after that, I sat down and relaxed a little in my command chair. We were safe, at least for now.

"I'll review all our scans and see what we can learn about what's going on in this system," Connor said.

"What's on the surface of the planet?" I asked.

"I'm putting the scans up on the screen now," Connor replied.

I stepped closer to the screens, so I could better take in what I saw. What I saw sent shivers across my skin. "It's a military base," I said.

"Yes, and a well-armed one at that. Look here and here," Connor said. "These are weapons turrets. This here looks like a shield generator. I would say this is a military base that expects to get attacked."

"Look at all the warships they have stockpiled. Let's get a count on those," I said.

"I think we've lost our element of surprise," Jeffery said. "They know we were here. They'll know what we are after."

"Yes, but they also know how far away from it we are. The question is, do we send in the Morag to eliminate this military base? Or do we hold off until we find their home system?" I asked.

"We'll need the numbers in their home system," Jeffery answered. "As much as it's tempting to attack the places we know are a threat, the greater threat comes from their home system. It is likely much more fortified than what we witnessed here."

"According to the scans, over two hundred of those orb devices were released from their shipyard," Connor reported.

"We must warn the Morag and the Federation about what we've found here today. They need to prepare on how to counter this newest threat," I said.

"I'll contact my father," Jeffery agreed.

"I'll prepare a report of what we've found and send it to the nearest Morag fleet and the Federation," I said.

"We will keep analyzing this data and see what else we can learn from our scans," Connor said.

"Bryce, how far are we from Maro's system?" I asked.

"Four hours, Captain."

I nodded. "Let's ensure we all have the chance to eat before arriving in Maro's system. The Jatarians know we are in the area and will be expecting our arrival. They'll be waiting for us. I'll need all hands on deck when it's time."

After that, I headed to my office. I had a lot of things to do.

Chapter Nine

I stayed in my office and poured over the data we had obtained. Our enemy had, indeed, grown stronger. Much stronger than I had anticipated.

I heard a knock at my door. "Come in," I ordered.

Jeffery walked in and sat down. "I informed my father of what we saw."

"What was his response?"

"Disbelief, anger, and finally acceptance. I told him we were sending the information we had obtained. I also informed him that I thought it best not to waste our resources attacking this system. We needed to wait and use the full force of our resources at the Jatarian home system," Jeffery explained.

"Good job keeping my name out of that. What did he say?"

"He said he would take the information to his war council, and they would decide what the best course of action was. I don't have that authority," Jeffery replied.

I shrugged. "All we can do is advise. Perhaps they will come to the same conclusion. By the time they can react, hopefully we will have found the Jatarian home system."

"Good point. I need to not be so frustrated at my father's dismissal of my recommendation."

"I am guessing they will come to the same conclusion. Yet this will be his decision, not one he will give you credit for. Although it would be wise for him to give you the credit, as you are the future of this Federation," I said.

"Assuming, when this war is over, there's still a Federation to protect," Jeffery replied.

Jeffery's comment caught me a little off guard. I couldn't imagine a future where the Federation no longer existed. "Do you think that's a possibility?" I asked slowly.

"Unfortunately I do. My father has no idea what's out here. To be honest, we don't either. That's only one of who-knows-how-many Jatarian military bases. One that you know didn't exist a few years ago. How many more are there? What will we find when we eventually do locate the Jatarian home system? If their military outpost bases are that well fortified, imagine what their home system looks like."

"Unless they intend to use these forward bases as a means to weaken whatever attacking warfleet heads their way. Then, whenever a warfleet does reach their home system, it is only a fraction of what it started as."

"I don't think any race would intentionally leave their home system underprotected. Do you?" Jeffery asked.

I shook my head. "I don't."

"Do you think there will be more Jatarian ships in Maro's system?"

"If they have this military base so close by, I don't see why they would use Maro's system. Unless they're using it for its resources or something similar," I reasoned.

"The Jatarians will be watching for us now," Jeffery commented.

"Yes. We must be more careful with our scans and movements, I'm afraid. Hopefully the Jatarians will not have those little orb devices in each of their systems."

"I would guess those orbs are what the Jatarians have developed to help them sense our stealthed ships. If I were them, I would have them in every system we had ships in, maybe even others as an early warning system. Like we have our buoys," Jeffery said.

119

"I know you're right. I'm just hoping it's not the case. Do you have any ideas on how we can neutralize the threat of the orbs?" I asked. No reason for me to solve this problem on my own. Jeffery was as likely to solve the problem as anyone.

Jeffery sat back in his chair, in the process of placing his feet on my desk. "Do you mind?" he asked, as he relaxed his feet on my desk.

I shrugged and did the same. I couldn't sit still long though. I had to get up and pace. I thought better that way. In my experience, walking and moving around always helped clear my mind.

After a few minutes, Jeffery said, "We need to find a way to make them detonate themselves while we are not in harm's way. In that last system, we released some of our waste and then jumped out. We could do that again. It worked last time."

"Possibly, but I'm afraid they will learn from their past mistakes. That didn't destroy our ship, and they no doubt realize that," I commented.

"You're right. The same strategy won't work again."

"I think we are deviating from our mission. Our mission is to find the Jatarian home system. Not to try to eliminate the threats along the way. We will scan the systems that the Jatarians are in, the best we can. We will avoid those orbs, as best we can. We will report everything we find pertaining to the Jatarians to the Federation. We will let them figure out how to deal with what we give them. We must figure out how we can gain the information we need *without* putting our ship—and, therefore, ourselves—at risk in the process," I said.

"You have a valid point there. I agree. Our mission is to find the Jatarians' homeworld. How do we scan the systems without engaging the orbs?"

"We didn't seem to activate their defenses until we were closer to their shipyard and military base. Maybe we need to remain farther out. We will be safer steering clear of any shipyards or military ships—although it would be important to know where the orbs launch from. Is it only from the shipyards?"

Jeffery frowned at me and said, "You're deviating from our mission again."

I laughed. "I'm going to struggle with that. Feel free to bring that up when it happens. I would imagine we will incidentally find out more about these orbs as we move toward the Jatarian home system."

"Assuming we are, indeed, headed in the correct direction," Jeffery commented.

I sighed. "Exactly."

"I see why you warned me that this mission might take a while."

"Are you missing your family?" I asked.

"Yes. This mission is important for their future though, for their safety."

"Have you spoken with your mother?" I asked.

"No, I haven't. Have you?"

I shook my head.

"I hope she remains as healthy as she was," Jeffery commented.

I debated whether now was the time I should mention our suspicions of the Averys or not.

"Do you still believe my father is behind her decline in health?" Jeffery asked.

No time like the present to bring Jeffery up to speed on what we had figured out, especially since he had brought it up.

"Actually, Jeffery, we think your father isn't the one behind it," I replied.

Jeffery looked puzzled. "Then who is?"

"Hear me out before you respond. Who has the most to gain from your mother's death?"

Jeffery shrugged.

"Who has the resources to pull off something like this?" I asked. I could tell Jeffery's mind was spinning, trying to figure out where I was headed with this.

Jeffery glared at me. "I have the most to gain, but I would never want any harm to come to my mother."

"I agree completely. Who else would gain from the situation?"

"Not the rebels. My mother is a supporter of them. I think I am too. It doesn't reason out that they would be behind it."

"What family stands to gain from you taking over your mother's position?"

A light bulb had gone off in his mind. "The Averys."

I nodded.

"But how could Lord Avery organize such a plot from his remote location?"

"We believe that he still has a network of loyal supporters and that he's getting word to them through the ships that bring new people to their location. He must have a contact on the transport ship. That person relays Lord Avery's orders to his network on Falton Two. It makes sense. Avery has the most to gain from your mother's demise. The Averys have always planned and plotted to get Eloise in that position. Just because they've been banished, that goal wouldn't change. Plus I'm sure Lord and Lady Avery believe that Eloise would bring them back from exile, as soon as she's the Empress. Just to be clear, we don't think Eloise is involved in any way."

"So who else have you shared your suspicions with?" Jeffery asked, slowly soaking in what I told him.

"Theodore and I figured it out. We've discussed it with your mother. She and Theodore made a list of everyone who she comes in contact with regularly, people who have access to Amelia to carry out the plot. Amelia and Theodore then planned to cross-reference that list with those known to be loyal to the Averys in the past," I explained.

"That's a good start. What about my father? Does he know?"

"I'm not sure. Amelia planned to speak with him about it. I don't know if that's happened yet or not."

"That's a lot to absorb. I do believe you're on to something though. I want to give it some thought too. Perhaps I can figure out who is behind the plot. Who is carrying it out anyway. I don't think we could ever prove it was coming from the Averys' direction though."

"I know. If we can stop the perpetrators though, then your mother would be safe. The longer we can keep her safe, the longer you can raise your family in peace."

Jeffery nodded. "I'll go to my quarters and give this some serious thought."

"Let me know if you need something," I replied, as Jeffery stood to leave.

Jeffery turned and said, "My in-laws are not only responsible for my brother's attempted assassination but now they're trying to kill my mother too. What kind of family did I marry into?"

"An ambitious one."

"And my father was worried about you. He should have had his gaze on Avery instead. And Avery was one of my father's closest allies. How will I ever know who I can trust, Slade?"

"I don't know, Jeffery. You can trust me, but I will never return to live at Falton Two. There's too much suspicion and mistrust. I don't want to live that way."

"Me neither," Jeffery replied, as he walked out the door.

When I sat back and thought about it, it was a little unsettling. Avery was one of the Emperor's closest allies and friends. Yet he was responsible for almost killing the Emperor's eldest son and for attempting to kill the Emperor's wife. It was easy to see why Jeffery might have some trust issues. And this was his father-in-law we're talking about.

I couldn't help but shake my head. I needed to go eat and to talk to Maro about what we might find in his system.

I got up and made my way to the cafeteria, and, sure enough, that's where Maro was, sitting and chatting with Parker. I couldn't help but smile. It was a great comfort to have Parker here.

I pulled up a chair and sat down. "Are you ready to see your planet again?" I asked Maro.

"Yes, but I'm also afraid of what we might find there," Maro replied.

"Like what?" I asked.

"Like maybe the Jatarians are using our system for their gain."

"You mean, using your resources?" I asked.

"Yes. There's nothing we could do about it, if they were."

"That's true. I guess we will know soon enough," I replied, looking down at my watch. We were under an hour from Maro's system.

"We've been discussing what we witnessed in the previous system," Parker added.

"I'm even more worried about what we might find as we get closer to where the Jatarian home system is. I would expect more fortified systems. Plus now they know we are in the area and will be vigilantly looking for any sign of us," I replied.

"They didn't seem to react to our scans from the outskirts of the system," Maro observed. "They only reacted once we were closer and did our more detailed scans. We might have to be satisfied with the scans from the outskirts of the systems."

"You're right, but that would be harder for us to figure out exactly what was going on there."

"Maybe we have to observe more and scan less," Parker suggested.

I couldn't help but sigh. "We will see as we move forward. It's important for us to get what information we need. But our mission is to find the Jatarian home system, not to document all their defenses."

"Maybe we can send the Federation scout ships to the systems that we need more information from. Leave that part up to them. We have a good excuse, after all. We do have the future Emperor on board. We can't take too much risk ourselves," Parker stated.

"Good point. Thanks, Parker. I've already sent the location of that system with the Jatarian military base to the Federation and to the scout ships. What they plan to do with that information, I am not sure," I said.

Summer walked up and said, "Slade, you looked like you might be hungry, so I made you a plate of food."

"Thanks, Summer. You know how I am. I'm always hungry." I looked down at the plate in front of me. I took a deep breath and savored the aroma of the meatloaf with mashed potatoes and gravy. I smiled. "It smells delicious."

Summer lit up. "I thought you would like it."

I didn't waste any time. I wanted to savor it while it was nice and hot. It tasted even better than it smelled. By the time I was done, I was stuffed. "That's just what I needed," I said to Parker and Maro.

"Summer's a pretty good cook. She learned from the best," Parker said, with a chuckle.

I laughed too. "You're absolutely right." Parker had taught Summer to cook. He still helped when he could, but the older he got, the less that was. Summer didn't mind though. She enjoyed having Parker around. We all did.

A quick glance at my watch told me that it was time to head to the Command Center. We would near Maro's system soon. What we would find there was anyone's guess. I hoped, for Maro's sake, the Jatarians weren't there. But, as Maro had mentioned, there really wasn't much we could do about it.

"I'll head to my post. I'll see you two when you join me in a few minutes," I said, as I stood.

Parker and Maro nodded, as I got up and left.

I took a quick stroll around the ship before going to the Command Center. Once inside, I sat down in my chair and surveyed the room. Not everyone was back at their posts yet. It wasn't quite time.

Bryce sat at his console, obviously deep in thought. He hadn't even looked up when I had come in.

"Is everything okay, Bryce?" I asked.

Bryce looked up, obviously startled. "When did you get back?"

"A few minutes ago," I replied, as I stood up and walked to where Bryce sat. "What's captured your attention?"

"I've been thinking about where we might find the Jatarians. I think we need the scout ships to head in this direction to do a sweep of the area. All systems around the one where we found the military base. I want to ensure we aren't missing anything.

We know their home system is not here, so it doesn't make sense for us to take the time to do the sweep," Bryce said.

"I'll talk to Jeffery about it. He can get ahold of the scout ships. I've already sent them the information we found and where we found the Jatarian military base. They may already be headed in that direction," I said.

Bryce asked, "How is it that we've been out here for less than two weeks and have already stumbled upon a Jatarian outpost? Those scout ships have been out here for two years and have found nothing. It just doesn't add up, Slade. Maybe there's something we aren't being told," Bryce said worriedly.

"You're starting to sound slightly like me there, Bryce. We have the locations the scout ships have searched. They are performing more of a grid pattern. It's slower but more methodical. They are sticking closer to the Morag borders and working out from the Federation. I do see your point that it's a little odd how we stumbled across the Jatarians so quickly, where we've heard of no other colonies from the scout ships," I replied.

"Exactly," Bryce confirmed. His attention momentarily went to the door to the Command Center, and a few more of the crew walked in.

"You think they're keeping us in the dark," I said quietly.

"Yes."

"We got this information from Amelia and Jeffery."

"Maybe they weren't given the full details, considering they planned to share it with us," Bryce said.

I shrugged. "It's something to think about. It doesn't add up to me though. It doesn't benefit the Federation to keep the information from us. The Emperor may need my help with the Morag to destroy the Jatarians. He gains nothing by keeping me in the dark. Right?" I asked.

Bryce shrugged. "I don't know. We just can't be that lucky. What are the chances?"

"Pretty slim." I didn't like where this was going. Was the Emperor hiding things from me? Was this mission far more dangerous than we initially thought? Maybe it was a good thing Jeffery was on board, after all. It might keep us safer.

As my mind started to veer down the paranoid path, Jeffery walked in with Parker and Maro. I took a deep breath and headed back to my seat. I would have plenty of time to mull this over later. I might bring it up with Jeffery.

First things first though. "How far are we from Maro's system?" I asked.

"Fifteen minutes, Captain," Bryce answered.

The paranoia kept rearing its ugly head at me. I kept pushing it to the back of my mind. If it had Bryce worried, it was definitely something I needed to put more thought into. He wouldn't have shared his concerns with me if they weren't seriously bothering him.

We had no way to know the actual location of the scout ships though. They would know where we'd been. By telling them what we found, they may ascertain our heading.

"Running scans now," Connor announced.

My attention moved back to the present. What would the scans show? Silence filled the room as we awaited the results. I found myself thrumming my fingers on the armrest of my chair. I made a conscious effort to stop. I needed to show my confidence. I was the captain.

Connor broke the silence and said, "The scans show eleven ships in the system."

My heart sank. The Jatarians were still in Maro's system. Why? What were they doing there? "Let's drop in and see what's going on. Do not run any scans once we exit hyperspace, until I give the order," I said.

Connor nodded.

I had decided we should charge our hyperdrive and be ready to leave the system, should any trouble arise from running our scans. We had to be more prepared. I knew we would be expected. It put me a little more on edge.

"Surely they do not have another military base so close to the other," Maro commented.

"Perhaps this will be a colony," Parker said.

"Or maybe a mining operation. Maro, did your people mine the system for its resources?" I asked.

"We took what we needed," Maro replied.

"I guess we will solve this mystery soon enough."

I had really hoped that the Jatarians had left this system alone. I knew Maro felt the same way. I also knew that, deep down, Maro had hoped to one day return to his homeworld. That wasn't even a possibility as long as the Jatarians were nearby, let alone in the system.

I was beginning to realize that this Jatarian problem wouldn't be solved by just destroying the Jatarian home system. It would be a much longer campaign that could possibly last years.

I patted Maro on the back. "We will figure out what they are doing in your system, Maro. Don't worry."

Maro nodded. "I know you will, Slade. Thank you."

I felt the familiar feeling in the pit of my stomach as we exited hyperspace. I took in a deep breath and slowly let it out. "What can we tell without doing any scans?" I asked the crew.

"Not a lot," Connor replied.

"Do we have a visual of any of the ships in the system?" I asked.

"No, we are too far out," replied Connor.

"Let's use our sublight drive and head toward Maro's planet. Once our hyperdrive is charged, we will do our first scan," I said.

It would be almost ninety minutes before our hyperdrive was charged. I also was aware the time would drag slowly by as we watched the system, waiting to see if any ships or orbs headed our way.

I stood and moved toward the viewscreen at the front of the room. I couldn't make out any ships. Even the nearest planet was little more than a small speck on the screen.

"I'm going for a walk. If anything changes, notify me immediately," I said. No use standing in the Command Center. I needed to move, to think.

I walked and sorted out my thoughts. Most of which I pushed off to worry about later. I also decided we might have to hold on to our information a little longer before sending it to the scout ships. If we weren't careful, the scout ships might catch up to us. If they did, would we be in danger? I wasn't sure. I would like to think we wouldn't be. We were on the same side, right?

What if the Emperor decided to use the Jatarians against the rebels? How could he do that? What if he ascertained the whereabouts of our settlements and traded that information to the Jatarians? Then the Jatarians would destroy our refugee settlements, and the Emperor would not look like the bad guy.

The Emperor had grandkids at one of those settlements. Did he care? I might be letting my imagination run wild again, but I also wouldn't put it past him to do something so underhanded like that.

Did the Emperor already know the location of our refugee villages? Would Amelia know? Would Jeffery? Or would the Emperor keep that information to himself for when he needed it one day?

I took a deep breath and slowly let it out. None of that was in my control. What *was* in my control was our actions in this system. Maro's system. Could I keep Jeffery from informing the Emperor and the scout ships about what we found here? Perhaps I could convince Jeffery to wait until we heard what the Emperor would do about the Jatarian military base we just found. Then we would report what else we'd found.

I could only control the release of the information we were gathering by controlling Jeffery. Could I do that?

"Hey, Slade. Are you okay?" Jeffery asked from behind me in the hallway.

Just the man I'd been thinking about. "Jeffery, are things okay in the Command Center?"

"Yes. I thought I would come check on you."

"I've just been sorting out things in my head. I think, until we know how your father will react to that military base we found, we might want to keep the other things we find a secret. Not permanently but just until we know what his plan is. What do you think?" I asked.

Jeffery thought it over. "I think you're right. No reason why we have to report everything we see exactly when we see it. We need to know what his plans are. We need him to remember that the goal is to first eliminate the Jatarian home system. Then we can go after all these outposts and military bases."

"There is something to having too much information. It makes you forget the main mission."

"Agreed," Jeffery said.

"I'm glad we're on the same page, Jeffery. I am so happy you got to come along on this mission."

"What do you think the Jatarians are doing here?" Jeffery asked, as he fell into step beside me.

"My guess is a mining operation. They already have a military base nearby. It wouldn't make sense to have another one so close. Perhaps a colony even. They would need raw materials for shipbuilding for that shipyard. If they can mine that from nearby, that would cut down on the time it takes to manufacture a warship."

"Very true. Will we investigate Maro's planet?"

"If we can. I know Maro would like to know how the planet has recovered since the attack. I can't blame him for that. We are here and so close to his homeworld. If it's feasible, we have to check it out. I won't put us in any unnecessary danger though. Maro understands that."

Jeffery nodded. "I really like Maro."

"The Federation would have deemed his race a threat, since they had ships, though unarmed, and could travel in hyperspace. They would have destroyed them too," I explained sadly.

"I think that policy needs to change, Slade."

"I agree. However, I doubt it will change under your father's rule."

"You're probably right about that. One day, when I take over, I will change it."

"I hope so, Jeffery."

Chapter Ten

Eventually I felt Cole trying to communicate with me telepathically. *Is everything okay?* I asked.

Cole replied, *Yes. I thought you might want to know that the hyperdrive is now fully charged.*

Thanks, Cole. I'll return then.

As I turned to go to the Command Center, I filled in Jeffery on what Cole had told me.

"Will we run the scans then?" Jeffery asked.

"Yes. I think we are safer running the scans from farther out than close in. We didn't get any reaction from those Jatarian ships, not until we ran the scans much closer in," I explained.

"That's true," Jeffery replied.

Once we arrived back in the Command Center, I had Connor start the scans. The rest of us waited in silence for them to come back. What types of ships were these?

"Scans are coming back. It seems only one of them is a warship," Connor reported.

"And the others?" I asked.

"A mix between freighters and transport ships. My guess is that we've found a mining operation," Connor stated.

"Where are these ships congregated?" I asked, as I hoped it wasn't on Maro's planet.

"Near the fifth planet from the sun, not Maro's."

"That's a relief. Maro, any idea what they might be mining?" I asked.

Maro shook his head.

"Let's keep moving toward Maro's planet. We want to see what it looks like now that it's had a few years to recover from the Jatarian attack. I'm also interested to know what exactly the Jatarians are mining for," I said.

"Should we do a microjump to save some time?" Bryce asked.

I hesitated. I didn't want to alert the Jatarians to our presence here, although they were likely already on the lookout for us. We couldn't waste too much time here though. We still had a mission to complete. "Let's do a microjump to put us closer to Maro's planet."

When that familiar feeling swept across my stomach, my nerves increased. Now we were closer to the Jatarians.

Maro's planet was the largest thing on the viewscreen now. No Jatarian ships orbited it. That seemed to be a good sign. Hopefully the Jatarians could get all of what they were after on the other planet and would leave Maro's untouched.

The mining had to be for raw materials needed for their warship-making endeavors at that shipyard in the last system. It made the most sense.

What if we destroyed that planet? Or the Jatarian mine there? Would that slow down their shipbuilding? I shook my head. That wasn't a part of our mission. Perhaps we could suggest it to the Emperor or possibly a Morag task group. Did I have enough data to send for a Morag task group? Or was this another diversion from our main target, the Jatarian home system?

It would take weeks to organize and to execute a Morag attack on any target. We were so far out already. Who knew how much farther out the Jatarian home system would be?

"Will we scan the planet?" Maro asked.

"Yes, once our hyperdrive is fully charged again, we will run the scans," I confirmed.

We continued to watch as Maro's planet came more into view on the screens. The atmosphere was not completely covered in ash and debris. In many places, the surface was visible. Everything we could see from our vantage point was positive. The planet looked much better than the last time we'd been here.

When we had confirmation from Cole that our hyperdrive was once again charged, we began the scans of Maro's planet.

Maro moved closer to the viewscreen. "Can we enter the atmosphere and get a better glimpse of the surface?" Maro asked.

"It depends on what the scans show. It might not be safe yet for us to enter the atmosphere," I replied.

"Scans show life-forms on the surface," Connor said, looking to Maro. "More of your people must have survived and stayed behind, when the rescue efforts had subsided."

"Where are they at?" Maro asked, intrigued.

"The scans show them congregated together here in this area," Connor said, as he showed Maro where the scans showed the life-forms.

"That's not near any of the cities," Maro explained.

"The cities still might not be safe places to go. The survivors might be congregated in the more rural areas," Bryce said.

"This is also near mountains with cave systems in them. This area is not near where you guys rescued me. Maybe this was an area they didn't attempt to rescue people from," Maro said.

"We will try to get a better view. Then we can see how well they're doing," I said.

"It appears it's safe for us to get a little closer," Connor said. "No point in taking any unnecessary risks though."

"Let's see if we can get a better view of the area where the life-forms are. Assuming, of course, that these life-forms are Maro's people and not something else entirely," I said.

Maro seemed surprised by my comment. I hoped the life-forms were his people, but there was also a chance it was a Jatarian group, scouting the area for one thing or another.

We moved in closer and could confirm that it was, indeed, a group of Maro's people. I was relieved. I knew he was as well. We watched them for a while. It boosted Maro's morale, seeing that some of his people were still alive and well on his home planet.

"Thank you," Maro said. "I'm glad my people still inhabit our planet. Perhaps one day it will become what it once was."

"Given enough time, I'm sure it will be even better," I replied.

"I guess it's time to go see what the Jatarians are mining here," Maro said, satisfied with what he'd witnessed on his home planet.

"Okay. Let's head that way. I don't want to use another microjump. Let's use our sublight drive to get closer. Then we will do our scans," I ordered.

"It'll take us at least a couple hours to get close enough to get the detailed scans we want," Bryce commented.

"Okay. I would rather it take longer, and we get what we need, than for the Jatarians to sense us. Let's stay as far away as we can to get those scans," I ordered.

"Yes, Captain," Connor replied.

I remained in my chair. Jeffery, Parker, and Maro stayed put in the Command Center too. We all watched as we headed toward the Jatarian ships. The closer we got, the more nervous I became.

Was knowing what exactly the Jatarians were mining for here imperative to our mission? I knew it wasn't, yet I knew it was important to Maro, which made it important to me.

Time seemed to drag on, until finally Connor announced, "I'm running the scans now."

I sat up in my chair and stared intently at the viewscreens at the front of the room. What would they show?

One viewscreen zoomed in on the lone Jatarian military ship. It was imperative that we keep a watch on what that particular ship did. If it went on alert and opened its weapons turrets, we would need to get out of here quickly.

Another one of the Jatarian ships was one I hadn't seen before. It must be a freighter, based on its size. It dwarfed the transport vessels. Whatever the Jatarians were mining from this planet, they got a lot of it. Especially considering that multiple freighters were in the system.

"Here is the mining operation right here," Connor said, as he indicated a particular area of the planet below.

From the looks of it, it was quite the endeavor.

"Another freighter ship is on the surface. Can we tell what they're loading up?" Bryce asked.

"It's raw materials for their ships," Maro said sadly. "It's a material we call *whampot*. It's a very strong material we used for our own ships. I didn't know there was any here."

Maro sounded so defeated to me. "Maro, it's not your fault the Jatarians are here, mining your resources," I said.

"No, but this will help them make more warships to use against you," Maro explained.

"Could we destroy this operation?" Jeffery asked. "It might slow down their ship-building process."

Jeffery had no idea our ship was armed, did he?

"How would you suggest we do that?" I asked him.

"This ship must have some weapon we can use," Jeffery said.

It did, but I didn't think now was the time. "We could send in a Morag task group. With only one military ship here, they shouldn't lose too many ships in the process."

"How close is the nearest Morag task group?" Jeffery asked.

"Slightly over two weeks away. It wouldn't be a bad idea for us to bring one closer anyway. Who knows what else we might find," I commented.

"Let's do that. Also let's not report it to my father."

"Are you sure?" I asked, a little surprised.

"I'm sure. We can tell him later. He doesn't have to know everything in every system. He has enough to worry about," Jeffery replied.

"Okay. Let's head out of the system, and I'll find the nearest Morag task group to send in."

"Will the Morag scan the system?" Maro asked.

"Not if I tell them not to," I replied.

"Can you do that, please?" Maro requested.

"Yes, I will, Maro."

"Thank you."

"Do we have everything we need?" I asked.

"I believe so," Connor answered.

"Bryce, please note our location so I can send it to the Morag," I ordered.

"Noted," Bryce replied.

"There's been no reaction from the military ship," Cole reported.

"Maybe we were only discovered by the shipyard and its technology. Maybe the military ships themselves can't sense us," Connor hypothesized.

"Should we test it?" Cole asked.

Should we? That answer was up to me. We had what we needed from here though. But what if more warships were in the next system? Was it best to test our theory here and now, when we had only one warship to worry about? "Let's test it. We might not have another chance like this, with just one warship in the system," I said.

The *Hunter* moved in closer to the warship. What if this was a trap to lure us in? The Jatarian ship pretended it didn't sense us, so we come closer.

I looked at the viewscreen again. The turrets remained closed. All evidence pointed to the Jatarians being oblivious to our presence here.

We continued to move closer. "Let's do the scans again. See if they react," I ordered.

"Running scans now," Connor reported.

My gaze stayed glued to the screen focused on the Jatarian warship. So far, so good.

"Maybe this is an older warship without the updated technology," Bryce suggested.

"It could be. Let's move on to the next system. We have the Jatarian home system to find. I'm sure there will be plenty more instances where we can test our theory," I ordered.

Shortly afterward, I felt us move into hyperspace. I sat back in my chair.

"How long before we reach the next system?" Jeffery asked.

"The next system we will pass by is in sixteen hours," Bryce answered.

"I guess I better go contact the Morag. Augusta, you're in charge. Connor, go get some rest." I walked straight to my office. I wasn't surprised that Jeffery followed me.

"How can I help?" Jeffery asked.

"We make note of where the larger Morag task groups are. I had the larger fleets stationed nearer to the Federation in case the Jatarians attacked. Smaller task groups are farther out. These are the ones we want to find and to make note of. Especially the larger task groups," I explained.

"How do I do that?" Jeffery asked.

This was a skill he needed to learn. It could come in handy one day when he was the leader of the Federation, as long as he never used it against the rebels.

"First, clear your mind and focus on your gift. Then reach out for a Morag mind. When you find one, listen in to his thoughts and words and figure out if that Morag is in a ship and if it's a military one. It's usually pretty easy to determine that. The harder part is determining which system they're in," I explained.

"It sounds complicated," Jeffery replied.

"It is, but the more you do it, the easier it is."

"I'll do my best," Jeffery said.

I nodded. It wasn't an easy task, but the more Jeffery tried, the better he would get.

I closed my eyes and cleared my mind. I reached out with my gift to find the nearest Morag mind. I knew about where they would be, which helped immensely. When I did find one, I noted the location and the number of ships in the task group. This continued for almost an hour.

As I opened my eyes, Jeffery was staring at me.

"You're really good at that, Slade."

"I've had a lot of practice. How'd you do?" I asked.

"Not great. I found a few minds, but none were Morag."

"No need to get discouraged. When I started, I was looking for Morag minds in the next system, not half a galaxy away. I'm not a very good teacher."

"You are, and I have no doubt I'll learn to do it. It'll just take some practice."

"How about you reach out to the system we are headed to next and see if you can sense any minds with your gift," I suggested.

"Okay. I'll try that."

I watched as Jeffery closed his eyes and focused on his gift. It was interesting to watch. I was usually the one using my gift, not waiting for the results.

After a few minutes, Jeffery said, "I did find some minds, but I did not know their language."

"That's a great start."

"So what about the Morag? How big of a task group will we send?" Jeffery asked.

I showed Jeffery my notes on my findings of the nearest Morag ships. After discussing our options for a few minutes, we made our decisions. Now to give the Morag commander his orders.

I again focused on my gift and reached out to the Morag commander. I gave him my orders to destroy the Jatarian mining operation and to stay away from any other planets in the system.

When I opened my eyes, Jeffery asked, "How long will it take them to get there?"

"Two and a half weeks," I replied.

"Maybe we will have found the Jatarian home system by then."

"I hope so," I replied. "We have a lot of systems to search."

"How do you guys decide where to search?" Jeffery asked.

"Maro and his people knew this area of space well. With them having traveled in this area often, we know the Jatarian home system is not in this area here," I said, pointing to an area on the map. "So we intend to search farther out. If Maro's people never happened upon the Jatarian home system before, it must be even farther out than they were. That's all we have to go on though."

"I guess that's better than nothing," Jeffery replied.

"We might still find plenty of Jatarian activity in this area, just not their home system."

"Do you think we can beat them?" Jeffery asked.

"Not on our own. Perhaps a united front between us, the Morag, and the Zator will put us on a better footing to come out of this war on top."

"And what if it doesn't?"

"I would rather not consider that outcome. We will deal with that if we have to down the line."

"Why do you think the Jatarians are building military bases farther out?" Jeffery asked.

"My guess is, they are preparing for a major attack. What do you think?" I asked.

"I can't think of any other plausible reason."

"The more I see, the more I worry about what we'll find when we do locate their home system," I said honestly.

"Me too. I'm glad I'm here to witness it myself. I miss Eloise and the kids, but I'm doing this for them. To help secure their future."

I nodded my agreement. I tried not to let my mind wander to my own family. I was using my gift every night to stay in touch with Hadassah. It helped, but it wasn't the same as being there in person.

This might be a good time to bring up Bryce's and my concerns about the scout ships holding back on us. "Jeffery, do you find it odd that we found the Jatarians within the first two weeks of our mission? The Federation scout ships have been out here for over two years and have found nothing."

"I noticed that myself. It makes you wonder if they aren't giving us all the information," Jeffery replied.

"But why wouldn't they? That's what I can't figure out."

"Maybe my father can't do much about it, as far away as he is. So he's just collecting information to use later?" Jeffery suggested.

"I don't know. I just can't figure it out," I said.

"So maybe we should hold our information a little closer," Jeffery replied.

"I don't see where this ends up in favor of us Humans, if we can't work together."

"Let's hold off on reporting for a few days. We don't want them to know exactly where we are and when. Just in case my father is plotting something," Jeffery said.

"Are you sure?" I asked.

"It doesn't hurt anything for us to wait a week or so to report what we've already found at that time. We would still be giving the Federation the information before they could possibly react to it."

"I agree. It doesn't hurt anything to wait. We will have that Morag task group nearer to us and can use them how we see fit," I replied.

"We are in control of our own destiny," Jeffery said.

"Yes, we are."

"So now what?" Jeffery asked.

"Now we wait and see what we find next," I replied.

"Are we now in unexplored space?"

I replied, "We're farther out here now than I've ever been. I'm not sure how far out the *Explorer* is, but it's pretty safe to say no Human ship has been here before."

"Have you tried to connect with your friend on the *Explorer*?"

"No, I haven't. I should though, now that we're farther out here. He could probably give us a better idea of where we should and shouldn't search."

"What are you waiting on then?" Jeffery asked excitedly. "Any information that we can get straight from the source would be very valuable."

"Good point. No time like the present."

I closed my eyes and focused on my gift. I reached out to Fritz. I had no idea where the *Explorer* was. They were farther out than we were though, so that's where I focused my attention.

Slade, it's so good to hear from you. I've been waiting and hoping you would find us.

Are you okay?

I think we just passed by the Jatarian home system.

What makes you think that? Did you exit hyperspace there?

No, unfortunately we do not have the stealthed capabilities of the newer ships. We passed by a system with thousands of ships in it though.

Thousands?

Yes. Who else can it be other than the Jatarians?

I hope it's not someone worse than the Jatarians, I answered. *Have you informed the Federation?*

No. It will take a long time for our message to reach them. We only just passed by the system about an hour ago. We plan to exit hyperspace in a nearby system that's free of any ships. Then we will do another flyby to confirm.

Are you afraid you're wrong?

I hope I am. I want to confirm before I send this message.

I understand. How far away is the next system?

Six hours. Assuming it's void of any ships.

What if it's not? I asked.

Then we'll go to the next one. At most I will wait twenty-four hours before I make my report.

Can you give me an idea of your location?

The Jatarian home system is in the Dremu system, Fritz answered.

I don't think that one's on my maps, I replied.

It's also known as AN2230.

I'll look for it and head that way. I'll check back in with you in about six hours.

Are you still within range of your gift and Falton Two? Fritz asked.

Yes.

Good. That'll be a much faster way to share our findings. Let me confirm though.

Okay. We will hold off passing on the information. I'll reach out to you again in a few hours.

Thanks, Slade.

I opened my eyes and grabbed the map. "Look for the system named AN2230."

"Why?" Jeffery asked, as he began looking at the map.

"My contact just passed that system. He believes it's the Jatarian home system," I explained.

"Why?"

"Thousands of ships are in the system," I said gravely.

"Thousands?" Jeffery asked in disbelief.

I nodded. I needed Bryce. He knew these maps better than me. "Come on. Let's go get Bryce. He's the map expert." Jeffery and I got up and went straight to the Command Center. Of course Bryce wasn't here. "Where's Bryce?" I asked Augusta.

"He went to get some sleep," Augusta explained. "Can I help you with something?"

"We need to know where the system AN2230 is," I answered.

Augusta moved from the command chair, where she'd been sitting in my absence, and moved over to Bryce's consoles. She typed in a few commands and waited. Then she typed in a few more things.

The viewscreen at the front of the room changed to a map. "Here is system AN2230," Augusta said, highlighting a particular system.

"How far are we from there?" I asked.

"Three weeks," Augusta replied.

"That's our new destination," I said. "My contact on the *Explorer* just passed that system and sensed thousands of ships there. We believe that might be the Jatarian home system."

Augusta looked alarmed. "That's a lot of ships."

"The *Explorer* will make another pass to double-check their findings," I answered. "How far off course are we?"

"Not much. We can course correct in the next system," Augusta replied.

"Okay." I took a deep breath. "I guess all we can do right now is get some rest." I would have difficulty sleeping, but I needed it. We still had another twelve hours before our next system.

Once I got to my quarters, I set my alarm so I could wake up and check in with Fritz again. I couldn't believe it. He had found the Jatarian home system. At least I hope he had. Who else out here would have so many ships?

Chapter Eleven

I woke with a start when my alarm went off. I shook off my confusion and remembered it was time to check in with Fritz. A quick glance at my watch told me the *Explorer* should be nearing the system Fritz hoped to stop in.

I closed my eyes, took a deep breath, and focused on my gift. I reached out to Fritz.

Slade, good news. This next system is empty. We are exiting hyperspace now.

Good. Do you plan to do some exploring while you're there?

We might as well, while our hyperdrive recharges.

Are you nervous about being so close to the Jatarian home system? I asked.

Yes. Any passing ship could sense us here. I don't plan to spend any more time here than I must.

How will you confirm it is the Jatarian home system? I asked.

We can't. I will confirm the large number of ships and then pass off the information to the nearest stealthed scout ship. They will come and investigate further. At least that's my plan.

It sounds like a solid one.

How far out is your ship? Fritz asked.

We are a three-week hyperspace jump away. We are headed in your direction, however.

Good.

What about the scout ships? Are any of them closer to you than we are? I asked Fritz.

I'm not sure. While our hyperdrive charges, I've got to locate all the scout ships and figure out which is closest to our location.

When was the last time you checked in with one?

It's been a good week, Fritz replied.

Have the scout ships found anything out there yet?

No, nothing of note. What about you?

See? That's what I find puzzling. We've been out here a little over two weeks and have already found a Jatarian military base and a mining operation. How is it that the scout ships have been out here for two years and have found nothing of note? I asked.

I'm not sure, Slade. When you put it that way, it seems whoever is telling the scout ships where to search is an idiot or someone is purposely hiding something.

Exactly. Have you found anything other than the home system?

Yes, I've found what I believe are four other colony systems. We couldn't exit hyperspace to find out, but I did send the information to the scout ships to investigate.

So what did the scout ships find?

I'm not sure. I doubt any has had the time to investigate yet. They were quite far from any of the systems, Fritz answered.

And you are sure you passed on the information?

Yes. It would have taken a while for my message to reach one of the scout ships. It was an encrypted message in the event someone else intercepted it. There's a lot of space between here and there.

So what are the scout ships doing then?

I don't know. What if something happened to them? Fritz asked.

Surely we would have heard. How long ago did you find the first colony?

About three weeks ago.

What's going on then? I asked.

Maybe the scout ship hasn't had time to receive the information and to arrive at the coordinates, Fritz suggested.

That could be. Could you tell me which systems you suspect the colonies are in? We could check them on our way to the home system.

I can do that. It wouldn't hurt to have you look. I trust you, Slade.

I trust you too, Fritz.

I assume you're in a stealthed ship?

Yes, we are.

Good. You'll need it.

How many planets are in the inhabitable zone in the system you're currently in? I asked. The explorer in me was too curious not to ask.

Two planets and three moons. We are doing a microjump now to check out one of them. We can never stop exploring, Fritz answered.

It's just part of who we are, I replied.

I know you're still far away, but how about you check in with me at least once daily? I would feel much better communicating with someone else more regularly.

I will. It's good to talk to you, Fritz. It's been forever since we got to see you. Hopefully we can arrange a remedy for that soon.

That would be great. Maybe even way out here, far from Federation space.

We will make it happen.

Oh no, Fritz said.

What's wrong? I asked.

The alarms are sounding.

Is it the Jatarians? I asked nervously.

Yes, it is. A group of twelve ships. I'm moving our ship closer to this moon.

Is it inhabitable?

Yes, our scans show it is.

Could you land the ship on the surface? Perhaps hide it in a cave?

We are headed closer to the moon. We will try to make it to the surface.

What are the Jatarians doing? I asked.

They are scanning the system.

How much longer until your hyperdrive is charged?

Too long. Slightly under an hour.

Is there anything between you and the Jatarian ships?

A planet thankfully.

That's better than nothing. Get to that moon quickly.

We are doing our best. Our shields are activated.

I stood up and paced back and forth. I was so worried for Fritz and the rest of the crew on the *Explorer*. What would they do? How far from the moon were they? The *Explorer* didn't have any weapons. At least it didn't the last time I was on board. *How far are you from the moon?*

We are almost there. Five more minutes until we enter the atmosphere.

And the Jatarians? Are they still scanning the system?

Yes. They're currently moving locations. I assume they'll scan again.

You've got this, Fritz. I know you can reach that moon before they realize where you are. I know you can do it.

Thanks, Slade. I pray you're right. I can't even fathom the situation that will unfold if we don't.

Me neither. I waited silently, letting Fritz command his ship during this time of extreme danger. I continued to pace in my quarters. Back and forth, time and again. *Status?* I asked. The pause before Fritz responded had my heartbeat quickening. I felt it thudding quickly in my chest.

We are entering the atmosphere of the moon. We are scanning the surface for a place to hide.

And what about the Jatarians?

They're headed our way, I'm afraid.

I ran my fingers through my hair. I was helpless to do anything to aid Fritz in this situation. *How far out are they?* I asked.

They just microjumped to the moon. I assume they'll begin their scans at any moment.

Have you found a place to hide?

We are moving the ship into a canyon area. You know the Explorer *is a large ship. It's not exactly easy to hide.*

Hopefully that'll be enough.

I'm afraid they will land and search for us.

They may, or perhaps they'll just wait until you leave to get you. If they can spare a few ships, they may just wait you out.

That would be the best-case scenario, Fritz replied.

I continued to pace and fidget. I was so nervous. I took several deep breaths to try to calm down. I was glad no one else was here to see me like this. *Update?* I asked.

We've found a cave in the canyon. It's a tight fit, but we are fully inside it. I'm grateful to find it under these circumstances.

It might be helpful if you powered down all nonessential systems. That way no power outlay exists for the scan to pick up on, I suggested.

Good idea. How will we know if they find us? Fritz asked.

You'll know. Nothing else you can do now but wait.

Good point. We are powering down all systems now. I pray it's not too late.

Me too, Fritz.

I'm thankful I've had you to talk me through this, Slade. If something happens, I want you to know I'm glad I had the chance to meet you, to know you. Even if you are considered a rebel, you're still my friend. You always will be.

Fritz, you will always be my friend. You'll make it through this. I know it. Have faith.

I do. I need to tell you where those four colony systems are, just in case, Fritz said.

I rushed into my office and found a paper and pen to write down what he told me. I knew none of the systems he mentioned. I jotted them down and hoped we would find them, based on what he told me.

I feel greatly relieved that you have the coordinates for the colonies.

I will feel greatly relieved once the Jatarians have left your system, I replied.

Ha, ha. Me too. Only I won't know it.

Wait twenty-four hours and then turn on only your tactical display, but only long enough to get a signal, I said.

It sounds as if you've done this before, Fritz replied.

I have multiple times. I'm still here, so it obviously worked.

That does make me feel marginally better.

Good, that's what I'm here for, I replied. *Maybe all those times we hid from the Jatarians were so we could help you make it through this alive.*

I hope your plan works.

It will.

Now all we can do is wait, right?

Right. You can post some guards outside your ship, toward the mouth of the cave. Is it daytime?

The sun is just beginning to set.

I wish we were closer and could come help.

How could you help? I doubt your one ship could take on twelve enemy ships, Slade.

Valid point. Now we wait, I said.

Do you think we can win this war? Fritz asked.

Not on our own. We need an allied force of the Morag, the Zator, and the Federation. What about those colony systems you found? Were a large number of ships in those systems too?

Yes. Not thousands of ships but hundreds. The more colonies we found, the closer we were getting to their home system. I'm sure more colony systems are out there.

We found a military base. I imagine more of those are out there too. We've debated whether it's best to wait and attack their home system or if we should attack the systems we find when we find them.

What did you guys conclude?

Wait for the home system. It will take all our ships.

If we wait and attack the home system together, those outpost military bases could send an attack on the Federation. They're much closer to the

Federation than the home system. So they could mount an attack, once we begin our attack on their home system, Fritz pointed out.

You're right. I hadn't considered that. Perhaps it benefits us to destroy these outposts that are closer to the Federation. Destroy what we can when we can. Except these decisions aren't up to me.

Aren't they though? You're here. The Emperor is not.

I don't know. Jeffery is with me. If I can get Jeffery to make the decision with me, that might take some heat off me later.

Would Jeffery stick up for you? If it came down to it? Fritz asked.

I would like to think so, but you never really know. I will discuss your thoughts with him and see what he thinks about hitting the targets closer to the Federation while we can.

How long do you think these Jatarian ships will stick around?

Until they have somewhere better to be. If they sensed your ship on their scans, they'll want to figure it out, especially being so close to their home system.

Our hyperdrive still isn't fully charged. We had to power that down though, Fritz explained.

Check once every twenty-four hours or so on the tactical display to see if the Jatarian ships are still out there. If they are, you'll have to wait longer. If they leave, power up your hyperdrive and let it charge. You'll have to be very careful. Err on the side of caution and not recklessness. No room for mistakes under these circumstances.

I agree. We must be very careful. Our lives are at stake here.

Patience. That's the key here, I said. *I understand how hard it is not knowing what's going on out there. I've been there before. You can do this, Fritz. You have to. I wish we were closer and could be your eyes and ears out there.*

You never know, Slade. We might still be hiding when you get here.

I know you have the supplies to last that long. We are coming, and, if you're still hiding when we arrive, we will do our best to free you from your hiding spot.

153

I've sent out a few guards to watch the entrance of the cave. I hope they don't see anything.

Ensure they stay hidden from view, Fritz. You know as well as I do that many dangers could be lurking out there, not just the Jatarians.

Good point. I will remind them.

We will win this war, Fritz. It might be long and hard, but, in the end, we will prevail. We have to. Humanity depends on it. The fate of the galaxy even.

Are you getting poetic on me, Slade?

Sorry. I guess I was trying to distract you from your current situation.

You're doing a great job at that, Fritz replied.

I am a man of many talents.

I've got to go take care of a few things, Slade. Will you check back in with me periodically?

Yes, I will. I'll check back in every half hour for now.

That sounds good. It's so encouraging to have the ability to communicate with you.

Would you like me to pass on the information about the Jatarian home system? I asked.

Why don't you speak to Jeffery about it? Perhaps the better strategy is to leave the Jatarian home system undiscovered, until we deal with all the military outposts and colonies. I'll leave that up to the two of you. I can't exactly report it right now. We must keep all communications quiet, so we will remain undiscovered.

Yes, you are right about that. You are stuck there, unable to relay any information to the Federation. Perhaps this gives Jeffery and me a little time to figure out the best strategy. But what if we are wrong?

I have every confidence in you, Slade. You'll make the right decision for the good of all. Not just for the Federation.

You think too highly of me, Fritz.

Maybe I should rephrase that to say, you will make the right decision for all Humans, whether Federation, Empire, or refugees.

That I can live with.

Good. You have some thinking to do. Good luck.

Stay safe, Fritz. I'll check in with you in half an hour.

I'll be here.

I'll count on it.

I opened my eyes and looked around my office. Now what? I needed to have a conversation with Jeffery. Where was he? I could easily find him by using my gift, but I had some deep thinking to do. Which meant I needed to move around. I could find Jeffery while I walked around the ship.

I had to decide what I would tell Jeffery and what I might keep secret from him. What should I do?

What did Jeffery already know? He knew the *Explorer* had found the Jatarian home system. He even knew the name of the system. So there was no hiding that from him.

After walking around the ship for half an hour, I decided to tell him everything. It would be too complicated to remember what I had and hadn't told him in the long run. I didn't want to alienate him. That was certain. This trip was supposed to help bring us closer.

I found a spot to sit down and focused once again on my gift. I had tried to distract myself from worrying about Fritz for the past half hour, but now my anxiety intensified, as I used my gift to reach out to him. *Fritz, are you okay?*

Yes. So far, so good. We've seen no sign of the Jatarians.

What a relief.

It's dark now. We are being vigilant to not use any lights that might give away our location.

Wise choice.

I think that, if the Jatarians had known our location, they would have attacked us by now, Fritz said.

Perhaps. It could be that they want the ship intact though. It could be a treasure trove of information about the Federation and our new ships and weapons. They might also believe you process the ability to sense the stealthed ships. No, I'm convinced that, if they do know where you are, it will be a ground assault.

They'll wait for first light then, Fritz commented.

That's what we would do. Who knows about them? Maybe they see very well at night. No way to know. We've not had enough experience to make that assumption.

That's true. Dang. I was hoping for a good night's sleep, Fritz replied.

I would at least try to get some sleep. Ensure your systems officer is alert and ready to activate your shield at a moment's notice, should you be found.

At least our ship is old and doesn't have that technology to sense stealthed ships.

The Jatarians don't know that though.

I think you're right. If they know where we are, it will be a ground assault. We don't have enough weapons to fend off very many hostiles.

Think outside the box, Fritz. Can you make more weapons? Some type of grenade or something?

I'll look into it. Hopefully they don't know where we are and will have to spend a few days finding us. Maybe we can figure out how to make some homemade weapons. Any ideas would be appreciated.

I will get my crew thinking about it too. Perhaps we can come up with something.

Thanks, Slade.

Oh, in that system where we found the military base, the Jatarians used these small orbs to try to find us. They might use them in this situation too. It would be easier than using the larger ships.

What do these orbs do? Fritz asked.

They have sensors on them. They are used to try to locate our stealth ship. They were pretty accurate at it. Ultimately we dumped some of our waste to see what would happen. The orbs detonated, causing small explosions. We weren't anywhere near there by that time.

Great. How small are these orbs?

About the size of a basketball. When activated, they have lights all over them though. So you'll see them coming. We also think they become activated when a ship nears them. Therefore, a dormant orb won't show up on a scan.

I'll tell the guards to be on the lookout for them. Any suggestions on how we can avoid being found by these orbs?

I would imagine that, since you have turned off almost all the ship's systems, the orbs won't pick up on any energy expenditure. They'll just have to do a thorough manual sweep of the area to find you.

Okay. We will be on the lookout.

We will try to help problem solve from our end. I'll check back with you again in half an hour.

I'll be here.

I opened my eyes and resolved to figure out how to help Fritz. I needed to get the crew together. The more minds thinking on this, the better. I would also reach out to Alex. I wasn't sure how much longer I could reach Elmania with my gift. Perhaps someone there could help. They did develop the weapons on our ship, after all.

I quickly found Parker and Maro and told them I needed a crew meeting in the cafeteria as soon as possible. Then I pulled out a chair at one of the tables and focused on my gift again. I reached out to Alex. Maybe he could help Fritz.

Slade, is everything okay?

My friend on the Explorer *is in trouble. He's hiding from a group of Jatarian warships on a remote moon. He only has limited weapons. I'm afraid the Jatarians will mount a ground strike to try to take the ship for the information that could be on board. We need to help them make some weapons. Can you get a team of people on this?*

We'll get started on this right away, Slade.

I'll reach out in another hour to see if you've come up with anything.
Okay. What type of weapons do they have now?
I believe only a few blasters and stun guns.
Any explosives?
I don't believe so.
I thought they might, since they're on an exploration ship. You should ask about that, the next time you check in. We will operate under the assumption they don't have them.

We will be working on a solution here too. I don't know how much longer I'll have the ability to contact you. I'll check back soon.

When I opened my eyes, most of the crew was already in the cafeteria. I took a deep breath. I might as well get started. Fritz might not have much time.

I brought the crew up to speed on the *Explorer's* situation and the need to improvise some weapons.

"Any ideas or knowledge in this area of expertise would be helpful. No experimenting here though. We can't risk our own safety. We might be their only hope of rescue. If you have ideas, I can pass them on to Alex back at Elmania. They can do the experimenting," I explained.

The crew began talking among themselves and brainstorming ideas. If only Fritz could see this, he would be encouraged. This same thing was happening back at Elmania and on the *Explorer*. Surely we could come up with something. We had to. I couldn't let Fritz down.

I glanced at my watch. Time to check in with Fritz.
Slade, we're still here and undiscovered still.
Good. We're considering solutions for you, as far as homemade weapons or defenses, and so is our team at one of our refugee villages. They were curious to know if you had any explosives on board.
Yes, we do. We have a small stash in case we need it, while exploring a planet or getting in a bind.

Is any of your crew trained to handle and use it?

Yes. That's Jerrod. He is already trying to figure out how to use them, if we have to, even if to self-destruct.

Self-destruct? Fritz couldn't possibly be considering it.

We can't let this ship fall into the hands of the Jatarians. If we have to, we will use the explosives to destroy the ship.

What if you used the explosives to close in the cave? Only if the Jatarians found you? It would seal you in and protect you, hopefully until we could get there, I suggested.

Maybe. I'll suggest that to Jerrod.

Okay. We will keep brainstorming ideas here and at our refugee village. If anyone can come up with something, it's them. They designed my ship. They can do anything. I know it.

Keep checking in. We'll figure out a solution. I just know it, Fritz replied.

We will. You can count on us, Fritz.

I know. Thanks, Slade.

I opened my eyes and looked around the room. Everyone was still talking and debating ideas. I felt very comforted by what I saw. We could do this. Together we could do anything.

Chapter Twelve

Hours passed, and we threw out many ideas on how to save the crew of the *Explorer*. Alex and the group at Elmania had a few ideas that I passed on to Fritz. So far, the Jatarians had not discovered the location of the *Explorer* and its crew.

We neared our next system. Here we would stop and course correct to make the fastest time to where Fritz and the *Explorer* were.

I sat in my command chair. The rest of the command crew were at their stations. Jeffery, Parker, and Maro sat nearby. We all awaited what we might find in the next system.

I hoped it would be empty. I didn't want to waste any time trying to figure out what was happening in any more systems, not until I knew Fritz and his crew were safe.

"Running the scans now," Connor announced.

I sat forward in my chair, watching the tactical display at the front of the room. I closed my eyes and reached out to the system. Could I communicate with anyone there? I hadn't found anyone, when Connor interrupted my focus.

"Captain, the scans show approximately two hundred ships in the system," Connor reported.

My heart sank. "Ensure our stealthed capabilities are online, and let's see what's going on."

Maybe this would be a quick stop. Perhaps while we were charging our hyperdrive, we could ascertain what was happening here. Could it be another military outpost? Maybe even a colony system?

Soon the familiar twinge in my stomach signaled our exit from hyperspace. My gaze stayed glued to the tactical display.

Were these Jatarian ships? Two hundred red threat icons were visible on the tactical display.

Connor reported, "The ships are Jatarian. They appear to be a mixture of military, transport, and freighters."

"What about a shipyard?" I asked. If so, we must stay well out of range of it.

"They do appear to be congregated around the same planet. As to whether a shipyard orbits it, I cannot tell from this distance," Connor replied.

"Let's use our sublight drive to move closer. We will not use a microjump. I want to know if a shipyard is here, but I'm not willing to risk our safety," I said.

"Hyperdrive is charging," Cole confirmed.

"What's the makeup of the ships, Connor?"

"The ships include six freighters, nineteen transport vessels, and the rest are warships of various sizes."

"Are any of those their smaller attack ships?" I asked.

"Yes. Six carrier ships and about seventy small attack ships," Connor said.

"Let's keep watch and monitor those ships. If any of them head this way, I want to know immediately," I ordered.

"Yes, Captain," Connor replied.

I stood up and moved closer to the screen. The ships were no more than tiny specks on the screen. We wouldn't be near enough in ninety minutes to see much more than we could now. Was this a colony? Was this a military outpost?

The more pressing question nagging me was why the Jatarians had so many colonies and military bases. What were they preparing for? An invasion? If so, from whom? The Federation? The Morag? Some other race we weren't even aware existed? The possibilities were endless and more than a little unnerving.

The time passed slowly, as we waited for our hyperdrive to fully charge. We still knew nothing more about what the system held than when we had arrived.

"Captain, the hyperdrive is fully charged," Cole reported.

I took a deep breath. Should we check out this system while we are here? It would only take another half hour. Could we spare it? I was torn about what to do. The explorer in me won out though. "Let's microjump in closer. Only close enough to figure out what might be going on here," I said.

I felt the jump, and, before I knew it, the ships on the screen were much closer. I swallowed down my nervousness. "Let's recharge the hyperdrive again before we run any more scans. I want to have the opportunity to exit this system immediately, if need be."

We watched and waited. The number of ships now visible in the system were much more intimidating than what had been previously shown on the tactical display.

Some of the ships were enormous. I assumed those were the freighters. Did these freighters come from the same mining colony we had witnessed previously? Or was another one nearby?

If we had happened on two military bases, how many more were out there? And my more intriguing question was, why hadn't the Federation scout ships reported any? What was going on here?

If the Federation had no intention of attacking the Jatarians, what were we doing out here? What was Fritz and the *Explorer* doing out here? What did this mean for our future?

I still needed to speak with Jeffery about the colonies Fritz had discovered. Maybe we should bring the Morag in to eliminate the nearer threats. But then what would we do about the thousands of ships in the Jatarian home system?

"Is this a new type of ship?" Bryce asked, pointing to one of the smaller ships.

I frowned. "It does have weapons, so it must be a military ship. It's bigger than the smaller attack ships. I wonder how maneuverable it is," I said.

"I count twenty of them," Connor said. "Without doing a more detailed scan, that's all we can say."

"I doubt we will see them in action, until we're in the midst of a battle," I replied.

"Do *we* have any new types of ships?" Cole asked Jeffery.

"No. We've focused on building the stealthed warships. However, for us to fire those weapons on the stealthed ships, the ships must lower their stealthed systems. The weapons draw too much power," Jeffery explained.

"What about a ship to transport the devastators to the Jatarian home system?" Bryce asked.

"We do have those. The last I heard, we had twenty of them. Each one will hold twenty-five of the devastators. It can also repair them, if need be," Jeffery said.

"What about weapons technology?" Bryce asked. "Have we improved in that area?"

"Yes, a little. I think our focus has been on the number of weapons on each ships. We've strengthen our shields and implemented the stealthed technology. We've added the carrier ships."

"What about the devastators? Are they stealthed too?" Bryce asked.

"Yes, as are their carriers," Jeffery replied.

"Well, that's a step in the right direction," I said.

"The question remains, is it enough?" Jeffery asked.

"We won't know until we are in a battle," I added.

"It might be too late then," Jeffery said.

"What about the Morag? Have they developed any new technology?" Bryce asked me.

"They've increased their numbers of ships and strengthened their weapons and energy shields. That's all I'm aware of," I answered.

"Let's hope they have enough ships," Bryce said.

I looked at the screen again. We were up against a very powerful foe, perhaps more powerful than any of us alone. However, together, we could probably make a stand. We had to. The alternative was unacceptable.

"Our hyperdrive is fully charged again," Cole announced.

"Run the scans, Connor. Be ready to leave immediately if we sense any of those orbs being released," I commanded.

We all waited in tense silence. I heard the *thud* from my heart beating rapidly in my chest.

So far, so good. No signs of any of the orbs.

Suddenly alarms blared, and red lights flashed. "Report," I said, as I returned to my command chair.

"The tactical display is filled with red threat icons. I think it's the orbs," Connor reported.

"Let's get out of here," I said.

"Scans have thirty more seconds, Captain," Connor said.

"How long until the orbs get here?" I asked.

"They are searching. They are currently not near us."

"Finish the scans and then prepare to jump," I said.

"Scans are complete," Connor called out.

"Let's get out of here," I said.

Once in the safety of hyperspace, I finally sat back and relaxed. We made it. We were safe.

"The scans show two shipyards in the system, Captain," Connor said.

"Two?" I asked, surprised.

"Yes. One orbits the planet, and the other orbits its moon. They seem to be fully functional. When they detected the scans, both shipyards released the orbs."

"How many?" I asked.

"I estimate one hundred from each shipyard."

"So it seems that the shipyards have the orbs. Maybe they won't be used to find the *Explorer* then."

"Those things could really do some damage to a fleet. We need to figure out a way to neutralize the threat," Bryce said.

"Any ideas?" I asked.

"None," Bryce said.

"We need to attract them somehow and then prod them to explode, once the orbs get close," Jeffery suggested.

"That's a good idea. Like what?" I asked.

"Not a clue. Maybe your guys back at the refugee camp can think of something."

"Why not the Emperor?" I asked.

"I'm not sure we can count on him," Jeffery replied quietly.

"Either way, let's brainstorm on our own and see if anyone can come up with an idea. I'll contact Alex and see what he says," I said.

"We are twenty-one hours from the next system," Bryce reported.

"Okay. Connor, you're in charge. Jeffery, let's go to my office." Jeffery followed me there. Once inside with the door shut, I asked, "Why do you think we can't count on the Emperor?"

"I think he's not sharing things with us."

"Me too. Yet I guess that makes sense. After all, he considers this ship and the people on it to be rebels. He doesn't trust us."

"But we are out here risking our lives to help the Federation," Jeffery replied.

"Yes, but the Emperor doesn't see it that way. He sees us as his enemy too. Which is why I'm hesitant to let the scout ships know where we've been, especially so soon after we've been there. I don't want the Federation to figure out where we are actually going."

"That makes sense, and I'm all for it."

"My contact on the *Explorer* informed me that they have come across four Jatarian colony systems and reported them to the scout ships," I said.

"We haven't heard anything about that from the scout ships," Jeffery replied, his concern evident on his expression.

"Maybe the last time you checked in with them, they hadn't received the information yet," I suggested.

"Let's see. I'll contact them now and see if they have any updates for me."

"If they say no again, you might have to be more specific and ask if there's been any sightings of the Jatarians," I said.

"Good idea. We will see if they're lying to us."

"Don't mention the Jatarian home system. To my knowledge, that has not been reported to anyone besides us."

"Maybe we should keep it that way. From what I'm learning, knowledge is power. Right now it seems we are being kept in the dark, but two can play that game," Jeffery said.

Jeffery closed his eyes and focused on his gift. I watched and thrummed my fingers silently on my desk. I didn't like not being the one using my gift. Waiting for Jeffery to get the answers we needed tested my patience.

I decided in the meantime I would check in with Fritz. I closed my eyes and focused on my friend.

Hello, Slade. We're still hiding here.

It's almost time to turn on your sensors. Are you nervous?

Yes. We've debated whether we should wait another twenty-four hours. We are in no hurry here. We don't want to risk being discovered. We can't think of any reason not to wait longer.

I can understand that. I know it's hard being in the dark and not knowing what's out there, I said.

But maybe being in the dark is better than knowing what's out there, Fritz suggested.

I guess I hadn't thought of it like that before. You do make a good point though.

Thanks. How are things on your end?

Good. We found another Jatarian military base. They have two shipyards in the system. Heavily armed, I should add.

This isn't looking good. They're obviously gearing up for a massive attack, Fritz said.

My thoughts exactly. How we should react to this information is anyone's guess.

What does Jeffery think?

He thinks we can't trust the Emperor. He also thinks the Emperor is withholding information from us. Plus Jeffery feels the Emperor has no intention of attacking the Jatarians.

Maybe he plans to use the Morag instead, Fritz said.

The Morag are not enough to face this enemy. Not alone.

I agree. The Emperor has not heard of the numbers we've found here in the Jatarian home system yet though. Maybe that will change his mind, Fritz said.

Perhaps. I guess we will find out soon enough. I'll contact you again soon. Stay safe out there, Fritz.

You too, Slade.

I opened my eyes and found Jeffery watching me. "Well?"

"They've had no reported sightings of any Jatarian ships or colony systems," Jeffery said. "Why are they hiding it from me?"

"Because you're with me," I replied.

"Is my father willing to lose this war because you're a better leader of his military than he is?" Jeffery asked, as he abruptly stood up.

I cringed at what Jeffery had said. "Maybe it's because your father can't control what happens way out here. It's beyond his reach. That could be why he's unwilling to commit the ships."

"And, in so doing, he's almost accepting defeat. How can we win this war if we aren't willing to attack? Does he plan to wait for the Jatarians to come to him?"

I could tell Jeffery was pretty worked up. I was having a hard time trying to figure out how to defend the Emperor's actions—or rather his lack of action. "Maybe he's hoping we will get the Morag to deal with the threat. It still looks good on him because the threat is neutralized. No one is the wiser," I replied.

"What will we do, Slade? I guess this is up to us."

"We already have a task group of Morag going to eliminate the one mining operation we've found. I'm guessing the Jatarians in the systems where we've been sensed will be on high alert. So do we have the Morag attack those systems too? Or do we wait and find others that we don't scan in as much detail?"

Jeffery shook his head. "I don't know. The element of surprise would be beneficial. But what if, by ordering a first strike, we are ultimately starting a new round of battles that ends up back in the Federation?"

"We have no way to know beforehand. Do we deal with the known threats while we can? Or do we wait and see what we find in the Jatarian home system?"

"At first," Jeffery replied, "I leaned toward waiting to use all our assets at the Jatarian home system. However, after hearing how many Jatarian ships were in that system, it gave me pause. Maybe we don't do it that way."

I shrugged. "If we wait too long, the Jatarians might strike first. If we strike first, at least we have control over when and where it will be," I added. "Now I'm not trying to tell you what to do. I'm just throwing out pros and cons."

Jeffery looked up at me and took a deep breath. "We strike while we can. Every enemy ship that can be destroyed now is one less that's available to attack the Federation."

"I think we'll need more Morag task groups then," I replied, shuffling the papers on my desk.

"We can always change our minds before the first attack. By the time the next Morag task groups arrive that we send this way, we will already be at the Jatarian home system. So just because we send the Morag today doesn't mean we are locked in later," Jeffery said.

"I agree. We still have a couple weeks to tweak our approach or to change it entirely."

"If we could hit all three of those systems at once, I think it would be a surprise. The Jatarians would probably expect one task group to systematically attack each of those systems," Jeffery said.

"You're right. Let's get some more ships headed this way." I had found my notes on how many Morag ships were where. "Do you want to try?" I asked Jeffery.

He nodded. "I do. I want to learn how and what to do."

"First, see if you can find the Morag in this system here," I said, pointing to a system where I had found the Morag previously. "It's much easier to communicate with them once you know where they are."

"What do I do once I find them?" Jeffery asked, unsure.

"You have to sift through their minds, until you find the commander. Sometimes it's hard to figure out. It's not a quick thing. It takes time to do. The more you do it, the better you will get," I explained.

"Okay. I'll try it."

I watched as Jeffery closed his eyes. It was hard for me to be patient and to wait to see if he was successful. I wanted to just do it myself and be done with it. I also knew that if I were patient and taught Jeffery what to do, then it would be beneficial in the future.

While I waited, I began to wonder if I should reach out to Amelia. Maybe she knew more about what was going on now. But, if I did, and she confronted the Emperor, he would know we were on to his plot. Maybe it was easier to operate on our own devices and without the oversight of Amelia or the Emperor. But what if we were wrong?

Jeffery's eyes opened, and he smiled. "I found them. I believe I found the commander in charge. His name is Commander Zohar."

"Let me confirm it." I closed my eyes and reached out to the Morag task group we were looking for. When I found it, I quickly confirmed what Jeffery had found out.

"Is it the right one?"

"Yes, that's really good, Jeffery. The first time I did this, I gave the command to the wrong Morag. He was a commander but only of the ship, not the task group," I said, as I laughed.

"That wouldn't get us very far, would it?" Jeffery joked. "So now what do I do?"

"Find Morag Commander Zohar and tell him a Jatarian military base has been discovered, and then give him the name of the system. Warn him of the heavily fortified shipyard and the orbs that can explode. We need the Morag to be ready for what they will face. The fewer ships they lose in these battles, the more they'll have to fight with in the next one."

"Okay. I can do that," Jeffery said.

We practiced his Morag phrases for a few minutes, before he closed his eyes again to focus on his gift. I watched and waited. After a few minutes had passed, I wondered if he was having trouble. Then his eyes opened, and a huge grin spread across his face.

"I did it," Jeffery said excitedly.

I couldn't help but give him a high five.

"I can't believe I did it. Can I do the other task groups too?"

"Sure." I looked down at my notes. "We must send this one here to the same system as Commander Zohar. And then these two task groups here and here to the last system we were just in."

"I can do that," Jeffery said proudly.

I couldn't help but smile at how excited and proud he was. I was proud of him too. Now to ensure he did everything correctly. We couldn't afford to make mistakes. I hoped I could check his commands without him realizing what I was doing. I didn't want to crush his confidence.

I quickly confirmed that the Morag task group had received the correct information. I opened my eyes and watched him, as he finished the other commands.

When Jeffery finally opened his eyes again, he said, "That is so exhilarating. Thank you, Slade, for teaching me how to do that. And giving me the chance to actually do it."

"I'm glad you can do it, Jeffery. I'm proud of you. I know it's not easy."

"So now what do we do?" Jeffery asked.

"Update our notes to when and how many Morag ships to expect in which systems. If we want to coordinate the attacks, we need to make adjustments when it gets closer to the attacks."

"Thank you, Slade, for letting me come along on this mission. I've already learned so much."

"I'm glad you're here. It's nice to have someone who I can bounce ideas off of and who will bounce back ideas."

"How much longer until we get to the next system?" Jeffery asked.

I checked my watch. "About eighteen hours."

Jeffery nodded. "I think I'll get something to eat and get some rest."

"Me too." I got up, and we started out the door.

Jeffery turned and said, "Do you think your friend on the *Explorer* can find out what the other scout ships have found?"

I raised an eyebrow. "Perhaps. Although if he knew, he would have already told me."

"I don't suppose you have other contacts who can find out somehow, do you?"

Jeffery was basically asking me if we had spies. I couldn't reveal that. I shrugged. "I have no idea. I could ask around. No harm in that."

"Do that. What if other military bases are in systems closer to the Federation?"

"I'll catch up to you," I said, as I returned to my desk.

Once Jeffery was gone, I closed my eyes and reached out to Kami.

Slade, how is the mission going?

Very eye-opening. The Federation scout ships aren't informing us of what they have found. Neither is the Emperor. So we don't know the full scale of what we're really dealing with out here. Also Jeffery doesn't believe the Emperor had any plans to attack the Jatarians on their home turf.

What? How will we defeat them then? Kami asked.

Jeffery and I will use the Morag to destroy what we find. That is already in motion. However, if we want to destroy all the Jatarian colonies and military bases nearer to the Federation, we need to know what those scout ships have found over the last two years. Do we have an inside guy?

Yes, we do. I don't want to risk exposing him though. How do we do that?

I have also been talking with Fritz. So that's just as likely the way I got the information. Jeffery may suspect it, but he won't know.

Okay. I'll see what I can find out. I suggest you wait to react to what we find out. Maybe these Jatarian systems the scout ships have found are the Emperor's responsibility. What if Jeffery has been given the information, but he's keeping you in the dark?

I hadn't really thought of that, Kami. He seemed genuinely upset with his father though.

Maybe Jeffery's a good actor.

Or maybe he's not acting at all.

I understand. I just don't want your judgment to be clouded. You must remember who his father is, Kami said.

I do. Don't worry.

I'll see what I can find out. Check back tomorrow.

I'm not sure how much longer I can use my gift to reach you. We are almost three weeks' hyperspace travel away from Elmania now.

I hope it will still be a while. Losing contact with you will not be very comforting.

I agree. Then we're truly on our own.

Out in the middle of Jatarian space, Kami noted.

True. Not very comforting.

I'll talk to you soon.

Stay safe, Kami.

You too, Slade.

Chapter Thirteen

Time dragged on. I worried about Fritz. Yet, as each day passed, I felt a little more relief when I checked in with him. The Jatarians must be waiting in orbit for Fritz's ship to leave. Otherwise the Jatarians would have found them by now with a simple ground search.

I wasn't sure what we would do, once we got to the system where Fritz and the *Explorer* were hiding, but we would figure that out when the time came.

Along the way to Fritz, we discovered four more colonies and six more military bases. These are just the ones we passed by. We did a minimal amount of scans in each system so we could remain undetected. If we had happened across this many of the Jatarian systems, how many more were out here? I was afraid to even consider the answer.

Kami had come through and informed me that the scout ships had found eight military bases and seven colony systems on their search so far. Jeffery and I still couldn't understand why the Emperor kept this a secret from us.

Jeffery and I agreed that we would return the favor. We would keep what we had found a secret too. Jeffery stopped checking in with the Emperor and the scout ships. It would likely be assumed that Jeffery had moved too far away to use his gift to communicate.

The time approached for the Morag to arrive and to eliminate the Jatarian activities in the first three systems we had found—the two military bases and the mining operation.

I wished we could be there to witness the battles, but we needed to get to Fritz. We also needed to see what the Jatarian home system held. I reassured Jeffery that we still expected to witness plenty of battles.

As time passed, Jeffery and I sent more Morag task groups toward our location. We knew we would need them. I refrained from taking any of the ships from the areas nearest the Federation. If the Jatarians decided a counterstrike was in order, we would need them back in the Federation.

When the time came for the Morag to attack the Jatarians, Jeffery and I met in my office. I wanted to teach Jeffery how he could essentially watch the battle from the minds of the Morag who were there. It wasn't exactly the same as seeing it firsthand, but the information gained from their thoughts was easy enough to decipher.

I closed my eyes and focused on my gift. The first battle to occur was the one in the mining system. The other two would commence prior to that one ending.

I found Morag Commander Zohar. Per his thoughts, he was preparing to exit hyperspace. Soon afterward the Morag task group of fifty ships exited in the mining system. Zohar noted his tactical display revealed the system now held twenty ships. I opened my eyes and checked my notes. When we had scanned the area earlier, the system held only eleven ships. Only one of those was a warship. The Jatarians must have beefed up security due to our presence there.

I focused back on Morag Commander Zohar. He was getting the results of his scans. The ships now stood at twelve warships; the rest were freighters and transport vessels. They shortly left the system. Now only twelve remained.

Zohar relished the idea that his superior numbers would plow through this small group of enemy ships.

The enemy quickly jumped out to engage the Morag ships. This told me that they had no defenses around the mining operations. Otherwise they would've drawn the Morag closer in before attacking.

The weapons fire soon erupted between the two groups. Energy screens lit up as they did their best to dissipate all the energy directed at them.

Ships began exploding, and debris spread across the area. I was thankful no Human lives were at risk here. Not yet. We would let the Morag destroy our enemy for us. At least as much as we could. I knew deep down it wouldn't be enough, but, for every Jatarian ship that the Morag could destroy, that was one less that could attack any Human settlement or planet.

The Morag made short work of the small number of warships in the mining system. I took the opportunity to remind Commander Zohar that he was there to destroy the mining operation and Jatarian warships. No need to scan the planets. His task group was needed in the next system.

I wondered if security had been beefed up in the other systems we had visited too. What would the Morag face there? We would know soon enough.

Once all the Jatarian warships were eliminated, the Morag moved on to the mining operation. I felt no compassion for those down below. Maybe I should, but I didn't. Was I turning into a monster? These were Jatarian lives, after all. However, the Jatarians had had no compassion for the lives of Humans. Why should I have compassion for them?

The Morag ships launched a bombardment of the surface, right where the mining operation was. It was safe to say that nothing remained. The entire area was decimated.

Having accomplished their goals, all the Morag had to do now was wait. Their hyperdrives had yet to fully charge. As soon as that was done, they would head to the next targeted system.

The Morag had lost only three ships. The Jatarians had lost twelve. So far, so good.

When I opened my eyes, Jeffery still had his closed. I waited quietly for him to open them.

When he did, he had a big smile on his face. "That wasn't quite like being there, but it was better than nothing."

"I'm afraid the other systems will be more prepared now for the Morag attacks," I said.

"They're already expecting them. They don't have much time before the other attacks start. Not much the Jatarians can do," Jeffery replied.

"That's true."

"How much longer until the next attack starts?" Jeffery asked.

I checked my watch. "About half an hour."

"Just enough time to get a snack," Jeffery commented.

"You go ahead. I'll try to contact my friend on the *Explorer*."

After Jeffery left, I once again focused on my gift.

Slade, it's good to hear from you. We're still hiding out.

Have you checked the scans lately?

Yes. Four Jatarian ships remain out there above the moon.

The Morag just attacked one of the mining operations we discovered. I'm hoping that might make the rest of the Jatarian ships head out of there. If not, the subsequent two attacks might.

Is the Federation military headed this way to attack what we think is the home system? Fritz asked.

Unfortunately no. Jeffery believes the Emperor has no intention of attacking anything outside of the Federation.

Why not?

My guess is he wants to use the Morag for that. He still hasn't shared the information the scout ships have found. So we've also stopped sharing what we've found.

177

That's not very productive for anyone.

At least we are using the Morag to eliminate all the targets we've found. That's the plan at this time.

It will heighten the threat level in the Jatarian home system.

Yes, but I don't think the Morag have the ship numbers to take on as many ships as you sensed in that system. We must do that attack in smaller chunks, where the Morag have the numbers advantage.

Do you have multiple Morag fleets inbound?

Yes, we do. Most of them are smaller task groups. I figured the more Jatarian systems we could hit simultaneously, the better. Within the next couple hours, two more strikes should happen.

The Morag have their work cut out for them. I'm sure the Federation thinks the Explorer *has been destroyed, since we've been unable to check in,* Fritz said.

I can no longer communicate directly with Falton Two. We're essentially on our own out here, I replied. *I guess if you ever had the desire to disappear from the Federation, now's your chance.*

Fritz laughed. *I wouldn't be an explorer anymore then, would I? Good point.*

How far out are you from the Jatarian home system?

Almost four hours.

Are you nervous?

No, not yet. I will be once we get closer, after the scans confirm the number of ships present.

So far we are still hanging tight here. We look forward to your arrival here. Although I'm not sure how you will deal with the ships in orbit.

Me neither. I'm hoping they respond to the more significant threat of the Morag and at least a few more of them leave the system.

I guess we might end up stuck here, until the Morag manage to attack the Jatarian home system.

I hope you're not, but it is a possibility.

Keep me posted on the Morag attacks. I'm glad we are at least making progress in destroying the enemy.

It's better than nothing, I replied.

When I opened my eyes, I checked my watch. Jeffery should be returning soon. Maybe he would bring me a snack. I stood and stretched my legs. I walked around my office a little.

We were making progress in destroying the Jatarians. It was about time they felt what it was like to have their homes targeted and destroyed. The tables had finally turned.

Jeffery walked back in then, pulling me from my thoughts.

"I brought you a little snack," Jeffery said, as he tossed me a muffin.

Summer had made a batch of blueberry muffins. I took one bite. They were delicious. "Thanks. Are you ready to see how things go in the first system where we found a military base?" I asked.

"I'm ready to see how the Morag react to those orbs. Plus to see how well-armed that shipyard is. I'm afraid the Morag will lose a lot of ships in this next battle," Jeffery said.

"I'm afraid you're right, Jeffery."

"How much longer do we have?"

"They should exit hyperspace within the next ten minutes or so."

Jeffery sat down and took a deep breath. Then he closed his eyes and began using his gift.

I sat down and did the same. This Morag task group was larger than the previous one. It took me a few minutes to find the commander. I hoped he was prepared for what he would shortly face.

Morag Commander Fantor prepared to exit hyperspace. The preliminary scans had shown slightly over one hundred ships in the system. He had one hundred powerful Morag warships with him. Fantor was confident he would win the battle. He knew he would take heavy losses but must destroy the enemy regardless.

Once Fantor's fleet had exited hyperspace, he quickly received more information about what he faced. The Jatarians had ninety-one warships in the system.

Shortly after the Morag's arrival, all the ships that were not warships had exited the system. Fantor couldn't help but smile. The Jatarians were already running scared from his mighty power.

Fantor had heard the Jatarians had a few surprises for his ships. A small orb that could explode, launched from a large shipyard. Fantor knew Morag planets had shipyards too. Yet they weren't heavily armed because nothing was out there to threaten them. These Jatarians must feel threatened to arm their shipyards. They'd known he'd come for them, and he would destroy them.

Fantor wasted no time jumping in closer to the enemy. The more time he gave them, the longer they had to plan for their defense. The time to prepare was over. It was time to fight.

Surprise overtook Fantor when he realized the size of the shipyard. Its turrets were already opening, and those orbs were launching from within.

He was prepared for the orbs. Fantor would wait until the right time and launch his attack. He watched as the orbs closed in on his fleet. Then he ordered his ships to launch their weapons. He had already had them preset to detonate, not on impact, but at approximately the location where the orbs would be. The math had to be spot-on, or his plan wouldn't work.

Fantor watched as the orbs closed in, and his weapons fire closed the distance. Any moment now his weapons would detonate, taking the orbs with them.

A chain of giant explosions ripped across his screen as his weapons detonated, causing numerous orbs to detonate too. The light was so bright from all the explosions, he had to close his eyes momentarily.

When Fantor opened his eyes, he was alarmed to see many of the orbs were still inbound. He ordered another round of weapons fire to destroy the remaining orbs.

This time when the orbs detonated, his ship shook. These explosions couldn't be any closer without weakening his energy screen. When the explosions died down, a few orbs remained. They were now reaching Fantor's fleet and beginning to detonate.

Fantor felt his ship shake, as seven orbs hit his energy screen simultaneously. Fantor quickly glanced at his damage console. His energy screen was still holding, for now.

A quick glance at the viewscreen showed all the orbs had detonated. The Morag had lost five ships to the orbs. It could have been much worse, if all those orbs had reached his fleet.

Their strategy had worked. Now to deal with the warships and the shipyard. Fantor was not surprised that the enemy fleet had not advanced toward his. The Jatarians would use the firepower of the shipyard to aid in their attack. Even now the Jatarian warships were forming up around the shipyard.

It was time to see what type of firepower this shipyard had. Fantor moved his fleet in toward his enemy. As soon as they reached optimal weapons range, the fighting intensified.

Fantor was a little surprised at the intense weapons fire coming to bear on his ships from the shipyard. He ordered his ships to focus all their firepower on the shipyard. It was obviously the biggest threat. After it had been eliminated, he would return his attention to the ships.

Fantor was also puzzled by the scans that revealed two ships had taken refuge behind the shipyard. Why would they do that? What were the Jatarians trying to hide? Those two must be warships, or they would have left when the Morag fleet arrived.

The battle continued, as Fantor focused all firepower on the shipyard. It obviously had very powerful energy shields. He was impressed that it was still online. There wasn't even a crack in its defenses for him to exploit.

Fantor angrily slammed his massive hand on the command console. He was losing ships, and the Jatarians still stood strong. How would he win this battle? He had to outmaneuver this enemy but how?

Did this shipyard have weapons on the other side? The side that faced the planet? Only one way to find out. Fantor commanded his fleet to change positions and to destroy any enemy ships in their path. If he intermingled the two fleets, the shipyard might have to stop its attack for fear of destroying their own ships.

As the Morag fleet closed the distance between them and their enemy, massive explosions rocked Fantor's ship. His fleet was paying a high price, but now the Jatarians were losing ships too.

Once Fantor's ship passed the shipyard, he realized what was hiding behind it. Jatarian carrier ships. Two of them. They began launching their small attack ships.

Fantor ordered their warbirds to launch. This was the Morag's response to the Jatarians' small attack ships. This would be the first time the warbirds had been deployed in an actual battle. Fantor hoped they performed as well as they were expected to.

As Fantor's fleet finished its formation change, he found the shipyard was just as heavily armed on the opposite side. That was disappointing. It had been worth a try, however.

The shipyard was now less focused on an overall bombardment and more focused on pinpoint targeting. It targeted specific ships, likely to avoid destroying the Jatarian carriers and their small attack ships.

Fantor had his ship focus on the carriers. If they could be eliminated, that would lessen the impact of the Jatarians' small attack ships, since it would keep them from reloading.

Due to the danger the shipyard represented, Fantor still had a majority of his fleet focusing on it. He also kept his ship far in the rear of his formation, away from the shipyard. He needed to survive this battle to report what had happened and what they'd learned. The Jatarians had adapted and had adjusted their tactics. The Morag must surpass them.

Soon the energy shield of one of the carriers was battered down and failed. Shortly afterward, a large explosion consumed the vessel. Then Fantor changed his sights to the other carrier. In a matter of minutes, it met the same fate. A fiery death. Now the small attack ships had nowhere to go.

Fantor soon realized that was a double-edged sword because now the small attack ships began ramming his ships, causing damage. In some cases, catastrophic damage.

The Morag's warbirds proved very effective in their pursuit of the Jatarians' small attack ships. Fantor was glad he had them at his disposal.

An idea came to mind. Perhaps he would take a play from the Jatarian playbook. He then ordered two of his warships to ram into the shipyard. Surely it was not made to withstand such an attack.

Fantor watched as two of his ships broke formation and headed straight for the enemy shipyard. The shipyard must have realized what was happening because it began targeting both ships. One soon exploded in a massive fireball. One was left, now too close to the target.

Fantor held his breath, as the ship collided with the shipyard. Explosions immediately shook the yard. One explosion after another ignited across the shipyard. *More.* He needed more ships to ram the shipyard.

Five more ships broke formation and headed to their certain deaths. It was a price worth paying, Fantor believed. Three of them impacted the hull of the shipyard. Massive explosions resulted. Shortly thereafter, the shipyard broke apart and fell toward the planet.

Fantor smiled. One target was eliminated. Now for the rest. His once-large fleet now consisted of only fifty-six ships and the warbirds. The enemy had seventy-six ships, plus a few of their small attack ships. The Morag were outnumbered. Fantor was not discouraged but still quite confident the Morag would win this battle.

The battle now came down to a ship-to-ship fight. The Morag were determined to destroy the enemy. There would be no retreat.

Fantor orchestrated the battle from the safety of the rear of his dwindling fleet. Weapons fire filled the area between the two fleets. Energy screens glowed, as they held their survival in their ability to dissipate the intense energy being directed at them. Occasionally one would fail, and, shortly after that, the ship met its end.

Ships on both sides of the battle succumbed to the intense amount of energy and weapons fire released by their enemy. Fantor focused his attention on destroying one Jatarian ship after another, never looking at the tactical display. He would fight to the bitter end, whether that be to his death or to the complete destruction of this enemy before him.

When the ships between him and his enemy disintegrated before him, Fantor moved more into their place. If Fantor died today, his ship would be the last Morag ship to die.

The battle waged on, as each side bared down on the other. Fantor thought he was gaining an edge on the Jatarians. The number of ships looked to be more even now. His warbirds had eliminated all the Jatarians' small attack ships. Now the warbirds worked together to target one Jatarian warship at a time.

As each Jatarian ship was consumed by weapons fire, Fantor grew more and more confident in his chances of surviving today. He finally decided to look over at the tactical display. The Jatarians were down to twenty-nine ships. The Morag held strong at twenty-three.

Fantor's confidence grew as the Jatarian ship numbers continued to diminish. Fantor had the edge now. He wouldn't have many ships remaining when this battle was over, but he would be one of them.

Once the battle ended, he would destroy whatever settlement or military base the Jatarians had on the surface of the planet below. Fantor smiled a sinister smile. Those Jatarians on the surface were breathing their last breaths. Soon he would rain down a fiery death upon them. But first he had to finish off the remaining fleet.

Fantor's warbirds were still wreaking havoc on the remaining Jatarian ships. It wouldn't be much longer now. Two more explosions flashed across the screen. A quick check of the tactical display showed only a handful of ships remaining on each side. This was a fight to the death.

The next he knew, Fantor found his ship the target of the remaining enemy ships' weapons fire. He gripped his command console tightly. Would his energy screen hold? His gaze traveled to the damage consoles. A few red lights angrily blinked at him.

Fantor quickly moved other ships in the way to protect his ship from certain destruction. Two of them immediately met their end. He felt no remorse. His life was more valuable than theirs. He was the commander of this fleet. They could be replaced, but he could not. At least not as quickly.

As the last four Jatarian ships exploded into oblivion, Fantor sat down and relaxed a little. He had only two ships remaining. His and one other. The other was a carrier ship thankfully that the warbirds could land in. The warbirds still numbered over a dozen.

Fantor moved his attention to the planet below. He would send in the warbirds to get a better peak at what was happening down there, right before he destroyed it. In the meantime, he sat back and relaxed. His job was done, well almost done.

Fantor laughed to himself. He had nowhere else to go at the moment. He would wait until Commander Amos finished his attack on the other military establishment, and then they would regroup.

The warbirds confirmed that the Jatarians did, indeed, have a military base on the surface. It even appeared they had a manufacturing facility, building the small attack ships. Fantor laughed. They wouldn't have it for much longer.

Fantor moved his large warship closer to his target. He wanted to see it decimated, to see the devastation he would soon create.

As Fantor gave the order to bomb the surface, he stood, smiled, and watched the mushroom clouds rise from below. His job here was done. Now he had only to wait for Commander Amos to contact him.

I opened my eyes and looked over at Jeffery.

"Wow," Jeffery said. "That was a lot of things. Scary, exhilarating, eye-opening, and so many more. I'm glad the Jatarian military outpost was destroyed."

"Me too. The Morag must adapt their strategy with those orbs and the shipyard in the next system. I'm interested to see how Morag Commander Amos handles it."

"That's true. I'm not sure the Federation would have fared so well."

"The Federation would have abandoned the attack. They would have never stayed until the last Jatarian ship was destroyed—at least not unless one of the Federation colonies or planets were at risk. Maybe not even then," I remarked.

"I've learned a lot today. I have many things yet to learn. This is an enemy that will take us a long time to defeat, I'm afraid," Jeffery said.

"Yes, you're right about that."

"How much longer before Morag Commander Amos arrives at his target system?" Jeffery asked.

I checked my watch and then my notes. "I estimate in another couple hours."

"I guess that gives us the chance to eat and to get in a little nap."

"That took a lot out of me," I admitted. "I could use a nap."

"I'll meet you back here in a couple hours then," Jeffery said, as he left.

I couldn't help but wonder if he would report what he had witnessed through Morag Commander Fantor to his father, if he could. Yet, if I was out of range to reach Falton Two, Jeffery certainly was.

Chapter Fourteen

Before long Jeffery returned to my office, as the time had come for Morag Commander Amos to arrive at his attack destination. As much as the last battle with Fantor had been epic, this one had the makings to be even more so.

This system was protected by even more ships than the last one. It held double the amount of enemy ships, plus two shipyards. The system even held a new type of Jatarian ship that we had yet to see in battle. All these ingredients would bring on an even more monumental battle than the previous one.

Knowing how things had gone down in the system Morag Commander Fantor had attacked, I was apprehensive about seeing what the Jatarian home system held, with its reportedly thousands of ships. Would we have the firepower and the ships to destroy it? I wasn't sure. First though, we would watch the Morag destroy this system.

Jeffery sat on the couch in my office, and I sat beside him.

"Are you ready for this?" I asked.

"Yes, I've already learned so much by tapping into Morag Commander Fantor's mind in that last system. My understanding of the Morag language has also improved. During our break, I looked up a few words I heard Fantor say that I didn't understand," Jeffery added.

"It is definitely an experience to follow the battles through someone else's mind, although tiring and mentally exhausting."

"Yes. I will admit I had a bit of a headache afterward. I'll need a longer break after this one."

"This battle should last longer too, with the extra targets and ships involved. I'm sure it will prove to be one massive battle," I shared.

"Is it time?"

I checked my watch and nodded. I took a deep breath and closed my eyes. I focused my gift on Morag Commander Amos.

The Morag fleet neared the system that they had orders to attack. The scans were just coming in. The system held 253 Jatarian ships. Which type of ships would be discovered upon arrival.

Morag Commander Amos relished in the thought of destroying his enemy. He'd already spoken to Commander Fantor, and together they had discussed what changes might be made for this next battle.

Amos knew he would be more successful than Fantor. These Jatarians were no match for the battle strategies Amos had in store for them. When this battle was over, he would have enough ships left to attack yet another system.

As Amos's fleet exited hyperspace, he waited for the scans to show the makeup of his enemy. He expected all the transport vessels and freighters to run. He had considered sending a small task group to follow them but then decided against it. He would hunt them all down sooner or later.

Twenty-seven civilian ships quickly left the system. Now all Amos had to do was destroy the remaining ships, which he assumed were all warships.

Amos was interested to see these highly protected shipyards. Surely Fantor had been mistaken about their potency.

The Jatarians also had a new type of ship in this system that the Morag had not battled against yet. What were the capabilities of this new ship? How strong were its weapons? Amos was curious but not concerned. He had the warbirds.

His tactical officer informed him the Jatarians had launched their small attack ships. They had eight carriers now in the system. Each held thirty attack ships.

Amos noticed the increased number of ships on the tactical display. Then they all disappeared. Amos smiled. So the Jatarians were bringing the battle to him. That would work to his advantage.

The warbirds were launched as soon as the Jatarians' small attack ships were. When the Jatarian ships exited hyperspace from their microjump, Amos's warbirds were there to meet them.

The battle between the small ships began. Amos sat back and watched. He knew his warbirds were superior to their opponents. Given enough time, his ships would eliminate all the Jatarian ones. No need to get in a hurry.

The Jatarians' small attack ships didn't engage Amos's warbirds, however. Amos was alarmed when the enemy's small ships ignored the presence of his warbirds and headed toward his main fleet. Now what?

Amos had his warbirds hunt down the Jatarian interlopers. Hopefully they could be eliminated before they caused any serious damage.

Then alarms rang out, signaling more ships had dropped out of hyperspace nearby. It was the new ships the Jatarians had. What did these ships have in store for the Morag fleet?

The Jatarians' small attack ships were intermingled among Amos's fleet now. It was impossible for the larger Morag ships to target the smaller vessels, not without taking down Morag ships too. Amos didn't want the newcomers to do the same thing, so he sent a wall of firepower their way to eliminate the threat.

Numerous explosions signaled the success of his strategy. Amos grew impatient now. He was ready to blow some larger Jatarian ships out of existence. He ordered his ships to advance toward the planet the Jatarians were orbiting.

When Amos felt his ship shudder, he checked to see what had happened. The Jatarians' small attack ships were now ramming into his larger warships. With so many of them available to do that, things weren't looking good. At this rate, the small attack ships would eliminate a majority of his warships. Amos needed to engage the larger enemy fleet and the shipyards *now*.

Amos gave the order to microjump to the main Jatarian fleet. He knew it wouldn't stop the attacks from the smaller Jatarian ships, but he needed bigger targets to hit.

When the fleet exited their microjump, Amos gave the order to begin the bombardment of the enemy ships. Explosions began dotting the viewscreen, as vessels succumbed to the ferocity of the Morag's firepower.

Amos smiled. This enemy would fall.

Alarms once again rang out, as the Jatarians launched those dreaded orbs. Amos continued to fire his weapons, hoping it would diminish the sheer number of the small weapons.

When Amos noticed that the enemy's small attack ships weren't merging into his fleet formation, he had a sinking feeling. Yet the orbs were moving in.

Then Amos sent his warbirds to help target the incoming attack of the orbs. Amos had to admit he was impressed with the number of different defenses and attacks the Jatarians had at their disposal. Amos needed more weapons at his disposal. It seemed the Jatarians had more options than the Morag. Amos didn't like it, not one bit.

Once the orbs managed to penetrate his formation, the detonations began. Amos wondered who controlled these small weapons. Was it controlled by an individual or a program?

In all, over three hundred orbs managed to detonate in the midst of his formation. This attack ultimately destroyed thirty-one of his prized warships.

Thankfully Amos had positioned his ship near the rear of the formation and was spared from any direct effects of the orb attack.

The battle continued between the two fleets. Amos was surprised by the intensity of the weapons fire from the shipyard. The other shipyard orbited the moon. It was a good thing they both weren't within range. His fleet would be demolished, if that were the case. He would eliminate this one and the Jatarian fleet, before turning his attention to the second shipyard.

A large explosion in front of his flagship brought his attention back to the battle. How could he outsmart this enemy? He knew Fantor had rammed ships into the shipyard to destroy it. Amos was resolved to try a different tactic. His would work much better. He was sure of it.

He microjumped his fleet to the rear of the shipyard and launched a couple rounds of weapons fire. Then, before the enemy fleet could react, he moved his fleet again. Amos was resolved to keep this tactic in use until it was no longer effective. If he kept his jumps random and unpredictable, it would last longer.

Soon the shipyard was surrounded by Jatarian ships. That's precisely what he wanted. The shipyard didn't have a clear path to launch its weapons at his ships, not if their ships were in the way. Amos smiled. His plan was going well.

The battle waged on as both fleets pounded the other with everything they had. Ships exploded all across both formations.

Amos had the Jatarian ships outnumbered, since the shipyard couldn't fire just now, not when surrounded by Jatarian ships. This kept many of the Jatarian ships out of the battle due to their positioning. If they decided to change positions, Amos would resume his microjumping strategy.

With the numbers advantage of the Morag fleet, the Jatarian fleet began to lose their ships much faster than the Morag. Amos noticed a few ships repositioned from their posts all around the shipyard. A little longer and Amos would have his fleet jump again. His tactic was working.

After a few more minutes, Amos ordered his fleet to jump again. When they exited, they were met with a wall of firepower from the shipyard. He hadn't been expecting that. Amos quickly returned fire and jumped again, only to be met with the same thing.

Anger filled Amos when he concluded that the best way to destroy this shipyard was the way Fantor had done. Amos would ram his ships into the shipyard, after all. He would lose fewer ships overall that way. Now to choose which ships to use.

Amos knew to send more than he needed. The shipyard would know what was coming. It wouldn't be a surprise this time. They were likely expecting it.

Twelve ships broke formation with their next jump and headed straight for the shipyard. Amos had selected a side of the shipyard that was less protected by enemy ships. Only three of his ships hit their mark, but the effect was enough to cause significant damage to the shipyard. It wasn't enough to destroy it though, not yet.

On the next jump, Amos sent in another twelve ships. This time only two hit their mark. Amos seethed in fury. He had sent twenty-four ships to their death, and only five had completed their mission.

Explosions rattled the shipyard, and the lights blinked. Amos held his breath. Perhaps they had hit something vital to the shipyard after all. Would it be enough?

The lights blinked again, and then the power failed. Amos saw this for what it was, time to press his advantage and to attack once more. With the shipyard now powerless, that meant it had no operating defensive weapons and no energy screen either.

The Morag fleet sent another round of weapons fire at the imposing shipyard. The firepower slammed into the side of the behemoth and detonated. A chain of explosions ignited and broke apart the vessel. When at last it was destroyed, Amos sat back, a satisfied smile across his face.

Weapons fire began anew from the enemy fleet. Amos returned his attention to the next phase of this battle. He needed to eliminate all these enemy ships. Then he would focus his attention to the surface of this planet. Also he would destroy the second shipyard that orbited the moon. No doubt the Jatarians watching the battle from that shipyard had already realized their doomed fate. Amos relished in the thought of their terror.

The tactical display showed more green icons than red. His warbirds had managed to finish off the Jatarians' small attack ships.

Amos noticed the new Jatarian ships were currently headed over to the remaining shipyard. These new ships were slightly larger than the small attack ships were. They must plan to make a last stand there.

As the two fleets continued to slug it out, Amos got more confident in his upcoming victory. Nothing could stop him now.

Two more explosions erupted near him, as adjacent ships met their end. Amos wondered if the Jatarians were trying to find his ship and destroy it. He moved more ships around him to help protect his position.

Amos had lost more ships than he had expected. These Jatarians had improved their abilities and strength since they'd last battled. Had the Morag? He was confident that they had. Would it be enough?

Alarms rang out once more.

Now what were the Jatarians doing? A quick look at Amos's consoles made him stop in his tracks. Another Jatarian fleet had arrived. He waited for his scans to confirm the number. He had a sinking feeling that he would have to retreat or die. Too many red threat icons were on that screen.

When the scans came in, he knew his fate. Over two hundred more Jatarian ships had arrived. Where had they come from? Were they nearby? Or had they realized that this system would be targeted?

With all the microjumps Amos's fleet had done, their hyperdrives weren't charged enough to make the jump to leave the system. Amos resolved to take as many enemy ships with him as he could.

Amos ordered his ships to advance toward the planet. He would destroy the settlement at least. That would hurt the morale of his enemy. He was comforted by the thought that his fleet had destroyed more ships than Fantor's. They'd also destroyed a shipyard. Now if only they could hit the surface and vaporize the enemy below.

Amos knew he only had minutes before the new Jatarian fleet entered the fray. He had to launch his missiles at the surface by then. He just had to.

With added determination, his fleet made their run for the planet, all the while still targeting any ship in their way. Amos witnessed more enemy ships exploding. He was almost close enough to launch his weapons at the surface.

Just as Amos gave the order to bombard the planet, the second fleet arrived within optimal weapons range.

Amos saw the mushroom clouds rising from the surface, just as his ship shook violently. He was knocked to the ground and felt blood dripping from a gash on his forehead.

With what time he had remaining, he ordered the warbirds to attack the remaining shipyard. The warbirds would die today too. They might as well die with honor, attacking the second shipyard.

Amos turned his ship to face the oncoming attack. He would meet his death head-on. He stood behind his command console. As his ship shook violently again, Amos held his ground. Sparks rained down from the ceiling, as his Command Center fell apart around him. Smoke filled the air. A moment later Amos was no more.

-

I opened my eyes and looked at Jeffery. He was staring at me, fear evident in his gaze. I suggested, "Let's find another Morag to witness what happens next. Maybe a pilot of one of the warbirds will get lucky and will destroy more enemy ships."

"Or the second shipyard," Jeffery suggested.

"I doubt that but maybe."

I closed my eyes again and focused on the Morag in the attack system. Which one could I find that was in a warbird? It didn't take me long to find one. It was intense watching the battle through this Morag's mind.

-

His warbird he piloted swerved and dove, trying to dodge the incoming weapons fire from not only the shipyard but also the other Jatarian ships positioned between him and the target.

The Morag pilot's intent was to ram his warbird into the shipyard. He knew today he would breathe his last. It might as well be in grand style. Not that anyone would know or would remember it. He would die with honor though, if only he could manage to avoid all this firepower that surrounded him.

Out of the corner of his vision, he saw one of his fellow warbirds get hit with weapons fire. The ship was quickly swallowed up in an explosion.

He had to make it to his goal. He was resolved and determined to last that long.

Another flash near him signaled another one of his comrades was gone. He would join him soon enough. He only had to make it a little farther.

He swerved and dove out of the path of another missile meant to kill him. He wouldn't let the Jatarians win this one. He would destroy them. His enemy would not destroy him first.

The shipyard grew larger out his window in front of him. Would he make it?

A quick look out his side window showed the diminishing number of warbirds. Did they have enough birds left? He knew he would never really know the answer to that. Regardless it just had to be enough.

As the first warbird slammed into the side of the shipyard, he saw the initial impact on the hull. An explosion occurred, sending debris flying.

Another bird hit and then another. He was almost there. The enemy's weapons fire had ceased. He was too close for the shipyard to target him.

The shipyard was all he saw now. He had only moments left.

-

I opened my eyes. That was the second Morag I had witnessed die today, while I was essentially in their minds, reading their thoughts.

Even though these individuals were Morag and not Human, it still took its toll on me. I looked over at Jeffery.

He leaned over his knees and had his head in his hands.

"Are you okay?" I asked.

"Yes, that was just a lot. I wonder if they were successful in destroying the shipyard," Jeffery said.

"I'm not sure. I guess we can see if any other Morag are left in the system," I suggested.

Jeffery nodded. We both closed our eyes again.

I found no Morag in the system. I opened my eyes.

Jeffery looked at me and shook his head. "Now what?" Jeffery asked.

"I don't know. I guess we need to send another Morag fleet to destroy what remains in that system."

"What if the shipyard is damaged enough that it is incapable of building more ships until it has had some repairs? Then we would be wasting Morag ships."

"Jatarian warships are still in that system. They need to be destroyed regardless."

"You do make a good point there," Jeffery replied.

"The Morag are very good at what they do. We've set things in motion. I would be interested to know what they have planned next," I said.

"We already have more Morag fleets headed this way. Should we just let them do their own thing? Do what they do best?" Jeffery asked.

"I think, for the meantime, yes. We need to give them an idea of where more target systems are. Then I suggested that we sit back and let them battle it out on their own terms. The good thing is, the battles are here in Jatarian space, far from the Federation. So no Humans are in the line of fire. In fact, right now, the only Humans in danger by the Jatarians are the ones on board the *Explorer*," I replied.

"I agree. Speaking of the *Explorer*, will we go rescue them first somehow, or are we checking out the suspected home system first?" Jeffery asked.

"With the *Explorer* still hiding and no sign of the Jatarians working to find them on the surface, I say we check out the home system first. Then we look to rescue the *Explorer*."

"I can honestly say I'm nervous about exiting hyperspace in the Jatarian home system. I expect it will be guarded much heavier than what we've already seen, with the best defenses and the most warships. What if they sense us before our hyperdrive has the chance to recharge? Then what do we do?" Jeffery asked, with a look of concern.

"Let's check the holographic display and see if another system is nearby, where we can recharge our hyperdrive before we enter the target system. Then it wouldn't take us as long to charge in the Jatarian system."

"Do you think the Jatarians will have sensors in the nearby systems though? To give them an early warning? Like what we do with the advanced detection buoys?" Jeffery asked.

"Yes, they might. That would explain how the *Explorer* was found. It's a pretty good possibility, when you think about it. Thanks for pointing that out, Jeffery." I got up and walked over to my desk. I pulled up the holographic display and looked carefully at it.

"Where are we now?" Jeffery asked, as he stood up and joined me to get a closer view.

"We're right around this area here. We are headed to this system here. Only a few hours to go."

"Any system near enough to make a difference in our hyperdrive charge time?"

"No, I don't think so. It looks like we may have already passed the nearest system. The Dremu system is the next one, where the homeworld may be. The only system near here and close enough to make a difference on our recharging time is the one the *Explorer* is in."

"And we know enemy ships are there," Jeffery stated.

"Yes, so not any safer than where we are headed. It only takes one ship to sense us and to destroy us," I pointed out.

"Yet facing only a few ships is better than thousands."

"True. We will plan to stay on the very outskirts of the system, until our hyperdrive is charged. We will make no microjumps. We will only use our sublight drive. We will be very cautious," I said.

"That's the best we can do. Hopefully it'll be enough. It will take a long time to get to their planet when using just our sublight drive."

"Yes, but we do have the time. We never expected to find their home system so quickly. Thanks to the *Explorer*, we have. We must remain patient to ensure our safety. Let's hope no shipyards are in the system."

"I would guess that multiple shipyards are staged throughout the system," Jeffery said.

"I bet you're right about that. We will see soon enough."

"How much longer do we have?"

I glanced at my watch and replied, "Four more hours."

"We should get some rest. I doubt I'll be comfortable enough to rest when we're in the enemy system, surrounded by thousands of enemy warships," Jeffery joked.

"Me neither."

Jeffery walked toward the door and said, "Thanks for teaching me how to watch the battles through the Morag's thoughts. I've already learned so much. I don't know what I would do without you."

"You would be living a life of luxury inside the palace walls."

"Ha. My life would be a lot different without you in it. I rather like how it's turned out so far."

"Me too," I said, with a smile.

After Jeffery left, I headed to the cafeteria. If I wanted to get some sleep, I needed a full stomach first.

I updated Bryce, Parker, and Maro on the Morag's activities.

"So what will you have the Morag do next?" Parker asked.

"I think I'll let them do what they do best, destroy their enemy. I informed them of multiple target systems. I think we can sit back and watch the Morag plow through the Jatarian systems. I'll keep tabs on them. With no Human lives at stake, I'll try to be more hands-off. The Morag are plenty capable of handling the situation on their own."

"Do you think they have enough ships?" Parker asked.

I sighed. "I have no idea how many warships the Morag will bring. I hope they have enough. It all depends on what we find in the Jatarian home system."

"The *Explorer's* report said they sensed thousands of Jatarian ships," Bryce reminded me.

"I know. I'm hoping a majority of those are their small attack ships. We will see in a few hours," I said.

"Yes, we will," Bryce replied.

After finishing my meal of fried chicken and mashed potatoes, I headed back to my quarters to get a couple hours' worth of rest. I needed it after using my gift so much. I needed more than a few hours, but I would take what I could get at this point.

Chapter Fifteen

I sat in my command chair, thrumming my fingers on the armrest. The command crew and a few extras were all in the Command Center. We were nearing what we expected to be the Jatarian home system, *if* this was, indeed, the Jatarians' home system. It was a little surreal to think about.

I never imagined we would find it so quickly. I estimated that this mission would last about one year. Not that it was over yet. We still had to defeat the Jatarians. I intended to stick around and watch their demise, hopefully at the hands of the Morag.

I still considered whether this might only be *one* of their core systems and not their actual home system. How would we know? We wouldn't, not unless we continued to look elsewhere. More Jatarian systems were surely out there.

"Fifteen minutes from the Dremu system," reported Bryce.

I took a deep breath and braced myself for what we would find on the scans. Fritz had sensed thousands of ships here. I hoped perhaps a majority of them were the small attack ships. If they were manufactured here, it would stand to reason that more would be in that system.

Not that going up against a large number of the Jatarians' small attack ships would be good. The Morag did now have their warbirds. I just wasn't sure they had enough of them.

If only the Federation would send their devastators to help the Morag destroy the enemy, then we stood a better chance.

It was still hard to believe that the Emperor had no plans to send his military here to help the Morag defeat the Jatarians. He didn't want to risk losing his ships. He would let the Morag handle it. I just wasn't convinced the Morag could handle it on their own.

"Running scans now," Connor reported.

I took a few deep breaths. This was it, the moment I'd been waiting on for years. I watched the monitors in front of Connor. What would they show?

Connor cleared his throat and said, "Scans are coming in. Initial scans say 3,568 ships are in the system."

Silence filled the room. A cold chill ran down my spine. That was a lot of ships.

I took a deep fortifying breath and said, "We will exit hyperspace on the periphery of the system. We will wait there while we charge our hyperdrive. Cole, are our stealthed systems activated?"

"Yes, Captain."

"We are ready then," I replied.

I swallowed the bile rising up in my throat. I was nervous. I was responsible for all these people on this ship. It was my job to keep them safe. However, finding this Jatarian system was what we were here for. We had to exit hyperspace and see what was there.

I felt that old familiar twinge inside, whenever we exited hyperspace. The Command Center remained eerily quiet.

"No scans, Connor. We will wait until our hyperdrive is charged," I said.

"Yes, Captain," Connor replied.

The viewscreens at the front of the room focused on the system. Yet it was hard to discern anything from our vantage point. We were so far out still. A good number of those reported ships would be transport vessels. At least I hoped they were.

Only two planets were visible. I couldn't make out any ships. We were even farther away from the inhabited area of the system.

Now all we could do was watch and wait. It was hard not running the scans to see where the ships were congregated. I couldn't take the risk. We weren't in a hurry. We had the time to wait, although the ninety minutes it would take to charge our hyperdrive would drag slowly on.

I focused instead on the two visible planets. The nearest one was smaller than the other. It had rings around it. I was reminded yet again of the beauty that surrounded me. This might be the home of my enemy, but it still held remarkable beauty.

It made me wonder what the Jatarian homeworld would look like. Would it be similar to Korah on Falton Two or Queen City on Golan Four? Would skyscrapers touch the clouds? What were their modes of transportation? Would they be similar to ours? Would seeing how they live their daily lives make them more relatable and humanize them? Could that make it harder for me to order the Morag to destroy them?

Maybe it was best not to look. I would be too curious though. The explorer in me would win the battle in my mind. We would get a view of the Jatarian planet, if we could. It might teach us many more things about them. We stood to learn a lot.

"This system will be very heavily fortified," Connor commented.

"Yes. It could have things we haven't seen yet. We will have to watch carefully," I replied.

"Do you think this is their home system?" Bryce asked. "It could be just one of their core systems, not their home system."

"I thought of that. No way to really know, other than the sheer number of ships in orbit. No matter what we find here, we still must search the area and see if we can find more Jatarian-occupied systems," I replied.

Bryce nodded.

"Maybe we can monitor their communications," Parker suggested.

"I'm not sure we have that good of a grasp on their language. We can try using our translators, but I'm unsure how well it'll work."

"We might as well do that while we wait," Graham offered. He pushed a few buttons on his communications console.

Soon a constant stream of voices could be heard. None of which we understood.

"The translator is a little slow. I'm looking at the translations now," Graham reported. "The translations are a little patchy. It appears they are talking about the Morag and the attacks."

"Perhaps, if we listen for key words, it would be easier," Parker suggested.

"Let's have the system listen for *Humans, Federation, Morag, attack, war, stealthed*, anything that might let us know that they realize we are here," I said.

After a few minutes, Graham said, "It seems they are mostly talking of the Morag and preparing for war."

"Let's hope they don't mention a spy ship or a stealthed ship or going to war against the Humans. Maybe the Morag attacking them will put the Morag more on their radar and the Federation on the back burner," I said.

We continued to wait. No ships headed our way, at least none that we could see on the viewscreen.

I was beginning to get restless but was doing my best to seem calm. I felt Jeffery trying to communicate with me.

How are you so calm right now? Jeffery asked.

I'm not at all. I'm glad it looks like I am though, I replied.

Well, you're doing a great job of appearing calm.

I am focused on it. I'm the captain. I have to seem calm, I replied.

I guess I should take a cue from you. One day when I'm emperor, people will look to me like this crew looks to you to lead them. I hope I do as good a job as you do here.

I have had a lot of practice, Jeffery.

Graham interrupted our conversation by saying, "They've mentioned Humans, Captain."

"What did they say?" I asked, as I moved forward in my chair. My anxiety level instantly shot up. Had they sensed us?

Graham answered, "It seems they are discussing if they should attack the Humans while the Morag are away. Or if they should ignore the Humans until the Morag are destroyed. Then, once their protectors are eliminated, they go after the Humans."

"Let's hope they choose *wait*. If we know they plan to wait, we can use more Morag ships in the attacks here," I said.

"I think they're just debating the subject. No definitive answer has been decided."

"Keep listening for those key words. Any advantage we can gain from eavesdropping, the better decisions we can make."

Jeffery turned to me and asked, "How do you get the Morag fleets that are nearer the Federation to come if they are out of the range of your gift?"

"Easy, I use the Morag leaders I can communicate with to get them to come," I answered.

"I guess that makes sense," Jeffery replied.

My attention went back to the viewscreens and the planets visible there. How many planets and moons would the Jatarians inhabit here? Would each one have a shipyard? Those things were formidable. The Morag had to figure out the best way to destroy them with the least losses. I had no idea what that way was.

Was this the majority of the Jatarian warfleet, or was this only a fraction of it? I had no clue how many ships the Morag had at their disposal. I hoped it would be enough.

I didn't even know the number of warships the Federation had. Would it be enough to destroy whatever enemy ships remained after the Morag were defeated? Could the Jatarians defeat the Morag? I had no idea.

I did know one thing though. I would have a front-row seat to the battle. How much longer would we have to stick around to witness that? I wasn't sure. We would eventually gather our information and then hopefully rescue the *Explorer*.

I had yet to figure out a plan for that rescue. I was confident I would know when the time came. First, we must survive our intelligence mission here in this system.

"Captain, should we start using our sublight drive to head toward the middle of the system?" Bryce asked.

"I think we will wait until we can run a scan. I want an idea of what we're headed to first. Cole, how much longer until our hyperdrive is charged?" I asked.

"About half an hour."

"We can wait that long," I said. "I don't want to take any chances that the Jatarians have some extra defense systems out there somewhere."

Bryce nodded his agreement.

It would take a long time to get to the inhabitable zone of this system using our sublight drive. It was the safest option, however.

My mind wondered to the vast possibilities that this system held. None were good. What types of defenses would we find here? Could we learn from them and use these defenses in our refugee villages?

What would happen when this Great War with the Jatarians was over? Would the Emperor turn his attention to us? To the people he considers rebels? I shook my head. That worry was for another day. We had to defeat the Jatarians first.

My mind kept thinking of the various possibilities this system held. I was surprised when Cole said, "Captain, our hyperdrive is now fully charged."

I took a deep breath and slowly let it out. It was time to see what the Jatarians had here. "Connor, let's run the scans."

I stood and walked closer to the viewscreens. Being on my feet and moving around helped to calm me and helped me to think better.

After a few minutes, Connor said, "The majority of the ships are clustered around the fourth and fifth planets. Based on where the remainder of the ships are, I would assume colonies are on three of the moons. I'll put the system up on the screen with the tactical display. It'll show you what I'm seeing."

The viewscreen switched to focus on a tremendous amount of ships.

"What's the ship makeup?" I asked.

"Sixty-one transport vessels and freighters. Another forty-three ships appear to be civilian in nature. The rest are all warships of varying sizes," Connor reported.

I sighed deeply. "What about shipyards?"

"From the scans, I believe this area has six shipyards," Connor replied, still analyzing the scans. "A lot of stuff is out there. The scans are picking up something not too far from our location."

"A ship?" I asked, puzzled, as nothing was visible on the viewscreens.

"No, much smaller, it seems," Connor answered.

"Like the size of an orb?" I asked.

"Similar but different."

"In what way?" I asked.

"Here is what an orb has looked like on our scans. Here is what this new thing looks like," Connor said, while showing us what he was talking about on the viewscreen.

"How many of them are there?" I asked, still puzzled as to what exactly we were looking at.

"Thousands," Connor replied.

Another cold chill ran down my spine. I looked over at Jeffery, standing beside me. "Thousands?" I asked slowly.

"Yes, Captain."

"Could they be sensors, trying to pick up on any ship exiting hyperspace in the outskirts of the system?" Bryce asked.

"Possibly, but I would imagine they wouldn't need so many in this type of formation. It's almost like a barrier," Connor answered.

"A minefield," Bryce replied.

I looked over at Bryce and then at Jeffery. "A minefield?"

"What a brilliant idea. We couldn't sense these from our long-range scans, could we?" Jeffery asked.

"No, they didn't show up on our long-range scans from outside the system," Connor confirmed.

"This idea hasn't been utilized in the Federation. It's been tossed around but always ruled out. The dangers had always outnumbered the benefits," Jeffery said.

"Can we get around it?" I asked.

"There does appear to be a path *through it*," Connor answered.

"I would be worried that leads us right into a trap," Bryce said. "Are any orbs out here?"

"Not that show up on the scans," Connor said.

An idea struck me. "Would the orbs show up if they weren't activated? Perhaps when something gets near it, something sets them off. Maybe this pathway takes us directly past one of the orbs."

"Or maybe it's just a way for ships that exited too far out to get through," Jeffery countered.

"What if you're wrong?" I asked.

"I see your point. We have to be careful. We can't take the chance that it's a trap," Jeffery replied.

"Any other ideas?" I asked the command crew.

"Maybe if we got a little closer, we would get a better idea of what we're dealing with here," Bryce said.

"How close can we get before we set off an orb or that minefield out there?" I asked.

Bryce shrugged. "No idea."

"Let's move a little closer. I would like to at least see them," I said. "No closer than we have to though."

The ship began to move forward. I scanned the viewscreens, looking for any visible sign of these mines. How lucky were we that we hadn't exited hyperspace in the middle of the minefield? I shuddered at the thought. We couldn't sense them from outside the system. How were we to know where it was safe and where it wasn't safe to exit hyperspace? I knew one thing for sure. When we exited hyperspace from now on, my anxiety level would be at an all-new level.

My eyes strained, concentrating on seeing the small mines on the screen. I was beginning to think they were farther away than we'd thought when Bryce spoke up.

"I see them." Bryce walked up to the screen and pointed them out.

It was like a wall in front of us. They were spaced far enough apart that perhaps a small ship could maneuver through but not one the size of ours.

The barrier wasn't a single layer though. The minefield spanned out farther than I could see with my naked eye. There were multiple layers that went as high and as low as I could see from my vantage point. It was literally a wall. "Can we tell the dimensions, how far out this goes? Can we map the distance so we can know next time where we can jump so that we're past the minefield?" I asked.

"Yes. I can do that," Connor replied, "but what if they can move this minefield whenever it is found? Just like we move, whenever found."

I groaned at the thought. "One step at a time," I whispered.

Bryce walked over to Connor's consoles to look at what Connor was doing.

Jeffery asked, "What if we microjump and find another minefield?"

"I wouldn't be surprised. Maybe that's part of the plan. Enemy ships would have to microjump farther into the system, perhaps nearer their orbs. The entire point has to be to sense our ships quickly and to have more time to eliminate the intruders, before they pose a real threat to the inhabited planets and moons," I said.

"We've got to get farther in and see what they have here," Jeffery said.

"I agree, which means we have to do a microjump. We have to get farther than the minefield but not close enough that the orbs could sense us."

"You're still convinced they've got orbs out there that will activate if something passes near them?" Bryce asked.

"That's what I would do if I had this arsenal at my disposal," I replied. "Wouldn't you?"

Bryce nodded. "I would. It might get pretty dicey, once we make this next microjump."

After determining how far we needed to go, we prepared for our jump. I sat in my command chair, trying to keep myself from depositing my dinner in the nearest trash can. I looked around quickly to locate the nearest one, just in case.

The twinge in my stomach was almost too much for my already anxiety-ridden stomach to handle. I managed to keep my dinner inside thankfully.

Once we exited, Connor immediately ran the scans. We had jumped to the nearest planet. We hoped that it would mask our presence in the system a little more. Hopefully no orbs would be in that area.

"Scans coming in," Connor reported.

"Are any orbs near us?" I asked.

"None show on the scans, but, as you mentioned before, if the orbs are not activated, they may not show on the scans," Connor said.

"Let's hold our position, until our hyperdrive can recharge again. It won't take long. Then we can use our sublight drive to head farther into the system," I said.

I looked closely at the viewscreen. The planet was even more impressive up close. The rings were made of rocks and ice. It was a sight to behold. Almost mesmerizing. Could an orb hide in the rings of this planet? My heartbeat sped up. I would feel so much better once we had the hyperdrive recharged.

No ships were visible from our vantage point. I knew they were there though. The tactical display was full of them. I felt like we were walking into a lion's den.

We had to get closer to investigate what this Jatarian system held, to figure out if this was their home system or just a colony system.

When we had the all clear, we began our slow journey toward our enemy. My nerves were shot, and we weren't close enough to see anything of note. "How long will it take us to reach the next planet?" I asked.

"Long enough for you to get some rest," Bryce said, giving me a knowing look.

He knew I was tired, but I also knew that he understood I couldn't sleep while we were in this system. "I'll go stretch my legs a bit. Connor, you are in charge while I'm gone. If anything is amiss, I need to know immediately."

Connor nodded.

I turned and headed for the door, and Jeffery followed.

"You like to walk a lot," Jeffery observed, as I started my lap around the ship.

"Moving helps me to think more clearly. It helps me expel some of my nervous energy."

"Well, you don't look very nervous."

"I'm glad you think that. I didn't know if I would keep my dinner from coming back up again."

"I would've never known it."

"Are you nervous?" I asked Jeffery.

"Yes. We are in the home of our enemy. It is heavily guarded. We know they are watching for us. This is the most danger we've been in yet."

"You're right. And we will be here for a while."

"Will my heartbeat ever slow down?" Jeffery asked.

I laughed. "I'm not sure. You're not alone. I'm certain we are all feeling the same way."

"Have you checked in on the Morag recently?"

"No, have you?"

"No, but it might distract us for a bit."

"Good idea." I quickly found a spot to sit down. Jeffery sat beside me. I closed my eyes and focused on my gift. Where were the Morag now? What were they doing?

It took me a few minutes, but I found them. I couldn't help but smile when I realized the Morag were accumulating a large fleet. What they intended to do with it, I wasn't sure. Should I tell them about this system?

I opened my eyes and looked over at Jeffery. "Do you think we should tell them about this system? It'll take them a while to get here. By then we should have more answers."

Jeffery nodded. "I think we have to. We can't count on the Federation. And honestly the Federation can't go up against an enemy of this size. We're not ready for that. I don't know if we will ever be."

"Okay. I'll pass along what we know then."

I once again closed my eyes and reached out to the Morag. I found the highest-ranking member, who turned out to be Admiral Wyn. I informed him that a Human ship had discovered a Jatarian system with over three thousand ships in it. Then I gave him the coordinates. I didn't tell him to prepare for an attack. That would be his decision, based on what he knew of his fleet numbers. I would check in with him in a few days to see what they were doing.

When I opened my eyes again, I told Jeffery what I'd done. He agreed. If the Morag wanted to destroy the Jatarians, they knew where to find them.

I knew the Morag would come. That's what the Morag did. They wouldn't rest until they had extinguished this threat. It might not be on my timetable, but it would happen eventually.

"I guess we better return to the Command Center and check in. Thanks, Jeffery. That was a good distraction—and one that needed to happen."

I couldn't stand being out of the Command Center any longer. I had to know what was happening, even if it was nothing.

Chapter Sixteen

The hours moved slowly, as we continued our journey toward the inner system. I left the Command Center only for short periods of time to eat and to stretch my legs. Once we left this system, I would sleep for days. I was exhausted but knew sleeping was futile. Not while we were here. Not in this system.

We were in the middle of the lion's den. Any wrong move and we could be discovered. Discovery would mean certain death. Even with our weapons, we were no match for these Jatarian warships, even just one.

We had finally made it far enough to see the ships on our viewscreen. None of the shipyards were within view yet. The ships were plenty intimidating though. I was thankful for our stealthed technology. Otherwise we could have never exited hyperspace.

"Should we run scans from here?" Connor asked.

"I don't think it'll give us much more information than what we've got. We know they have warships of varying sizes. What we don't know is where they live and how they live. We've got to keep our chances of making those scans higher by not running the scans here," I answered.

Connor nodded. "That makes sense."

Connor was used to running lots of scans. Not doing so went against his training.

We studied what we could see on the viewscreen. The ships in view looked similar to the ones we'd seen before. That didn't make them any less intimidating. There were just so many of them.

Suddenly alarms rang out.

I stood up. "What do we have?" I asked, while turning to the tactical display. I assumed it would be more Jatarian ships arriving in the system. I was wrong.

"Captain, we seem to have activated one of those orbs you were afraid was waiting out here for something to pass it," Connor said.

An explosion rattled the ship before we had the time to even react to what had happened. "Status of our stealthed capabilities," I asked.

"Still intact, Captain," Cole answered.

"Let's jump back behind the minefield. It appears those warships are headed our way."

Before we jumped, another orb exploded near us. I didn't have time to check the damage control console before I felt that familiar twinge, signaling our jump.

Once safely on the opposite side of the minefield, I said, "Connor, run the scans. We need to know what's going on."

"Yes, Captain."

"Mariat, what does our damage control console show?" I asked.

"No systems were harmed. Our energy screen took a hit though."

"Cole, what's the status of our energy shield and our stealthed capabilities?"

"Energy screen is holding at 75 percent. The stealthed capabilities are still online," Cole answered, while checking his consoles.

"What about our hyperdrive? How long does it need to charge?" I asked.

"Thirty minutes, but, for some reason, it's not currently charging."

"Jeffery, go to engineering and see what's going on. There may be some damage to the hyperdrive," I ordered.

Jeffery immediately got up and headed out the door. I could have just asked Samson through our gift, but I had other things to tend to. Plus Jeffery could learn a thing or two in this situation.

"Scans show hundreds of orbs scanning the area where we were. Plus eleven warships responded to that location," Connor reported.

"So they know where we've been but hopefully not where we are now. Let's keep a close watch on those orbs. If they head this direction, I want to know," I said.

"The scans show that orbs all over the system have now been activated," Connor added.

"Tell me none are out here on this side of the minefield," I said.

"None show up on the scans."

"Why wouldn't they put some out here?" Bryce wondered aloud.

"That's a good question," I replied.

Jeffery returned, out of breath. "Samson and Wyatt said they have identified the problem and are working to fix it. They estimate half an hour until it's fixed."

Cole added, "Plus another half hour after that to charge our hyperdrive. So we are stuck here for at least an hour."

Everyone turned their attention to me.

I took a deep breath and slowly let it out. This was not a position I wanted to be in. "At least the minefield gives us a barrier of protection."

"Unless they jump out here too," Bryce commented.

"Surely they think we've left the system," Parker said.

"Unless now that they're on the lookout for us, they realize we are actively running scans from out here," Bryce said.

I didn't like the sound of that. What should we do? We needed to know what threats were near and what they were doing. We might have to move our position.

"Captain, the orbs are headed toward the minefield," Connor said.

"Seriously?" I asked.

"Can they get through it?" Bryce asked.

"They are small enough," Connor noted. "I think it would slow them down at least."

"Can they make a microjump?" Bryce asked.

"We haven't witnessed them do that, but who's to say they can't?" Connor answered. "There's just so much we don't know about them."

"What if they could track a ship into hyperspace?" Bryce asked.

"That would be disastrous, especially if they can identify a stealthed ship," I said.

"Our enemy is advancing their technology. We assumed they would try to develop stealthed ships themselves. It turns out we're wrong. Instead they focused on how to identify them and to destroy them," Bryce said.

"With this system so heavily guarded, I'm not sure we will get close enough to their inhabited planets and moons to scan them. We may have to wait until the Morag show up and destroy their main fleet," I said.

That situation wasn't ideal, but it's what made the most sense. We could scan the planets later, after the big battle. We just had to be more patient. Patience was not one of my strong suits.

"We have plenty of other systems we can check before the Morag have time to assemble and to get here," Bryce said, looking over his notes. "Who knows. We might find more systems just like this one."

"You're right about that. Our job is to identify the targets. We know this is a system we have to send the Morag to. There will likely be more. We might have to prioritize them, before all is said and done," I added.

"We've already found more than I thought we would," Bryce said.

"Me too," Jeffery agreed. "I have to admit that being on a ship like this is very addictive. The adrenaline courses through my veins. The danger, the new discoveries, the learning? I can't imagine life *not* on a ship anymore."

"I think Eloise would have something to say about that," I said, with a laugh.

"Not to mention my parents," Jeffery added.

I was glad Jeffery had tagged along. We had grown closer over the last few weeks, and he had learned a great deal. All of these experiences would help make him a better leader one day. It also would help solidify his relationship with my crew and then, by extension, the rest of the refugees.

Jeffery was seeing things from my perspective—even the scenario where his father was hiding things from him. I knew Jeffery questioned whether or not we could even trust the Emperor. As much as I understood how that was a hard thing to question, it was a good learning experience. You always had to consider someone's motivations.

The Emperor, for example, wanted to protect the Federation. The rest of the galaxy he could care less about. This was why he was willing to let the Morag do his dirty work for him, which I didn't disagree with. I just think it would take more than the Morag alone to win this war with the Jatarians.

Jeffery could see the good and the bad effects of policy decisions. That rules made by politicians way back on Falton Two influenced how the Federation's ships operated way out here—not necessarily on our ship but on the *Explorer* and the scout ships. How little those politicians knew about what actually happened out here, yet they held the keys to how things should be done. It didn't add up. Jeffery was seeing that firsthand.

We continued to scan the area for any change in activity. The orbs were still headed our way. It would take them a while to get here. Just knowing they were on their way to us made me nervous. We should be ready to leave before they could arrive here.

I closed my eyes and focused on Samson. I wanted an update on the repairs of the hyperdrive. *Samson, how are the repairs coming along?*

It's taking a little longer than we expected. Can we try to avoid those orbs in the future? Next time it might cause us more damage than we can handle.

We will do our best to avoid them. What does your timetable look like?

Give us another fifteen minutes, and we'll have the repairs wrapped up, Samson replied.

Okay. We do have orbs headed our way. Anything you can do to speed up the process would be appreciated.

I'll keep that in mind.

I'll check back with you soon, Samson.

When I opened my eyes, my gaze moved to the viewscreen. The minefield filled the screen. Where earlier it was a barrier to keep us out, it now acted as a shield to keep our enemy away.

"The warships near the orbs are charging their hyperdrives. I believe they're about to do a microjump," Connor said.

"What about the orbs?" I asked.

"They appear to be loading up into the ships."

"So they're hitching a ride?" I asked.

"Looks like it," Connor replied.

"I guess we now know the orbs can't make hyperspace jumps," I said.

"That's a relief," Bryce added.

"All the orbs have now loaded on the ships. They're making their jump," Connor announced.

The big question remained. Where would they end up? Would it be near us? Which side of the minefield would they emerge on? Our side or their side? I hoped it wasn't on our side. We still couldn't even charge our hyperdrive.

"Look. There they are," Bryce said.

I breathed a sigh of relief. The Jatarian ships ended up on the opposite side of the minefield. A buffer still remained between us.

It was clear to see on the viewscreen when the enemy ships released the orbs. A cold shiver flowed down my body.

"Our hyperdrive is now charging," Cole reported.

"Good. I'm not sure how much time we will have before they find us," I replied.

We all watched as the orbs fanned out to search the area. Our scans gave away our location. "Connor, no more scans. We will use only what we can see on the viewscreens. We can't risk them pinpointing our location."

"Do you think they'll go through the minefield?" Connor asked.

"I would think the orbs would. They are small enough to make it through."

"Do we have anything small we could send out there to distract the orbs? Maybe make them set off the mines in the minefield?" Jeffery asked.

"That's an interesting idea, Jeffery. Let's go talk to Samson about it quickly. If we can use something on this ship, he would know," I shared. What a great idea. If we could get one of the orbs to detonate while in the midst of the minefield, it would likely set off a chain reaction. It would take out a majority of the orbs, not to mention the minefield.

On the flip side, it would then clear the way for the warships to reach our location. Either way, it was worth a try.

Jeffery and I walked quickly to engineering.

"I think this idea could really work," Jeffery said excitedly.

"Me too. Brilliant idea, Jeffery."

When we reached engineering, we quickly filled in Samson and Wyatt on Jeffery's idea.

"We do have a few explorer pods that can be used. The pods are small remote-controlled vehicles, designed to be used in places we might believe are unsafe. We have three of them," Samson explained.

"How small?" Jeffery asked.

"Follow me, and I'll show you," Samson said, as he headed out of engineering.

"Alex designed these?" I asked.

"I'm sure it was Alex and his team. They tried to think of every possible scenario and what we would need to navigate through it."

"Are the pods stealthed?" I asked.

"No, they are not. Yet one pod might be small enough that the Jatarians won't realize it's there."

"How small is it?" I asked.

"It's right here," Samson indicated.

This explorer pod was about the size of the orbs we had seen.

"It looks like a basketball," Jeffery said.

"Yes, and very similar to the orbs. I don't suppose it can scan and explode?" I asked.

Samson laughed. "No, all it can really do is take pictures and send them to the ship. The Jatarians are a few steps ahead of us with their orbs."

"Won't the Jatarians realize where we are, once we release this explorer pod?" I asked.

"Yes, but that minefield is currently between us, correct?" Samson asked.

"That is correct," I replied.

"Maybe we release the explorer pod and then move the ship. That way we're not in the same location as before," Jeffery suggested.

"We couldn't move far, not with our sublight drive."

Samson said, "Maybe the explorer pod will be enough to distract the Jatarians. If we're lucky, they'll think this little thing is more advanced than it truly is. Maybe they'll think this is what they sensed earlier and not an actual ship."

"As if this were some small scouting device. More advanced than their orbs. This just might work," I said.

"How quickly do you want to release it?" Samson asked.

"As soon as possible. Will you operate it from here?" I asked.

"I can operate it from the Command Center, if you like. I just need a few things," Samson said.

"Can you maneuver it through the minefield?" I asked.

"Yes, I believe so, if I can get a good view."

"Let's get this process started then," I said.

"I'll get it ready. I'll have to launch it from the small launch bay we have. Then I'll head to the Command Center."

"Do you need any help?"

"No. Wyatt can help me."

"We will return to the Command Center then and watch for any reaction from the Jatarians," I said.

Jeffery and I raced excitedly to the Command Center. Once there, we filled in the crew on what we had planned. Would it work? We had no idea. Was it worth a try? Absolutely. Was it risky? Yes, but shortly we would have the option of leaving the system whenever we needed to.

We all waited anxiously yet hopefully to see our little explorer pod head toward the Jatarians. Would they think it was a weapon? Perhaps one even more potent than their own? We could only hope.

While we waited, we moved the *Hunter* slightly farther away from the minefield—in case something did happen. We might need to make a quick getaway.

Connor announced, "I see our explorer pod. It's right there."

I moved forward to see the viewscreen a little closer. I could just barely make out our little pod.

Samson came in then, with his equipment.

"Feel free to set up wherever you want, Samson," I said.

"Let me get this settled, and then we should have a live view from the pod itself," Samson said.

I watched as Samson quickly set up everything and typed in a few commands. Shortly afterward one of the viewscreens changed to a view from the explorer pod.

The pod was just entering the minefield. It was definitely an interesting view. So much danger all around. If Samson made a wrong move, it would set off a serious chain of events. I was confident we were outside of the blast zone, but I wasn't ready to find out yet.

We continued to watch as the pod closed the distance between itself and the orbs. I had no doubt the Jatarians now knew of its presence. What they thought of it, I had no idea. Graham was listening at his comms, but the translations were not making much sense.

Without running scans, it was hard to determine how far out the pod was from the orbs. It was moving slowly, partly to draw the orbs into the minefield. The more orbs we could get in the danger zone before we set off our chain of explosions, the better. At least we hoped it would set off a chain of explosions.

The time seemed to stand still as we waited for the events to unfold. Would it go as planned? Or would we be running scared from the system?

I tried to keep my mind from spiraling down a dark hole of possibilities, none of which were good. I focused instead on what was next. One step at a time. First, the orbs had to enter the minefield. Then the other orbs had to follow.

Once the majority of the orbs were in the danger zone, the pod would ram into one of the mines. This would hopefully cause a chain of explosions that would destroy all the pods in the blast zone. It was the best we could hope for.

The Jatarian warships would stay clear of the minefield, at least until we blasted a hole through it, which they could then use to come through and to hunt us down.

One step at a time, I kept reminding myself.

The pod was now closing in on the orbs. It had obviously piqued their interest. Many of them were headed toward the pod.

"I'm in the middle of the minefield," Samson said. "Do you think I should stop?"

"Maybe just go slowly parallel to their location. Keep moving, as if you don't sense them. Let them slowly gain on the pod's location. Then when they all get near, *bam*, hit a mine," I said.

Samson smiled. "I like the sound of that. I hope Alex won't mind too much that we destroyed one of his explorer pods."

"I'm sure he's already working on making them better for next time," I replied. "I think he will be glad we found a way to use them efficiently."

Samson changed the direction the pod was moving. We could still see a side view from the pod, which showed the orbs. They took the bait. The orbs continued to move deeper into the minefield. I couldn't help but smile. They were headed right into our trap. It's too bad they were only orbs and not warships.

The warships appeared to follow the pod too. They were moving away from our location. A few more minutes and our hyperdrive would be charged. If we could string the Jatarians along long enough, we might get out of this system relatively unscathed.

The orbs were slowly gaining on the explorer pod. The viewscreen, showing the angle of vision from the pod, revealed just how close the orbs were getting. Any minute now, we would set off the explosions. Well, what we hoped would be a chain reaction of explosions.

One orb was getting very close to the pod. Would the orb set off itself to destroy the pod? In doing so, would it detonate the mines in the minefield?

Suddenly a bright light had all of us shielding our eyes. What was happening?

When I looked back at the viewscreens, the one screen that had the view from the pod was black. I moved my gaze to another screen. Explosions were spreading all throughout the minefield and were headed our way.

"What happened?" I asked.

"I believe the orb detonated itself when it got close enough to the pod. When it did, the nearest mine was also ignited. Then it spread from there, just like we thought it would," Connor explained.

"Are we far enough away?" I asked.

"I think so," Connor said.

The Command Center fell into a silent state, as we watched the mines detonate, one after the other. I felt my heart beat faster, as the mines ignited closer and closer to our position. Where would it stop? Would every single mine be destroyed? That would help out the Morag, at least if we rid the system of the minefield in its entirety.

How long would it take the Jatarians to deploy another minefield? Would they put it in the same location? Or would they move it? I had a sinking feeling about it.

The explosions got brighter, as the detonating mines exploded closer and closer to us. Our ship was in the process of moving farther away from the blast zone and the resultant debris. I didn't want any of that to hit our ship, energy shield or not.

As we watched the minefield disintegrate, I felt a rush of relief. So far, so good. We had remained outside of the blast zone.

When all the explosions came to an end, all the mines in our view had been destroyed.

"Captain, the warships are preparing to launch their weapons," Connor yelled.

"At what?" I asked.

"At what they believe is out here but are unable to see," Connor answered.

"Cole, how much longer on our hyperdrive?" I called out.

"Two minutes," Cole answered.

"Let's keep moving away from the area and hope the random shots miss us," I said.

We all watched the screens, as the Jatarian warships sent a wall of weapons fire in our general location.

I swallowed to soothe my dry throat. Would we make it out in time? Would we get hit before we could make our jump?

Time seemed to slow as we awaited our fate. Were we breathing our last breaths?

The weapons fire was closing in on our location. Without using our scans, which could give away our location, it wasn't easy to tell how close the weapons fire would get to our ship.

I looked around the room, taking in my crew. This was my family. Had I brought them to their deaths?

Cole interrupted my thoughts by saying, "Hyperdrive is fully charged."

"Let's get out of here," I ordered.

I felt an extreme weight lift off my shoulders as the ship entered hyperspace. We had made it. My family was safe, at least for now.

Chapter Seventeen

After a good nap and a full stomach, I returned once again to my post in the Command Center. I still had moments where I could hardly believe that I was the captain of this vessel. I shook my head. Here I was living my dream. I was in unexplored space, at least to Humans, and I was captain of my own ship. I had an amazing wife and children, who I adored and missed terribly.

I blew out a long breath. I had to ensure the Jatarians were no longer a threat before I could return home. This would secure a better and brighter future for my children and, for that matter, all Humans.

The last time I had checked in with the Morag, dozens of fleets were headed this way. It would still be a couple weeks before they were ready to mount the attack on the Jatarian home system. I had a sinking feeling that we might find similar systems to the previous one out there somewhere. If the Jatarians had more heavily populated systems, they could be nearby. I was resolved to spend a few weeks, checking each system in the area, before heading home.

However, now we had to rescue Fritz and the crew of the *Explorer*. How exactly would we do that? I had no clue. I needed to see what we were up against first. At my last check-in with Fritz, only four vessels showed on his scans of the system. What could we do up against four heavily armed Jatarian warships? Not much, I was afraid. We had to do something though.

"Running the scans of the system now," Connor said, interrupting my thoughts.

Would more ships be there now? Maybe the ships here had left to help secure the Jatarian home system. Numerous scenarios ran through my mind.

"Captain, four vessels are in the system," Connor reported.

I nodded. "Just as we expected."

"Five minutes until our exit from hyperspace," Bryce announced. "What's our plan?"

"I want to confirm what types of ships are present in the system, before we make our final decision on how to handle the rescue operation," I replied.

Bryce nodded. "Maybe we will get lucky, and they won't be the large Jatarian warships."

"We'll see shortly." I hoped that Bryce would be right and that those four ships wouldn't be the large warships. Not that our ship could go up against the smaller warships either. Not four of them anyway.

As we exited hyperspace, my gaze moved directly to the viewscreens that filled the front of the Command Center. What would I see?

"Running scans," Connor said.

I bit my lip idly, as I awaited the news. What would we find here?

Alarms rang out almost immediately. "What's going on?" I asked, as my heart leaped into my throat.

"The ships in the system have launched the orbs," Connor answered.

Was this a trap? Did the Jatarians assume we would come here to this system to try to rescue our fellow Human ship? Of course they would, and we landed right in the middle of their trap.

I ran my fingers through my hair. Now what? "Cole, how long on our hyperdrive?"

"With the short jump from that last system, we only need an hour to recharge," Cole answered.

Well, that was better than ninety minutes. "How many orbs are there?" I asked Connor.

"Close to two hundred. They're headed our direction."

"Let's use our sublight drive and move away from this area. We know that when we run our scans, they can sense where we are or at least get an idea of our location. So, Connor, let's stop running our scans for a bit. We need to stay away from those orbs for the next hour."

"Then what? How do we rescue the *Explorer*?" Bryce asked.

"I'm open to ideas," I responded.

"If the *Explorer* could remain in hiding for another couple weeks, these ships here might head to the home system to help defend it when the Morag attack," Jeffery suggested.

"Or we could have the Morag stop here first and free the *Explorer*," Bryce said. "It would only take a small task force. The rest could continue with the attack on the Jatarian home system."

"I like that idea," Jeffery said. "It frees our ship and destroys these enemy ships. Is a small task group closer than two weeks away that we could send here?"

"Possibly but do we want the Jatarians to realize that the Morag know where their home system is and are en route to attack it?" I asked.

"Surely they already believe that now when we were sensed in their home system," Jeffery replied.

"Good point," I answered. "Let's see how things go with these orbs. It's too bad we can't somehow use their own orbs against their warships."

"Like implant a virus into their programming? Maybe one that would make them explode when they return to their ships?" Bryce asked, intrigued.

"Yes, exactly," I replied.

"Do we have anyone on board with that type of knowledge and skill?" Jeffery asked.

I looked around the room. "I don't suppose any of you do?" I asked.

Everyone shook their heads.

"What about Samson?" Bryce asked. "He has many skills."

"I'll ask him." I closed my eyes and focused on my gift. Samson was easy to communicate with, as he was so close. *Hey, Samson. I don't suppose you have any skills in programming computer viruses, do you?*

No, I'm afraid not. What's going on? Samson asked.

The Jatarians in the system launched their orbs. Bryce had an idea to program a virus in the orbs, so they would explode in the warships when they returned, I explained.

That would be a great tactic. Unfortunately I can't help with it. I'll ask around and see if anyone else has those skills.

Thanks, that would be great.

When I opened my eyes, everyone in the Command Center looked at me. "Samson does not possess that skill set, but he will ask around."

"It might be something to keep in mind for future battles, even if it's not something we can implement today. Surely someone in the Federation would have the skills to make that come to fruition," Bryce said.

"I'm sure you're right, Bryce. Our only limitation would be the programmer. If we could gain access to one of the orbs, it would be helpful, but I don't see that as a possibility," Jeffery replied.

"That's definitely not a possibility," I noted. "I'm glad we have an idea for a way to combat these orbs in the future. They could really do some harm to a system, if they were released to attack the surface," I said, my concern evident in my tone.

"It would be an easier way for the Jatarians to find any hidden settlements too," Bryce pointed out.

That's something I had already thought about but hadn't voiced. It's one of the numerous things that haunted my dreams. Another reason why we had to ensure the Jatarians were destroyed. "So that idea is out for now. Any others?" I asked.

Everyone shook their heads.

I looked closely at the viewscreens. The orbs were so small that it would be hard to see one before it was too late. "Let's stay on the move, and hopefully we can avoid these guys for the duration of our stay in this system. It appears the *Explorer* just might have to wait for the Morag to rescue them," I said.

I took a deep breath. I needed to check in on Fritz and see if they could handle another two weeks hiding in their current spot.

"Could they make a run for it?" Bryce asked. "Hear me out. What if we wait until our hyperdrive is charged? Then we show ourselves and distract the Jatarian warships. That would give the *Explorer* the perfect opportunity to make a run for it."

I mulled over Bryce's idea.

Connor added, "We must be far away from the warships. They would jump to our location very quickly. The *Explorer* would have to be ready to act immediately."

"They could be waiting just inside the atmosphere. We could appear and disappear a few times. Keep the Jatarians guessing at our location," Bryce suggested.

"What if the Jatarians have left orbs stationed across the surface? Or in the atmosphere?" Jeffery asked.

"It's a chance we take. Perhaps once they realize we're out here, they'll use all the available orbs to hunt us down," I said.

"The *Hunter* becomes the hunted. I'm not sure I like the sound of that," Bryce commented.

I didn't either. The *Hunter*'s appearance and the *Explorer*'s escape would have to be well-timed, which Fritz and I could handle directly with our gift. "Let me discuss it with the *Explorer* and see what their thoughts are on our plan. In the meantime, let's move around and keep away from those orbs."

I took a deep breath and focused once again on my gift.

Hello, Slade. It's good to hear from you.

It's good to know you're still alive, my friend.

You too. Especially since you're my only contact right now, Fritz said.

I guess I hadn't thought of it like that. We have a plan.

Good. I can't wait to hear it.

Four Jatarian warships remain in the system. They are also loaded with orbs, which are currently hunting us.

We hadn't sensed any of these orbs, Fritz said.

The Jatarians didn't release them until we arrived and scanned the system. We believe that's how they can sense our presence, when we run our scans.

I guess we will stop running scans down here then. That's the last thing we need. We are sitting ducks right now. We are pretty defenseless against a weapon of that nature.

We hope to stay away from the orbs while our hyperdrive recharges.

So what's this plan you've come up with? Fritz asked.

We will distract the warships, while you make a run for it.

And how exactly do you plan to distract the warships?

Easy. We show ourselves.

The Jatarians would be at your location in a heartbeat.

236

Yes, but we will jump somewhere else and make another appearance. We can do this cat-and-mouse game until the Explorer *is safely out of the system.*

What if a Jatarian ship follows us?

You can lead them back to a Morag task group that will happily rid you of your tail.

And what if something happens to you, Slade? You'll have to recharge your hyperdrive again.

Yes, but we can be stealthed, once your ship is safely out of the system.

What about the orbs? Fritz asked.

They can't travel in hyperspace. At least not that we've witnessed. We've observed them loading on a ship, right before the ship enters hyperspace. This is what makes us believe they are unable to make the jump themselves.

Sounds accurate. At least that's something we have going for us.

Do you think the plan could work?

Yes. How much longer until your hyperdrive is charged? Fritz asked.

Approximately forty-five minutes.

We will begin getting the ship ready. Give me a fifteen-minute warning.

I can do that, I replied.

I hope this works.

Me too.

Good luck up there, Slade.

Thanks. I think we could use a little luck.

When I opened my eyes, my gaze returned to the viewscreen. I searched intently for any sign of an orb. I saw none. It didn't help relieve the tension in my head. I rubbed my temples with my fingers, trying to discourage some of the looming headache. I knew the orbs were out there. I just couldn't see them. "Do we know at what rate these orbs can travel?" I asked.

"No. It's varied," Connor replied.

"I guess what I'm asking is, can the orbs catch us at their top rate of speed compared to our sublight speed?" I asked.

Connor, Cole, and Bryce quickly did some calculations. "Yes, I believe they can," Connor spoke up first.

"I agree," added Cole.

"Me too," Bryce replied.

That's not the answer I was hoping for. Quite the opposite. "Let's ensure we keep moving."

"We should be good if we refrain from running any scans," Bryce said, trying to ease everyone's minds.

I continued to study the viewscreens at the front of the room. I watched carefully for any sign of the orbs, but I also knew that, for me to see one with my naked eye, they would be way too close.

We needed to keep the Jatarians in the system busy. Not just the orbs but the warships also. To do that, we must show ourselves. That sounded like a terrible idea, but I was confident it would work. In order to keep Fritz and the *Explorer* safe, I must put my crew and the *Hunter* at risk.

Numerous things could go wrong with this plan. They'd all been running almost continuously through my mind. What if our stealthed capabilities malfunctioned? I knew, if we had to, we could leave the system and lead the Jatarians into a Morag trap.

If our hyperdrive failed for some reason, we were doomed. Considering this was a new ship though, I was relatively confident that wouldn't happen.

This plan had to work. Otherwise the *Explorer* would be stuck here for another couple weeks, until the Morag arrived. Every day that the *Explorer* and its crew remained holed up in that cave, the higher the chance they would be discovered. Especially now that we knew that the Jatarians had the orbs here as well. Had they had them the entire time the *Explorer* had been here? If so, why hadn't the Jatarians used them to locate the *Explorer* already?

I was puzzled but knew I wouldn't get an answer to my question. Perhaps the orbs had only arrived a short time ago. Maybe to help detect us when we arrived and not to help hunt down the *Explorer*.

Either way I was determined to help Fritz get the *Explorer* safely out of the system. Not to mention our ship shortly afterward.

I glanced back at the viewscreens. Cole had put up a timer, so we could all easily see how much longer it would take until our hyperdrive was charged. We still had over half an hour to go.

Now was as good a time as any to check on how the Morag task groups were faring. I closed my eyes and focused on Morag Admiral Wyn. It took me a few minutes to find him, but, when I did, I was pleasantly surprised at the progress they'd made. I tried to determine the number of ships now with his fleet but to no avail.

I was satisfied that at least the Morag were still inbound toward the Jatarian home system. Well, at least the system we believed to be their home system. I sincerely hoped that it was and that there wouldn't be another even more heavily fortified system to deal with.

The Morag didn't have the fleet numbers to deal with multiple heavily armed systems, at least not like the one we had witnessed before. As to how many ships the Morag actually had, I hadn't a clue. I just didn't imagine it would be enough.

When I opened my eyes again, I searched the viewscreens for any trouble. I saw none. It still didn't help relieve any of my tension. If I could spot trouble, it would be too close.

The time dragged on, until finally the clock ticked down to fifteen minutes remaining, before our hyperdrive was fully charged. That was my signal to contact Fritz again.

I closed my eyes and focused on Fritz.

Is this my fifteen-minute warning? Fritz asked.

Yes, are you ready? I asked.

We are.

Is your hyperdrive charged?

Yes, we've been charging it incrementally over the last few days. Ten minutes here and another ten minutes there. We wanted to be ready if we needed it.

Good. I'll let you know once we have the Jatarian warships preoccupied. Be ready to make your getaway.

I will.

Whatever you do, don't do any scans. It will alert the Jatarians of your presence.

Need I remind you, Slade, that my ship is not stealthed. The Jatarians will be alerted to our presence as soon as we leave the planet's atmosphere.

You're right. However, I'm not sure if doing a scan might activate the orbs though and put them on your trail. So, to be on the safe side, refrain from doing any scans. Just focus on getting out of here.

Do you have a suggested direction or rendezvous location? Fritz asked.

Head toward the Morag, just in case you are followed.

We will do that. If we get lucky, and no Jatarian ships follow us, then we will continue exploring this segment of space.

That's our intention too. We need to figure out if more Jatarian-occupied systems are out here. We need to know what we're up against, I replied.

Agreed. Let me know when it's time for us to launch.

I will.

Good luck, Slade.

You too, Fritz.

I opened my eyes, took a deep breath, and slowly let it out. It was almost time. "Bryce, have a few coordinates picked out for our microjumps."

"I already have them ready," Bryce replied, a big smile on his face.

It was great working with a team of people who basically knew what I needed before I even asked. We were family, and I was grateful for each and every one of them. It was my responsibility to keep them safe. Were we doing the right thing? Was this too risky?

I shook my head to clear away my thoughts. I had to think about the plan, not how many ways it could go wrong.

A quick glance at Bryce helped strengthen my confidence. He smiled at me and nodded. He knew me better than anyone. No doubt Bryce realized that I was questioning my choices and our plan. I tended toward worry and paranoia. I knew it, and Bryce knew it.

He was always my voice of reason. I truly valued that. Especially right now. Bryce didn't even need to say anything. Just smile and nod. I understood that he was trying to tell me to not worry and that everything would work out.

I had to believe that.

The time on the clock was ticking down to zero. Our hyperdrive was charged. "Is everyone ready?" I asked.

Everyone nodded.

I took a deep fortifying breath and said, "Let's do it. It's time to disengage our stealthed capabilities. Connor, run a quick scan, and then we will begin."

I practically held my breath, as Connor initiated the scans. Would the orbs be near? How close would they be?

"Scans are coming in," Connor said. "The orbs are here in this area." Connor put the scans on the viewscreen. "The warships are over here."

None of them were near our current location. I breathed a sigh of relief. I knew that was about to change.

"The orbs are headed in our direction now," Connor announced.

"Let's disengage our stealthed screens and get the warships distracted. Are you ready, Bryce?" I asked.

Bryce nodded.

"Cole, it's time."

I stood and watched the screen. How long would it take the enemy ships to react? I watched as Cole input the commands to lower our stealthed capabilities. Then I waited for Connor to inform us that the Jatarians' warships were headed our way. It didn't take long.

"The Jatarians are making the jump," Connor announced.

"Bryce, let's make our first jump," I said quickly. I felt relieved when that familiar feeling came in the pit of my stomach.

I closed my eyes and focused on Fritz. *It's time to leave the cave and enter the atmosphere. We've got the Jatarians following us.*

Okay. Here goes nothing.

Soon after we exited from our first microjump, Connor did another scan. "The Jatarians are at our last location. It appears they are preparing to make another jump."

"I'm not sure how long the Jatarians will play this game of cat and mouse with us," I stated. "I just hope it's long enough for the *Explorer* to get out of here."

"If we time it just right, the *Explorer* can make its jump into hyperspace right when the Jatarians come after us," Bryce said.

"That's the plan. The *Explorer* is getting into position just inside the planet's atmosphere. Once I have the confirmation they are in position, I'll let the *Explorer* know when to jump," I explained.

"The Jatarians are jumping," Connor reported.

"Let's make our next jump," I said. We were moving farther away from the planet, farther from where the *Explorer* was hiding. Anything we could do to help Fritz have a better chance of escaping, we had to do.

Once we exited from our second microjump, I felt Fritz trying to communicate with me. I closed my eyes and focused on him.

We are in position, Slade, Fritz said.

Okay. We just made another jump. The Jatarians just arrived at our previous location. Get ready to enter hyperspace. I'll let you know when the Jatarians make their next jump.

We will be waiting for your signal.

I opened my eyes. "Are they preparing to jump again?" I asked.

"No, not yet," Connor said, puzzled.

"What are they waiting on?" I asked, now more worried that something would go awry with our plan.

"They've likely realized we will just keep making jumps, and they won't have the chance to catch us. They're probably trying to figure out a better strategy," Bryce said.

What now? How could we get them to chase us at least one more time? We had to give the *Explorer* an opportunity to make a run for it.

"The Jatarians are charging their hyperdrives," Connor announced.

I breathed a sigh of relief. Maybe this would work after all. "Tell me when they jump," I said, as I closed my eyes. *Fritz, the Jatarians are about to jump,* I said.

We're ready, Fritz replied.

I heard Connor say, "They're jumping."

So I passed the message on to Fritz. *The Jatarians are jumping.*

Here we go, Fritz said.

Good luck, I replied.

I felt the sensation in my stomach as we once again made another microjump. Hopefully this would be the end of our cat-and-mouse game.

I opened my eyes and looked at the viewscreen. Then over to the tactical display. It showed the four Jatarian warships. Only the four ships weren't together anymore. They were all spread out across the system. The Jatarians were adapting.

"Did you see the *Explorer* leave the system?" I asked Connor.

"Yes. It was only on the scans for a few minutes," Connor replied.

"Long enough for the Jatarian ships to sense it?" I asked.

"I would assume so. The Jatarian ships exited from their microjump just before the *Explorer* made its jump. I guess the Jatarian ships couldn't follow the *Explorer* because their hyperdrives need charging," Connor said, with a big smile across his face.

"Engage our stealthed capabilities and let's make one last jump. Now we only need to stay hidden long enough for our hyperdrive to recharge," I said.

"Reengaging stealthed capabilities," Cole confirmed.

"Making our last microjump," Bryce said.

"No scans, Connor," I ordered.

We exited hyperspace shortly after that. I studied the viewscreen for any threats nearby. I saw none.

"Stealthed capabilities are online," Cole confirmed.

I breathed a sigh of relief. "How long until our hyperdrive is charged?" I asked. We had made four microjumps. It wouldn't take ninety minutes to recharge, but I was also aware it wouldn't be only a few minutes.

"Thirty minutes until we can leave this system," Cole reported.

Okay. We could stay hidden for that long. Yet I couldn't relax until we were safely in hyperspace. "What's our next destination?" I asked Bryce. If I could keep myself occupied for the next half hour, I would be much better off.

"A system nine hours from here," Bryce answered.

I nodded. I was thankful for the longer jump. It would give us ample time to sleep and to eat. We needed it.

I closed my eyes and reached out to Fritz. *Our plan worked on my end. How about yours?* I asked.

Yes, it did. We have no ships following us, Slade. I owe you big-time for this. I'll never forget it.

You owe me nothing, Fritz.

What about you guys? Are you safe?

For now. We've reengaged our stealthed capabilities and are recharging our hyperdrive now. We have under half an hour before we can get out of here.

Good. Let me know once you've left the system. I'll sleep better knowing you're safe, Fritz explained.

I will.

Be careful, Slade.

You too.

I opened my eyes and walked closer to the viewscreen. I wondered what the Jatarians thought about what happened. Did they think we had a malfunctioning system that caused us to lose our stealthed system? Or did they realize it was all a ruse to ensure they couldn't follow the *Explorer* when it left? Either way the plan had worked. So far, so good.

Now all we had to do was stay away from the orbs in the system. Surely we could handle that, right?

I sat back down in my command chair. I was exhausted. I couldn't wait to crash in my nice warm bed and get some shut-eye. Maybe a nice warm meal first. Then off to dreamland for me.

Alarms sounded, waking me from my dreams of sleep. "Report," I commanded.

"Jatarian warships are exiting hyperspace," Connor reported.

"How much longer on our hyperdrive?" I asked worriedly.

"Fifteen more minutes," Cole answered.

I looked at the screen. Connor had known it was Jatarian warships because we could see them on the screen. They were way too close for comfort.

"Maybe they're too close to target us," Cole commented.

"True. As long as they don't run into us," I added. I could see twenty Jatarian warships on the viewscreen. A cold shiver ran down my body. "Let's use our sublight drive and move away from these warships. It won't be long before they release their orbs."

Bryce was moving us toward the inner system instead of the outer part of the system. I wondered why but assumed he had good reason.

"Surely the Jatarians believe we are headed toward the outskirts of the system and will send their orbs in that direction," Bryce shared. "That's why we are headed in the opposite direction."

I smiled. Smart move.

It didn't take long for the alarms to sound again. I knew what that meant. The Jatarians had released the orbs. I closed my eyes and said a silent prayer. We had to remain safe for ten more minutes. That's all, ten more minutes.

When I opened my eyes, I studied the viewscreens carefully. None of the orbs were near enough yet to see with the naked eye. Of that I was grateful. Would that stay true for the remainder of our time here? We would soon find out.

Eight more minutes now showed on the countdown. Cole had moved it to one of the viewscreens. The crew in the Command Center went eerily quiet, as we watched each second tick by.

I took a few deep breaths and stopped myself from thrumming my fingers on the armrest of my chair.

Seven minutes. We were still moving toward the inner system. The nearest planet came more into view. Perhaps if I focused on it for a little while, it would help pass the time.

Six minutes. How many of the planets and moons in this system were inhabitable? We already knew the moon Fritz and the *Explorer* had taken refuge in was inhabitable. Were there more? Why hadn't the Jatarians colonized this system? It was nearby their home system. It was a puzzling thought.

Four minutes remained on the timer. If this system held inhabitable planets, why would the Jatarians not move here? If it were the Federation, we definitely would have colonized such a nearby system. Perhaps Fritz would have an answer to my mystery.

Two minutes. I sat forward in my chair as the last remaining minutes disappeared.

When we made the jump into hyperspace, I couldn't help but smile. We had made it. The plan had worked. We were now safely in hyperspace for the next nine hours.

"Let's get some rest," I said, as I stood to leave.

Chapter Eighteen

When I woke seven hours later, I felt much better. I had already communicated with Fritz a couple times.
The *Explorer* would continue exploring this area of space alongside us. We would cover more ground that way. We would work together and trade information.

I would check in with Fritz again in another hour, after we pass this next system. What would we find there? We would know soon enough. Fritz was still four hours from his first system.

Since the *Explorer* was not stealthed and could be seen by the enemy, Fritz would keep his ship in hyperspace, while we did any investigating to be done. We had plenty to do over the next couple weeks to keep us occupied, until the Morag arrived at the Jatarian home system. I had every intention of being there to watch that fight play out. The Jatarians would finally get what they deserved—death and destruction of their planets, instead of ours.

As for the Federation, we were too far out to use our gifts to communicate. Any communication had to go through the scout ships between us and the Federation. Jeffery took care of that.

We would have no communication with Elmania or any of the rebel bases until I returned within range of my own gift. It was hard being in the dark, so to speak. Not knowing if my family was safe was hard. I also knew that Hadassah would be far more worried about me. I was out in the unknown, while she cared for our growing family.

I quickly got ready and headed to the cafeteria to eat my breakfast. I smiled when I walked in and saw Maro and Captain Parker sitting together, deep in conversation. They were like two peas in a pod. I was glad they were here. I could depend on them both for support and reason. They were each wise in their own ways. Plus, truth be told, if we ever got stranded on an unknown planet, they would be vital to our survival, as both had been in that situation before.

Once my tray was filled with several delicious food options, I sat at the table with Parker and Maro. "Don't let me interrupt. Please keep discussing what you've been talking about," I said, as I ate my omelet.

"We were debating why the Jatarians had yet to colonize that last system," Maro said.

"I'd been wondering that myself," I replied. "What did you come up with?" I leaned forward in anticipation of their answers.

Parker spoke up first. "It's hard to say. It was hospitable to Humans, but perhaps the Jatarians' needs differ slightly from ours."

"Did your friend happen to mention anything suspicious that he may have noticed while they were hiding out there?" Maro asked.

"No. I asked for his opinion on the matter too, and he couldn't figure it out either," I responded.

Parker sat back and folded his arms around his chest. "We've got a mystery on our hands. Did the *Explorer* take any readings from the surface while they were stuck there?"

"I don't think so. They were trying to hide. The best way to do that was to power down all nonessential systems, which would include all types of scanning and sensors, I'm afraid. At that point it was more about surviving than exploring," I answered.

Parker and Maro both nodded in understanding. "Perhaps we will not find any more inhabited systems of the Jatarians," Maro suggested.

"Or perhaps that was their home system, and they have all the available resources there to protect it," Parker remarked.

"We have almost two weeks before the Morag arrive to figure that out," I said. "Maybe during that time, we will understand why the Jatarians don't colonize the system nearest their home system."

"I'm worried about these orbs, Slade," Parker said. "They're small and likely relatively easy to mass produce. I'm afraid we will see more and more of them as time passes."

"I agree. This is why it's vital that the Morag eliminate the Jatarians. The sooner, the better," I replied.

"We need to figure out how to defeat these orbs," Parker said. "Even if the Morag are successful in defeating the Jatarians, I doubt it would be the last we hear of them."

"I'm trying not to think about that, Parker. One step at a time. That's my thought process. Speaking of, I believe we better head to the Command Center and see what this next system has in store for us," I said, as I glanced at my watch.

The three of us got up and headed toward the Command Center. Once there, I took my seat in the command chair.

"We are about fifteen minutes from the system," Bryce reported.

I nodded. I had mixed feelings about what to expect. I didn't want to find any more Jatarians. I'd had enough excitement for the week. A part of me though *did* want to find more Jatarians. I wanted to find them all and to mark their systems for destruction.

A thought occurred to me. Was I becoming like the Morag? Was I to the Jatarians what the Morag were to the Human Empire? I shook that thought from my head. This was different. The Jatarians were a threat to Humans everywhere, Federation and Empire—even though the Empire had no clue the Jatarians even existed.

My thoughts were pulled back to the present when Connor announced, "Running the scans now."

I could practically hear my heart beating loudly in my chest. I waited patiently for the scans to come through. Surely if other Jatarian systems were out there, they would be relatively nearby the home system.

"Scans are coming in," Connor reported. "The scans show twenty-one ships in the system."

I sighed heavily. "I guess we better check it out. This time though, we will not run any scans until our hyperdrive has recharged. That way we can leave at a moment's notice. We will assume from now on that each system with a Jatarian ship also has orbs. We will operate with the utmost care to not activate those orbs until we are ready to jump into hyperspace."

Everyone nodded in agreement. No more hoping the orbs won't catch up to us while we wait for our hyperdrive to charge.

"Exiting hyperspace in five minutes," Bryce said.

We waited. Twenty-one ships was not an intimidating number. Was there a reason for that? Was this a trap? Perhaps the system was full of orbs or mines.

The more I thought about it, the more worried I became. The list of possibilities was endless.

I was surprised when the twinge in my stomach brought my attention directly to the viewscreens. No scans meant we wouldn't know what we were actually dealing with for ninety minutes. It would be a tense ninety minutes.

We had opted to exit hyperspace on the outskirts of the system. The possibility of a minefield was fresh in our memories.

"Anyone see anything?" I asked.

"No," multiple people replied.

Not much to see with our viewscreens from this far out. I sat back in my chair and waited.

Cole put the timer on one of the viewscreens at the front of the room. This was the countdown for when our hyperdrive would be charged. Watching that thing would drive me nuts. So I closed my eyes and focused on Fritz.

Did you find anything? Fritz asked.

Twenty-one ships are in the system. We exited hyperspace but will wait until our hyperdrive is charged before doing any scans. That's what seems to activate the orbs.

Smart choice. We are still a few hours from our first system.

I'll check back in with you later, I replied.

Twenty-one ships didn't seem like enough to protect an inhabited system. So what exactly did this system hold? It was hard not doing the scans.

Out of the utmost precaution, we held our position in the far reaches of the system. Without the scans, it was too risky to advance toward the inner system. There could easily be a minefield out there. If we waited to see it on the screen, it would be too late.

While we waited, my mind sifted through the possibilities that this system might hold. *A mining operation, a new colony, a small military base, even a prison.* We simply didn't know enough about the Jatarians and their culture to understand what we might find. "Anything on the comms?" I asked Graham.

"Not that I'm picking up," Graham replied.

We still didn't have the most accurate grasp of the Jatarian language. Our translation system was constantly learning and updating. Eventually we would have the ability to eavesdrop on their conversations. But, for now, it was too confusing. Hopefully the Jatarians would be destroyed soon enough, and we didn't need to learn more about their language.

The ninety minutes finally ended, and we ran our initial scans.

"The ships are assembled around the third planet from the sun. Only six of them are military ships. The rest are transport vessels and freighters," Connor reported.

"Any minefields?" I asked.

"Yes, closer to where the Jatarian ships are. It's between the third and fourth planet," Connor explained.

I nodded. "So my best guess would be that this system holds a mining operation. Anyone else have another idea?"

"I agree," Bryce chimed in. "With this many transport vessels and freighters, it must be a mining operation or a small colony. I don't think we need to spend time checking into it."

"I agree," Jeffery added. "We can mark this on our notes and see what the next system holds."

"Anyone object?" I asked. Not that I ran my ship with votes, but, if someone opposed, I wanted to hear their reasoning. No one did.

"Where to next?" Jeffery asked.

"The next system is twenty-seven hours away," Bryce answered.

"Let's head that way then," I said.

We were soon back in the safety of hyperspace. We returned to our rotations, and I waited a few hours and then contacted Fritz. By now he would have already passed by the nearest system to their location. I hoped they hadn't found anything significant. I closed my eyes and focused on my gift. *Did you find anything?* I asked.

Only a handful of ships were in the system. So it wouldn't make sense for it to be a core system. I noted it, and we can check it out later, Fritz replied.

We concluded our system was a mining operation or a small colony. We are already en route to the next system.

How many ships were in the system?

Twenty-one ships, mostly transport vessels and freighters, I replied.

I would assume a mining operation, as you did. How far out are you from your next target system?

About twenty-three hours, I replied.

Okay. We will pass by our next system in approximately nine hours.

I will check back with you in a few hours then, I said.

Fritz and the *Explorer* were the only other Humans who had any idea where we were. If something happened out here, we might need help. It was reassuring to know the *Explorer* was within a couple days' hyperspace jump from us.

It was unsettling being so far from any Human settlement and also being out of range of my gift. I did not want to get used to that feeling.

I passed the time with my crew and got some rest. I spent a few hours with Captain Parker and Maro. They were always great at helping the time pass faster.

Before long I was back in my command chair, awaiting the scans from our next target system.

Fritz had found nothing in their last pass by. Is that what we would find?

"The long-range scans are coming in," Connor announced.

I waited to hear what they would reveal.

Connor remained silent.

"Is everything okay?" I asked.

Connor took a deep breath. "The scans show over one thousand ships in the system, Captain."

I sat back in my chair and ran my fingers through my hair. What had we found now? I swallowed to soothe my parched throat. "One thousand ships?" I asked to confirm that I had heard Connor correctly.

"Yes, sir," Connor replied.

"We will need to investigate the system then," I replied.

"We're eight minutes from our exit from hyperspace," Bryce confirmed.

"Cole, are all our systems operating as they should?"

"Yes, Captain."

"We will exit hyperspace in the periphery of the system. There we will not run any scans until our hyperdrive is charged. I expect this system to be heavily guarded by orbs and mines. If you notice anything odd or out of place on the viewscreens, report it. We can never be too careful," I ordered. I already felt knots in my stomach, as my level of anxiety grew. I knew it wouldn't dissipate for hours. Not until we were safely back in hyperspace.

A few minutes passed, and I felt the ship exit hyperspace. Something caught my attention on the screen. "What's that?" I asked, pointing to the viewscreen. Flashes of light could be seen on the distant horizon.

"I can't know for sure without doing scans," Connor replied.

I was torn. The sensible thing to do was wait and charge the hyperdrive. Then run the scans. My curiosity was starting to get the best of me though.

"Shall I run the scans?" Connor asked hesitantly.

"No. We will wait a bit," I replied. I was dying to know what was going on, but the safety of this ship and the crew on board was my responsibility. I had to be cautious.

"Is it a battle?" Bryce asked.

"It could be," Connor replied.

I closed my eyes and reached out with my gift. Were there other species here in the system? Perhaps ones who I could communicate with?

After a few minutes I opened my eyes again. I looked over at Jeffery. He looked puzzled.

"What is it?" Bryce asked.

"It's the Zator," I replied, surprised by what I had found. "The Zator are here, attacking the Jatarians."

"Are you sure?" Connor asked.

"Yes. It's not Zator Commander Tao. I didn't know any of the Zator minds I looked into. They are Zator though, of that I have no doubt."

"Maybe the Zator from their real home system?" Bryce asked. "Remember how Zator Commander Tao mentioned to that Jatarian military leader that the Zenyan system was not their home system, and we wondered if he was bluffing?"

"He must not have been," I replied.

"Do you think it's safe enough then to run our scans? The Jatarians seem to have their hands full at the moment," Connor commented.

I took a deep breath. Connor was right. The Jatarians were a bit preoccupied at the moment. "Run the scans. I want to know where the minefield is and where this battle is happening. I want a better view of what's going on."

Connor smiled and turned and punched in a few commands into his console.

I sincerely hoped I had made the right choice and wouldn't soon regret my decision.

Connor pointed. "I'm putting up what I found on the viewscreen. A minefield surrounds the planet. A majority of the Zator fleet has held back and is watching a small contingent of fifty ships currently attacking the Jatarians," Connor informed us.

"Let's move in closer then. I want to see what's happening," I ordered.

After our microjump, we had a much better view of the battle. I stood up and moved closer to the viewscreens at the front of the room. I studied the scene. "How many ships do the Zator have?"

"A little over four hundred," Connor answered.

"So they're outnumbered," I replied, with a heavy sigh.

"They are, but these Zator ships are much larger than the ones in the Zenyan system," Connor said. "I wouldn't assume that just because they're outnumbered that they'll lose."

"You're right," I replied. "Can you bring up a closer look at one of the Zator warships? Let's see what they've got."

As Connor changed the view to one of the Zator warships, I was taken aback by what I saw. It was massive. Larger than any ship the Federation had. I automatically wondered if the Zator were truly our friends. What if they were only using us to help rid themselves of their enemies? Had those battles in the Zenyan system been the first meeting between the Zator and Jatarians? Everything that I could remember pointed to it being their first exposure to the other race.

I shook my head. I couldn't let my imagination wander toward paranoia. The Zator were our allies. I wished I could speak with Zator Commander Tao. I would feel much better if I could talk to him, but that was quite impossible at the moment. "Are all the Zator warships this size?" I asked.

"No. The Zator have three sizes of ships showing up on the scans. This one is the largest. Let's call it a battleship. They have seventy-five of those. The next size smaller, we will call cruisers.

Here is one of those," Connor said, as he pulled up a view of one of the cruisers.

The cruiser was more along the size of a Federation warship. "How many cruisers do the Zator have?" I asked.

Connor replied, "The Zator have 255 cruisers. The rest are the small attack ships we are used to seeing in the Zenyan system."

Jeffery spoke up then and said, "So perhaps the Zator are more of a threat than we realized."

I turned to Jeffery. "Not if they are our allies."

"They are our allies, until they decide we have something they want," Jeffery replied.

"We have an agreement with them. Perhaps we should strengthen that relationship. They could be very useful to our defense now and in the future," I suggested. "It never hurts to have allies—ones who you can depend on. The Morag might not always come to our rescue, if they are too far away or otherwise detained."

Jeffery nodded. "It is something I will need to think about some more."

That had to be enough for me right now. Everything depended on what we would witness here today. How powerful was this Zator fleet? "So the Jatarians have six hundred ships?" I asked.

"Yes, of varying sizes. None are new. We've seen them all," Connor reported.

"I guess that's something," I replied.

"Why do you think the Zator sent in only a fraction of their fleet?" Jeffery asked.

"Perhaps to size up their opponents," Bryce suggested. "If this is the first meeting of these two species in the Jatarian area of space, there could be a lot of unknowns. Before committing their larger ships, the Zator might be trying to determine the strength of the Jatarians' defenses."

"Look. The Jatarians are sending out the orbs," Connor announced.

I had a sinking feeling. I closed my eyes momentarily. Then I watched as the Zator ships sent out a flurry of weapons fire at the incoming threat. Did the Zator know what those orbs were capable of?

A chain of small explosions across the space between the advancing Zator and the orbs signaled the destruction of a number of the enemy orbs. Would it be enough?

The Zator continued their attempt to ward off the threat by sending a massive amount of firepower toward the orbs. Could the orbs maneuver around the threat? It didn't appear so. More explosions dotted the area. It wouldn't be long before the orbs reached the small task group of Zator ships.

Once in range of the Zator's small attack ships, the orbs began their final mission of destroying their targets. It took multiple hits to take down one of the Zator's small attack ships. Thankfully a large number of orbs had been eliminated before they could do much damage to the task group.

It was fascinating to watch the battle unfold. I wasn't sure what we had witnessed earlier when we saw the flashes of light from far away. Had there been more ships that had already battled?

I waited anxiously for the battle to begin in earnest. What were they waiting on? Did the Zator have backup en route? I prayed they did.

If only the Zator and the Morag would cooperate and work together to destroy the Jatarians, we might really have a chance to win this war.

"What are they waiting on?" Jeffery asked.

"Reinforcements would be my guess," I replied.

"Do you think the Zator have their home system near here?" Jeffery asked.

"No, I don't believe so. If that were the case, I think the Zator would have already destroyed the Jatarians. So the Zator must not occupy the same area of space," I replied.

Jeffery nodded. "That makes sense. So who do you think has reinforcements coming?"

I hadn't thought about that. Did they both have reinforcements coming? I shuddered to think about it.

"The Jatarians have released more orbs," Connor reported.

"Perhaps the Zator are trying to force the Jatarians to deploy all their orbs before they commit their larger warships to the battle," Bryce commented.

"Either way," Jeffery replied, "hopefully we will see Jatarians destroyed here today. However many enemy warships can be destroyed before we face them in the next battle is a good thing," Jeffery added.

The Zator were already launching their strike against the orbs. Small flashes of light signaled their success. How many orbs did the Jatarians have? Wouldn't it be more effective to launch them all simultaneously to ensure more made it through to their target?

We watched as the remaining orbs arrived at their targets and detonated. More Zator small attack ships exploded in small infernos.

"How many do they have left?" I asked.

"The Zator still have thirty-three small attack ships remaining," Connor reported.

"Why don't they attack the front line of the Jatarians' formation?" Jeffery asked.

"I think they're trying to draw out all the orbs," I replied.

"Do you still think they are waiting on reinforcements?" Jeffery asked.

I frowned. "No. The Zator may be trying to draw out all the orbs before they send in the larger warships."

We watched and waited. Who would make the next move? The Zator or the Jatarians? How long would we have to wait to find out? Things seemed to be at a stalemate.

Chapter Nineteen

The stalemate didn't last long. The Jatarians sent in their small attack ships to destroy the remaining smaller Zator ships. How would the ships match up? I hoped the Zator ships in this fleet were more advanced than the ones in the Zenyan system.

I wondered if Zator Commander Tao knew of this attack. Had he tried coordinating a joint operation between the Zator and the Federation? Had the Emperor refused? What would that mean for our future alliance with the Zator?

None of these answers were easy to get, especially not as far away from the Federation as we were. I was thankful for the long distance between this Jatarian stronghold and the Humans of the Federation. The Humans of the Empire, where I grew up, were even farther away.

Jeffery would surely speak further with the Emperor about the Zator. They would be considered a threat now, knowing they had a massive fleet. We did have the ability to use our gift on them, but their language was not an easy one to learn. It was far easier to use the translators and to speak audibly to the Zator of the Federation.

Perhaps I could save the Zator from the destruction I knew the Emperor would want to rain down on them. If I could spin the scenario to Jeffery that it's helpful to have powerful allies, it might work. The Zator can stand between us and any trouble we may face in the future.

A flash of light brought my attention back to the viewscreens. The two fleets of small attack ships had begun their dance of death. It was fascinating to watch them spin and weave and try to gain the upper hand in the dogfight. It was a fight to the death. It was hard to determine which side had the upper hand in terms of maneuverability. Each side seemed very skilled in this area. As for weapons, that too seemed pretty evenly matched. The Jatarians would win this small battle, for they possessed a larger number of ships.

It was hard to keep up with what was happening and who had destroyed the most enemy ships. Debris littered the area. I watched one Zator ship navigate its way through the battle. When it met its end, I found another to watch. Eventually none remained. Round one was over.

"I wish we knew if the Zator did have reinforcements inbound," Bryce commented.

"I can use my gift on the Zator, but I don't think it would do us much good. I do not have a good grasp of their language. I know a few words here and there but not enough to decipher to make any sense," I replied.

"I guess we will have to sit back and continue to watch the show then," Bryce replied.

I did have to admit that it was nice not being hunted for once. The Jatarians hadn't noticeably reacted to our presence. Perhaps they had overlooked our scans due to the Zator fleet's presence here. Either way, it was nice not to be concerned for our safety. Currently we were out of the way of any weapons fire. Yet we were close enough to get a good view of the battle with our viewscreens.

What would happen next, now that the Zator were out of the small attack ships?

We watched and waited for someone to make the next move. Who would it be? The Jatarians didn't seem to be in any hurry either. This led me to believe that they too had reinforcements headed here.

As the minutes ticked by, the Zator began to change their formation. I knew little about battle formations and strategy, so one formation or another wasn't an obvious advantage in my mind. This one reminded me of one that I'd seen the Morag use. A wedge-type formation, with the larger battleships toward the inner formation and the battle cruisers taking up flanking positions around the larger ships.

Once in their desired formation, the Zator advanced toward the Jatarians.

My Command Center went eerily quiet, as we awaited the eruption of the weapons fire from both fleets. We all knew that, any moment now, the screen would be lit up with various colors of deadly weapons.

"Why do they wait to fire? Why not just begin the bombardment now?" Jeffery asked.

"The closer they are, the less time the enemy has to shoot down their incoming firepower. Essentially more firepower makes it to the enemy if they wait until they are a little closer. It gives the Jatarians less time to react and to shoot down the threats," I answered.

"That makes sense. I haven't witnessed very many battles firsthand," Jeffery replied.

"I've seen more than I would like. It's different though when the lives at risk are not Human. Not that they are valued less, but I feel it more when those explosions signify the death of our race as opposed to others," I said. I did feel guilty when those deaths resulted from my meddling with the minds of commanders, like the Morag for instance.

Jeffery nodded. "I'm glad those aren't Human ships. Hopefully between the Zator and the Morag, not much will remain of the Jatarians for us to clean up."

I looked over at Jeffery. His words sounded so cold. I agreed with his sentiment, but his delivery could use some work. A little more compassion could be shown, even if it was only for show.

Had Jeffery changed? Or had he only been playing me all these years? Was he more like his father than I realized?

"It's starting," Connor called out.

My attention returned to the viewscreens just in time to witness the trail of weapons fire headed toward the Jatarians. "They must have reached their optimal weapons range," I commented.

Almost immediately the Jatarians returned fire. Explosions erupted between the two fleets, signaling the success of the weapons' targeting systems. No way to determine which side had targeted the other. Either way, less firepower would reach the other side.

Energy screens began to glow brighter, as the weapons fire impacted them. My gaze shifted from the Zator side of the battle to the Jatarian side. Multiple screens glowed brightly on each side. Who would be the first to lose a larger ship?

The answer came with a brilliant explosion, as one of the Jatarian ships succumbed to the onslaught of firepower hitting it.

I couldn't help but smile. One less enemy ship.

Several large explosions signaled the death of ships on the Zator side of the conflict.

"Connor, can you put up a ship count on one of the viewscreens?" I asked.

"Yes, Captain, right away."

The numbers popped up on the screen. The Zator's ship count showed in green and the Jatarians' in red. So far, not many ships had been eliminated. This would change as time wore on.

I mentally prepared myself for the sensor alarms to sound. One side or the other must have reinforcements nearby. I hoped, when that alarm sounded, more green icons would appear on the tactical display. Yet I knew the Jatarians had more ships not too far away.

As we had no idea the Zator would be here, we had no way to determine how far any reinforcements could have come from or could be coming from.

The battle waged on. The sheer amount of firepower between the two fleets was mind-blowing.

Was this the largest fleet the Zator had? Was this the only fleet the Zator had? I sincerely hoped not. I had no way to find out.

Either way, the damage the Zator would do to the Jatarians today was significant. Even if no reinforcements arrived, the Jatarians would suffer heavy losses today.

The battle seemed pretty even. Losses on both sides mimicked the other. It wasn't obvious that one side was more powerful than the other. The only difference was in the number of ships.

The Zator's large battleships rivaled anything I'd seen regarding size and firepower. Each was heavily armed and well-armored. As of yet, the Zator had not lost a single one. Their losses came from the battle cruisers. It was only a matter of time before the larger warships succumbed to the relentless storm of weapons fire from the enemy.

The Jatarians' small attack ships, what was left of them, now headed toward the frontline of the Zator. Once the Jatarians penetrated that line, the Zator would find them nearly impossible to destroy. Small targets weren't an easy kill, especially not when they were intermixed with your fleet.

The Zator must have realized what the Jatarians had planned. They changed the focus of their firepower to this incoming foe. A wall of weapons fire was sent toward the small attack ships. Multiple explosions resulted. A large number of the ships made it through, only to be met with another wall of firepower.

While the Zator fleet was focused on the threat of the small attack ships, the larger Jatarian ships were taking full advantage of the opportunity to target the larger Zator ships unencumbered.

More and more Zator ships were consumed in giant explosions. The Jatarians now seemed to be targeting the larger battleships of the Zator.

I watched in dismay, as dozens of them were overcome by the intense firepower directed at them.

Now the Jatarians' small attack ships had reached the frontline of the Zator fleet. The Zator would suffer greatly from the cost of allowing those small attack ships into their ranks. I doubted they could do much else to prevent it, however.

The Jatarians' small attack ships began focusing their firepower on the larger Zator battleships, as the main Jatarian fleet focused again on the entire frontline of the Zator. It was easy for the Jatarians' small attack ships to meander through the formation and to pick their target.

Once the target was selected, they all began bombarding it with their weapons. The energy shield began to glow ever brighter, as the small attack ships continued to focus all their weapons fire on one single ship. Suddenly a hole opened up near the rear of the ship, and the enemy's small attack ships quickly capitalized on the opportunity and sent multiple missiles through the hole.

The missiles slammed into the hull of the powerful battleship, causing explosions. It wasn't enough to take down the ship though. It was only a matter of time.

Given the chance, the entire Zator fleet could fall to these small attack ships of the enemy. They were like little bees. Annoying and potentially deadly when they worked together to attack their enemy.

We watched as more and more missiles made their way through the various holes that had opened up in the energy screen. Finally the screen failed altogether, and the missiles detonated against the side of the ship. Explosions began and fanned out all across the ship.

I imagined the panic of the Zator on board, smelling the smoke, seeing sparks and fires throughout the ship, knowing these were their last moments of life, wondering how they would be remembered.

The ship was engulfed in a massive explosion that sent debris flying all around. It was over. At least for those on board the once-massive ship.

The debris impacted the energy screens of neighboring ships and even hit a few of the enemy's small attack ships. A few were eliminated. Unfortunately not enough to matter.

The Jatarian small attack ships picked their next target and repositioned themselves around it.

I imagined how the crew might feel, knowing they were next.

Alarms blared, and red lights flashed.

I shook my head and focused on the tactical display. The moment had arrived. Reinforcements were here. Who would it be? Zator or Jatarian? Would the icons remain red or turn to green?

My gaze shifted from the tactical display to Connor and back again. I practically held my breath, waiting for the answer.

"It's Zator ships, Captain," Connor confirmed excitedly.

The icons began to turn green. They kept appearing on the screen, as more exited hyperspace. How many would there be? Would it be enough to win this battle?

I found myself crossing my fingers, as more appeared on the screen. A smile spread across my face. Hope filled my thoughts. This may turn out to be a good day for Humans after all.

"Another four hundred Zator ships, Captain," Connor reported.

"That'll help," I replied. My attention refocused on the battle between the two fleets still going on. Explosions dotted both sides.

I hoped the Zator had brought more of their smaller ships to challenge the Jatarians' small attack ships. "Any of the smaller Zator ships with the new arrivals?" I asked.

"Yes, about one hundred of them. The Zator have another seventy-five of the large battleships, and the rest are the battle cruisers," Connor reported.

"Fantastic," I replied.

Now the battle would be much more even in terms of ship numbers. It would be a battle to the death. Neither side would have much remaining when this day came to an end.

Unless the Jatarians also have reinforcements coming. Maybe they were too far away. Perhaps the Zator would have the time they needed to annihilate the Jatarians before any help could arrive for them, if luck was on our side.

It didn't take long for the newcomers to join the battle. They jumped in and began their attack. The fighting grew more intense as the firepower ramped up.

The Zator's smaller ships immediately began hunting the Jatarians' small attack ships.

I couldn't help but smile.

With the Zator hot on their tails, the Jatarians' small attack ships stopped their attacks on the larger battleships and focused instead on their new foe. Now that their dance of death was taking place among the Zator fleet, it was even more interesting to watch.

The smaller ships now had plenty of things to swerve around and to use as cover. I found myself watching this part of the battle more than the larger battle. It was very fascinating to study. The maneuverability of these ships was impressive. I wasn't sure how our devastators or strikers would match up.

Was I a good enough pilot to maneuver around this battlefield, while ensuring no one was targeting me, yet targeting an enemy ship myself? I was not confident in my ability to do that. I think that's what drew my attention. These pilots were way more adept at this than I could ever expect to be. The hours of training it would take to even be on the same level intimidated me.

There really was no amount of simulator training that could prepare you for this real live battle situation. Danger was everywhere. You might not even see the opponent targeting you.

Small flashes of light signaled the success of the pilots. Which side of the battle they'd fought for was hard to tell. The only way to tell was by the ship count.

The numbers now dwindled much faster, with more ships in the battle. I was anxious to see if the Zator could pull off this win before any Jatarian reinforcements arrived.

I wondered if the Zator would stay and fight *if* more Jatarian ships arrived. Would they abandon their fight and try again another day? Or were they here to make their stand? I hoped we wouldn't have to find out.

Every enemy ship destroyed was one less that could attack the Federation. Maybe now that the Jatarians had been attacked in their area of space, they would keep more ships closer to home and would leave the Federation out of it altogether, especially since we weren't the ones attacking them. Maybe the Emperor had thought this out more than I had realized.

The battle drew my attention back to the viewscreens and away from my thoughts. Ships all across both frontlines were dying. Debris was strewn about in all directions. Such death and destruction.

I wondered about the planet the Jatarians appeared to be protecting. Did Jatarians live down there? Did a large population call that planet *home*? Were they aware that their fate was even now being decided above the planet?

What would the Zator do to the planet if they succeeded in eliminating all enemy ships? Would they bomb the surface? Or would they be satisfied with the destruction of the fleet alone?

No shipyards nor space stations orbited this planet. I was curious about what the planet held. It was protected by a massive fleet and a minefield. The possibilities were endless. I hoped we'd the chance to figure it out. First things first though, this battle had to end in favor of the Zator.

The viewscreen showed one of the larger Zator battleships. Its energy screen glowed brighter and brighter, as the Jatarians focused the firepower of multiple ships on the stronger Zator ship. The shield would fail. It was only a matter of time.

The battleship put up a good fight, targeting a ship aiming at it. The smaller ship exploded, reducing the number of weapons fire targeting the Zator battleship. It didn't take long for another enemy ship to move up and to take its place.

The Zator battleship took out four enemy ships before succumbing to its wounds. The massive explosion forced me to close my eyes momentarily. "Connor, how many Zator battleships are remaining?"

"Currently 151 Zator battleships are still in the fight," Connor replied.

I smiled. "If it takes four Jatarian ships to destroy one of those, the numbers are on our side."

"Let's hope they all fare that well," Connor replied.

Weapons fire filled the viewscreen. Explosions dotted the area of both fleets. Energy shields glowed, as they worked to dissipate the energy hurled at them. It was a fantastic site to see.

My gaze moved from one thing to another. Space travel was pretty amazing. I never imagined I would witness something like this. On this scale even.

I shook my head and looked over at Jeffery. His attention was focused on the battle playing out on the viewscreens. He seemed entranced by what he saw. Would this make him crave war? Make him to want to see more battles? Had I made the right decision in bringing him along on this mission? I reassured myself that I had. Jeffery had to know what was out here. To see that the galaxy was a much bigger place than the Federation. Jeffery needed the bigger perspective, especially if he was to rule the Federation one day.

I closed my eyes and thought of Amelia. I prayed she was doing well and that she and Theodore were keeping her safe from whomever had been poisoning her. We had no way to know from out here. The last time we tried our gift, even the scout ships were unreachable. Had the Emperor moved them closer to the Federation? If so, why?

I didn't like being in the dark, with no safe way to communicate with our fellow Humans. Only Fritz and the *Explorer* were near enough to communicate with.

I opened my eyes and focused again on the battle. Ships were dying in large numbers. I was relieved that no alarms had sounded again. If only the Zator could finish off this Jatarian enemy fleet quickly.

The ship count constantly changed, as ships on both sides of the battle were destroyed. The small attack ships from both fleets had all but eliminated each other. Only a handful of the Zator small attack ships remained. None of the Jatarian small attack ships were left.

I watched the formations, as each side changed tactics. Was one formation better than another? I didn't think so. I also wasn't in the military, so what did I know?

Would the Jatarians abandon this battle and let this planet fall into the hands of the Zator? I doubted it. No, this would be a battle to the death. The Jatarians would remain until every last one of them was destroyed.

An enormous explosion took my attention. Another of the Zator battleships had been eliminated. From the looks of things, the number of battle cruisers and battleships were almost even. At the beginning of this battle, the battle cruisers had more than double the number of the battleships.

It was too bad the Zator did not have a fleet of battleships. That would be a force to be reckoned with.

The battle continued its deadly dance, and more and more ships disappeared from the tactical display. I constantly watched those ship numbers. Currently the green icons outnumbered the red ones. The tide had turned. The Zator were defeating the Jatarians.

Now that the numbers were uneven, more Jatarian ships were destroyed than Zator ones.

Jeffery said, "I think the Zator will pull this off."

I cringed at his statement. "Don't count it as a win until all the enemy ships are destroyed. At any moment more Jatarian ships could arrive, and the tide could turn again."

"You're right. I was just getting excited," Jeffery replied.

We watched as the once-massive Jatarian fleet dwindled to only a few. When the last remaining enemy ships died their fiery deaths, the Command Center erupted in applause.

"They did it," I said excitedly.

"That they did," Bryce answered. "Now what will they do?"

"Surely they will destroy the planet, right?" Jeffery stated.

I shrugged. "Who knows? That's what the Federation would do. These are Zator. We don't know what drives them or what their policies are."

"Look. They're firing on the minefield," Connor pointed out.

Hundreds of missiles were aimed at the minefield. Once there, the missiles detonated, triggering multiple mines to explode. One after another exploded, making a significant path to the planet, free from any threats.

Now what? Would the Zator take aim at the surface?

Two of the smaller attack ships went through the cleared area of the minefield and onto the planet. They even flew down into the atmosphere.

"I wonder what's down there," Bryce said.

"We might not ever know," I replied.

We watched and we waited. After a couple hours, the ships returned. We then waited to see what would happen next. Would the Zator strike the planet?

"Captain, the Zator are charging their hyperdrives," Connor said.

"Should we follow them?" Bryce asked.

I was torn. I was very curious about where the Zator were going, where their home system was. How far away was it? "No, that's not our mission. Hopefully in our explorations one day, we will see the home system of the Zator. I am confident this will not be the last we see of this fleet," I said.

I watched the viewscreens as the Zator ships entered hyperspace. As the last one left the system, I sat back in my chair. *Now what?* "Let's see what's on the planet's surface. It must not be a military base or anything threatening, or I'm sure the Zator would have eliminated it," I said.

Excitement buzzed around the room. Everyone was curious to see how the Jatarians lived.

We slowly moved the ship through the opening in the minefield and to the planet beyond. From space, only a few things were visible. It was easy to see that the Jatarians had a large population here on this planet.

"Let's enter the atmosphere and get a better view," I said. "We might not get another opportunity like this one."

The *Hunter* moved through the planet's atmosphere. Eventually a city came into view. It was similar to a Human city in that the buildings were built high into the sky. Their building material was unlike anything I'd seen before. I couldn't describe it. It seemed as if mud had been made into buildings. They rose high into the sky, rivaling buildings I'd seen in Korah.

As for their transportation, I saw ships and aircars, similar in design to our own. They seemed well advanced. I don't know why I was surprised since the Jatarians were well advanced in their warships and weaponry.

I saw nothing like a military base or any type of threat. Perhaps this was why the Zator had decided not to bombard the planet. This appeared to be a civilian planet. No threat to the Zator. At least not that could be seen.

After observing our enemy for an hour, we decided it was time to head out. No doubt Jatarian warships were even now closing in on this system.

Although why guard it, if you now know that the Zator won't target the planet? That couldn't be said for the Morag though. They would hit the surface without a second thought. Surely the Jatarians were aware of that.

Perhaps this would take more resources out of the home system. If they reassigned another fleet here, less would be around to defend the home system when the Morag arrived, which would mean a more likely scenario for the Morag to pull off the upset.

We made our way back out of the planet's atmosphere and then out of the area where the minefield was.

"I guess it's time for us to head on to the next system," I said.

Before Bryce confirmed my command, alarms sounded.

All of our attention moved to Connor.

Connor put the tactical display up on the viewscreen again. "Seems the Jatarian reinforcements have arrived."

"A little too late," Jeffery smirked.

"Let's continue to move away from the planet but wait and see how many ships exit hyperspace. Hopefully these ships came from the home system and will weaken the defenses the Jatarians had there," I said.

"Maybe they'll use their resources to hunt down the Zator," Jeffery replied.

"Maybe, but the Zator did spare the planet. So perhaps the Jatarians will keep that in mind," I commented.

"I doubt it," Jeffery responded.

"Captain, the Jatarians have stopped exiting hyperspace," Connor reported.

"How many ships do they have?"

"Six hundred, Captain."

"Wow. They may expect the Zator to return and want to be ready to defeat them this next time," I stated.

"If the Zator do return, they better bring more ships," Jeffery said.

"Can we warn them?" Connor asked.

"I don't think so. They'll know when they scan the system. We don't know this commander, and we have no relationship with these Zator. For all we know, this group of Zator is completely separate from the Zator group we know. This group might not know we have an alliance," I explained.

"I hadn't thought of that," Jeffery replied.

"It's similar to the Human Empire and the Human Federation. They're the same species but have no alliance. One doesn't even know the other exists," I explained.

"True," Jeffery added. "I guess you're right. That's a good analogy too. One we can relate to."

"Let's get out of here," I said. "We have other systems to check."

Once in the safety of hyperspace, I sat back and thought about what we had witnessed. The Jatarians had suffered a significant loss today. How would they react to that? I was afraid we might not like the answer.

Chapter Twenty

The following three systems we passed were clear of any ships. I was beginning to believe that we were headed in the wrong direction, when our luck changed.

"Captain, the long-range scans show over one thousand ships in this system," Connor reported.

I sat forward in my chair. "Must be another core system for the Jatarians."

"Only one way to find out," Bryce joked.

"We will investigate. We need to know. Remember. No scans until our hyperdrive is charged, once we're in the system," I said to Connor.

"Yes, Captain," Connor confirmed.

My mind raced with the possibilities. Chances were, this was another core system of the Jatarians. Yet it could be a Zator fleet preparing for battle though. That's what I was really hoping for.

We exited hyperspace in the far reaches of the system. No planets were visible from our vantage point. No ships could be seen either. We must wait ninety minutes to find out where they were and if they were friend or foe. It would be a tense ninety minutes.

We held our position for fear of setting off a mine or an orb. There was too much risk. We would wait until our hyperdrive was charged. Then we would see what was happening out there.

"I'll go stretch my legs. I'll be back in a few minutes," I said.

Sitting still for the next ninety minutes would be really hard. I might as well move around a little. I could sort through my thoughts and plan for what would come next. Walking always helped me clear my mind and think better.

The ninety minutes passed relatively quickly. I know it helped that I had not sat in my command chair the entire time, just staring at the viewscreens and imagining what could be out there.

"Let's run the scans, Connor," I said, as the countdown clock passed the ninety-minute mark.

We all waited for the results to come in. What was out there?

"Jatarian ships, Captain. Mostly warships, with a few transport vessels in the mix," Connor reported.

"Where are they?" I asked.

"All over the system, with the most activity around the fourth planet and a moon around the fifth planet," Connor replied.

I debated whether we should explore the system more closely or just note the system data and move on. There really was no reason we needed to see things up close. We knew this was a Jatarian fleet. A rather large one. Could the Zator handle this many ships?

"What's our plan?" Bryce asked.

"No need to explore this system further. We know who's here. We don't need to waste any more time here," I said slowly.

"Captain," Connor spoke up, "a group of the Jatarian warships are charging their hyperdrives."

I was alarmed. Had they sensed us? Were they coming to destroy us? "Let's prepare to enter hyperspace," I ordered.

"They're beginning to make their jump," Connor said.

I gripped the side of my chair and held my breath, expecting the ships to surround us. Nothing happened.

"They must be headed to another system," Connor commented.

"Should we follow?" Bryce asked.

"Yes, let's follow. They might lead us to another one of their systems," I said.

We quickly followed the enemy fleet into hyperspace.

"Scans show six hundred ships," Connor said.

"Left in the system or in hyperspace?" I asked for clarification.

"In the system, Captain."

I nodded. Which would mean four hundred had left the system. Based on our direction, these ships weren't headed to any of the systems we'd already explored.

We had no idea how long we would be in hyperspace. It could be hours, or it could be days.

"Let's start our rotations. Augusta, you're up first," I said, as I stood to leave.

Augusta walked over and took my place in the command chair. "Don't worry, Captain. I'll let you know immediately if anything changes," Augusta said, as she gave me a reassuring smile.

"Just remember. No scans once we exit hyperspace," I said.

"Yes, Captain."

I headed to the cafeteria. Now that I was relaxed again, I could use a good meal.

Connor and Jeffery joined me.

"Do you think this Jatarian fleet is headed to attack the Zator?" Jeffery asked.

"It could be or might be headed to another of their core systems. Either way, it'll be interesting, that's for sure," I answered.

"Never a dull moment around here," Connor joked.

"I can't imagine being on the surface and not on these adventures," Jeffery said.

Connor and I exchanged a look of concern, but Connor spoke up first.

"Jeffery, our time on the ship isn't always so exciting. There are a lot of mundane and boring days sometimes. It's not all discoveries, battles, and danger at every turn," Connor commented.

Jeffery replied, "I understand. I know this mission isn't what you guys typically do. I'm along for the ride. I'm glad I am. I've already learned so much."

"I'm sure you miss Eloise and the kids," I said.

"Of course but it is nice to get away. I don't mean that to sound bad. I love my family. It's just nice to have a little break every once in a while."

I nodded. "I can understand that."

Jeffery gave me a puzzled look. "What do you mean?"

"That it's good to get away from home. If I'd never ventured away from my parents, we wouldn't be here now," I replied. I thought I had done a pretty good job of covering myself. I couldn't believe I almost told Jeffery that I had a family.

I looked over at Connor.

He lifted an eyebrow. "I, for one, am glad you decided to leave the Human Empire. You've definitely made my life more interesting, Slade."

We all laughed at that. I was thankful for Connor to help move the talk away from Jeffery's suspicions.

"Do you think we could get the Zator and the Morag to work together to coordinate their next attack?" Connor asked, changing the subject.

I shook my head. "These Zator may have had no interaction with the Morag before. We can't control the Zator with our gift, as we don't have a good grasp of their language. At least I don't. I've always relied on the translator for my conversations with

Zator Commander Tao. We could control the Morag side of
things by suggesting they work together with the Zator, but I'm
not sure how this particular Zator group would react."

"I wish we could get a message to Zator Commander Tao
and see if he knows these Zator. Like you said before, they might
not even know these Zator exist," Connor replied.

"Or perhaps this is their fleet from their homeworld, and
Tao knows everything about them and these attacks," Jeffery
suggested.

"Have you looked for Tao using your gift?" Connor asked
me.

I shook my head. "No. I never thought it might be him out
there. The commander I did find was not Tao."

"He could be out there. You should look next time we run
into that Zator fleet again," Connor said.

"I will do that," I replied. Could Zator Commander Tao be
out here, closer than I'd imagined? And, if so, what were the
implications of that? Would Jeffery feel they were a threat and
report this to his father? Were the Zator a threat to the
Federation? The Zator I had experience with was not a threat.
These Zator might be completely independent of that. It was an
unsettling thought.

What if these Zator planned to expand their territory and
rule more of the galaxy? Even if they were not a threat today,
what about in another one hundred years? I took a deep breath
and slowly let it out. That was a worry for another day.

"What's on your mind, Slade?" Jeffery asked.

"I was just thinking about the Zator and the Morag. Even if
they don't work together, even independently, they could do
significant damage to the Jatarians. Hopefully by the time they're
both done, whatever remnant of the Jatarian warfleets that are
left can be managed by the Federation," I said.

"I wish we could talk to my parents and see how things are going back home. It's so weird not to talk to them whenever I want," Jeffery said.

"It would be nice to know that the Federation is safe and that your mother is well," I agreed. On the other hand, I was glad the Emperor had no idea what was going on out here. By the time he did, it would all be over. One way or another. We didn't need another war after this one with the Jatarians. Perhaps I could persuade Jeffery to keep quiet about the Zator's role in this war.

"I am worried about my mother," Jeffery said.

"I'm sure she's fine," I replied. Of course no way would we hear otherwise. What if something had happened? With Jeffery out of the Federation and out of range of his gift, what would the Emperor do? How would he handle everything? I wouldn't worry about that now. We would mostly likely finish our mission before we heard anything from the Federation.

I did wonder why we could no longer communicate with the scout ships. It either meant they had returned to the Federation or we'd moved too far from their current locations. Why would the Emperor pull the scout ships back to the Federation? This line of thinking wasn't a healthy one. I didn't need more things to worry about and to lose sleep over. It had to be that we had moved too far from the scout ships.

"The Morag and the Zator will have their hands full destroying all these Jatarian warships we've found," Connor stated.

"Let's hope that they can get the job done and that no Human ships have to clean up what's left," Jeffery said.

"Do you think your father would send a fleet all the way out here?" I asked.

"It's doubtful. He would rather send more Morag ships. That way our ships can stay and protect the Federation. We have no business sending them all the way out here. We have the Morag for that," Jeffery replied.

I nodded. That's precisely what I thought he would say. I wondered if Jeffery would make the same decisions if he were in charge. Hopefully by the time that happened, this Great War with the Jatarians would be over with and a distant memory.

After I finished my meal, I headed to my quarters. I had some notes to make on that last system. I wanted to study the maps and then see if I could figure out any pattern to the systems the Jatarians had selected to inhabit.

Bryce joined me, after I'd been at this for over an hour.

"Have you made any grand discoveries?" Bryce asked.

I sighed. "Unfortunately, no, I haven't."

"Let me have a look," Bryce replied.

After reviewing the information for a few minutes, Bryce replied, "I don't see any pattern. What I see is a heavily fortified enemy, with multiple core systems. How many more do they have? If you consider the Human Empire, we had numerous core systems and many others that were a part of the Empire. If the Jatarians resembled that, this war might last much longer than we'd hoped."

"You're right. If we continue following these ships and find even more core systems, it just adds to the list that the Morag must destroy. I don't know that they have the ships for that big of an attack. It could take years."

"What will we do?" Bryce asked.

"First, we keep looking for more systems, while the Morag are en route. Hopefully the Zator will take out a few of the systems in the meantime. Then the Morag will do what they do best when they arrive. They will destroy the enemy. Once that time comes, we will evaluate the situation and what we should do next."

"Any word from the Federation?"

I shook my head. "Both Jeffery and I are out of range of our gift. Even the scout ships are beyond our reach. The only ship we have contact with is the *Explorer*."

"Has the *Explorer* found anything of note since we rescued them from that moon?"

"The last time I checked in with Fritz, they had discovered two systems with a few ships and one major system," I replied.

Bryce rested his head in his hands for a moment. "The Jatarians are much more powerful than we had realized. We need a larger Morag offensive."

"I am out of range of any more Morag fleets. I've sent as many as I could in this direction. I've shared what I know with Morag Admiral Wyn. Hopefully he has called in reinforcements."

"I guess we will find out eventually."

"We may be here a while," I replied.

"We did expect this mission to be a long one," Bryce commented.

I agreed. We had warned Jeffery of that exact thing. We never knew how long a mission like this could last. It could be weeks, months, or even years. My heart ached at the thought of not seeing Hadassah and my children for years.

"With the Zator and the Morag both fighting the Jatarians and in different systems, perhaps they will make faster progress than we anticipate," I said.

"I hope you're right," Bryce said.

"I also hope the Zator have more ships. They lost a significant amount in that last battle."

"Could you use your gift to check?" Bryce asked.

"I don't think so. I'm not proficient in their language. I only know a few words. I might make out a few things but not enough to make sense out of."

Bryce nodded. "Do you think the Morag would bring in help from the other races of the Confederation that they rule?"

I thought over that idea for a few minutes. "I doubt it. But, if the Morag feel the threat is warranted and more than they can handle, they might. The big question would be if they believe they needed help. Knowing the Morag as I do, I would venture to guess the Morag would believe they could handle it. Asking for help is not something they do."

"I was afraid you would say that. With the combined effort of the Seven Great Races of the Confederation, the Morag could easily destroy the Jatarians."

"I don't see that happening," I replied sadly. "A new enemy to the Confederation might keep them busy and away from the Human Empire for a while longer."

Thinking of the Human Empire had my thoughts wandering to Charlotte. I hoped she was well and safe. She and Mathew would have a great life in the Empire, away from the political dangers that they would face here in the Federation. I wondered if Mathew even remembered Amelia.

"You're thinking of Charlotte, aren't you?" Bryce asked.

"Yes, I am."

Bryce smiled. "I'm sure she and Mathew are doing well."

"I hope so. I'm not certain though that I've done a great job protecting Phoebe, like I'd promised Charlotte."

"Only so much you can do, Slade. Phoebe is safe for now. At least until Jeffery takes over, and you've offered to give her a new home when that time comes. I would say you've done an excellent job of looking out for Phoebe, given the circumstances," Bryce replied.

"I guess you're right. Not much I can do right now, besides eliminating the threat the Jatarians pose."

"Exactly. We can worry about Phoebe later. She's safe, as long as Amelia is alive, and Jeffery is with us."

I nodded. Bryce was right. Phoebe was a worry for another day.

"You might want to get some sleep while you can," Bryce commented, as he stood to leave my office. "No telling how much longer we will remain in hyperspace."

"You're right," I agreed, glancing at my watch. "My shift will start in a few hours."

"Don't worry. We will wake you up if needed."

I laughed. "I'm pretty easy to wake up."

Bryce got a good laugh out of that. "Quite the contrary, based on the number of times I've pounded on your door to wake you up."

We both laughed as Bryce headed for the door.

"Thanks, Bryce."

"Get some sleep," Bryce replied.

After Bryce left, I looked around my office. I needed to sleep while I could. Other than following the Jatarian fleet, not much more I could do until we exited hyperspace.

I moved to my quarters and laid down to rest. I hoped I could calm my mind enough to relax. Various thoughts and worries kept coming to mind. I did my best to dismiss them but to no avail.

I must have dozed off at some point because I woke suddenly to alarms blaring. I shook my head and jumped up. I ran through my office to the Command Center.

"What's going on?" I asked, still trying to fully wake myself up.

Connor replied, "We've exited hyperspace with the Jatarian fleet. The sensor alarms triggered, once we exited hyperspace."

"Did you do any scans?" I asked worriedly.

"No, none. But we can easily see the Jatarian ships on our screens," Connor said, as he pointed to the viewscreens at the front of the room.

A cold shiver ran down my back. We were very close to the Jatarian fleet. Too close. My heart beat rapidly in my chest. I felt the sweat beads forming on my brow.

Connor stood from the command chair, where he'd been performing the captain duties while I slept, and moved to his station.

I took my spot at the command console. I looked at all the viewscreens. The Jatarian fleet was very close. Should we use our sublight drive to distance ourselves from our enemy? Or should we remain in our current position and try not to bring any attention our way?

"Cole, how's our stealthed capabilities?" I asked.

"They're online, as is our energy screen."

"Shall we put some distance between us and the Jatarian ships, Captain?" Bryce asked.

"Yes, we should. If we plan to do any scans once our hyperdrive is charged, we need more distance between us," I replied.

Bryce nodded.

I felt the ship begin to move. I watched for any reaction from the massive warships surrounding us. We were safe as long as we didn't use our systems to scan the area. That's how the Jatarians figured out we were in the system. At least that's what we had assumed. I hoped we were right.

It was a little intimidating, being amid a Jatarian warfleet of four hundred ships. I was also well aware that this might not be the only fleet in the system.

Why had the Jatarian fleet exited hyperspace in this particular system? Was this another one of the Jatarian core systems? Was this a Zator system? Were Zator ships here?

One thing was for sure. I didn't want our ship to get caught in the crossfire if Zator ships *were* here. I would feel much better once we were well clear of this enemy fleet. "Is the Jatarian fleet moving toward the inner system?" I asked.

"It appears they are stationary," Connor replied.

Was this only a pit stop? Is that why the Jatarian fleet remained in the outskirts of the system and did not move inward? Or were they waiting for the Zator to make the first move? It was hard not knowing what else was out there, *who* else was out there.

I hoped the Jatarians would not launch their orbs. If they did, we would be in serious trouble. I swallowed and took a deep breath. So far, so good. The Jatarians had made no moves since we'd arrived here. If only that would continue, I would be happy.

We watched the Jatarian fleet slowly became smaller on the viewscreens, as we moved farther and farther away. Time seemed to drag on, while we impatiently waited for our hyperdrive to charge.

The Jatarian fleet continued to hold their position. As time progressed, I was more convinced that no threats to the Jatarians were in this system. I would assume that, if there were, the Jatarians would have already attacked. This strengthened my belief that this was yet another core system of the Jatarians.

Once I could see the entire Jatarian fleet on the viewscreens, I felt some weight lift off my shoulders. The farther away we got, the better I felt.

When at last our hyperdrive was charged, Connor asked, "Captain, are we ready to run the scans?"

Were we far enough away? What if the Jatarians realized we were here and sent out the orbs as soon as we exited hyperspace in the next system? We couldn't risk it. "Let's wait and see what the Jatarians do next. Their hyperdrives should be charged by now. Let me know if it looks like they're going to jump."

We watched and we waited. My curiosity was beginning to get the best of me. I wanted to know what was in the system. I had to know. "Connor, did we scan the system before we exited?" I asked.

"Yes, two hundred ships showed on the scan. I made a note of it. Of course no way to tell whose ships they are, not unless we do a scan in the system," Connor replied.

"They must be Jatarian. If they were Zator, surely the battle would have already begun by now. Especially since the Jatarians would have the numbers advantage," I said.

"Captain, it appears the Jatarian fleet we followed here is preparing to jump," Connor said.

"Run the scans quickly. Then let's continue to follow this fleet and see where they lead us next," I ordered.

I watched the screen as the Jatarian ships began to enter hyperspace.

"Scans complete," Connor said a few minutes later.

"Okay, let's follow those ships," I said.

A moment later I felt the familiar twinge in the pit of my stomach as we entered hyperspace. "So what did the scans show?" I asked.

"The two hundred ships in the system were Jatarian ships. They were spread out around the middle of the system," Connor confirmed.

"Just as we thought," I said.

"I just ran another set of scans since we left the system. Three hundred ships are now in the system," Connor said, puzzled.

"So the Jatarians left part of their fleet back there. Now only three hundred are in the fleet we are following," I said.

"Why would the Jatarians leave some behind?" Jeffery asked.

"Perhaps to bolster the number of ships in the system. Maybe they are expecting an attack and are, therefore, redistributing some of their fleet numbers," I explained.

"That would make sense," Jeffery replied.

I sighed. We'd found yet another Jatarian-inhabited system. Where were we headed now? To yet another one? What would we find there? How many more Jatarian-inhabited systems were there? I would have my answers in due time. For now though my crew must get some much-needed rest.

As for me, it was my shift to be on duty in my favorite part of the ship. Right here in the Command Center.

Chapter Twenty-One

Two days passed as we followed the remaining Jatarian fleet through hyperspace. So many thoughts drifted through my mind. Plus worry and speculation on what we would face once we did exit hyperspace. Would we get lucky this next time and remain undetected? Or had the Jatarian fleet realized we had been with them in the last system, when we did our scans as we left it? This was the thought that cost me the most sleep.

If the Jatarians released their orbs upon exit from hyperspace, we would be in trouble. We would be stuck in the system for the ninety minutes it would take to charge our hyperdrive. Without the option of scanning the system, we would basically be blind to what the Jatarians were doing.

I was on my shift when Connor said, "Captain, the Jatarians are exiting hyperspace."

"Scan the system and see what's there," I ordered. I bit my lip as I waited for the scans to come in. What would they show?

"Scans show two hundred ships in the system," Connor answered.

"Let's exit with the Jatarian fleet and see what we've got. Remember no scans once we exit hyperspace," I said.

Connor confirmed, and then shortly I felt that familiar feeling as we exited hyperspace. My gaze immediately went to the viewscreens. What could we see from our vantage point?

Thankfully this time the entire Jatarian fleet was in view. We hadn't exited in the middle of their formation, like last time.

"Let's put more distance between us and our enemy," I ordered.

The ship moved slowly away from the enemy fleet.

"So, if two hundred ships were already in the system and now an additional three hundred just exited from hyperspace, that would give the Jatarians five hundred ships in the system," I reasoned out.

"As long as that first two hundred were, indeed, Jatarian ships," Connor replied.

"If not, I think we will learn that soon enough," Bryce added. "I doubt the Zator would allow this fleet to sit out here unchallenged in their system for very long."

"Unless the Zator are waiting for reinforcements," Connor responded.

I absorbed everything being said, while I studied the viewscreen. Did this Jatarian fleet exit hyperspace here because they had sensed a large fleet that shouldn't have been here? The Zator, perhaps?

"Captain, the Jatarians are preparing to jump," Connor said.

"Well, they can't jump far without fully charging their hyperdrives. They must be moving toward the other fleet in the system," I said.

I watched the viewscreen as the Jatarian ships entered hyperspace. Without scanning the system, we wouldn't know where they ended up. Should I tell Connor to scan the system?

"Shall I see where they ended up?" Connor asked.

"No. I will use my gift to see if any Zator are in the system," I said.

I closed my eyes and focused on my gift. It didn't take long for me to find the Zator. They were nearby but not yet in the system. I searched for more Zator nearby but found none already in the system.

"It's not the Zator, but they aren't far away," I told the command crew.

"Do you think the Jatarians had a warning that the Zator would soon strike, and this is why this extra Jatarian fleet came to enhance the fleet stationed here?" Jeffery asked.

"I'm not sure how they would get a warning, unless they were somehow monitoring the Zator's communications," I replied. "Graham, have you intercepted any Zator communications?"

Graham shook his head. "I haven't."

"Maybe it's just luck then," Connor added.

"Could you tell how far away the Zator were?" Bryce asked.

"No, only that they weren't far."

"Maybe they won't exit hyperspace here if they'll be outnumbered," Jeffery commented.

"I wouldn't if I were them and didn't have the numbers advantage," I said.

We all watched and waited. Now that the Jatarian fleet had moved toward the inner system, nothing of interest was visible on the viewscreens. At least not yet.

I hoped that we could get a good amount of charging time on our hyperdrive before the Zator arrived, if the Zator even arrived at all. If they didn't have a larger fleet than what the Jatarian had gathered here, the Zator would likely keep on going. Why face an enemy that outnumbered you?

Twenty minutes passed, and then suddenly alarms rang out.

I wasn't alarmed in the least. I knew who it was, the Zator. And, since the Zator had exited hyperspace, it could only mean one thing. The Zator had over five hundred ships.

The viewscreen showed the Zator fleet. It was massive and not far from our location.

"Shall I run scans, Captain? The arrival of our allies might mask our presence," Connor said.

"Yes, run the scans. The Jatarians will have bigger problems than us on their hands," I replied.

Connor reported, "The scans show 578 Zator ships. The Jatarians stand at 511 ships. The Jatarians are currently nearest the fifth planet."

"It seems we will see a battle today," I told Jeffery.

"Any Jatarian ships destroyed are one less that can threaten the Human Federation later," Jeffery replied.

I nodded. With the ship counts so close, it would be a tough battle. I was confident that the Zator would pull through, but it would cost them significantly.

"The Jatarians are preparing to jump," Connor said.

"Cole, are our shields up?" I asked.

"Yes, Captain."

"We need to move farther from the Zator fleet. We don't want to accidentally get caught in the crossfire," I said.

We headed toward the nearest moon and away from the Zator.

The viewscreen showed the Jatarian fleet as it emerged from its microjump. Immediately shots were fired.

Weapons fire was targeted and destroyed before it hit its mark. The Zator were prepared.

The Zator couldn't destroy all the weapons fire aimed at them. Eventually some began to get through and struck the energy shields of their targets. The energy crawled across the screens, creating brilliant fingers of light.

Explosions began to rattle the front lines of both fleets. Debris was flung in all directions.

I sat forward in my chair, as the battle heated up. This was slated to be another fight to the death. Both fleets would pay dearly for the win today. I expected the Zator to win out with superior numbers, but reinforcements could arrive at any time for either side.

By now, we were well out of harm's way. We need only watch the battle unfold before us.

"The sensors show that the Jatarians are releasing their orbs," Connor called out.

I sucked in a quick breath of air. The orbs could be a game changer if enough of them could penetrate the Zator lines and could coordinate an attack.

Thankfully the Zator had experience with this weapon of the Jatarians and focused their firepower into one large wall of death and destruction.

A few hundred orbs survived the attempt and made their way toward the Zator front line. The Zator continued to try to stop the orbs from reaching their formation but to no avail.

Once the orbs reached the middle of the Zator formation, they formed into small groups and surrounded their prey. Soon explosions erupted as the orbs detonated themselves simultaneously. This coordinated attack was successful in destroying over thirty Zator ships.

It had me wondering yet again if these orbs were controlled by a Jatarian or a computer system. Could we somehow create something similar for protection at our own systems back home?

If someday we faced an enemy of large numbers, it would be nice to have various ways of defending ourselves. I was confident that, with enough information, Alex could make almost anything.

"The Jatarians are launching their small attack ships from their carriers," Connor reported.

I enjoyed watching the small attack ships duke it out. A lot more skill went into that fight than in any with the larger ships.

I picked out one of the Zator's small attack ships to keep my eye on through the battle. I watched as it made its way toward the enemy, all the while avoiding the weapons fire from the larger ships. Once within range of its foe, the real duel began.

The ship spun and dove, trying to avoid being hit by enemy weapons fire. It found a target of its own and locked on. Two small missiles fired from its weapons tubes and headed for an enemy target. A small explosion confirmed that the hit was successful.

With one target down, the small Zator ship quickly found another. I watched as it maneuvered around the fleets and weapons fire to eliminate its targets. Its luck would eventually run out, and, when it did, I was sad. Such talent was not easy to come by. I was sure of that. In total, that one ship had eliminated six of the Jatarian's small attack ships. A job well done. Now, if only the rest of the ships in the fleet could have that large of a kill number, then this battle would go our way.

The larger ships continued to slug it out. When one was consumed in a large explosion, another ship would move forward and take its spot.

"Do you think the Jatarians will stick out the fight, once they realize they will not win?" Jeffery asked. "The Jatarians know from the last system that the Zator will not attack the planet. So at what point do you cut your losses and run?"

"You do make an excellent point, Jeffery," I said. "The Jatarian ships we followed would be unable to leave, as their hyperdrives wouldn't be charged yet. The only fleet in this system that can leave was the original two hundred that were here before we arrived."

"Good point. How much longer until our hyperdrive is charged?" Jeffery asked.

Cole replied, "We're about halfway done, so we've got another forty-five minutes."

"The Jatarian fleet microjumped to the inner system and back again, so they would take a bit longer than us to charge their hyperdrives," I said.

The battle continued in full force, but I did wonder if the Jatarians would consider retreating from the battle, especially once they realized their fight was futile.

Connor had put the ship count up on the screen. The Zator had the advantage by eighty-three ships.

It had me wondering if perhaps this battle would last long enough for the Jatarians to abandon the system. Would they do that? I just couldn't comprehend that possibility.

How many more ships did the Zator have? How close were more reinforcements? I hoped there were plenty more where this fleet came from. We would need them.

A large explosion engulfed one of the larger Zator battleships. I imagined how deafening that explosion would be if it were on the surface.

More ships succumbed to the bombardment of the enemy. The ship numbers were falling quickly. The Zator were focused on their mission. It's almost like they knew they only had a small window of time before the Jatarians would have reinforcements arriving.

"Do you think the Jatarians have more ships en route?" Jeffery asked.

"If they did, I would have thought they would have stalled for time before engaging the Zator. The Jatarians are the ones who initiated this battle, right when the Zator arrived. I bet the Jatarians wish they hadn't left part of their fleet in that last system. If they hadn't left so many ships behind, this battle might not turn out as we hoped. So my best guess is that no one else is coming," I explained.

Jeffery nodded. "That makes sense. This Zator fleet is pretty potent. I hope this sect of the Zator realizes they have an agreement with the Federation and that we are allies."

"It is something we should speak with Zator Commander Tao about. It could be that Tao's group is separate from the one we see here. Or they could all be part of the same," I said.

"Do you think this Commander Tao would tell you the truth?" Jeffery asked.

I considered Jeffery's question for a few moments. "I can see why Tao might hesitate. If he informed us that his group has no relationship with this group, the Federation might decide the Zator are not our friends. At least not this particular sect here. So I can see Tao wanting to protect his people. On the other hand, he may trust me enough to tell me. We've seen many battles together."

"I'll be interested to see what this Commander Tao has to say," Jeffery replied.

I would be too. I also hoped, when I had the opportunity to speak with Tao, that Jeffery wasn't around. I wasn't sure that was possible though.

I took the opportunity to close my eyes and to reach out to the Zator with my gift. I wanted to ensure Tao wasn't with them. I was slightly relieved when I didn't find him. If I had found Tao, I couldn't talk to him with my gift, not with the translation difficulties regarding his language. Therefore, I would be forced to speak audibly with him, using the translator, which meant Jeffery might hear both sides of our conversation. This was one discussion I would like to keep more private than that.

Jeffery was watching me when I opened my eyes. "What did you figure out?"

"I didn't find Zator Commander Tao. He is not with this fleet," I replied.

I returned my attention to the battle. I was relieved no Human lives were at stake here. I rather enjoyed these battles that were out of the Federation. Knowing no Human lives would be lost here today made watching this battle much more enjoyable.

It was not lost on me though that thousands of Zator and Jatarians were losing their lives here today. The Zator were our allies. We needed them and their numbers to help the Morag eliminate this threat.

The explosions continued to spread across both formations, as energy screens failed due to the intense energy directed at them.

"I'm sure glad I chose to be an explorer and not in the military," I said, as yet another ship was engulfed in an explosion.

Everyone else nodded in agreement.

Captain Parker noted, "Space is a very dangerous place, Slade—whether you're on a military ship or a civilian ship."

"Yes, I've had my fair share of adventure and danger. Still I haven't experienced anything like that," I replied, pointing at the viewscreen in the front of the room.

"Remember when the Jatarians fired on the *Explorer*?" Bryce asked.

"I remember like it was yesterday. I thought we wouldn't make it out of there alive. That was definitely a close call," I replied.

Parker said, "Thanks for letting me tag along and experience these adventures with you and your crew. I never imagined I would witness something like this."

"Hopefully, very soon, this will be a thing of the past, and our children will never see something like this," Jeffery said. "I want the Federation to be a safe place, like when I was growing up."

I bit my tongue and refrained from mentioning the fact that Jeffery's own brother had to worry about his sibling getting rid of him. Jeffery's own mother sent his baby brother to live in the Empire to get away from Jeffery. Not exactly how I want my kids to grow up.

Parker added, "A future free of the threat of the Jatarians does sound good, although we may never know who the Jatarians might be keeping in check by their actions. Once the Jatarians are defeated, another race could rise up and become a threat. We must always remain vigilant and not grow complacent," Parker stated.

Parker had voiced something that I'd thought about often. How had the Jatarians gotten so much war experience? Perhaps they had another enemy besides the ones I knew of? What if we eliminated the Jatarians? Would it open the way for an even worse enemy?

Jeffery replied, "One good thing about the Jatarians is, they have lessened the political turmoil we had between the loyalists and the rebels, at least from what I've heard. My father has been more focused on defeating the Jatarians than on his paranoia that the rebels are planning an attack." Jeffery looked around the room carefully.

I knew that Jeffery tried his best to refrain from reminding people who he was and who his father was.

I reminded him, "I can assure you, Jeffery, that the so-called rebels have no plan to attack the Federation. They are just refugees, trying to live out their lives in peace. A few bad apples might be among us, but, for the most part, everyone is peaceful."

Jeffery nodded. "Yes, I've seen that firsthand. I'm really glad you rescued me from Tyrus before the plot to kill me was carried out. I've thoroughly enjoyed my time among the refugees."

I felt slightly uncomfortable about the mention of the plot to kill him that I had fabricated to make Jeffery think I was saving him instead of abducting him.

A large explosion drew our attention to the battle still playing out on the viewscreens. Sometimes it was hard to imagine that the battle was really taking place and not just some movie on the screen.

I checked the ship counts. The Zator were pulling even farther ahead. They now had over one hundred ships more than the Jatarians.

"How much longer until our hyperdrive is charged?" I asked Cole.

"Half an hour, Captain," Cole answered.

The Jatarians couldn't leave the system yet. They were stuck here. At least part of the fleet.

We watched as the energy screens for both Jatarians and Zator alike grew tired of all the pounding they were receiving. I was thankful our energy shield was not being hit by weapons fire.

The Jatarian energy shields grew brighter with each subsequent hit. We all knew what was coming. With enough energy hitting it, the screen would ultimately fail, leaving the ship exposed to a certain death. We had watched this scene unfold time and time again.

"Do you think the Jatarian ships will leave?" Jeffery asked.

"No, I don't," I answered. "They'll stay and fight until the very end. I wouldn't be surprised if the leader of this fleet leaves before he's destroyed though. That's what the Morag would do."

"Speaking of the Morag, how close are they to the Jatarian home system?" Connor asked.

"After this battle I will check in with them and see," I replied.

"Will we have the time to return there to watch the battle unfold?" Connor asked curiously.

"I don't think any Jatarian ships will be left in this system for us to follow when this battle ends. We will check the timing of everything and see what our plans will be next," I said.

I tried to remember how far from the Jatarian home system we were. It was at least five days hyperspace travel.

I also needed to check in with Fritz and warn him. He must keep the *Explorer* far from these systems. If something malfunctioned, it wouldn't be wise to be near these systems, especially in the middle of a battle.

The viewscreens showed the carnage that this battle had created. Pieces of debris floated all over the area. Some hit nearby ships, momentarily causing a small flash in the energy screens.

I wondered what it would feel like to fight in a battle where you would not survive. For facing certain death was the fate of most of the ships here today and their crews. Would I be so brave?

I swallowed the lump rising in my throat. I hoped to never find out how I would react to that particular situation. We would defeat this enemy, and then the Morag would watch and ensure that the Jatarians never rose up again. The Morag were good at that.

With the battle still raging outside, I wondered how many of these battles we would see. With both the Zator and the Morag soon attacking targets in the Jatarian-held space, we would no doubt miss some of the action.

I couldn't influence or affect the outcome of the battles the Zator fought in. I could possibly help the Morag though. So that's where we needed to head next. If there was even a chance I might see something that could help influence the battle in the Morag's favor, that was something I *had* to do. However, first this battle had to wrap up.

The weapons fire between the two fleets was quite a sight to see. So beautiful yet so deadly. Deliverers of death, that's what it was.

Each fleet was suffering from the loss of their numbers. The fighting slowly lost its intensity as more ships were destroyed. Yet the battle continued, and the Zator continued to gain an upper hand in the numbers. With that came more ships to target the dwindling enemy ships.

Before the Jatarians had time to finish charging their hyperdrives, their fleet was destroyed. No Jatarian ships escaped the system, not even that of the leader.

"Now what?" Jeffery asked, as the last remaining Jatarian ship was eliminated.

"Now we wait and see what the Zator will do. Will they send ships to the surface again to identify any targets to be destroyed?"

Connor announced, "The Zator are charging their hyperdrives."

"Are they leaving? Or just moving closer to the inhabited planet?" Bryce asked.

"I would say the planet," Connor replied.

We watched and we waited. The Zator ships entered hyperspace and then shortly exited near the planet.

"Shall we move closer too?" Bryce asked. "It would be nice to know what the Zator do here."

"I agree. Let's follow them to the inhabited planet."

A few minutes later, we emerged from our microjump near the Jatarians' inhabited planet. The Zator were already sending their smaller ships to investigate the surface.

Alarms sounded, signaling a new threat had arrived. "What is it?" I asked Connor.

"Orbs are launching from the planet," Connor replied.

"Move us farther back," I said. I didn't want an orb to find us.

The orbs headed straight for the Zator fleet. The Zator fleet immediately opened fire on the incoming threat. The Zator didn't have much time to react. They had already moved into a close orbit around the planet.

Many orbs were destroyed by the defensive fire of the Zator fleet, but enough made it through to eliminate another thirty-nine ships.

The Zator in turn bombarded the surface of the planet. I'm not sure if it's because of what the smaller ships had found there or in retaliation for the orb attack.

After the firing stopped, thirty-nine mushroom clouds rose from the planet's surface. "Those thirty-nine bombs were clearly a retaliation for the thirty-nine ships the Zator lost in the orb attack," I said.

"Perhaps the Jatarians also had a military base or two down there. The orbs must have launched from some type of military installation," Bryce replied.

"That's true. Either way, the Zator exacted some revenge today," I added.

"And the Zator eliminated over five hundred enemy ships," Jeffery commented.

"All in all, I would say it was a pretty good day," I said.

"What's next for us?" Bryce asked. "Do we follow this Zator fleet to their next destination, or do we return to the Jatarian home system?"

"We have a few more days before we return to the Jatarian home system, so we can assist the Morag, as needed. Meanwhile, we will follow the Zator fleet and see where they go next. We must pay close attention to our timetable though, so we don't miss the massive battle between the Morag and Jatarians in their home system," I answered.

"Captain, the Zator are preparing to make their jump into hyperspace," Connor said.

"Let's follow them," I said.

I watched as the Zator fleet entered hyperspace. We followed shortly behind. Where we were headed, I had no idea. I only knew we were going in the direction we'd been before, which provided more Jatarian systems for the Zator to target.

Whatever the Zator had in store for the Jatarians, we would be there to watch.

Chapter Twenty-Two

I woke from my dreams with a start. We had just exited hyperspace. I jumped, straightened myself up quickly, and ran to the Command Center. "What's going on?" I asked, as I burst into the room.

Augusta was in my command chair, as it was her shift in charge. "Captain," Augusta said, standing to move, "the Zator exited hyperspace, so we followed suit."

"What did the long-range scans of the system show?" I asked, as I took my seat.

"No ships in the system, Captain," Augusta replied.

I breathed a sigh of relief. It didn't take long for the rest of the crew to arrive. They'd all felt the ship exit hyperspace too.

The Zator ships were prominent on our viewscreens at the front of the room.

"Why do you think the Zator stopped here?" Jeffery asked.

"Likely to make repairs on their ships," Bryce answered.

"They could also be planning to rendezvous with another Zator fleet, before they attack their next target," I suggested.

"Let's hope that's it," Jeffery replied.

We watched and waited. We weren't in any danger. At least that's how we felt. What would the Zator do if they knew we were here? What if they *did* know we were here? We hadn't run any scans, as there was no need. We had nothing to worry about, with no other ships in the system.

Three hours later, our sensor alarms sounded, and the red warning lights began to flash. I sat forward in my chair. Had a Jatarian fleet happened by the system and sensed the large fleet here? Had they come to destroy them?

I watched the tactical display intently, as the new ships were identified. I breathed a sigh of relief when the icons on the tactical display turned green.

"More Zator ships," Connor confirmed.

"How many?" I asked. I hoped it would be a significant amount.

"Three hundred new ships, Captain."

"Great. I would feel better with even more, but I guess that will have to do."

"What if these ships are from Commander Tao's group?" Bryce remarked.

"I'll see if I can find him." I was still doubtful that the two Zator groups even knew of each other. I closed my eyes and focused on my gift. I reached out in the system to see if Zator Commander Tao was there. I couldn't find him, however.

I opened my eyes and shook my head. "No sign of Commander Tao."

"Now I guess we wait for the newcomers to charge their hyperdrives. Surely then we will be underway to our next Jatarian target system," Jeffery said.

"I would imagine you're correct, Jeffery," I replied.

Half an hour later our sensor alarms sounded yet again. I stood up and moved closer to the viewscreen. Was this more Zator ships?

I watched the tactical display intently and waited for the icons to turn green. When they did, I breathed another sigh of relief.

"Captain, another two hundred Zator ships have arrived," Connor reported.

"Wow, they're amassing quite the fleet," I said.

"Now we wait for these guys to charge their hyperdrives." Jeffery sighed.

"Remember, Jeffery. Not all space travel is action-packed. We go through some mundane and boring times."

"Yes, I know. I'm just ready to get underway and on to the next battle," Jeffery replied.

I was too. I was ready to end the Jatarian threat once and for all. Then I could return to my family. I didn't like being cut off from them. I knew they would be worried. We had discussed that my gift might not be strong enough to reach them, but knowing it was a possibility and having it actually happen were two very different things.

After getting a proper breakfast and walking around the ship for a few minutes, I returned to my post. It had almost been enough time for the newest Zator ships to have fully recharged their hyperdrives. "Did I miss anything?" I asked, as I returned.

"Not a thing," Connor replied.

"How much longer do we expect they have left?" I asked.

"About five minutes," Bryce replied.

I enjoyed the view for the last few minutes, while contemplating Jeffery and what he could learn from this moment. The viewscreens showed the Zator fleet in its entirety. "They are impressive. I am glad this fleet fought against the Jatarians and not with them. The Zator were definitely a powerful ally to have. Jeffery, I believe it would do the Federation good to cultivate this friendship in the future. We definitely want the Zator on our side and not against us."

Jeffery frowned, as if considering it.

I thought I could make a case for the continued friendship with both categories of the Zator. "We could in time learn their language. Therefore, I could use my gift on the Zator, if I had a better understanding of their language. It could be a language taught in flight school."

"Captain, the Zator are preparing to enter hyperspace," Connor observed.

"Let's follow them," I replied. "I would guess they are headed to one of the Jatarian systems we've been to."

The twinge in my stomach signaled our jump into hyperspace. I sat back and relaxed. We were safe, for now. "How far are we from the systems we visited before?" I asked Bryce.

"Not far from the one where we followed the Jatarian fleet, and they left behind two hundred ships. I estimate we are about six hours from there," Bryce answered.

I nodded. "Good. I guess that'll be the Zator's next target."

"The Zator have many Jatarian systems they've got to fight through before this is all said and done," Bryce replied.

"They've got their work cut out for them. Hopefully, once the Morag arrive, and they're both hitting Jatarian systems, this will progress faster," I said.

Connor nodded. "The Zator hitting these systems before the Morag's arrival might help pull more Jatarian ships out of their home system. The Jatarians might redistribute their fleets to cut off this attack before it gets to their home system," Connor remarked.

"*If* that's their home system," I pointed out. "Still we can only hope. We have no idea how many ships the Jatarians have—or the Zator for that matter. We will definitely witness some epic battles in the near future," I replied.

Jeffery added, "I'm so glad I get to see this."

"We all need to get a little rest before we exit hyperspace. I want everyone well rested for the battle," I said.

I encouraged everyone to take time to rest and eat, and we all returned refreshed to our posts in the Command Center. It was almost time for the Zator to reach the system we expected them to attack.

"I'm running the scans now," Connor said, as we came in range of our long-range sensors.

It was hard to guess how many Jatarian ships might now be in the system. When we had left there, the Jatarians had six hundred ships. How many they may have now was anyone's guess.

"Scans show seven hundred ships in the system," Connor said, amazed.

"I guess they've redistributed ships again," I replied.

"Do you think some of those could be their small attack ships?" Jeffery asked. "Perhaps they're using their smaller ships to inflate their ship count. It might make the Zator second-guess their decision to target this system."

"It could be. Not a bad idea. I hope the Zator aren't intimidated by the ship count," I replied.

"We will know soon enough," Connor replied. "I'm running my scans again. If the Zator are exiting hyperspace, it should show on my scans."

We all waited in anticipation. Was another battle soon at hand?

"Captain, the Zator are exiting hyperspace," Connor reported.

"Let's follow them. Don't run any scans until I tell you. Our scans should be masked by the Zator's activities, but hold off until I give the order."

I felt our ship exit hyperspace. I immediately stood and moved toward the viewscreens. The Zator fleet was prominent on the viewscreens. I couldn't help but wonder what the Jatarians were thinking.

With our position behind the Zator fleet, I felt safe enough to run our scans. I wanted to know what the Zator would be up against.

"I show a few Jatarian ships preparing to leave the system," Connor reported.

"Why would they do that?" Jeffery asked me.

"Probably some civilian ships and transport vessels. They don't want to get caught in the crossfire. If they can leave, they will," I replied.

"You are correct, Captain. No warships left, only civilian ships," Connor stated.

"Are there any mines or orbs in the area?" I asked.

"No, Captain. The scans show a minefield nearer to the sixth planet. The Jatarians have ships on the opposite side of the minefield. It appears that the mines are spaced farther apart than what we've witnessed previously," Connor reported.

"Perhaps the Jatarians have learned from the previous battles and are attempting to implement a new strategy," I suggested.

"It will be interesting to see how the Zator handle it," Jeffery stated.

I watched the viewscreens. The Zator made no move toward the enemy fleet.

"What are they waiting on?" Jeffery asked impatiently.

"I'm not sure," I replied. What *were* they waiting on? Were the Zator rethinking their plan of attack? Were they waiting for their hyperdrives to recharge first? Was this some type of intimidation tactic? *Let the enemy see your fleet and make them wait for their impending death?*

"I wish the Zator would get on with it," Jeffery said.

"The Zator ships are preparing to jump," Connor announced.

"Yes. Let's get this party started," Jeffery said excitedly.

"Shall we follow them?" Bryce asked.

"Let's wait and see what the Zator do first. Then we can decide where to best view this battle," I ordered.

I watched as the Zator made their microjump closer to the Jatarian fleet. Time for the battle to begin.

Yet the Zator did not exit hyperspace where I expected them to.

Connor stood, and I did too and walked closer to the screen.

"Where did they exit?" I asked, frowning at Connor.

Connor had a big smile on his face. "The Zator exited on the opposite side of the Jatarian fleet. Essentially pinning the Jatarians up against their own minefield."

"Brilliant." Jeffery laughed.

"The Jatarians have nowhere to go," I remarked.

"Now they will be more desperate," Bryce added. "Where should we move to? We want a good and safe vantage point," Bryce said.

"Let's jump in on the right flank of the Zator fleet. A good distance away of course. We can't afford for any stray weapons fire to hit us," I said.

I felt the *Hunter* make the quick microjump to where we could safely watch the action unfold. Things had already heated up between the two fleets. The Jatarians had wasted no time in firing their weapons. Space was already lit up with the various weapons at both fleets' disposal.

Connor put up the ship counts on the screen for all to see.

"When do you think the Jatarians will launch their orbs?" Jeffery asked.

"I would wait until my enemy moved in closer," I said. "It would give the Zator less time to react and to eliminate the threat. That situation would allow for a bigger chance that more orbs would make it through to their targets."

"You're a wise man," Jeffery said.

I turned to Jeffery and shrugged. "I guess I've learned many things by watching so many battles."

Did Jeffery feel I was a threat to him with all my knowledge? My military knowledge? I shook my head. I couldn't worry about that right now.

Energy screens lit up as energy crawled across them, looking for a weakness to exploit. When one was found, the enemy didn't take long to capitalize on it.

One thing was obvious. The Jatarians and the Zator had experience in battle. Had they fought each other in the distant past? Or were they new enemies? Would Zator Commander Tao tell me the truth about what we've witnessed here? Or would he hide behind a mask of ignorance? That may be the safest route to take. I had to be at peace with the thought that I may never know the answers I seek.

A giant blast caught my attention, as a Jatarian ship was blown into millions of pieces. Thousands of lives were being lost out there, but none of them were Human.

What did that say about me? That I value Human lives over the Jatarians and the Zator? Was I heartless? Had I lost touch with my humanity? Had I grown callous to the loss of lives in the large number of battles I had now witnessed? I took a deep breath. I needed to focus on what was happening around me. I couldn't let my mind go down the rabbit hole of paranoia. It wasn't a productive way to spend my time.

I glanced at the tactical display and the ships represented there. Many new ships appeared while I was watching. It had to be the small attack ships from each fleet. They would soon enter their own dance of death.

I wondered how I would fare as a pilot in one of the Federation's devastators or the *Defender*. Could I match the skills of those I watched on the viewscreen? How long had it taken those pilots to develop such skills? Was it mainly learned in a simulator or in the throes of battle?

The small attack ship I currently watched blew up before my eyes, and I knew what my fate would be if I were the pilot of a small attack ship. It would be certain death, no question about it. I think in the future I should stick to transport vessels and stealthed ships. I could never step foot in a simulator again, let alone a striker, not after what I'd witnessed here.

I also decided to talk to Colin about what I'd seen here. Our striker pilots needed many more hours of training.

I thought about the numerous striker pilots I knew—including Bryce's brother Peter and my good friend Teryn. Both were still stuck at Dove Two. That was another situation that had to be rectified soon. The Federation or the Morag had to rid that system of the Jatarian colony or military base that had been established nearby the refugee settlement.

Why we had allowed that to continue was beyond my understanding. No more though. Even if I had to take a Morag fleet there myself, I would do it. Well, the Morag would do it at my command—if there were any Morag ships left after this war here in the Jatarian systems.

Explosions rattled both sides of the battle. The Jatarians were losing a few more ships than the Zator. Not by much, however.

I also noticed that the Zator had come to a stop. They were no longer moving toward the enemy. Perhaps they had realized what I had. The Jatarians hadn't launched their orb strike yet. The Zator needed space to react and to maneuver and to counteract that type of attack.

As if on cue, alarms rang out. I looked at Connor.

"It's the orbs. They've been launched," Connor said.

I stood and walked toward the viewscreens again. Would this even the playing field? Had the Zator figured out a way to fend off this type of attack?

"Look. The Zator are widening their formation. They're putting more space between each ship," Connor observed.

Would this keep the orbs from hitting multiple ships as they exploded? It would be interesting to see if this tactic worked.

The Zator sent a wall of firepower toward the incoming orb attack. They were so small that it was hard to hit them directly. Nearly impossible really. It all came down to the weapons exploding near the orbs to take them out.

The Zator had become reasonably good at this strategy and destroyed almost half of the incoming orbs. It still left far too many though. The Zator did not give up. They kept firing their weapons and targeting the orbs. A few more were destroyed.

In the end far too many orbs remained. They were now too close to target. There was nothing left for the Zator to do besides weather the attack.

"Captain, the Zator are preparing to jump," Connor reported.

"Where are they going?" Jeffery asked.

We watched as the Zator fleet disappeared and quickly reappeared behind the Jatarians' ships. Now the minefield separated the two fleets.

The Zator immediately began firing on the Jatarians. Many mines were destroyed in the process. The Jatarians lost many ships before they could turn their fleet to face the Zator fleet.

Once the Jatarians had readjusted their formation, the battle intensified. The orbs also headed toward their prey. Now they had to cross through their own fleet, a field of mines, and then to their enemy. The Zator had many more chances to reduce the number of orbs before they reached their targets. I also would guess that the Zator might microjump again to get away from the orbs, once they reached them.

The Zator still had a numbers advantage. If they could keep away from those orbs, that advantage might last.

The carnage of the battle was evident all around them. Pieces of what once were powerful warships, both Jatarian and Zator, floated in space. I thought about how long both fleets would take to rebuild their fleet numbers. How could we stop the Jatarians from rebuilding their military might?

I was getting ahead of myself. First, we had to eliminate the current threat of their warships. Not only here in this system but all across this Jatarian stronghold.

The Morag would know how to keep the Jatarians from rebuilding. The Morag were good at suppressing the power of all others to keep them from becoming a threat. I could see why this was important. At least for those who might one day become your enemy. But how could one tell who might one day become our enemy?

Why did the Morag believe the Human Empire were their enemies? I had to laugh. I knew why. My father would build up a fleet, believing he could challenge the dominance of the Confederation one day. Especially now that he had freedom without the total oversight of the Confederation.

Had my interference in influencing the High Council of the Confederation been a mistake? Had I given my father the freedom to build a fleet that could one day cause the Empire to be destroyed? A cold shiver ran down my spine. Goose bumps rose on my skin. Had my actions opened the door to the end of the Human Empire?

I felt a great weight on my shoulders. I didn't like it. What could I do? I only had one option, which was to contact my mother when I could and remind her of what would happen if my father got too ambitious. I couldn't do that now. All I could do now was watch these two races kill each other and then be thankful neither one had their sights set on Humans right now.

My attention returned to the present and the orbs that had made it through the Jatarian fleet. The orbs now had to navigate the minefield. All the Zator had to do was wait for the right time and set off the mines. A few perfectly timed explosions were key. If the orbs used the areas where the mines had already been destroyed, the Zator would have to funnel the orbs in closer together, making them easier to eliminate. What a brilliant plan.

I watched as the orbs drew closer together to avoid the mines still in place. I smiled. That was a mistake. Of course their other option wasn't a good choice either.

The Zator fired away, focusing their firepower on the densest area of orbs moving through the minefield unscathed. Once the Jatarians realized their mistake, the orbs spread out.

Then the Zator changed their targeting to the minefield. A dozen perfectly timed explosions ignited the entire area, detonating mines all around the orbs. I couldn't help but smile. Now only a small fraction of the original number of orbs remained.

"The Zator are preparing to jump again," Connor announced.

My smile grew bigger. "I think the Zator have figured out how to neutralize the orbs. All they have to do is microjump when the orbs get near. If the orbs can't get close, they can't fulfill their job," I said.

"I think you're right," Bryce replied.

The Zator fleet disappeared and then reappeared on the left flank of the Jatarian fleet. As soon as they exited from their microjump, the Zator ships began firing on the Jatarians. The strategy was effective. Before the Jatarians could change their formation, at least a dozen of them were blown to oblivion.

The orbs, the few that were left, changed their path and headed toward the Zator's new position. They would never get there though. The Zator would move again.

I was relieved that the Zator had figured out how to neutralize the threat of the orb attack. I could use their success to help the Morag eliminate the orbs when they reached the Jatarian home system in a few more days. I imagined the number of orbs that would be deployed in the Jatarians' home system would be drastically more than we'd seen to date. Now I knew how to help the Morag weather that orb attack without losing any ships.

Once the Jatarians adjusted their formation, the Zator moved again. The explosions spread across the enemy fleet. One ship after another was destroyed. The Zator now outnumbered the Jatarians two to one. It was only a matter of time before the enemy was defeated.

I sat back down in my command chair and enjoyed the show. I'd learned many things from watching the Zator battle the Jatarians. I hoped I could use it to help the Morag. We could do this. We could defeat the Jatarians, especially if we all worked together.

I hoped this Zator fleet would continue their rampage of death on the Jatarians in another system. They would need reinforcements to do it. While they would win the battle in this system, it still came at a heavy price.

When the last Jatarian ship succumbed to the enemy firepower, the Zator had only ninety-six ships remaining. They'd lost a majority of their fleet.

No orbs were left to threaten the Zator either. The Zator had been pretty effective at eliminating all threats. Now what would they do? Would they destroy the inhabited planet and moon? Or would they move on to the next target system?

"Why aren't they moving toward the inhabited planet?" Jeffery asked, after a few minutes had passed.

"I'm not sure," I replied.

"Surely the Zator will send a ship to scan the surface to determine its threat level, right?" Jeffery asked.

"That's what they've done previously," I answered. "I don't know why they wouldn't do that here."

Another few minutes passed, and twelve of the Zator ships broke formation and headed toward the inhabited moon and planet. Once they were closer, the twelve ships split into two groups, with six headed to each target.

Would they scan the surface first? Or would they bombard the surface without looking any closer?

It didn't take long before I had my answer. The six ships reached the moon first. Since they didn't immediately launch their weapons, I had to assume they did scan the surface first. A few minutes later, they sent sixteen missiles to the surface. Large explosions detonated above the surface. Massive mushroom clouds rose to the sky above.

I didn't feel any triumph in my enemy's moment of death. Even though that moon was home to my enemies, not all of them had anything to do with the attacks on the Human Federation. They'd likely never even heard of Humans before. Innocent lives were being lost on that moon. This was not something to be celebrated.

I turned my head and looked over at Jeffery. The smirk on his face sent shivers down my spine. He looked so much like his father sometimes. I quickly looked away. Jeffery obviously liked what he witnessed. He reveled in the death of the Jatarians.

Soon afterward the other six Zator ships reached the planet. A similar chain of events ended with the destruction of the Jatarian lives on the planet. I guess that was one way to ensure the Jatarians didn't rebuild their military ships. If they had no planet from which to rebuild, not much could happen. Or at least not quickly.

Once the twelve ships returned to the fleet, the Zator left the system. We followed closely behind. Thankfully the Zator still traveled in the direction of the Jatarian home system.

I couldn't help but worry about what would happen if the Zator and the Morag met in the Jatarian home system. Would they work together to eliminate the Jatarians? Or would they find they had new enemies? I would lose sleep over these thoughts.

Chapter Twenty-Three

We continued to follow the Zator toward the supposed Jatarian home system. We passed by numerous systems that held ships. Why had the Zator not stopped? Were they headed to a rendezvous system to meet up with more ships? No way they could challenge the Jatarian fleet we had witnessed earlier in what we thought of as the Jatarian home system. Over three thousand ships were there. With the attacks in this area of space, I would assume the Jatarians had beefed up security even more since we'd left there.

I'd kept tabs on the Morag. They would arrive in the Jatarian home system in just under twenty-four hours. I still worried about how things would go if the Morag and Zator picked the same time and the same system to attack. The likelihood was remote, but the closer we got to the Jatarian home system, the more likely it became.

Could I keep the Morag and the Zator from attacking each other? I had no connection to this group of Zator. Commander Tao was not among them. Should I try to reach out and warn the Zator that the Morag were near?

I paced my office, deciding how to handle the situation. Do I interfere? Or do I just let things play out, the chips falling where they may? As long as it ended with the Jatarians' destruction, I was good with it. I didn't, however, want the Zator and the Morag to realize they had another enemy in each other.

The Morag had attacked the Zator group in the Zenyan system multiple times. More recently though they'd worked together to fend off the Jatarians, with their common enemy bringing them together. Would that be the case here? Or would the Morag realize the Zator were more of a threat than what they'd seen in the Zenyan system? How would this play out? I didn't know, but I lost many hours of sleep over it.

I was pacing in my office when I felt our ship exit hyperspace. I quickly made my way to the Command Center. "What's going on?" I asked, as I walked in.

Augusta replied, "The Zator have exited hyperspace, so we followed them."

"Any ships in the system?" I asked, while checking the viewscreens for the tactical display.

"None showed on the long-range scans of the system," Augusta answered.

I breathed a sigh of relief. I didn't think this Zator fleet was large enough to challenge any sizable Jatarian fleet. The Zator fleet numbered less than one hundred. They needed more reinforcements first.

"Perhaps this system is where the Zator intend to rendezvous with more fleets to increase their numbers before their next attack," I commented.

"Let's hope so," Bryce said, as he walked over to his console. "I was midbreakfast when I felt the ship exit hyperspace."

"At least the sensor alarms didn't sound," I joked.

"No kidding. I might have choked on my bacon," Bryce joked back.

I couldn't help but smile. It was so good to have Bryce here. He was like a brother to me. I didn't know where I would be without him. "So where exactly are we?" I asked Bryce.

Bryce typed in a few things on his console and replied, "We are in a system some twelve hours' hyperspace jump from the Jatarian home system."

"Wow, that's pretty close. Surely the Jatarians are running patrols to nearby systems. I'm afraid the Zator might be discovered here," I commented.

"You might be right. It would be wise for the Jatarians to run patrols to nearby systems. It would all be in the timing. Is the patrol large enough to challenge this Zator fleet, or would they have to call in reinforcements? If it's the latter, then the Zator might be gone before the Jatarian reinforcements arrive," Connor said.

"Let's hope the timing runs in our favor," I replied.

"If the Morag and the Zator both attack the Jatarian home system, we might just defeat them," Bryce said.

"It all boils down to the timing. Will it play in our favor or against us?" I muttered.

"Let's hope the Zator accumulate a larger fleet while they're here," Connor added.

"Why else would they stop?" Bryce asked.

We all knew the answer. It could be to make repairs or to recharge their hyperdrives before they make their last jump to the Jatarian home system.

I tried not to worry about the timing of everything. I could do nothing to change the timing of the Zator's attack, unless I contacted them. If I did that, I might scare them away. They might not want the Morag to know they are in the area.

The information might totally change their strategy. I didn't want that to happen. The Zator had developed a good battle strategy to face the Jatarians. They might have a better chance than the Morag at defeating the Jatarians, once and for all, which is what we needed to happen.

No, I would not interfere. Not with the Zator. I couldn't help but wonder if Zator Commander Tao had sent this command to attack the Jatarians. Was he behind it all? I hoped so. I also hoped I would get the chance to ask him one day.

"Is anything interesting on the scans?" I asked Connor.

"Maybe," Connor replied.

I sat forward in my chair. "What is it?"

"I'm sensing something near the third planet. It's very small though," Connor replied.

"Let's go check it out," I said. "I'm certain this fleet will be here longer than ninety minutes."

I couldn't stop my imagination from running wild. What could it be? An orb? A mine? Some type of early warning system, like the Federation had? A small attack ship left here to report any activity in the system? The possibilities were endless.

I felt a twinge in my stomach as our ship made the short jump closer to the unidentified object. "If our scans don't know what it is, it must be something we've not encountered before," I commented. That in itself narrowed down the possibilities.

When we exited hyperspace, we were still not close enough to visually see the object on our screens.

"Let's slowly move toward the object. We've got to figure out what it is," I said.

"It's larger than an orb or a single mine," Connor confirmed. "It's too small to be one of the small attack ships the Jatarians have too."

"Is it active? Is it running scans?" I asked.

"It's doing something. That's why I picked it up on my scans of the system," Connor said.

"If we've picked it up, then the Zator have too," I said. I wondered how long we would have to figure out what it was, before the Zator jumped closer and blew it to oblivion.

"It's sending some type of signal," Graham reported. "I can't figure out what it is exactly. It's not in the Jatarian language or any others that our translator knows."

"It's got to be some type of early warning system," I said.

"Like the buoys the Federation has," Jeffery added.

"Exactly. Maybe they learned it from us," I said. What else had the Jatarians learned from us? Stealthed technology? A cold shiver ran down my back. If the Jatarians had developed a way to sense our stealthed ship when we ran scans, it wasn't too far out of the realm of possibilities that they'd had some success with stealthed systems. They would have to start small, right?

"What if it's not Jatarian?" Bryce asked. "Maybe it's a sensor for another race, warning them when the Jatarians entered their system."

"Scan the nearby planets and moons and see which ones are inhabitable," I ordered. Just what were we dealing with here?

I watched the viewscreens as we grew closer to the unidentified object. It was just coming into view.

"Captain, two planets and four moons are capable of sustaining life," Connor reported.

"That's a lot of options. Let's move in a little closer to this object. I don't want to get too close in case it's a weapon of some type," I said.

Many of the command crew exchanged glances at the mention of *weapon*.

"I'm just being overly cautious," I assured them.

"Captain, three Zator ships just entered hyperspace," Connor reported.

I looked back at the viewscreen just in time to see the three Zator ships appear between us and the unidentified object. We were far enough away from both that we could stay right where we were.

"I guess we will see if it's a weapon soon enough," Bryce said.

A hush fell across the Command Center, as we all intently watched what would happen with the three Zator ships.

"The Zator might destroy it before the object has a chance to do its thing," I said.

"Is that a bad thing?" Jeffery asked.

"I would like to know what it does first. We need to know if it's a weapon or merely a way of communicating," I replied.

"Surely the Zator will want to know the same thing," Jeffery noted.

I shrugged. I would think so, but other alien species didn't necessarily think like we did.

"Look. Something is happening," Connor said, pointing to the screen.

The Zator ships had moved in fairly close to the object. Suddenly the object seemed to activate, and then it detonated, sending a blast of energy toward the Zator ships. To be fair it wasn't only toward the Zator ships but in all directions. All three Zator ships were disintegrated.

My eyes grew wide in horror. That could have been us. If we'd been much closer, we would be dead right now. I felt my heart beating rapidly in my chest. Sweat pooled on my forehead. I took a couple deep breaths to ward off the oncoming panic attack. We were alive. We had to be cautious. Space *is* a dangerous place.

I looked around the room. I wasn't the only one shocked by what had happened.

Finally Jeffery broke the silence. "I'm glad we weren't any closer."

"No kidding," I replied. "It must be a self-destruct system that activated when the Zator ships got too close."

"Let's make a note of that so we avoid that object in the future," Bryce said.

"We've got to give it a name," Connor said.

"*Hmm,*" Jeffery said. "What about *death probes?*"

"That sounds like a good name. It should be obvious that it's a deadly object and should be avoided at all costs," I replied.

"Death probes it is," Connor said, keying in some commands into his console.

"What if the Jatarians have these death probes in their home system?" Jeffery asked.

"These probes are similar to mines but larger and more powerful," I said. "When we were there before, we didn't sense anything like this, right?" I asked Connor.

"I will review our scans from the Jatarian home system to confirm that, but I don't think so," Connor replied.

"Perhaps this is a new weapon," Jeffery suggested.

"I hope not. Right now we don't even know for sure if it was a Jatarian object. Graham, have you picked up any communications between the Zator ships about what just happened?" I asked.

"There is a lot of chatter about the object. The Zator assume it is Jatarian since we are in their area of space," Graham said. "It also sounds like the Zator are waiting on reinforcements."

"Connor, scan the system again and look for any more of these death probes. Perhaps we can't sense them on our scans if they aren't activated yet."

"I've run the scans now multiple times. I've found no more evidence of any more death probes," Connor replied.

Bryce spoke up and said, "Should we warn the *Explorer* about this device?"

"Yes, we should," I replied. I definitely didn't want Fritz to come across one of these and try to figure out what it was. Fritz might not end up as lucky as we did.

I closed my eyes and focused on Fritz.

Slade, it's good to hear from you. I was beginning to get worried.

Sorry, we've been busy following this Zator fleet. How is the Explorer *faring?*

We are well. We're making note of all systems with ships in them, whether large or small. You will have many systems to check out.

Good. In every system we've followed the Zator to so far, the Zator have reigned supreme. They've eliminated all Jatarian ships they've come across.

That's excellent news, Slade. Maybe the Zator will turn out to be a stronger ally than we thought.

Perhaps. It appears this fleet is headed toward the Jatarian home system next. They're currently rendezvousing with more ships. We're about a twelve-hour hyperspace jump from the Jatarian home system.

Wow, that's close. Do you think the Zator will attack before the Morag arrive?

I'm not sure. I'm keeping tabs on the situation.

Will you inform the Zator that the Morag are coming and that they could work together to destroy the Jatarians?

No, I do not plan on it. I'm afraid it might scare off the Zator. I'm also not certain that this group of Zator has ties to Zator Commander Tao. They could be two totally separate groups.

Yes, you're right. Better to be cautious.

Speaking of cautious, we ran into something new in this system and wanted you to be aware of it. We're calling them death probes. They're larger than a single mine or orb but smaller than the small attack ships. Our scans picked it up as it seemed to be transmitting something, but we could not decipher it. When the Zator got too close to the death probe, it self-destructed, taking the three Zator ships near it. There was no sign left of the three Zator ships or the death probe.

Wow, that's scary. I'm glad your ship wasn't nearby.

We were pretty close but thankfully not close enough, I replied. *So, if you come across something of that nature, stay away. It did not register on our long-range scans of the system. Those scans came up clear. Maybe it was inactive or something. So possibly you could enter a system with one or more of these probes and not necessarily know they were there.*

What do you think their purpose is? Fritz asked.

My guess is some type of self-destructing early warning system. Something to let the Jatarians know that something or someone is out here. Give them a warning that danger is coming. Yet we haven't confirmed it is a Jatarian device yet. This one is new to us and to the Zator obviously.

You've never seen this before?

No, we haven't.

So these death probes weren't in the Jatarian home system? Fritz asked.

No, not the last time we were there. I'm having Connor reexamine the scans to double-check. With the mines and so many ships in that system, maybe we missed something.

Thank you for the warning, Slade. I'll be on the lookout for these death probes you speak of. When do you expect this attack on the Jatarian home system to commence?

The Morag were under twenty-three hours away at my last check-in. The time is finally coming. I'm jealous I won't get to witness it.

We plan to watch, I replied.

Good. I know you've already learned a great deal by watching what works for the Zator against the Jatarians. Not to mention, you've been present at numerous Jatarian battles yourself. If anyone can help this attack be more successful, it's you, Slade.

Thanks. I'm hoping it will go well, and we will be on our way to ridding the galaxy of the threat of the Jatarians for good.

I hope you're right, Slade. Keep me posted, and let me know when you head toward the target system. Stay safe.

I will. I'll talk to you soon, Fritz.

When I opened my eyes, I looked at the viewscreens. The nearest planet was coming into view. My curiosity got the best of me. "Let's see if that planet is inhabited," I said.

A short microjump later, the planet was prominent on the viewscreen. It was a beautiful planet. The explorer in me was excited. No reason we couldn't explore a little, while we waited for the rest of the Zator to show up.

"Running scans of the planet now," Connor said.

My mind filled with the possibilities. Could this be inhabited by Jatarians? Perhaps they thought if no ships guarded the system, we wouldn't bother to look. I shook my head. That would be too risky.

"Scans show the planet is inhabited," Connor said excitedly.

A smile spread across my face. "Let's get a closer look."

As we moved closer, the sensor alarms rang out. "Connor, let's confirm those ships are Zator, and then we will continue our exploration."

A moment later Connor replied, "Scans confirm the newcomers are Zator ships, two hundred of them."

"So the Zator fleet is up to just under three hundred. Let's hope more Zator ships are on the way," I said.

With the arrival of this newest fleet, we had at least ninety minutes to explore. I couldn't hide my enthusiasm. It seemed to be contagious. The overall mood in the Command Center had changed. Considering that we had recently come very close to incinerating with that death probe, the mood had definitely shifted for the better. Everyone was excited to get a good look at the inhabitants of the planet.

The Command Center buzzed with energy the closer we got to the planet. When we were finally close enough to get a view of the surface, what we found surprised us all. It was home to a species we'd seen before. The planet was inhabited by Jatarians.

"Why would the Jatarians not protect this system if it's occupied by their own people?" Jeffery asked.

"If no ships are in orbit here, no reason for enemy fleets to stop here and check the planets," I said. "It's sort of like our refugee systems back home. We don't fly many ships there, so it goes unnoticed by any ships passing by."

I immediately regretted my words. Jeffery now knew that our systems would have no ships in them. The Federation would have to scan the planets to find the refugee villages. We still hid in the caves when any unknown ship exited hyperspace. So the villages should still remain safe.

Surely Jeffery already knew we don't keep ships in orbit in space above our villages. It didn't make sense to do that when someone wants to remain hidden.

"It doesn't appear the Zator have any interest in scanning the planets here," Jeffery replied. "So I guess their plan worked."

"That's so risky though, leaving a planet unprotected like this," Connor said.

"Maybe it's more protected than we realize," Bryce said. "Perhaps other defensive mechanisms are hidden here."

That made all of us a little more nervous. We held our position above the planet and observed the Jatarians below. I still couldn't wrap my mind around the fact that this planet appeared to be so defenseless.

"Do you think the other inhabitable planet and moons also have Jatarians living on them?" Bryce asked.

"That could be," I replied.

"Should we scan the surface to see if anything threatening is down there?" Connor asked.

I thought it over for a minute. We were very close to the planet. "Let's not risk it. I don't want to cause an unknown defensive mechanism to activate," I said.

"What if we moved farther away and then initiated the more detailed scans?" Connor suggested. "We need to know whether this planet needs to be destroyed."

He had a point. If we eliminated all military ships and ignored this Jatarian system, they could rise again. We didn't want that. "Let's move back as far as we can to still get the detailed scans of the surface. Look for military bases or ship manufacturing facilities," I said.

The mood in the Command Center had grown more tense. A danger could possibly be here that we couldn't see.

After moving and running the scans, nothing threatening showed up on the surface.

"Maybe this system doesn't want to be involved in the war," Jeffery said.

"Or they are really good at hiding it," I replied.

"We can't destroy a planet of defenseless people can we, even if they are our enemies?" Augusta asked.

"Well, *we* can't do anything," I replied. "The Zator don't seem interested in scanning the planets. So, for now, we will make note of this finding. While we have more time, we should scan the other inhabitable planet and the four moons. You never know what we might find there," I said.

"Do you think we have enough time to recharge our hyperdrive if we do a microjump before this Zator fleet leaves?" Bryce asked.

"Yes, the Zator do not have enough ships yet. If they go to the Jatarian home system with only three hundred ships, they'll be annihilated," I replied.

"Plotting our microjump now," Bryce replied.

A few minutes later, we exited our short jump near the second inhabitable planet. Our sensor alarms sounded again. My gaze shifted to the tactical display. I assumed it was more Zator ships, but I also wouldn't be surprised if Jatarian ships showed up. That death probe surely had transmitted information to someone somewhere. That had to be a new Jatarian security device, with them inhabiting that planet. So the Jatarians knew the Zator were accumulating a fleet here in this system. The big question remained whether the Jatarian could get a fleet here before the Zator were ready to leave.

"It's another Zator fleet, Captain. They've added another three hundred ships," Connor reported.

"So that brings their numbers to almost six hundred ships. This might be it. We need to ensure we are ready to jump in ninety minutes," I said.

"I'll keep watch on our hyperdrive. We will be ready," Cole confirmed.

"I'm scanning the planet now," Connor said.

We waited with mixed emotions. Did we hope to find more Jatarians?

"The scans show the planet is heavily populated," Connor reported.

"Move in closer and scan for military installations," I ordered. "How many inhabitants?" I asked.

"Over six billion," Connor replied.

"Wow. That's a lot," Bryce said.

Was this system the Jatarian home system and all the others were outposts or distractions? The large Zator fleet had no idea what was going on here. Was a population of Jatarians a threat if they didn't possess military ships? Was everything run from here?

Connor interrupted my thoughts and said, "I find no evidence of any military installations or manufacturing facilities."

"Okay. Let's see who lives here," I said, as we continued to move in closer.

A few minutes later we confirmed what I already suspected. This planet was inhabited by Jatarians. We investigated all the moons in the inhabitable zone. Three of them were inhabited by Jatarians.

Meanwhile another one hundred Zator ships arrived, bringing the total to almost seven hundred ships.

Once the latest Zator ships had time to charge their hyperdrives, they entered hyperspace. We followed right behind them.

"Captain, we're headed toward the supposed Jatarian home system," Bryce confirmed. "We will arrive in twelve hours."

I closed my eyes and reached out to Morag Admiral Wyn. I needed to know how close to the target system they were. It took me a few minutes, but I was happy to see the Morag would arrive one hour after the Zator.

Maybe by the time the Morag arrived, the Zator would have the battle well in hand. With as many ships as the Jatarian home system had the last time we passed by, I was surprised the Zator hadn't accumulated more ships. Maybe the Zator were unaware of how many ships awaited them.

I still worried about the undefended Jatarian system we had just left. We had decided to call it Jatarn, as we suspected it may actually be the true home system of the Jatarians. In total it was home to almost twelve billion Jatarians, with no obvious military installations or weapons manufacturing facilities.

Unless they were hidden or underground, and that thought sent a shiver down my spine. What exactly we were dealing with there in Jatarn, we might not ever know. Should I have the Morag go there and destroy the surface of the two planets and the three moons? Was that the right thing to do? If I did, would it haunt me forever? If I didn't, would that haunt me forever?

I needed to get some rest. In twelve hours the biggest battle I'd ever witnessed would begin. I could use some rest. I needed to be on the top of my game when the time came.

It was hard to fall asleep, with my mind wandering to the upcoming battle and concerns about what to do with the Jatarn system. Eventually I fell into a fitful sleep.

Chapter Twenty-Four

We were closing in on the vastly defended Jatarian home system. We would exit hyperspace in the next fifteen minutes. I'd done my best to stay in my office and to do my pacing there. I didn't want the command crew to see how nervous I was. Why was I nervous? I had no power or influence over this Zator fleet. I had nothing resting on my shoulders, except keeping my crew safe.

I knew, however, that in this Jatarian home system, we would find a defensive fleet ready to die for their people. They would do anything to eliminate any threat. This was their system. They had everything to lose.

Would the Zator even exit hyperspace when they did their long-range scans and realized they were so greatly outnumbered? I think this worried me most. I kept telling myself it was out of my control, and, therefore, I shouldn't spend any of my time thinking and worrying about it. That didn't work though.

I watched our progress and the time from my office. When the fifteen-minute mark arrived, I composed myself and walked into the Command Center.

Immediately I could tell that everyone was worried. I felt the nervous anticipation of what we were about to witness. We were about to watch the most epic battle ever witnessed by Humans before. Were we lucky? Would we tell our grandkids about this one day? Would we even live to see our grandchildren?

As I sat down in my command chair, I looked over at Connor. It was almost time to run our long-range scans. What had the Jatarians added to their defenses since the last time we'd been here? It wouldn't be the same. The Jatarians knew this attack was imminent, either from the Zator or the Morag. The Jatarians had to be reinforced to the max.

I tapped my foot, trying to release some of my nervous energy. My heart beat quickly in my chest. I glanced over at Connor. He was watching his consoles.

"I'm commencing the long-range scans now," Connor announced.

I focused on my breathing. I took deep breaths in and slowly let them out, trying to gain control of my nerves.

"Scans are coming in, Captain. They show 2,106 ships in the system," Connor reported.

I was surprised. That was over one thousand less than when we'd been here before. If we were lucky, perhaps some of them would be transport vessels that would leave the system, once the Zator arrived. Still, the Zator would be drastically outnumbered.

"Maybe they redistributed ships to other systems to help reduce the number of enemy ships as the Zator made their way here," Bryce suggested.

"Or this is a trap," I said. "Make the Zator think they can win, so they go ahead and exit hyperspace. Then nearby fleets make their way to the system before the Zator can charge their hyperdrives and have a chance of retreat."

"I don't like this. I have a bad feeling," Bryce replied.

"Me too," I said.

"Five minutes to our exit from hyperspace."

"Scans show the Zator are exiting hyperspace," Connor reported.

"They must not be intimidated by the fact that they'll be outnumbered three to one," I said.

"Maybe they know something we don't," Connor suggested.

"Let's hope so," I replied.

When we exited hyperspace, we were behind the Zator fleet. From this position, I felt safe enough to run the scans. We needed to know what was out there. "Connor, let's run the scans of the system," I ordered.

"Running scans now."

I watched the viewscreens at the front of the room. They were filled with Zator ships. The tactical display was filled with red and green icons. The red icons were positioned well toward the inner system.

"Will the Zator wait to charge their hyperdrives before they attack?" Jeffery asked.

"I doubt it. They don't want the Jatarians to have time to get reinforcements here," I replied. "I'm guessing they are scanning the system and making a plan of attack."

"That's why you feel comfortable running our scans? It's because you believe ours will be masked by the Zator's scans?" Jeffery asked.

"Yes, exactly."

Jeffery nodded. "Now what?"

"We need to decide where we can watch the battle between these two fleets without being in any danger ourselves," I replied.

"But we don't know what the Zator will do," Jeffery said.

"You're right, but we do know what the Zator have done in the past. Although their strategy may change slightly, I'm sure it will be similar."

Connor reported, "I'm getting the scans of the makeup of the Jatarian fleet. No civilian vessels are in the system. All of them are warships of some nature. We have four hundred of the larger ships, six hundred warships, and over one thousand small attack ships. Minefields are throughout the system. One must be very precise to make microjumps to avoid them all. Orbs are also spread throughout the system. I imagine more than we can sense is out there too. Some of those devices will be inactive, until a ship passes nearby and activates it. I'm also sensing ten of the death probes scattered throughout the system," Connor reported.

Bryce nodded. "I'm reviewing the scans now. I would guess that those places where it appears safe to jump to are traps with multiple inactive orbs hiding nearby. I'm not sure *where* we can watch this battle safely," Bryce said, the concern evident in his tone.

"We might just have to stay right here and move closer as the Zator clear the way," I said.

"If they have to make their way through this obstacle course, the Morag will definitely be here before the Zator are finished," Bryce said.

"I wonder how the Zator will approach this?" I asked. I had many things I could learn here. I was mapping out in my mind where I would jump, if I had a fleet at my disposal. In one short hour, I would have precisely that.

The Jatarians held their position, waiting for the Zator to make the first move. Where would they go? Where would they jump to first? Anywhere they went was fraught with danger. We would shortly see how good of a strategist the Zator were.

I was in way over my head.

"The Zator are preparing to jump," Connor said excitedly.

"Don't follow. We will wait and see how it goes first," I ordered.

The Zator ships on the viewscreen started to disappear but not all of them.

"Captain, the Zator sent twenty-five of their cruisers to an area near the eighth planet," Connor said.

"Run the scans and see what's happening there. Did they make it?" I asked.

"They made it initially. Scans show orbs activating in that area. The orbs are headed for the ships now," Connor said.

I wished we had a better vantage point. We couldn't see much from our current position, as we were too far out. Our only view of what was happening was the tactical display. Or my gift.

I closed my eyes and focused on the Zator. I might not understand their language, but I could still see more of what was happening.

The Zator in the cruisers began firing at the incoming orbs. A few were hit and destroyed. More came in their place. It seemed orbs were coming at them from all around. The defensive fire continued, as the Zator attempted to destroy as many of the orbs as possible. Then the Zator ships entered hyperspace again and exited somewhere else in the system.

I opened my eyes and looked over at Connor. "Where are they now?"

"Those twenty-five ships are now near a moon of the sixth planet," Connor reported. "Orbs are activating there too."

I closed my eyes again and focused on my gift. It was easy to find the Zator commander I had just been watching.

The orbs were activating all around his small task group. The Zator launched their defensive fire, hoping to eliminate some of the threats. While some exploded, far too many didn't. After another round of defensive fire, it was time to make another jump.

I watched as the small Zator task group jumped to twenty different locations all across the system, never getting close to the Jatarian fleet.

"What are they trying to do?" Jeffery asked.

"I assume the Zator are trying to activate as many orbs as they can. That way the orbs move and will create a safe space for the fleet to jump to. Connor, where are the orbs currently headed?" I asked.

"Unfortunately the orbs deactivated, once the threat moved away."

"Dang. The Jatarians are learning. The Zator's orb strategy will have to change," I said, as I hit the arm of my command chair.

"They'll figure something out," Bryce said.

"It looks like the Zator are making another move," Connor said.

This time we watched the viewscreens, as fifty ships entered hyperspace. It didn't take long to figure out their target. They were after the minefields. They traveled in task groups of ten ships. They targeted minefields all over the system. When they were done, they had destroyed thousands of mines, making the system safer for the larger fleet to move about.

The orbs would still be a problem, but I couldn't think of much more that the Zator could do to help that.

"I think the entire fleet is preparing to jump," Connor said.

I watched the viewscreen, as the Zator fleet slowly disappeared. I waited to see where they ended up.

"The Zator jumped to a position near the sixth planet. All but one hundred ships made the jump," Connor reported.

The Zator fleet was not within the optimal weapons range of the Jatarian fleet. I wasn't sure why they'd picked that particular location. There were still plenty of orbs and a few minefields between the two fleets.

"Orbs are activating in the area," Connor informed us.

The Zator launched their defensive weapons multiple times, thinning out the orbs inbound to destroy them. Before the orbs could get close enough to detonate, the fleet moved again.

This time the Zator jumped near enough to the Jatarian fleet to launch their attack on the ships.

The Jatarian were taken off guard by the closeness of the enemy fleet. I'm sure the Jatarians had expected to watch the Zator move about their system, destroying more mines and orbs before engaging the main fleet. They were wrong.

The Zator opened fire upon exiting hyperspace from their microjump. Space was lit up with various colors of weapons trails and explosions. The energy screens of numerous Jatarian ships glowed as they were struck with the enemy firepower.

The Jatarians reacted swiftly and launched their defensive fire, destroying numerous weapons fire from reaching their ships.

Orbs activated all around and headed toward the Zator fleet. I guessed the fleet had only a few minutes before they jumped away from the orb attack.

A portion of the Zator fleet changed their focus to the incoming orbs, doing their best to eliminate as many of the small threats as possible.

Jatarian ships found their energy shields battered down, and, when they failed, the enemy wasted no time striking the killing blow. Large explosions erupted all across the front of the Jatarian formation, sending debris flying in all directions.

It was the carnage that we craved. As much as I didn't want to admit it, I enjoyed seeing my enemy destroyed in epic fashion. Especially an enemy that had harmed my people. The Jatarians had attacked the Federation without restraint, destroying and killing more people than I wanted to admit. I tried hard *not* to think about.

It still haunted my dreams though. Seeing the colonies destroyed. Watching Tyrus bombed. Today was the day that the Jatarians would finally receive the retribution due them. And I had a front-row seat to watch it all unfold.

Was I heartless? Was I cold like the Emperor? I looked over at Jeffery. He obviously enjoyed watching the bloodbath unfolding before us. Would Jeffery develop a taste for war? Was this a mistake to bring him along?

I shook my head. It wasn't a mistake. Jeffery had learned so much already. Things he would never learn in the safety of the palace or the Federation. I reassured myself that I had made the right choice in bringing Jeffery.

"The Zator are preparing to jump again," Connor announced.

We all watched, as the Zator fleet disappeared from the epicenter of the battle and reappeared behind the Jatarian fleet.

The excitement changed to horror, once we all realized the fatal flaw the Zator had made. The Zator had jumped into a field of unactivated death probes. As soon as the Zator ships exited hyperspace from their microjump, the death probes activated and detonated themselves. They took out ships in all directions. With one giant explosion, massive holes were ripped in the Zator formation.

"How many ships did the Zator just lose?" I asked in shock.

"Over one hundred," Connor said, shaken up from what he'd witnessed.

The death probes had decimated all the ships around them. Nothing was left.

"Can we sense these death probes if they're not activated?" I asked.

"None of those were on our scans, not until they came online," Connor replied.

"Guess that confirms that we are staying right here," I said.

"The Jatarians were just out of the blast zone of the death probes," Connor explained. "It's like the Jatarians knew the Zator would jump to their rear and attack."

"The Zator had done it before. It was in their playbook. So the Jatarians made it appear to be an option, then set a trap. I'll admit that's a pretty brilliant plan. Set a trap for your enemy in a place you know they'll go," I said.

"Now the death probes are gone at the rear of the Jatarian fleet, so it's safe for the Zator to fight from there," Jeffery said.

Jeffery was right. The fighting had already started anew. It had taken the Zator a few minutes to recover from the death probe attack, giving the Jatarians the time they needed to turn around.

Energy screens lit up on both sides of the fleets. It wouldn't be long before more ships succumbed to the onslaught of enemy weapons fire.

I was still in shock about what had just happened. How many more death probes were out there? "Connor, I need you to track where the Zator go when they make their jumps. We need to know which areas are safe, for when the Morag arrive. We can't afford to make mistakes like that if we plan to win the war," I said.

"Yes, Captain."

The small attack ships from both fleets launched and began their attack runs. It was easy to get entranced by their intricate moves and skill at what they did. It was an absolute dogfight.

The Jatarians outnumbered the Zator in their small attack ships. It didn't seem to faze the Zator at all. Their small ships fought hard and were determined to destroy their enemy.

"Captain, I've got a group of orbs inbound to the Zator fleet's location," Connor reported.

I watched as some of the Zator ships turned to face the incoming threat of the orbs. They launched defensive fire and began eliminating the new threat.

Where would the Zator jump to next? I knew they would jump before the orbs arrived but where? Would they jump back to where they were before?

"The Zator are preparing to jump again," Connor announced.

The Zator disappeared and then reappeared in their previous position.

"Captain, the Zator left something behind," Connor said, puzzled.

The orbs moved toward the object, and just as the first one came within range of its blast zone, the object exploded with a bright flash of light. I shielded my eyes from the flash, and, when I looked again, most of the orbs had been incinerated.

"What was that?" I asked. The Zator had left behind a device similar to a death probe. It had taken out most of the orbs in the area.

"It's some type of weapon we've not seen the Zator use before," Connor answered.

That was a little scary, but maybe it was to help combat the orbs. Yet, for the Zator to have the time and the resources to build a weapon to counter the orbs, then this was definitely not the first time the Zator have attacked the Jatarians here in their area of space. The ramifications of that thought were not settling at all. It was more than a little disturbing.

Was this battle the culmination of years' worth of battles? Was this the last stand or another attempt to defeat the Jatarians? Had Zator Commander Tao battled the Jatarians before the battles that transpired in the Zenyan system?

My mind spiraled again. I couldn't let that happen. I had to stay focused. We needed a weapon like that. How long had the Zator had one?

346

I focused on the screen. I had to concentrate on the battle playing out before my eyes. I looked over at the tactical display and to the ship count Connor had put up on the screen. I didn't like what I saw.

That death probe attack had really done a number on the Zator fleet. The new Zator weapon they had deployed helped rid the system of a large number of orbs, but none of the larger warships.

How could the Zator use that type of weapon to destroy the Jatarian ships? That's what the Zator needed to figure out. Surely they were working on that now.

"Captain, look. Those small Zator attack ships are flying in formation, like they're protecting the middle ship," Connor observed.

"Why would they do that?" I asked. "That ship must be important. Can you zoom in on it more?"

"No, not from this far out. I just noticed the odd formation the small attack ships were flying in," Connor replied.

"It seems they've caught the attention of the Jatarians. All of their small attack ships have changed their focus to that Zator squadron," I observed.

"It must have some important mission," Bryce said.

"What if it has one of those new Zator explosive weapons on board?" Jeffery asked.

I nodded. "That's it. That has to be it. The Zator put one of those special weapons on the small attack ship. The goal would be to get that ship as far into the Jatarian formation as possible, before detonating it," I said. "That's brilliant."

"Look. Now seven more squadrons are flying in that same formation," Connor said excitedly.

"This could be the game changer," I said. "This is exactly what the Zator need."

"I don't think the Jatarians are planning to let them just fly right in," Bryce said. "They've changed all their firepower to focus on those eight squadrons."

"That's a suicide mission," Jeffery said, as he realized the ramifications for the pilots of those ships.

"Possibly for all the squadron working to protect them too," I added.

We all sat in silence, as we watched those small Zator attack ships head to their death. I hoped they would make it to the Jatarian fleet formation. Their timing had to be precise, or they would destroy the other squadrons with one premature release of the new weapon.

"What should we call the Zator's newest weapon?" Jeffery asked.

"Incinerators," I replied.

"Good one," Jeffery replied.

The Jatarians were throwing everything they had at the incoming threats. A few of the protector small attack ships were hit, but, so far, not the ones carrying the incinerators.

"Just a little bit farther," Bryce said.

The fleet of small attack ships from both fleets engaged each other. One side trying to eliminate the other, while the Zator tried to defend the eight ships.

"Do you think the device will detonate if the ship carrying it gets hit?" Jeffery asked me.

"That's a good question. The eight squadrons are pretty spread out, as if cautious to not be too close to each other, if one were hit," I said.

"That first squadron doesn't have many left," Connor said.

"But look. I think they have reinforcements moving in to replace those that have been lost," Bryce said.

This could be a turning point in the battle. This just had to be successful.

A bright flash had all of us shielding our eyes and blinking quickly. What had happened?

"One of them got hit," Connor said. "It still detonated, taking many small attack ships from both sides."

Now only seven more of the incinerators were left. Were these all the special weapons the Zator had? Was this their Hail Mary? A last-ditch effort to turn the tide of the battle in their favor?

It had to work. It had to.

"Look. The squadrons have reached the Jatarian formation. Now all that can destroy them are the enemy's small attack ships," Connor said.

The Jatarian fleet had changed its focus again to the Zator fleet. The Jatarians could do nothing more to stop the small Zator attack ships.

"The Jatarian fleet is preparing to jump," Connor said, as he stood to his feet.

"Now, now," I said. The Zator had to detonate *now*.

An intense light swept across the viewscreen. It was so bright it temporarily gave me a headache. All I could see were spots when I dared open my eyes. I blinked rapidly. Was I blinded? Had that device caused such a bright light that it blinded us? Slowly my vision returned, and I looked around my Command Center. Everyone else seemed to be experiencing the same effects as I was.

Once I could see more clearly, I looked up at the screen. The Jatarians were gone. Was it because they'd microjumped somewhere else in the system? Or had they been incinerated?

"Where did they go?" I asked Connor.

"The Jatarian fleet, or should I say what's left of it, exited their microjump near the third planet," Connor answered.

"I'm sure that's their fallback position. I would guess that area is fraught with mines, orbs, and death probes," I said.

"I'm scanning the area now," Connor said.

"How many ships did those incinerators take out?" I asked.

"Slightly over 150 ships," Connor replied.

"That still leaves the Jatarians with a higher ship count than the Zator," I noted, as I tried to figure out what else could be done.

"How much longer until the Morag arrive?" Bryce asked.

I glanced at the clock on the wall. "Within the next twenty minutes."

"So the Zator only have to hold on a little longer, and then, once the Morag arrive, the battle should go quickly," Bryce said.

I nodded slowly. I had a bad feeling growing in the pit of my stomach. I didn't know why, but this battle was far from over.

"The scans don't pick up anything dangerous near the Jatarian fleet," Connor said. "So whatever is there is not currently activated."

"Surely the Zator realize this," Jeffery said.

"What can they do about it?" I asked.

"Send in a small group of ships. It would be better to lose a few than the entire fleet," Bryce said.

"What are they waiting for?" Jeffery asked.

"The move falls to the Zator. The Jatarians have set up traps all over this system. It's truly a death trap. I wonder how many Jatarians even call this system home?" I asked.

"According to my scans, only two planets and three moons fall into the inhabitable zone," Connor said.

"What if this isn't even their home system?" I asked. "What if this is just a decoy system, and no Jatarians even live here."

Everyone in the Command Center slowly turned and looked at me.

"Only one way we could find out," Connor said.

I shook my head. "We aren't moving. Not until this system is clear of any danger."

Everyone went back to their consoles and their jobs. I wasn't the only one who still wondered what was happening here.

What if this was only a decoy system and the Jatarn system was truly the home system of the Jatarians?

Chapter Twenty-Five

"Part of the Zator fleet are preparing to jump," Connor announced.

I leaned forward in my chair. Things were about to heat up. I watched the ships disappear from the tactical display and then reappeared near the Jatarian fleet.

Seven ships made the jump and almost immediately were incinerated by a death probe.

Shortly afterward, seven more ships made the jump a little farther over. Their fate was the same as before.

I glanced at my watch. The Morag would be here in under ten minutes. I wondered if what they saw on their long-range scans scared them. I couldn't imagine the Morag being scared or intimidated by anything.

I closed my eyes and focused on my gift. I reached out to Morag Admiral Wyn. He was close.

The Zator have brought a fleet to the suspected Jatarian home system. This is why so many ships are in the system. When you arrive, you must reach out to the Zator and inform them the Morag have come to defeat the Jatarians. The Zator have already reduced the number of enemy ships in the system. Remember the Morag and the Zator share a common enemy in the Jatarians. Destroy the Jatarians.

I repeated my message a few times to ensure my message was getting through.

I watched the tactical display as another seven ships made the microjump to the same area near the Jatarian fleet's current location. This time the seven ships were met with weapons fire from the enemy fleet.

The Zator commander must have taken this as a sign that the death probes had been eliminated—as the rest of the fleet had been engaged in the battle before also made the jump.

One hundred Zator ships remained near our location. I wasn't sure why this group hung back. I assumed the commander was in one of these ships. The rest of their fleet would greatly benefit from another one hundred ships though.

Once the Zator exited from their microjump, they immediately fired their weapons. Of the seven ships that had been there first, now only three remained.

I could only imagine how relieved those three ships were when the rest of the fleet showed up.

I held my breath, waiting for more death probes to detonate, but none did. I let out a sigh of relief after a couple minutes.

"Orbs are launching," Connor reported.

It's always something. "How many?" I asked.

"Nearly two hundred," Connor replied.

"Perhaps the Zator have another one of their incinerators to use on them," Jeffery said.

Sensor alarms started sounding, and red lights blared. I knew it was the Morag. I wondered what the Zator and Jatarians thought of the newcomers.

"The Morag have arrived," Connor said excitedly.

"How many ships do they have?" I asked.

"The Morag have just over one thousand ships," Connor answered.

"I'm intercepting a transmission between the Morag and Zator," Graham reported.

"Let's listen in," I ordered.

The viewscreen changed to a view of who I could only assume was Morag Admiral Wyn and the leader of the Zator. I was thankful for our translator device, so we could better understand both sides of the conversation.

"The Morag have come to eliminate the Jatarians," Morag Admiral Wyn said.

"Welcome to the battle. I am Zator Commander Raone. We have been hunting down Jatarian systems and destroying them. It is useful for us to have more help in this endeavor. We welcome your addition to our numbers."

"We will fight our battle our own way. We will not fire upon your vessels, unless fired upon," Wyn replied.

"Good. We are of the same mind then. Good luck. This system is a death trap, as I'm sure you will soon learn."

With that, the transmission ended. I looked around the room. That had gone decently well, considering the circumstances.

"Will you let the Morag do what they do, or will you help them?" Jeffery asked me.

"I will give them the coordinates to the areas we know are safe, but the Morag cannot effectively engage the Jatarians from any of those locations," I said.

"The Morag are preparing to jump," Connor called out.

"What? That was fast," I replied. I hadn't had the chance to tell the Morag admiral where the safe areas were. I couldn't believe he was already jumping his fleet into the battle. I was sure he would watch and learn first. The Morag were a very logical race.

I watched the screens as the Morag ships disappeared. Where would they end up?

"The Morag just exited near the right flank of the Jatarian fleet," Connor said.

We all looked hesitantly at the screens, expecting a bright flash of light. It didn't take long. Three bright flashes told us what we already knew. The Jatarians had death probes all around them. Well, not anymore, at least not on two sides.

"How many Morag ships did that eliminate?" I asked.

"Sixty-two," Connor replied.

The Morag began their attack on the Jatarians from that side. The Jatarians were now heavily outnumbered. With this advantage in numbers, it wouldn't take much longer to destroy them all.

I knew the Jatarians wouldn't stick around. Why would they? Especially if this wasn't their home system. Once they realized this was a fight they couldn't win, they would be gone. Why stay and fight?

None of the ships in the system could follow them. At least not yet. If the Jatarians wanted to preserve their fleet, now was the time to do it. I hoped they didn't.

Explosions filled the front lines of the fleets as the Jatarians turned and battled their enemies on two fronts.

The orbs made it to the Zator fleet. This time the Zator ships stayed to continue the fight against their enemy. They would lose more ships by jumping near the death probes than what these orbs could do. It took multiple orbs to destroy one ship, whereas the death probes took out twenty ships with one blow.

The orbs selected their targets and then detonated. Only twenty ships were lost. It was easy to see that the Jatarian's orbs were much less effective than the Jatarians' new weapon. It also appeared that the Zator had used up all their new weapons. Otherwise they would have used them on the orbs. Or perhaps they were saving them for another attack on the main Jatarian fleet.

"How much longer until our hyperdrive is charged?" I asked Cole.

"Another fifteen minutes," Cole answered.

"I'm afraid this Jatarian fleet won't stick around much longer," I said.

"If this is their home system, they will," Connor said.

"If it's not, they have no reason to," I said. "I guess we will know soon enough. With the combined attack of the Zator and the Morag, the Jatarians won't last long, and they'll lose their entire fleet to defend this system, which may be just some decoy, a death trap."

"The Jatarians have made a few microjumps, so they might not yet be ready to leave the system," Cole said.

"You are right. Maybe we will be ready to follow by then," I said.

Would the Jatarians stay and fight or leave to preserve their fleet?

The Zator and Morag continued to pound their weapons into the Jatarian fleet. No way the Jatarians could come out on top of this fight. The odds were totally stacked against them, especially now with the arrival of the Morag.

"Captain, the Jatarians are preparing to jump," Connor said.

"Will it be a microjump, or are they leaving the system?" I asked.

The Jatarian ships began disappearing. We all watched the tactical display. Were they gone for good? I stood up and walked closer to the viewscreens.

"Captain, the Jatarians have exited hyperspace on the opposite side of the Morag fleet," Connor said.

I was relieved the Jatarians had not retreated. What did this mean? Did it mean this *was* their home system? Or were they trying to eliminate more of their enemy with the help of their death probes?

The Jatarians immediately opened fire on the Morag. The Morag quickly readjusted their formation to face the Jatarians' new positions.

The Zator were forced to stop firing, as the Morag now stood between them and their enemy.

"What will the Zator do?" Jeffery asked.

"They must reposition. If they don't, the Morag will get angry that the Zator are not helping," I said.

"You're right. The Zator fleet are preparing to jump," Connor said.

I shielded my eyes from what was about to happen. Even with my hands in front of my eyes, the flash was still evident. It was so bright.

"How many ships did the Zator lose?" I asked.

"Eighty-four," Connor replied.

"Dang. We can't continue like this. If the Jatarians keep repositioning, which I believe is their strategy, the death probes will decimate both of these fleets," I said.

"How many probes do you think they have out there?" Jeffery asked.

"I don't know, but it would take less than one hundred of them to eliminate both the Zator and the Morag fleets. The Jatarians just have to get the Zator and the Morag to jump to certain locations," I said.

I was frustrated and didn't know how to help the Morag. The death probes were a game changer. We couldn't sense them unless they were activated. They stayed idle until a ship neared them, then activated. By that time, it's too late.

"What if the Morag and the Zator spread their formations out larger? If there are death probes, they will destroy fewer ships at a time. Instead of getting around twenty with the closer formation, maybe the death probes would only destroy ten," Jeffery suggested.

"Unless the larger formation activated more of the probes," Connor replied.

"Only one way to find out. Seeing that we can't suggest the Zator do that, we can only try the strategy on the Morag," Jeffery replied.

I looked over at Jeffery. He was right. What did we have to lose? If the strategy worked, then it might make the difference we needed in this battle. "Let's try it," I said.

I closed my eyes and used my gift to reach out to Morag Admiral Wyn. *What if the next time we follow the Jatarians to a new location, we spread out our formation? Perhaps then the deadly weapons the Jatarians have will be less effective. There won't be as many ships near each one at detonation.*

I made the suggestion but didn't make it an order. I wanted Morag Admiral Wyn to consider it but not feel compelled to listen.

"The Jatarians are preparing to jump again," Connor said.

We watched as the Jatarian ships disappeared. Where would they end up now?

"The Jatarians exited their microjump near the fifth planet," Connor informed us.

Now the Zator and the Morag would have to change locations. Both hesitated. It was almost as if they waited on the other to make the first move.

"The Morag are jumping," Connor announced.

When the Morag emerged from their microjump, their formation had changed. Perhaps it had changed before, but their formation was now drastically more spread out.

Everyone in the Command Center shielded our eyes from the light we knew was about to burst from the death probes.

When I dared open my eyes again, I looked over at the tactical display.

Connor said, "That tactic worked. They activated more of the devices, but each one destroyed fewer ships. Half as many. The Morag only lost sixty ships this time."

"I guess we can call that a win. Let's see if the Zator executed the same strategy," I said.

"We're about to find out," Connor said.

All gazes were on the viewscreens and the tactical display. Would the Zator learn from the Morag's technique?

We shielded our eyes from the intense light that the death probes created as they detonated. When I opened my eyes, I looked over at Connor.

"The Zator spread their formation too," Connor said. "They only lost forty-nine ships."

That was better than before. Now if we could just destroy more Jatarian ships than we'd lost with this move, we would make more progress.

The tactical display confirmed that we had more green icons than red, but not by a lot. That was a little comforting. These death probes were really wreaking havoc on the Zator and the Morag ships.

"That was a great idea, Jeffery, to spread farther apart the ships in the formation. Do you have any other ideas?" I asked.

Jeffery shook his head. "Afraid not."

"The Jatarians are preparing to jump again," Connor said, obviously frustrated.

"If we keep going like this, all of our allies' ships will be destroyed before the Jatarian ships are," I said.

The Jatarian ships disappeared again from the tactical display.

"What if we have the Morag scan the planets and the moons in the inhabitable zone? If they find where the Jatarians live, the

Jatarians will have to stay and fight to prevent the Morag from destroying their colonies. No more of this jumping around," I said.

"Great idea," Jeffery said. "Do it."

I quickly relayed my thoughts to Morag Admiral Wyn. It would only take a few ships. If one were hit by a death probe device, then we would know that spot was safe afterward. Send one ship to each location, while the others continued to fight the main Jatarian fleet.

We watched and waited to see if this new plan would work. If no Jatarians were found in the system, we would know we weren't in their home system after all.

It didn't take long for the Morag to send ships to investigate the inhabitable planets and moons in the system. They sent one to each spot.

"The Jatarians are now near the third planet," Connor said. "It appears the Morag are preparing to hunt them down again."

The Morag made their microjump. We all braced ourselves for the intense light that would come when the death probes detonated.

Connor said, "It's safe to look. The Morag lost forty-two ships."

The Morag began their attack and launched their weapons at the Jatarian fleet. Energy screens began to light up as they were hit. Eventually it was too much for them. The energy screens failed, and the next weapons fire struck the ship's hull, causing massive damage. Explosions spread across the vessel, until the entire thing was consumed.

The Zator fleet remained where they'd been. This puzzled me. What were they doing?

The Morag continued to hammer the Jatarians with every weapon they had. Orbs were activated and headed toward the

Morag fleet. I quickly used my gift to warn the Morag admiral of the danger of the orbs. The Morag commander changed some of his targeting to the orbs but kept most of his targets on the enemy fleet. He would not be distracted. His goal was to kill the Jatarians. Nothing would stop him.

The Jatarians stayed longer than usual and fought back against the Morag. I wondered if it was because they were more evenly matched. When both the Morag and the Zator challenged the Jatarians, it seemed the Jatarians moved more often.

The orbs arrived at their intended targets and detonated. It only destroyed thirty-two ships. The good news was that no more orbs were currently in the area.

The Morag continued to duke it out with the Jatarians. The Zator continued to watch. It was an amazing sight to see. Both fleets fought hard. No one seemed to back down.

Connor interrupted my focus and said, "The Jatarians are preparing to jump."

We all watched as the ships disappeared.

"The Jatarians are now near the seventh planet," Connor said. "The Zator are preparing to jump."

We all braced for the intense light that would follow.

"The Zator lost thirty-two ships," Connor said. "They used the same strategy again of spreading the ships farther apart in their formation."

"Look how close they are to the Jatarian formation," I said, as I looked at the tactical display.

"They are very close," Connor said.

"It appears the Zator ships are moving toward the Jatarian ones," Bryce said.

"Why would they do that?" Jeffery asked.

"I have no idea," I replied.

We all watched to see what would happen. The Jatarians focused their weapons fire on the nearest ships of the Zator. The Zator focused their firepower on the Jatarian frontline.

Were the Zator planning to ram the Jatarian ships? Why would they do that? It didn't make any sense to me at all. I shook my head. What was going on?

Jeffery said, "What if those larger ships have the incinerators on them? Maybe the Zator intend to penetrate the Jatarian fleet and then detonate their remaining incinerators."

I turned and looked at Jeffery. He had a good point. "I don't know what else it could be," I said.

We continued to watch, as the Zator fleet closed in on the enemy. The Jatarians did their best to destroy the Zator ships.

"They're almost to the Jatarian frontline," Connor called out.

"Why don't they jump?" Jeffery asked.

"I don't know," I replied. All of my attention was on the two fleets now coming together.

An intense light filled the Command Center. It was so bright my head ached, and my eyes saw only darkness with spots of light. I blinked several times, trying to see again. Was this temporary?

After a few minutes of blinking rapidly, my sight began to return. I looked around the room. Most people were holding their heads and rubbing their eyes.

I looked up at the viewscreen and the tactical display. No red icons showed on the screen.

"Where did the Jatarians go?" I asked Connor.

"They're gone," Connor replied.

"Did they jump? Or were they destroyed?" I asked.

"I'm not sure. Let me review the information that the scans and the tactical display picked up," Connor said, as he began typing things into his console.

I noticed a large number of green icons were missing too—the Zator fleet that had been engaging the Jatarian fleet.

"The Jatarian fleet was destroyed, along with most of the Zator fleet," Connor said.

A strange feeling crept up on me. I was glad the Jatarians had been destroyed, but what about the Zator? Why sacrifice your fleet like that? It was a win but left a bad taste in my mouth.

"Captain, I'm intercepting a communication between the Morag and Zator," Graham reported.

"Let's see what they have to say," I said.

The viewscreen switched to a view of Morag Admiral Wyn and Zator Commander Roane.

"What happened?" Morag Admiral Wyn asked.

"We used our secret weapon to eliminate the enemy. We had to sacrifice a majority of our fleet to do it," Roane responded.

"That leaves you with very few ships to continue on," Morag Admiral Wyn replied.

"We will make do."

"Where will you go now?" Wyn asked.

"The Jatarians inhabit many other systems that must be dealt with, before we can put this war behind us, once and for all. We will systematically destroy each of them. We could use your help, since we've lost a majority of our fleet."

"We would be happy to eliminate more Jatarian strongholds. You only need to give us the coordinates to these systems, and we will take care of the rest."

"This system here held the Jatarians' largest fleet and their most powerful defensive weapons. We presume this to be their home system. Did your ships scanning the surface of the planets and moons confirm this?" Roane asked.

"On the contrary. My ships found no Jatarians living in this system," Morag Admiral Wyn replied.

Roane looked shocked. "None at all?"

"None."

"This must be a decoy system. One the Jatarians could make into a death trap but didn't stand to lose any of their planets or colonies."

"That must be. We will search each system in the area until we find their true home system and then destroy it," Morag Admiral Wyn stated.

"We will aid you in this endeavor. We will not rest until all Jatarian systems have been destroyed," Zator Commander Roane said.

"We will end this Great War once and for all. We appreciate your efforts to rid this galaxy of the Jatarians. From now on, we will consider the Zator as our allies."

"We will hold the Morag as our allies."

The communication ended then.

I was still in shock by what I'd witnessed. The Jatarians had made this system into a trap, one where none of their civilians would be at risk. I had no doubt the Zator and the Morag would hunt down every last Jatarian ship.

From what I'd witnessed today, surely the Federation would not want the Zator nor the Morag as their enemies. I hoped Jeffery had learned the same.

"Now what?" Bryce asked me.

I took a deep breath. "Our mission is done. Now we tell the Morag where the real Jatarian homeworld is. The Zator and the Morag will hunt down the Jatarians. I can check in with Morag Admiral Wyn to ensure this happens. I see no reason why we can't return home. Any objections?"

I could tell everyone was still in shock by what we'd witnessed here today.

"Bryce, let's head home. I'm confident that, before we get there, all of the Jatarians will be no more."

Bryce nodded. He turned to his console and typed in a few commands. A few moments later, we entered hyperspace. I could relax. The Jatarians were living their last days. Of that, I had no doubt.

Chapter Twenty-Six

We headed back to Elmania. It would be a long journey. This would give me the time I needed to reflect on what I'd seen and what I'd learned.

The more I thought about what the Zator did in that last battle, the more intelligent I realized it was. The Zator had a weapon the Morag had never seen before. Zator Commander Roane had to realize that, by deploying this weapon in front of the Morag, that act alone would make the Morag realize that the Zator were a bigger threat than the Morag had thought.

By using his fleet to deploy the weapon, Roane ensured the weapon could successfully reach its target. It also took a majority of the fleet with it. Both Jatarian and Zator. What this did was make the Morag think the Zator no longer had much of a fleet left with which to battle.

All of Zator Commander Roane's actions were to destroy the Jatarians, while also ensuring the Morag did not then see the Zator as a legitimate threat. The Morag ended the battle, still thinking the Zator were less powerful than them, since they had a significantly depleted fleet. Brilliant in my opinion.

I checked in with the Morag regularly on our return. I would eventually get too far away and would be unable to connect with Morag Admiral Wyn. So far the Morag and the Zator had gone through each system, scanning the surfaces of all inhabitable moons and planets. If Jatarians were found, they were destroyed.

For as many systems that we knew held Jatarian colonies, there were likely just as many we didn't know about.

The Morag had plans to permanently monitor the Jatarian activity to ensure the Jatarians couldn't rise up again. Having the Morag as our watchdogs really was beneficial.

I tried each day to reach Kami on Elmania. Since that was the farthest outpost of the refugee camps, she would be the first one I could communicate with.

Jeffery tried to communicate with the scout ships but had no luck. He was frustrated that the scout ships had been pulled back to the Federation. I'm also a little worried as to why that would be.

I spoke with Fritz a few times. The *Explorer* was headed back to the Federation. Fritz knew it was time to check in and to report on what had happened out here. His report would refrain from any mention of us. It would only say the Zator and the Morag worked together to defeat the Jatarians.

My time with Jeffery was coming to a close. I'd enjoyed my time with him and ultimately was glad he had tagged along. Jeffery had learned a lot, from working in engineering with Samson and Wyatt to watching the battles unfold. He even had the opportunity to work with the Morag.

We all missed our families and couldn't wait to return to them.

I had two stops along the way that I wanted to make. One was in the system where Phoebe's and Charlotte's family had been. I needed to ensure the Jatarians hadn't destroyed their colony. I also wanted to pass on the news that the Jatarians had been defeated.

The other stop was in Maro's home system. We had sent the Morag to eliminate the Jatarian presence there, but I wanted Maro to see it for himself. He would rest better knowing the enemy had been eradicated from his home system. Would he ever return there? I was relieved when Maro said he'd found his new home with us at Dove One.

I was in my office, reviewing my notes, when I decided to reach out to Kami again. Perhaps we were finally close enough that I could use my gift.

I closed my eyes and cleared my mind. I focused on Kami.

Slade, I'm so happy to hear from you. We've been so worried about you and your crew.

We are safe. We are headed back to Elmania now. Although it will still be a few weeks.

Have you spoken to anyone else yet? Kami asked.

No, you are the first. Elmania is the farthest outpost. I figured I could reach you with my gift before I could anyone else.

I feel honored. How did things go out there?

The Morag and the Zator have defeated the Jatarians and are working to eradicate any remaining threats.

What a relief. The Jatarians in the Dove Two system still need to be dealt with.

Yes, I plan to ensure that happens once I return. I'll figure out where the nearest Morag fleets are, and we will eradicate the Jatarians from their last colony, I replied.

That'll be a relief. I'm sure those stuck at Dove Two are ready for things to change. Have you spoken with Colin?

I have not.

I think you should try to reach out to Colin and check in, Kami said.

Any particular reason?

He's your family, and I'm sure he'll be relieved to hear from you directly about the Jatarians.

Okay. I will try to reach out to him shortly.

Good. I will pass on your safety to Hadassah and Dove One. Also to Eloise. How's Jeffery?

He's well. I'm glad he was able to come along. I think he learned many things that will help him in the future.

Good. I'm glad to hear that. Stay safe, Slade. Check in with me periodically. We will be happy to welcome you back to Elmania in a few weeks.

Thank you, Kami.

I sat there thinking about what Kami had said. Why would I need to check in with Colin? Something just wasn't sitting right with me. I felt like something was wrong, something that Kami didn't want to tell me yet. Would Colin know what it was? Kami had mentioned he was a part of my family. She usually didn't say things like that. Something was going on, and I had to get to the bottom of it.

I took a deep breath and closed my eyes. I tried to clear my mind but struggled a bit. I concentrated on Colin.

Hello, Slade. It's good to hear from you. I assume you are safe? Colin asked.

We are. The Zator and the Morag have defeated the Jatarians. They're currently hunting down all the outposts and destroying them. We are headed back.

That's excellent news. What a relief. I'll be happy when this outpost of Jatarians here in the Dove Two system is dealt with.

That is one of the first things on my list to do.

How's Jeffery? Colin asked.

He's well. Jeffery's learned a lot out here. Things that I hope will help him in the future. How are things there?

Not great.

What do you mean? What's happened?

Has Jeffery contacted his father yet?

Not that I'm aware of. I am just getting to where I can communicate with you and Kami. Falton Two is still farther out than that.

I don't know how to tell you this, but Amelia has died.

I immediately threw up my lunch in my trash can. I took a few deep breaths and focused back on Colin. *What? I can't believe this. What happened?* I asked.

She was poisoned.

Do they have a suspect?

Thankfully it's not you. You were far from the Federation when it happened, so no way the Emperor could pin this on you, Colin replied.

When did this happen?

Two weeks ago.

How'd you find out?

I have my contacts. I couldn't go to the funeral obviously because I am stuck here at Dove Two.

My mind went to Phoebe. Was she okay? *Who is accused of the crime?* I asked, fearing the answer.

You and I both know it was the Averys, but that narrative does nothing to benefit the Emperor.

My fear grew, and I took several deep breaths, slowly in and slowly out. I knew it wasn't me, but there could still be a few others who could be falsely blamed for this crime. *Colin, I need to know everything.*

I don't have all the details. The Emperor spins things to his own advantage, as you know.

My mind filled with the possibilities and the ramifications of what Colin told me. *Who is taking the blame, Colin?* I asked.

Phoebe and Gabriel.

What? Why Phoebe and Gabriel? I asked in shock.

The Emperor says that Phoebe and Gabriel worked in conjunction with the rebels. After Amelia returned from her time with Jeffery and Eloise, things were never the same between her and Phoebe and Gabriel. Gabriel wanted to take over and found the perfect opportunity while his brother was being held captive by you, Phoebe's good friend. What better time than while his brother was off saving the Federation from the Jatarians?

I can't believe this. The Emperor is making it sound like Jeffery is a hero. He did help, and his presence did make a difference here, but it was the Zator who did in the Jatarians, with help from the Morag.

Let's hope Jeffery remembers that and doesn't let this go to his head.

The Emperor knew Jeffery could be gone a long time on the hunt for the Jatarians. Colin, do we need to stay gone longer? Or get back and get this sorted out?

Get back. I'm afraid for Phoebe and Gabriel.

What's been done to them?

They're under arrest, being held in the palace until their trial.

When is their trial?

Next week. It begins in five days.

We won't be back by then, I said desperately.

This is likely what the Emperor is counting on. If you can't influence the outcome, he can take care of Phoebe once and for all. He's never liked her since she was friends with you and from the Human Empire. He never thought she was worthy of his son.

What about their children?

They are being held separately from their parents. The Emperor refuses to let them see their parents. He will keep them and raise them in the palace.

No, no, no. This can't be happening.

Slade, I need to remind you that you hold all the cards here.

What do you mean?

You have Jeffery. You know where Eloise and the children are. You have the power. You must use it, and use it wisely.

How do I do that? Contact the Emperor myself?

You can't go through Jeffery. How would you know what was really being said? Colin asked.

Good point.

You must negotiate for Phoebe, Gabriel, and the children. And don't think for a second that the Emperor will make it easy. Don't give him all he wants until you have all he wants. Do you understand?

371

I think so.

The Averys are already on their way back. Well, a ship has been sent to retrieve them from Earth, Colin explained.

What? They took the fall for the attack on Gabriel. How can they be allowed to return? I asked.

The Emperor said that they were only trying to protect their daughter from a plot to poison her. Phoebe and Gabriel had a plan to kill Eloise, to poison her. The hit was supposed to be on Phoebe, the mastermind behind the plot, but Gabriel pushed her out of the way.

Wow. I don't even know what to say to that.

The Emperor is brilliant at spinning his webs of lies, Slade. He's been doing it for years. Plus no one even questions him or challenges him. What he says goes.

That's scary.

Yes, it is, which is why you have to be very careful. How you handle this will decide the future for Phoebe and Gabriel, Jeffery and Eloise, and the entire Federation.

I will be careful.

Remember. You have all the power. Keep it and get what you want. Don't give Jeffery to the Emperor until you have what you want.

Do you have the connections we need to get Phoebe and Gabriel out of there?

Yes, but not the children. They're being held only with the Emperor's most trusted people.

I don't want to alienate Jeffery in this. We've become very close. I think our friendship will be useful to us in the future.

Then you'll have to walk a very thin line. Good luck. Feel free to bounce your ideas off me anytime. I know this is a lot. So much is on your shoulders. Not to mention the loss of Amelia. I know you two were close, especially after the time you two spent together at Elmania.

Yes, we were close. She was an amazing woman. Does my mom know of her death?

No. My gift is not strong enough to reach her. Maybe it's best if she isn't told until we have this all worked out. We don't want her to worry more than is necessary.

You're right, Colin. I guess I have a lot of things to think about.

Yes, you do. Good luck. I'm proud of you, Slade. You found the Jatarian home system, and you ensured they were destroyed. Even if Jeffery gets credit for it, we all know who was really behind it.

I'm not sure I did much.

Did you find the home system?

Fritz found the decoy home system, where the main Jatarian fleet set a trap. And we found the true home system.

Did you give the Morag those coordinates?

Yes.

Why were the Morag in the area?

I had them come.

Exactly. Thank you, Slade, for all you do for us. I know you'll figure out how to best navigate this situation.

Thanks, Colin. I have to go. Someone is knocking on my door.

Okay. Good luck.

I took a deep breath and said, "Come in."

I was relieved when Bryce walked in. "You don't look good. What's wrong?"

I quickly brought Bryce up to speed. He was visibly upset about the news.

"You have to tell Jeffery. If he hears it from you, that'll be better than his father. You know his father will spin it in his favor. You have the opportunity to spin it yourself. You have to tell him before his father," Bryce said.

"I know you're right. It's just not a conversation I want to have."

"I'll go find him and send him this way," Bryce said, as he stood to go. "The longer you wait to tell him, the more he will wonder why."

"Okay." Bryce left. I sat here and stared at my desk. It seemed like only a couple minutes before another knock sounded on my door. "Come in," I said.

Jeffery walked in. He took one look at me, and his face went pale. "What is it? What's wrong?"

"I think you should sit down, Jeffery."

Jeffery sat down and looked me straight in the eyes. "Tell me."

"Your mother has passed away. Two weeks ago. I just heard the news myself from Colin."

Jeffery sat back in shock. "What happened?"

"She was poisoned."

Jeffery stood abruptly, sending the chair toppling over. "We know who is behind this."

"The Averys," I answered.

"Exactly. I will never forgive them."

"Jeffery, that's not who your father is putting the blame on," I said carefully.

Jeffery turned and looked at me, obviously surprised. "Who could he possibly pin this on?"

"Think about it. What would benefit him the most?" I asked. I had to be careful here. I was walking that thin line.

"Not by blaming the Averys. They're already banished to Earth. If he wants me to take over, which last I spoke with him, that was the plan. He needs to discredit anyone who might try to make a claim on the inheritance," Jeffery said and looked at me carefully. "We both know that's not you."

"Definitely not me," I confirmed.

"So that leaves Gabriel and Emma. Mom said Emma wasn't cut out to lead the Federation, so I don't see Emma trying anything. So that leaves Gabriel."

I could tell Jeffery was deep in thought. He had a look of concentration on his face. "The easiest way to discredit Gabriel would be through Phoebe, since she is from the Empire and good friends with you. My father would see your connection to Phoebe as a threat. So my best guess is he's blaming Gabriel and Phoebe for the poisoning. Am I right?"

"Unfortunately you are. From what Colin has gathered, Phoebe is being blamed. The story goes that she and Gabriel decided now would be the perfect time to try to overthrow the succession, since you are out of the Federation and being held hostage by the rebels."

"Wow. Gabriel and Phoebe would never do such a thing. I know they want nothing to do with Eloise and me, but they would never harm my mother. My father maybe but not Amelia. Who does my father think will buy this story?"

"I don't know, but their trial starts in five days. We won't be back by then."

"What can we do?" Jeffery asked.

"Do you trust me, Jeffery?" I asked.

"Yes, of course."

"Will you help me ensure Phoebe, Gabriel, and their children can get safely off Falton Two?"

"I'll do anything I can to help," Jeffery replied.

"I'll have to negotiate with your father. A trade. I have what he wants the most, *you*."

Jeffery nodded. "You can say that for their safe transfer to you, you will ensure our transfer to Falton Two."

"Do you think we could trust your father with a deal like that?" I asked.

"No. He will double-cross you the moment he has me. And he'll try to capture you, given the chance."

"So we have a problem to solve. How can we do this, where no one gets hurt? Where you, Eloise, and your children safely get to Falton Two. Where Gabriel, Phoebe, and their children safely get to Elmania."

"We have some thinking to do."

"Yes, we do. I'm glad we are on the same side here, Jeffery."

"Me too. I'm glad you're in my corner, Slade. I hope you always will be."

"I'm glad I've gotten to know you better, Jeffery. I'm glad we're cousins. But, more important, I'm glad we're friends."

Jeffery uprighted the chair that he had knocked over and sat down. He rested his head in his hands.

I stood up and walked around the desk to him. I put my hand on his back. "I'm so sorry about Amelia."

Jeffery nodded. "I'm so glad I got to see her and to spend time with her at Elmania. Thank you, Slade, for bringing her there."

"I'm glad it worked out. I'm just sorry this happened."

"We only have a few days to figure this out. We have to outplay my father. He's the master at this, and we must beat him at his own game. That won't be easy, Slade."

"I know, but we have each other. Together, we can do it. I know we can."

"We have to," Jeffery said. "For our future and for the future of the Federation."

"Partners?" I asked, as I held out my hand to Jeffery.

"Partners," Jeffery agreed, as he shook my hand. "It's time we beat my father at his own game."

I smiled. "Let's do it."

Epilogue

I opened my eyes and looked around the room. My sister, Layla, was crying. Emira was as well. She knew my aunt Amelia, so I understood her tears.

That was the part of the story I didn't want to share. The part where Amelia left this life. It was so long ago now, but the pain in my heart felt as if it had only happened yesterday.

The joy of victory over the Jatarians was short-lived, as we returned and found Amelia had died.

"I can't believe the Emperor is blaming his own daughter-in-law," Layla said, through her tears.

"Not to make light of your aunt's death, Soren, but what about the Jatarians? You said the Morag would watch them to ensure they didn't rise back up. Do you think that's still the case? Still after one thousand years?" asked Human Empire Admiral Cleemorl.

"Do you want my honest answer?" I asked him, as I looked him straight in the eyes.

"Yes, I do."

"The Morag do have a fleet that patrols the Jatarian area of space. Admiral Adali seems to believe that this will continue, that the Jatarians won't know the Morag have been defeated and are no longer strong enough to hold them back. Adali is not in the least bit concerned," I said.

"But you are?" Cleemorl responded.

"Yes, sir. Very much so. Seeing what the Empire was able to build under the watchful eyes of the Morag and the other races of the Confederation makes me think the Jatarians are likely doing the same thing, biding their time and waiting for the right opportunity to strike. I'm also concerned that the Morag fleet might leave the Jatarian area to begin a new colony of their own. Away from the watchful eyes of the Empire, who I'm sure intends to keep tabs on the Morag to ensure *they* do not build back a strong warfleet. Without the Morag fleet patrolling the Jatarian systems, things will surely change," I explained.

"Is the Federation sending a scout ship to check on the Jatarians?" Cleemorl asked.

"I'm not sure. I've tried to make the Federation understand the danger that the Jatarians pose. The Federation doesn't take it seriously. *The Morag have it in hand* is what I'm told. I'm hoping to persuade Emperor Rowan when we get back, even if I have to go check it out myself."

Layla spoke up. "So the Human Empire defeated the Morag, who were keeping the Jatarians in check. Now that the Morag are on the run and defeated, they will stop watching the Jatarians. Which means it's our fault if the Jatarians rise again?"

"The Human Empire knew nothing of the Jatarians. You defeated your enemy, the Morag. You fought for your freedom."

"Why did you not tell the Morag to stay away from the Empire again?" Emira asked.

"By the time I was taken out of cryo, it was too late. The Empire had already launched their attack on the Morag. The Confederation had already split. I was a little behind," I said.

"What now?" Cleemorl asked.

"We try to make Emperor Rowan see the danger of the Jatarians," I replied.

"What does he want with Layla?" Cleemorl asked.

"He has a proposition for Layla and the Human Empire. While you believe you are strong and have a strong military, that is not the case when compared to the Human Federation. You need the Federation as an ally," I explained.

"So what does the Federation need from the Empire?" Cleemorl asked hesitantly.

"That I am unsure of. My best guess has something to do with the gift. The telepathic gift some of us have. As the generations have continued, the Federation gift has become rarer. Not only rarer but weaker. Very few can use their gift outside of Falton Two, let alone across systems, like I can. I'm sure Emperor Rowan is curious if Layla has the gift—not to mention the baby she carries."

"Will he take my baby?" Layla asked.

"No, he won't. He promised me that no harm would come to any of you. You will be safely returned to the Empire," I said.

"How do we know he will stick to that deal?" Cleemorl asked, concerned.

"He has to. He needs me. I'm the strongest person with the gift. He needs me to keep the Federation safe from outsiders, from other races who might try to attack the Federation."

"You have a stronger gift than Emperor Rowan then?" Layla asked.

"Very much so," I replied.

"What makes him believe you will help him?" Cleemorl asked.

"I protect all Human lives. Whether it's Federation or Empire, I do what I can."

"But you just watched Golan Four get destroyed," Cleemorl said. "How is that protecting Empire Humans?"

"The citizens are in bunkers. They had plenty of warnings to get to their safe spots. Adali only bombed the countryside, where it would appear to anyone looking at the planet that the surface had been destroyed. The cities will be intact. The clean-up will be faster than usual, as the minimum number of bombs were used to cloud the atmosphere. Very few Humans died on the planet."

"Not true for my fleet," Cleemorl said angrily.

"If you had been willing to give up Layla, your fleet would have survived," I reminded Cleemorl. It wasn't the nicest response I could give, but it was the truth.

"What will Rowan want when he realizes I do not have the gift?" Layla asked.

"He will want to run a few tests to see if you possess the gene that passes the gift to your children. Once your child is born, he will want to do the same to the baby. A few tests can be run to determine if the gift may be present in your child. If you are not a carrier, it won't matter," I explained.

"What if I'm not? Then what? We don't have anything to negotiate with," Layla replied.

"You still have Mathew. Even if he does not possess the gift, he may be a carrier."

"I thought you wanted to keep his existence a secret?" Layla replied.

"I do, for now. We may have to use it in the future."

"What about you? Are you a carrier?" Layla asked.

"Yes, I am."

"So you have the power to keep us safe?" Layla asked.

"Yes, I believe so. If I didn't, I would never have agreed to bring you back to Falton Two," I explained.

"Will you marry again?" Layla asked.

"I hadn't thought much about it, until you said that Mathew was alive. I hope his guardian, Charlotte, is too. If Charlotte still lives, I would love to see her," I said.

I felt a pang of guilt, as my mind drifted to Hadassah. She was long dead though. I hoped she had lived a happy life, after I was put in cryo. I might never know the answer to that.

I tried not to hold out much hope about Charlotte either. Layla had said the name wasn't familiar. Surely if Mathew was around and was dating Layla's cousin, they would have met Charlotte.

I looked over at Emira. Wouldn't Emira know? She said she didn't. Was she being honest?

"What about your children you had with Hadassah?" Cleemorl asked.

"They did have the gift. Their descendants likely do too, but it might not be as powerful as it once was. I have had no contact with my descendants yet. My children would have died almost one thousand years ago. That's a lot of generations to dilute the gift."

A knock sounded at the door. Cleemorl answered.

"Admiral Adali wants Soren to report to the Command Center immediately," the man said.

I stood and walked to the door.

"Soren," Layla interjected, "I still want to know the rest of the story. Did you rescue Phoebe and Gabriel? Did Jeffery and Eloise take over? What happened?" Layla said.

"I'll get to that. I promise. Let me see what Admiral Adali needs, and I'll return later."

Layla nodded.

I walked out the door. I slowly headed to the Command Center and reflected on what I'd discussed with Layla. I couldn't get my mind off Charlotte. Could she still be alive? Could she have been in cryo for one thousand years, like me? If Mathew had been rescued and had been taken to the Earth system, did Charlotte go too? Could she be there?

When I arrived at the Command Center, Admiral Adali sat in his command chair.

"You wanted to see me?" I asked.

"Yes, have a seat," Adali said.

I sat down in the chair he had indicated.

"I've received word from Emperor Rowan that he has sent a scout ship to check on the Jatarians. Also on the Morag. I assumed you would want to know."

"Thank you. That does make me feel better. I hope they find the Jatarians still under the Morag influence," I replied.

"I'm confident they will."

"What if they don't?" I asked.

"Then we will squash them before they realize what's going on," Adali replied.

"I like your confidence. I'm sure the Federation has spent the last one thousand years developing incinerators, plus weapons similar to those we saw the Jatarians use—the death probes, mines, and orbs. It'll be an easier battle if we have a few of those ourselves."

Adali studied me closely. "I don't even know what you are talking about."

It was my turn to eye him closely. "We haven't developed a weapon similar to the death probe?"

"What is a death probe?"

"It's a device that, when detonated, completely incinerates twenty or more ships within its range," I said.

Adali obviously didn't like the sound of that. "Perhaps the research and development team has been working on a similar device. I've never personally seen one deployed."

"I hope our R&D team is working on that," I replied.

"That type of device in the wrong hands could be disastrous," Adali said.

"Yes, it could. I've seen that firsthand."

"I'm sure we have nothing to worry about," Adali commented, with a wave of his hand.

"Is that all?" I asked.

"Yes, you are dismissed."

As I left the Command Center, I became increasingly worried. Surely the Federation had been developing new weapons. If not, we could seriously be in trouble, should the Jatarians rise up again. I had no doubt the Jatarians had spent the last one thousand years developing more advanced weaponry. If the death probes were that potent one thousand years ago, I didn't even want to consider what the Jatarians had in their arsenal one thousand years later.

That would keep me up at night. Another thing I would ask Emperor Rowan about.

I went to my quarters. I was exhausted. I needed some rest. I fell asleep and dreamed of Charlotte.

Other Books by Raymond L. Weil

And Julie Weil Thomas

Available on Amazon

Moon Wreck (The Slaver Wars Book 1)
The Slaver Wars: Alien Contact (The Slaver Wars Book 2)
Moon Wreck: Fleet Academy (The Slaver Wars Book 3)
The Slaver Wars: First Strike (The Slaver Wars Book 4)
The Slaver Wars: Retaliation (The Slaver Wars Book 5)
The Slaver Wars: Galactic Conflict (The Slaver Wars Book 6)
The Slaver Wars: Endgame (The Slaver Wars Book 7)
The Slaver Wars: Books 1-3
-
Dragon Dreams: Dragon Wars
Dragon Dreams: Gilmreth the Awakening
Dragon Dreams: Snowden the White Dragon
Dragon Dreams: Firestorm Mountain
-
Star One: Tycho City: Survival
Star One: Neutron Star
Star One: Dark Star
Star One
-
Galactic Empire Wars: Destruction (Book 1)
Galactic Empire Wars: Emergence (Book 2)
Galactic Empire Wars: Rebellion (Book 3)
Galactic Empire Wars: The Alliance (Book 4)
Galactic Empire Wars: Insurrection (Book 5)
Galactic Empire Wars: Final Conflict (Book 6)
Galactic Empire Wars: The Beginning (Books 1-3)
-
The Lost Fleet: Galactic Search (Book 1)
The Lost Fleet: Into the Darkness (Book 2)
The Lost Fleet: Oblivion's Light (Book 3)
The Lost Fleet: Genesis (Book 4)

The Lost Fleet: Search for the Originators (Book 5)
The Lost Fleet (Books 1-5)

-

The Star Cross (Book 1)
The Star Cross: The Dark Invaders (Book 2)
The Star Cross: Galaxy in Peril (Book 3)
The Star Cross: The Forever War (Book 4)
The Star Cross: The Vorn! (Book 5)

-

The Originator Wars: Universe in Danger (Book 1)
The Originator Wars: Search for the Lost (Book 2)
The Originator Wars: Conflict Unending (Book 3)
The Originator Wars: Explorations (Book 4)
The Originator Wars Explorations: The Multiverse (Book 5)
The Originator Wars Explorations: The Lost (Book 6)

-

Earth Fall: Invasion (Book 1)
Earth Fall: To the Stars (Book 2)
Earth Fall: Empires at War (Book 3)

-

The Forgotten Empire: Banishment (Book 1)
The Forgotten Empire: Earth Ascendant (Book 2)
The Forgotten Empire: The Battle for Earth (Book 3)
The Forgotten Empire: War for the Empire (Book 4)
The Forgotten Empire: The Confederation and The Empire at War (Book 5)
The Forgotten Empire: War in the Confederation (Book 6)
The Forgotten Empire: The Path to Victory (Book 7)
The Forgotten Empire: The Fall of the Confederation (Book 8)

-

All Dates are Tentative
Forges of the Federation: Explorer
Forges of the Federation: Oasis
Forges of the Federation: Rebel One
Forges of the Federation: Spirit of Rebellion
Forges of the Federation: Defender

Forges of the Federation: Hunter
Forges of the Federation: Guardian (December 2024)

ABOUT THE AUTHORS

Julie Weil Thomas lives in Tulsa, Oklahoma with her husband Barrett and two boys. She attended university at the University of Oklahoma in Norman, OK where she received a degree in Finance with a minor in Accounting.

Her hobbies include watching her boys play numerous sports, reading, camping, and scuba diving. She got her imagination from her dad. Julie grew up listening to Raymond's many imaginative stories and watching anything and everything science fiction.

Julie is honored to carry on her dad's stories as best as she can. For as long as the fans are interested in reading the stories, Julie will continue to write in the worlds that her dad created.

Raymond Weil lived in Clinton, OK with his wife, Debra, of 47 years and their beloved cats. He attended college at SWOSU in Weatherford, Oklahoma, majoring in Math with minors in Creative Writing and History.

His hobbies included watching soccer, reading, camping, and of course writing. He also enjoyed playing with his six grandchildren. He had a very vivid imagination, writing more than 47 science fiction novels over his writing career.

He was an avid reader and has a huge collection of science fiction/ fantasy books. He always enjoyed reading science fiction and fantasy because of the awesome worlds the authors would create. He was always amazed that he was creating these worlds too.

Made in the USA
Las Vegas, NV
25 October 2024